"A true Gothic romance, deliciously written in a modern setting. Death, kissing, and a smoking hot mystery boy: what more could you ask for?"
Amy Plum, author of the bestselling Die For Me *and* Until I Die

"*Broken* is a devastatingly haunting love story where nothing is as it seems – and your heart is not your own."
Michelle Zink, author of the Prophecy of the Sisters *trilogy and* A Temptation of Angels

"Darkly romantic, *Broken* is an intense, beautiful, and intricate story of love that knows no bounds. Even death can't stop it."
JA Souders, author of Renegade

"Brilliantly dark, creepy and atmospheric, *Broken* is a love story that will hold you captivated until the stunning conclusion."
Justina Ireland, author of Vengeance Bound

"*Broken* contains all the mystery and romance I love in a YA novel. A delicious and haunting read."
Elana Johnson, author of Possession

"Hauntingly beautiful, achingly romantic, and edge-of-your-seat scary, *Broken* will keep you up way past your bedtime. I loved this book!"
Trinity Faegen, author of The Mephisto Covenant *series*

A E ROUGHT

Broken

STRANGE
CheMISIRY

STRANGE CHEMISTRY

An Angry Robot imprint
and a member of the Osprey Group

Lace Market House
54-56 High Pavement
Nottingham NG1 1HW
UK

4301 21st Street, Suite 220B,
Long Island City,
NY 11101
USA

www.strangechemistrybooks.com
Strange Chemistry #6

A Strange Chemistry paperback original 2013

Copyright © A E Rought 2013

A E Rought asserts the moral right to be
identified as the author of this work.

Cover by Steven Wood.
Set in Sabon by THL Design.

Distributed in the United States by Random House, Inc., New York.

ISBN 978-1-908844-31-6 ·
Ebook ISBN: 978-1-908844-32-3

Printed in the United States of America

9 8 7 6 5 4 3 2 1

For my daddy, gone but never forgotten.

And for Lexie. Without her, this book simply wouldn't exist.

Did I request thee, Maker, from my clay
To mould me Man? Did I solicit thee
From darkness to promote me?

John Milton, PARADISE LOST (X. 743-5)

Chapter One

Cold seeps through my jacket while I lean on the wrought-iron gate, staring at the rows of headstones parading across the lawn of Memorial Gardens Cemetery. Lanes of crushed gravel snake in white paths through the grass. Fading daylight spills down an angel's robe, collects in a puddle at the foot of a chipped urn, and glances from headstone engravings. At night, when I'm alone, it's easier to fantasise about who's buried there.

I drift along the sidewalk skirting the graveyard toward the mausoleums, chain-link fence clinking beneath my dragging fingers. I've haunted this place, lingering on the border between the living and the dead, wishing for a grave that will never exist. Two yards from the gate, a broken link cuts my finger. Same spot's been cut three times already. Thank God I had my tetanus shot recently.

Absentmindedly sucking my finger, I wander until I'm even with the tomb farthest from the gate. The bones of some of the area's wealthiest residents are interred within its gleaming white walls – self-important snobs who even have a wrap-around porch on their mausoleum. Daniel and I used to sit there, cracking inappropriate jokes, facing the trees and drinking the whiskey he stole from his parents' liquor cabinet.

Not anymore.

Echoes of us fill our seats now, Daniel's long legs whole, not broken, and stretched across the polished stone. One of his hands holds the glass, the other hand curls over my shoulder. My profile is clear, aimed at him, beaming love brighter than the fading day. Curls muss his nearly black hair and cast his face into shadow. A chill October breeze stirs the trees. Branches clack above my head, brittle as old bones. Goosebumps coat my skin, my pulse jumps. When Daniel's echo turns to me, his face is broken and bleeding, red shiny trails streaming from the crack in his skull, coursing into his hazel eyes.

My breath escapes in a rush. The same loss tears through me. And here I am again, living the hurt over and over, like constantly ripping off a Band-Aid to feel the sting.

Hurting is better than forgetting.

Daniel wouldn't want me living in this limbo. He would've screwed up his face into a comical mask long ago and shooed me away from here. I'm so weak without him. I struggle to keep my chin up, and lose the sudden battle with my tears.

After backhanding moisture from my cheeks, I jam my hands into my pockets and turn from the fence. We'll never sit together again, and someday I'm going to have to accept it. He would want me to move on, not haunt the graveside his parents will never give his ashes. Heart heavy and somehow empty at the same time, I drift toward home. Fall leaves whisper beneath my steps. Jack-o'-lanterns leer from porches, glowing faces following my every step, as if they see the hollow space in me and find it familiar. The Peterson's pumpkin is particularly vicious looking, with narrow pointy teeth and angular flaming eyes, squatting like a gargoyle on the front step. Drew, a junior at Shelley High like me, really went all out with the carving this year. He's always had a flair for darkness and drama.

The front porch door opens with a screech of hinges. Mrs Peterson shuffles out, flowered house coat catching the breeze and showing her corpulent pasty white legs. She gives me a wave and sympathetic smile when she stoops in her housecoat to blow the candle out.

Shrinking deeper into my coat, I keep my eyes forward and hurry toward home. My loss bleeds out a little at a time through the mesh of the Memorial Garden's fence, but it doesn't mean I like walking by myself in the gathering twilight. I'm skilled at scaring myself with what I think might be watching me. Even now, I feel the weight of a stare on my back. At least, I *think* I do. Of course, when I was five I'd convinced myself there were monsters, too.

A ring from my pocket shatters the silent laughter of carved pumpkins and tacky plastic Halloween lawn ornaments. Letting out a little groan, I fish out my cell phone, and then squint at the screen.

Bree Ransom.

I click to accept the call, then hold it to my ear and try walking and talking without tripping in the fading light. "Hey, Bree, wassup?"

"Loitering is against the law, you know." I can almost hear her eyes roll. Bree's one of the few people who understands why I spend so much time outside of the cemetery.

"Only if I get caught."

"Well, that'll never happen. That neighborhood you hang out by is dead quiet." OK. So Daniel and I aren't the only ones to crack inappropriate jokes. The *snap* of a pop can opening punctuates her sentence. "Those people aren't going to tattle on you."

"You won't either." I hop a pile of leaves on the sidewalk.

"Who am I to break up your mournfest? Just tell me you're willing to wear a costume to the dance Saturday and I'll quit pestering you." The papery sound of flipping pages comes through the phone. Knowing Bree, she's paging through the sale flyer for the pop-up Halloween store in downtown White River. "We can coordinate if you give me enough time."

Which is exactly why I hadn't said anything. Bree might be a genius in the costume and make-up department – comes with the territory for a theater major – but she's not a miracle worker. The longer I hedge, the less time she has to force me into being a Zombie Twin, or Bad Faery Twin, or What-everelse Twin she's plotting on subjecting me to. With us both being about five-foot-five, with blonde hair – mine natural, hers what my mom calls bottle blonde – and average curves, Bree has a lot to work with in the Twins department.

"I'll let you know."

"Dying of antici-PATION," she says, dragging out the last word like Frank-N-Furter in *The Rocky Horror Picture Show*.

"Can we discuss this tomorrow? I'm walking and talking and can hardly see the sidewalk…"

"Say no more." She takes a swig from her pop, then says, "See ya in the morning, Em."

"Bye, B."

Bree may be my best friend, but she will never let me forget my walking, talking, tripping over a fire hydrant incident of last year. To return the favor, I often remind her of her orange Kool-Aid hair-dyeing event.

A branch swings in a sudden breeze and knocks the phone out of my hand. Spitting swear words, I squint at the ground, covered with a layer of gold, browns, and red. It didn't hit the sidewalk – no horrid *crack* followed the fall. My backpack slides to the ground when I bend down, scoping the yard to either side. Then I see the faint glow of the screen display reflecting from the underside of an oak leaf.

The screen goes dark before I can grab it, and I fumble in the leaf litter, through another string of cusswords, before wrapping my fingers around the hard plastic case.

Standing, I feel the same heavy stare wash across my face like a warm damp cloth. Prickles crawl over my skin, my scalp tightens, and I'm sure if I could see myself, the blue of my eyes would be swallowed by my pupils. I spin slowly, taking in every inch of Seventh Street and its shadows. Comfortable two-story houses, some with open porches, most with narrow siding and painted trim. Grinning pumpkins, a skeleton in the Millers' yard, Mrs Jones' witch-in-a-tree…

As far as I can tell, I'm alone. The feeling of being watched isn't easy to shrug off. I square my shoulders, tuck my aching loss away where my mom won't see it, and trudge the last two yards worth of sidewalk to my house.

My trio of jack-o'-lanterns sits on the edge of the wide steps of our two-story Victorian, the candlelight welcoming me home. Under the waning light, the house has a morose quality, the dove gray siding and black trim and shutters making it look almost emo. Through the big living room window I can see Mom curled up on the sofa, nose buried in a book. I'm sure Dad's in the basement, tinkering on some project. Renfield's sinuous white cat body is curled in the window, crammed behind couch.

Burnt pumpkin stink rises with each lid as I lift them from the jack-o'-lanterns to blow out the candles. Porch boards creak beneath my Converse sneakers when I walk across to the door. Dad's been forever planning to fix them, but never has. He'd much rather make picture frames and cabinets in his downstairs workshop. Carpentry is his escape, like Mom's is the next best romance novel on the shelves, and mine used to be my bedroom and the Internet. Hand on the handle, I pause and cast one last look at Seventh Street.

Still vacant, though a presence seems to thicken the shadows.

The door opens onto the smell of bread and pot roast. Gray and black carpet anchors the rooms. Walls, ceiling and trim all match; a stark, blaring white. Furniture squats around the room, a conclave of fat, bloody trolls, in varying shades of burgundy. Mom's evening show chatters to itself in the wavering light of the TV. She looks up from her novel, a smile softening her brown eyes and deepening the wrinkles around them.

"How was the library?" she asks.

"Silent as the grave." I pull Renfield into my arms. He squirms, skewers me with a cat glare of discontent at his up-side-down position. One gold eye has a black freckle in the iris, like one of Daniel's hazel eyes did. Kind of ironic. Other than me, Daniel was Renfield's favorite person. The cat's purr matches the rumble of my stomach, finally growling to life under the smell of food. "Any leftovers from dinner?"

"Of course." Mom scans her page, then points in a general kitchenly direction. "There's a warm plate in the oven for you."

At home, with normalcy crashing in, it's easy to shut out my loneliness and let the reality of the weight of my backpack press against my spine. A heavy backpack equals lots of homework. Trig, Social Studies and an essay on Machiavelli and the humanist movement are not going to do themselves.

Resigning myself to a night of hitting the books, I grab an oven mitt and pull my dinner from the oven.

Instead of settling in the living room and watching Mom read while I ignore the TV, I sit in my normal seat at the dining room table. It's quieter here, and the faint smell of fresh-cut wood from Dad's latest project drifts up the basement stairs. A wide window gapes across the table from me, an evening view of the side yard and the skeletal trees reaching skyward. The branches jerk back and forth in a sharp wind, a limb cracking and plummeting to the ground – a macabre combination with the scent of wood death curling in my nose.

My cell comes to life, the vibrate setting making the pink thing look like it has legs. It jitters across the table, the screen flashing green. I don't need to look at the display to know it's Bree calling again. Shoveling in a forkful of potatoes and gravy, I let the call go to voicemail.

Hopefully I'll dodge her Zombic Twins bullet tomorrow morning. Homework is on my dance card for tonight, then shower and sleep.

Chapter Two

Tuesday morning dawns chilly and dry. Frost glitters on the lawn, delicate and sharp. Crisp air steals through the little crack I left open between my window and sill, and billows the sheer curtains.

Indian summer has definitely given up the ghost.

I pull my bare legs from the tangle of sheets and blankets shackling them and immediately regret it. Cold air swishes around me when I fling off the rest of my covers and dash for my walk-in closet. The sweet, fresh smell of Mom's dryer sheets greet me behind the door, and shadows obscure the familiar shapes of my clothes... perfect for hiding things.

The deep red sweatshirt I've worn every night since June leaves residual warmth on my skin when I pull it off. I run my finger along the hood's edge – then, standing in the privacy of my nearly closed closet, I fold it and tuck it away where no one will see. The only soul who knows I have that shirt is gone. Goosebumps razz my skin, stealing the heat left behind. I hop into a pair of jeans, pull on a T-shirt, and add a black zip-up hoodie with splashes of filigree embroidery on it.

Mom has her famous Walking Breakfast Taco, or WBT
as I like to call it – crumbled sausage, scrambled eggs, and
cheese, added to a snack bag of corn chips – in her hand,
with my backpack in the other, when I shoot from the stairwell. With a spin-and-grab move, I slide into my backpack
and grab breakfast. Plastic spoon included.

"Thanks, Mom!"

She smiles, and reminds me I wouldn't always be in a
hurry if I'd just set my alarm. I've listened to it so many times
all I really hear anymore is "Nag-nag, Emma, nag-nag."

While I can't walk and talk on the phone, I have no
problem walking and spooning food into my mouth.
Maybe eating is mindless, and conversations aren't if you
do them right. Either way, my WBT is nothing but a bag
and spoon by the time I reach the walk-up window of the
Mugz-n-Chugz coffee shop. They installed the walk-up on
the opposite side of the drive-through for the safety of the
students too stubborn to walk inside and order their caffeine fix.

Sunlight beats down, deceptive and taunting, all sharp
light and no warmth.

The glare bounces my reflection back from the walk-up
window, and I take advantage of the moment to run a
comb through my hair. Then on a whim, I pull eyeliner
from my backpack pocket and line my right eye in black-
blue. I have the other started when Tiny, who is *not*, shoves
the window open. He reminds me of the fat Buddha statues, only Tiny is crammed into a tacky, sweat-stained
Fifties-style uniform shirt.

"Hey, Em," he says in a voice incongruously high-pitched
for his size. "The usual?"

"Yes, please."

"OK." He nods like I asked him a question. "I'll get you that breve, and let you finish your make-up routine."

"Thanks."

Daniel turned me onto M-n-C's breve with caramel a month before his fall. We got them every May morning it wasn't raining. I can see a ghost of him beside me, laughing at my use of the window as a mirror as I hastily line my left eye in the dark color Bree says makes my blue eyes "really pop."

Just then, Tiny pushes the window outward. I catch a reflection of a guy superimposed where Daniel's echo was a moment before. He wears inky dark jeans, a T-shirt-weight hoodie with the hood up, under the kind of battered brown leather jacket that's scuffed in all the right places. Then the window moves farther and a blare of sunlight burns his reflection. Shocked, I spin to the side, hair whipping out, and expect to see the guy beside me.

No one's there. Not even Daniel.

Someone disappears into the cedars just across the parking lot drive, and then crosses the street yards away. They were close. A shudder ripples down my spine before I can pull myself together. *So weird*, I think. Blinking, and wishing I had sunglasses, I trade cash for coffee, avoiding the lingering gaze of the guy three years older than me in the window. Tiny takes a shaky inhale, holds it, and then says, "So... um... I was thinking if you weren't busy, maybe we could–"

"Gotta go, Tiny. Don't want to be late for class." I cut him off before he tries to ask me anything awkward.

People clutter the campus, busses pulling up to the drop-off corner, knots of girls, clumps of guys, all jostling closer to the doors. Right across from me stands nearly half the Shelley High Ravens baseball team, tossing a freshman's lunch back and forth.

Catching sight of Bree, all in blues and pinks, I hustle to cross the street. Brakes squeal, and Josh Mason lays on the horn when his crappy Z-28 nearly sideswipes me. He shoves his head out the window and yells something less than nice about me being in my "proper spot on the curb." People freeze up and down the block, and all eyes turn toward me. With a half-smirk, I rail him about the vehicular compensation for his lacking manhood. Slinging insults is better than wasting my coffee on his windshield.

Josh takes it well. We've been playing the insult game since Daniel beat him to the "Dating Emma Gentry" punch. Feet from the curb, I shoulder between Josh's baseball teammates and hear, "Good comeback, Gentry."

"It's a finely honed skill," I say, flicking a glance up at the team's spare pitcher.

No. That's not right, I think, *it was more than just dating.* I'd dated other guys. Hand-holding, a few kisses, a feel or two, but none of them affected me the way Daniel did. With Daniel, it was so much more. He wasn't just in my heart, he *was* my heart.

"Hellooo?" Bree's face is suddenly inches from mine, her ice blue eyeshadow glinting in the sunlight. "Earth to Emma."

"Sorry," I mutter, and sip my coffee. "Guess I was spacing out."

"Guess? There's no guess about it."

"OK, OK." I drop to my knees, coffee cup raised, other hand wrapped around it like I'm praying. From this position, I'm suddenly aware how short her skirt is and what an awkward position I put myself in. "Forgive me, oh Bree, for I have sinned!"

"Ha!" she snorts, checks blushing scarlet when she hooks

her hand in my elbow and hoists me to my feet. "Get up before the new guy sees you down there and gets the wrong impression."

"New guy?" A shard of the reflection I'd seen earlier flares behind my eyes.

"New to our school, anyway." She wraps her hand in mine and drags me toward the wheelchair ramp leading to the side door. Once in the fractured shade of the maple tree, she points along the sidewalk, halfway down the gym complex. "Mr You-Don't-See-Me with his hood up." She leans around me, does a little wiggle meant to hike her skirt higher hands-free. "And I wanna see what he's hiding under there."

I follow where she's pointing. Coming toward us walks the 3-D version of the reflection I'd seen. His entire look seems crafted to both draw and shun attention. His clothes are definitely designer, but with the hood up and shoulders hunched he appears to not want the attention the girls at Shelley High are going to give him. His head tips up just enough for me to catch a glint of his eyes. The world narrows, everything falls away, cleaved from existence the moment he meets my eyes.

Then his gaze falls and life crashes back.

Rumors whisk in front of him, brittle as fall leaves, darker than crows in a murder.

"He's been in juvie," says the baseball player a few feet away.

"No way," the third baseman says. "He was in jail."

"I heard he killed someone with his bare hands," one girl says. Her friend argues, "Not with his hands. With a knife!"

"Back from the dead," another Ravens baseball player murmurs behind me.

"Weird day to start school," mutters Bree.

"Yeah," I agree. "In the middle of the semester, too."

Then Sam Ashton – last semester's Sadony Academy transfer – says, "Hi, Alex."

Alex nods his head, gives them a short wave, and the flock of biting words die at his feet. Guys appear to shrug off his arrival, but still pin Alex with sneaky, kill-the-interloper glares. Girls – despite still whispering – slather on predatory smiles, thrust up their boobs, and tip their hips in curvy poses. Alex's appearance may have shaken up the quad, but it settles back to a more normal morning routine quickly.

"Alex?" Bree whispers to me, her brown eyes wide. "As in Alex Franks?"

I shrug. Doesn't sound familiar to me. I'm too busy trying to figure out what happened when he looked at me to worry about his last name. Something tingled deep in my chest, a sparking wire with a faulty connection. Bree's saying something about recognizing him from elementary school, thinking out loud that she pulled his hair in a sandbox. The only coherent thoughts I can formulate are: *What's he doing here now?* And: *Why is he coming this way?*

Alex whoever-he-is walks closer, and the tingle in my chest becomes a steady electric current. Slowly, every gaze on the high school campus zeroes in on us. A hot blush reddens my cheeks. With everyone looking in our direction, I feel like one of those bugs on display, skewered to a corkboard in the biology lab. Only a livewire buzzes in me instead of a stick pin. The sharp elbow nudge Bree gives me registers in the same way movement registers in peripheral vision.

A couple of steps away, Alex stops.

Cold sunlight reaches inside his hood, washing his features. A nervous twitch at the corners of his full lips could be a smile. Then he looks at me, I mean, really *looks* at me, like he's counting every freckle the DNA faery rudely splattered across my nose. An expression of wonder, disbelief maybe, lights his face. My head's a mess, my chest's tingling, and all I can think is that he feels like an echo ringing through the hollow left inside me, undeniable and utterly dwarfed by Daniel's memory.

I want to speak. I should. A muscle twitches on his jaw like he does, too.

Bree, of course, beats us both to it.

"Hey, Alex. Remember me? We went to kindergarten together. I think I pulled your hair..." she says, sliding close to me and edging closer to Alex at the same time.

"Bree, right?" The corner of his eyes crinkle. "Yes, you did."

"Sorry about that." Red floods her cheeks. "Do you and Emma know each other?"

"No," comes out in stereo, his a velvet tenor and mine a thin soprano.

I drop my gaze, pretending interest in his overpriced shoes. His jacket creaks like new leather, and I look up when Alex lifts his arm and shoves off his hood. Longish brown hair shot through with natural coppery highlights tumbles loose, dusting his collar, brushing his cheekbones. He shoves a long, thin hand through his hair.

The electrical current shorts out, and I'm hollow again.

"So," he says, then points at the coffee cup in my hand that's twitching slightly, "Mugz-n-Chugz has the best coffee, right?"

Realization slams into my gut. The shudder I felt before slides down my spine. Alex watched me at the Walk-Up window. He must've been right behind me. He'd had to have, otherwise, how would he know I was holding a coffee? *Why was he watching me?* Before I can formulate the question, Alex gives me a short wave, identical to the one he gave the guy who called his name. He hides his face in the shadows of his hood, then leaves. The scent of leather lingers in my nose, and unconsciously I draw another deep breath of it after the side door slams shut behind him.

"What was that all about?" Bree's eyes are wide pools of confusion.

"You tell me." I hike my backpack and chug down the rest of my coffee in the hope of burning the smell of leather and the taste of embarrassment from the back of my throat. "Remember I moved here in sixth grade? I've never seen the guy."

"Well, he certainly acts like he's seen you before." Then a Cheshire grin spreads over her glossy lips. "Are you hiding secrets? Bet you are! You know him. You had a hot summer fling, never expecting to see him again, and now he shows up here—"

"Shut up, Bree." I chuck my cup into the trash can. A satisfying hollow *bang* rings from it. "That's the plot to *Grease*. I know your group did the show last year, but all life doesn't fit one musical."

"Maybe you two are star-crossed lovers, and he's finally found you on his soul's ageless search—"

"Maybe," I hit her with a narrow look when we reach the door, "or maybe he has a girlfriend—"

"Not the way he was looking at you." Utter conviction in her voice.

"Fine." I'm not winning this one. Arguing with Bree when she's entrenched is a lot like arguing with a brick wall. "Then how about you get your own boyfriend and quit dumping your fantasy relationships on me?"

"That's always a goal of mine."

"Mine, too."

Inside, Shelley High is hell on the eyes. Bright lights, chipped flooring, battered lockers, and neon flyers litter the walls. And people everywhere, milling in the halls like cattle in slaughter pens. The popular crowd I'll never be a part of and never want to, Bree's theater nerd friends and fellow thespians, and half a dozen other cliques jostle and shout, close to half of it in abbreviated text lingo.

I tuck my arms in, and weave through the throng. My locker is close to the main office. Usually it smells like coffee at this end of the hall. Not today. A lingering wisp of leather hangs close. I bend my head to my locker door, spin the combination, and tug. It's no use. Damn thing's stuck, again. It's only October and I've already had to get help from the janitor five times to force it open.

Josh Mason breaks free of the surge behind me. He leans his frame against the locker beside mine. I shoot him an exasperated look, then spin my combination again.

"That was a nice insult," he says.

He's trying to be sexy, I can tell, with his casual slouch and plaid button-down shirt open to show a little skin at his neck. For me, a six-foot ginger with curling hair and freckles is *so* not sexy. Cute, annoying, but never attractive like Josh wants to be to me.

"Yeah?" I slam my palm on my still-locked locker. "Well, you make it so easy."

He snorts, and has the decency to look like he's struggling for a nasty response when Alex Franks glides from the rabble and push of bodies and says, "You're on my locker."

No preamble, nothing polite. I think I could learn to like this guy.

"Sorry, man." Josh raises both hands and steps back. "Just making small talk."

Alex tips his head slightly, then turns from the curly-haired redhead. Josh puffs his chest out and clenches his jaw. A vein stands out on his forehead. The building tension must be obvious to Alex, too. He slowly faces back to Josh and asks, "What?" in that knowing, try-and-push-me tone.

"Nothing," Josh almost spits, then adds, "See you later, Emma," before walking away.

Alex watches Josh until he disappears around the hall corner, then turns back to his locker. He exudes mystery where he stands, drawing female gazes like an electromagnet. Brown hair obscures his face while he bends over his lock.

He opens his locker, shuffles stuff, deposits paperwork on the top shelf, and then shuts it while I still struggle to liberate my door from the steel grip of the locking mechanism.

"Want help?" he asks, a spark of amusement in his voice.

"Sure." I flick him a grateful glance, then look at my hands and rattle off my combination. Simple hope morphs to shock as he spins the numbers, pushing in with each one, then nudges the door with his hip.

The locker springs open.

My jaw drops.

In the two years I've had the same locker, only Daniel worked that damn lock as easily as Alex.

A tickle thrums across my skin when he swings the door open, his arm inches from mine, like he's a Tesla coil. Then with a slight nod and slighter smile, Alex pulls his hood back up and plunges into the churning masses. He cuts a path, heading towards the performing arts hall – our halls have names, like we can't figure out all the maths, literary, or arts classes are gathered in one area. Funny, he's getting along just fine, but since he arrived this morning I feel like I'm the one being suffocated.

Chapter Three

Halfway through first hour, my butt's numb from the hard plastic seat and I'm afraid the numbness is leeching up my spine and affecting my brain. I heave a sigh, chew my pencil, and try to pay attention while Mrs Johnson writes Trig problems on the dry erase board. Between the marker squeaks stabbing my eardrums, and thoughts of Alex and how he stared at me like I'm not supposed to be real, focusing on classwork is impossible

My cell phone vibrates in my backpack, a chaotic buzz and clatter, like bees and chicken bones. Half the class is texting or talking, taking advantage of Mrs Johnson's stubborn refusal to treat her hearing loss with hearing aids. I certainly wouldn't be the first to whip it out in class.

Casting a glance at her shoulders working under her sweater, I slide my phone free of the inner pocket, clicking a few pencils together. I stow the pink thing on my thigh, under my desk. When someone's at a desk, looking down with both hands in their lap, you know what they're doing. I join the ranks of the obvious.

Bree Ransom, the display screen reads.

What does she want? We just parted about ten minutes earlier. Sighing, I slide the phone open.

Alex's in my first hour! He's H.O.T. & single!

Well. That answers the girlfriend question I posed earlier. It also makes him extremely eligible in Bree's mind. A girlfriend would be a speed bump in her acquisitions pursuit, but she is one of the most determined people I know. I'm sure Bree's wondering if he's going to the dance this weekend, and if she can get him in a costume. I steal another peek at our hearing-impaired teacher before replying to the text.

His locker's next to mine.

Her response must have burned wires somewhere with its speed: *LUCKY!*

I silence my phone, slide it shut, and slip it back into the little pocket. At the head of the class, Mrs Johnson waves a marker at the string of gobbledygook numbers and symbols that I'd understand if I had paid attention earlier. I try to force my brain into logic mode – it's not happening. Ducking my head, I pray to not get called on to solve the equations. Images of Alex stab into the static noise in my head: standing next to my locker, spinning the combination like he's done it dozens of times before.

Luck has nothing to do with it.

Second hour passes in a classical literature fog.

Given the season, Mr Hansen is tormenting us with classic horror and Gothic fiction. We've read, discussed, and acted out bits of Bram Stoker's *Dracula* – my favorite book and the reason my cat's name is Renfield. After watching the second half of the latest Hollywood attempt at capturing the novel, Mr Hansen reaches around his paunch to hand out Further Reading lists, complete with samples of some

of the more popular choices. He looks like he might be sali-
vating with delight, and an errant thought careens through
my head: Mr Hansen dressed as an executioner, pulling a
lever...

On the Further Reading list are Hawthorne, Shelley, Poe,
and many others. Our task for the week, according to our
teacher, is to choose a title for class reading and use the week
to read it. The first week of November, we're to prepare a
thesis and report, comparing and contrasting *Dracula* with
the title of our choosing.

I run my finger down the list, names blurring into an il-
legible smudge.

The bell rings without me making a choice. Looks like I'll
have to visit the library after school. For once, I'll be doing
just what my mother thinks I am.

Hair down, head down, I leave class and aim for third
hour by way of the catwalk between the second floors of
the main building and the sports complex. Air whistles in
my ears when I open the door, then my heart clenches and
throat tightens. Last fall, on a sunny cool day like today, I
had met Daniel about three feet from where I stand. Sunshine had beat down, warming the hallway, separating the
red carpet into swaths of light and shadow, like puddles of
new blood bordered by old. Daniel had lounged against a
metal support, bathed in white light, looking better than any
senior should. I was awkward and shy, and a little in awe
of him.

His friend was all in red, from his hair to his shirt to his
shoes, reminding me of fire. The guy listened to headphones,
music loud, howling along and flailing around.

Playing the damsel in distress is way passé, but I was a le-
gitimate victim of a dance-by whacking from his oblivious

friend and his swinging arms. Daniel whipped off the T-shirt he wore over his thermal undershirt and packed my gushing nose in it. On the way to the office, when the stairs swirled at my face, Daniel saved me from falling. Then he'd carried me the rest of the way.

Today I walk in the opposite direction, heart aching, knowing Daniel is forever gone, as I aim for the torture chamber the staff of Shelley High likes to call the gymnasium.

Group and Individual Sports takes up my third hour. Normally I hate it, but hope bubbles up, thinking it's a chance to get physical and forget about Shelley High's latest addition to the student body. The locker room floor is made of mini-tiles, which are variations on brown, beige, and pukey pink, the lockers are beige, the rest is white. An ugly room, and exactly the reason my friends and I call it the Ugly Room. Usually filled with gossip, and this morning's no different.

Alex, Alex, Alex.

Alex Franks, his height, his leather jacket and the way his jeans hang on his butt are the main topics of conversation in the Ugly Room. Nikki Cummings has him in her second hour. "He wears his hood up all the time," and she thinks "it's sexy, even if he is a killer." Faith Lewis ran into him in the hall, "accidentally," she swears with a giggle, and her "cell phone hasn't worked right since." Marin Rhodes places bets with a few of her friends as to how soon she can get him to date her.

Rolling my eyes, I pull on my gym clothes. I wish I could be like them, excited about a boy, whispering about his looks, gossiping over whether he has a girlfriend. Daniel was that guy for me. His hazel eyes were so easy to get lost in. He held me and the world disappeared. Daniel was the one to carry me home when I tripped over that hydrant and broke my ankle. He was mine and losing him the way I did ripped a hole in me.

No new guy was ever going to fill the void he left.

My cell phone comes alive in my locker, a swarm in a metal can. I ignore Bree this time, and whip my hair into a ponytail. Our gym Drill Sarge is neither understanding nor accepting of phones, iPods, or any other portable electronic device in his class.

There is no mercy in Mr Ashford's eyes when we walk in, nor in the way he uses his shiny whistle. A mesh bag of basketballs rests at his feet in the middle of the gym. The gel in his buzz cut bounces back the overhead lights as he struts back and forth, barking orders. A full class hour of running and shooting baskets – my most dreaded activity. Running, dribbling a ball I lose as much as keep, and missing the baskets I shoot at anyway. *Dear God*, I think, *just kill me now*.

Slicked in sweat, ponytail slid halfway down the back of my head, I stagger through the showers after running so much I thought I'd puke. Lather, rinse, repeatedly curse the Drill Sarge.

Somehow, the student body seems to double during the lunch hour, collecting in one hall and one big room. Voices echo in the side hallway, dismembered and blurry with volume. Laughter punches through the cacophony, an occasional squeal slashes above the din. The sound batters my ears, and I quash the urge to skip lunch to avoid the throng.

The lunch line is ridiculously long, as always. The queue snakes out the door and down the hall. Tired and wringing shower water from my hair, I take last position.

"Emma!" Bree pokes her face out of the doorway. Her fake blond hair swings out like a flag. "Didn't you get my text? I'm saving you a spot."

That was what the text was about? She always saves me a spot in line, I just forgot. Good thing Bree's parents put her on an unlimited plan for her phone. I look up, blink and try to focus – when tired and a tad flustered, I run on autopilot, which includes standing in lines.

"Hey," whines a zit-faced, greasy-haired freshman, "no saving spots."

"When you're an upperclassman," comes a smooth tenor voice behind him, "you'll use the same unwritten privileges."

Heads swivel toward the source. Mine, too.

Tall, hood up, long sleeves pulled down over his wrists and thumbs shoved through holes in the cuffs. Sadly, I look to see how well Alex Franks' jeans look on his butt. The girls in the Ugly Room didn't lie. He wears them well, fills them in all the right spots. No sooner does the admiration of Alex's butt form, than a twinge of guilt pinches my heart. A ghost of Daniel's memory glides behind my eyes. I don't need to look at another guy, especially Alex Franks, when I have perfect memories.

Shaking my head, I schlep along the queue of shocked faces, then pause by his shoes.

Alex wears a bemused smile in the shadows of his hood. "Thanks."

He nods. "No worries."

The strange tunneling sensation strikes again when his eyes meet mine. Under the garish bright lights, it's easy to see their color, a rich hazel. Then he blinks, ducks deeper into the fabric surrounding his face and adds, "If you're really grateful, you can save me a seat."

Shock silences my tongue. It's not strong enough to muzzle some of the harpies with their sights obviously set on Alex, though. Hissed mutters remind me of vipers in movie scenes of Egyptian tombs. A couple of unkind things are muttered. Lots of heavily painted eyes glare daggers at me. I'm tempted to give them all the middle finger.

"Not sure about grateful, but I'll save you a seat," I say, then toss my wet hair over my shoulder and claim my spot behind Bree, nearly at the head of the line.

"Well, well," she simpers. "Looks like someone has a crush."

"What are you talking about?"

"Hellooo." She scoops up a tray and turns into the alcove containing hot foods. I snag a tray and follow. "First he stops and openly stares at you, then he asks to sit with you for lunch?"

"Yeah," I say, layering sarcasm into my voice. "I'm sure he's talked to lots of other girls in a friendly manner, too."

"Not that I've seen. He hardly talked to anyone in first hour." She loads her tray with French toast sticks, Tater Tots and applesauce. I opt for tots and applesauce – my stomach hasn't liked me since memory caught up to ogling, and I wrenched my gaze from Alex's back pockets. Bree pauses at the drinks cart, tosses a casual look toward the line where he clutches a tray. "Normally introverts don't take theater and drama. Someone must've screwed up his schedule. And for not crushing on you, he sure looks at you enough."

I jab her in the back with my tray, hard enough for her to gasp and stage whisper a cussword. Despite my desire to stay loyal to Daniel's memory, I find myself peeking over my shoulder. The shadows of Alex's hood aim directly at me.

I'm not sure, but I think there's a ghost of a smile hiding in there, too.

Forcing my eyes back to my lunch, I grab a water bottle, and traipse after Bree.

The wretched brown/beige/pukey pink color scheme of the locker rooms repeats in the cafeteria and the bathrooms; basically any place at risk of getting wet has the horrible vomit-colored mini-tiles. We weave between battered faux wood tables crammed with people shoveling food, or picking at it, or sitting there drinking Diet Coke like that's enough for them. Cliques spill in puddles from the food service doors; the in crowd, the sports crowd, the out crowd, and the thespians. Being Bree's best friend, I'm an honorary theater nerd. Plus, I've been to every performance since we moved here in sixth grade.

"Wassup, Em?" asks Bree's friend Jason Weller, pretty in a not-interesting way, and normally the leading man in any Shelley High theater production. "You going to the dance this weekend? I hear Bree has some kickass costumes picked out for you guys."

"I don't know." I turn it around on him. "What's she dressing you as?"

"Oh…" His smile is perfectly practiced when he feigns interest in buffing his nails on his sleeve. "We have a theme this year. It will be ah-mazing."

With Jason, everything good is "ah-mazing." And for a straight guy, he has damn good taste. Well, not in girlfriends. When it comes to girls, his taste is somewhere between airhead and bitch. But I don't judge…

"Maybe, then."

Bree's pink-clad arm snaps across the table and she smacks Jason's shoulder. "Leave it to you to pique her interest."

A sarcastic grin tugs at Jason's lips. "That's because you don't know how to sell it, B. She's probably scared you were planning on Zombie Twins."

I don't make an effort to hide the relief in my voice. "You weren't?"

Bree's laugh is bright enough to light a dark room. "Not this year." Then she sobers, and nudges me. "Look who's coming this way."

Alex, holding his tray in front of him like a shield, negotiates his way around the drinks cart, and almost clears the in crowd's ring of tables. Almost. Marin Rhodes, looking more perfect than I ever would after gym class, pops up from her seat and hurries over to Alex. She coos something not quite audible, then hooks her arm around his and takes his tray from him.

I cross my arms and lean back in my chair, watching him be dragged away.

He looks back over his shoulder, hood obscuring half his face when he shrugs. I lift one eyebrow and one shoulder. Doesn't bother me that he's falling prey to a girl placing bets on him. He wants to play Marin's little pet, then let him. At the head table of the in crowd, Marin motions imperiously for people to make room, then with one last glance at our table, he settles in with them.

"Ooh, girl," Bree says, dragging out the *girl* part. "That puppy's going to get tired before you have a chance to play with him."

"Who said I wanted to?" So I'm huffy. Sure, it's my fault I let my hopes climb out of the hole Daniel isn't buried in. Marin Rhodes booted them back in.

"Puppies as cute as that one don't last in the window very long."

"Awesome," I deadpan. "At least you didn't compare this moment to one of your stage productions."

"No," Jason cuts through the rising tension. "But I bet we could."

The entire drama club leans toward the center of the table, all pitching in play names that might match the new guy being sucked into the popular gang, while secretly in love with the outcast. I tune them out, and chew each Tater Tot with force, trying to grind out my frustrations. My applesauce is woefully inadequate for stress chewing, though.

Uncapping my water bottle, I scoop up my tray and promise to call Bree after school.

She knows I mean I'll call her after I leave the cemetery.

Tonight, I'll really need the solace.

Chapter Four

Lunch was awkward. Fifth hour knocks awkward out of the park.

The classroom looks like the rest of the classes in the sciences wing. A long black table stretches at the front of the room, with gas hook-up for Bunsen burners at one end and a small sink at the other. Industrial-grade gray flooring gleams beneath our feet, miniature versions of Mr LaRue's big lab table cluster in the back, and rows of wingtop desks march in formation between.

Our seats are not assigned in Dune Ecology. Mr LaRue says we're "up and running enough that assigned seating is a bother." Which translates to a one-desk ring of empty space circling Asia Foley, who's been coughing all day and is said to have puked between first and second hour. No one wants to get sick before the play-off game and dance on Saturday. It also means a free pass for that carrot-top Josh Mason to park himself somewhere close, usually one seat over.

"So," he says, dropping into the vacant seat in front of mine. I suppress the urge to groan, but just barely. His gaze rakes me. "When'd you hire the guard dog?"

"Excuse me?" I arch one eyebrow, despite my intentions to ignore him.

"Y'know..." He pulls his shirt collar onto the nest of his ginger curls. "Lurch. With his hood up?"

Wait. He thinks I asked Alex to run him off? My jaw clenches; I exhale an angry little puff I'm surprised doesn't carry steam. My instinct is to deny it with enough venom to melt his exposed skin. I don't need a guard dog, I can bite his ankles by myself. And I certainly wouldn't hire the new guy. He... puts me on edge. Instead of denying Josh's claim, I relax into our insult game.

"What?" I cup a hand to my ear, megaphone style. "I can't hear you over the red in your hair."

His brown eyes widen; his eyebrows go up, too. Then a slow poisonous smile spreads across his face. Not the response I was hoping for. Josh leans forward, his cologne assaulting my nose as I tilt in the opposite direction. His voice slips down in timbre when he whispers, "You know you like it."

"Hardly."

I'm tempted to tell him where he can shove his red hair, but I've tried that once. He grinned and offered to show me the hair already growing there. Cocky bastard won that round, and I've been playing catch-up ever since. At times I thought I hated him for not helping Daniel that night – maybe I just wanted to hate Josh because he didn't fall. Either way, sniping at each other is our best way of coping with surviving Daniel's loss.

Before I can formulate a good comeback, the door opens and Alex Franks walks in. He's thinner than I thought, now that I see him without his leather jacket. His black hood and sleeves cover as much as possible, but still can't camouflage the long lines of a swimmer's build. Girls' breaths catch classroom-wide – Asia's too, then she coughs a nasty wet bark of a sound. Josh snorts something less than nice, his grip white-knuckled on the edges of his desk.

Mr LaRue's dress shoes slap the floor as he hurries to take Alex's transfer slip. Our new student must stand a head higher than the rail-thin, balding teacher. Alex reaches one hand near the light switch to place his paperwork into the spidery waiting fingers. Above our heads the banks of fluorescent lights surge in brightness, a hum rising to a complaining pitch. The lights burn bright enough to sting my eyes, then die back to normal.

Heads tip up, faces turn toward the lighting fixtures. If possible, Alex sinks deeper into his hood. Mr LaRue smooths his tie, a nervous habit, and then says, "Welcome to Dune Ecology, Alex. Hopefully you'll enjoy our many preservation projects." He waves the papers toward the class in a vague gesture. "We have open seating."

"But not open season," Josh mutters, just loud enough for Alex to hear. The pesky redhead shifts his bulk in between me and the front of the room, and then flings his legs across the aisle. His sneakers land with a bang in the seat opposite him.

I shove the back of his desk with a foot, sending the metal legs on a screeching skid far enough for Josh's feet to drop from the seat. Alex turns his shadowed face toward us. And I'm sure I see a flicker of a grin, one that seems to radiate, "Game on" toward Josh. The air turns frigid between the two guys when Alex strides even with Josh and eyes him. Neither moves. Josh's normal smirk shrivels, the corners of his mouth sinking when he curls his long legs back under his desk. Alex hikes his backpack and steps right to left over the seat, making a point to step through where Josh's feet had been moments before.

He stands one aisle over, still eyeing Josh, who looks back and doesn't respond. Satisfied, I guess, Alex walks one more desk back to the last empty seat outside of the sick zone around Asia, and directly across from me. My gaze is drawn to him, the smooth movements, and quiet confidence. As if Alex can feel me gawking, he turns his hood my way, and his calm smile falters. The earlier look of disbelief widens his eyes, then he blinks and ignores Josh. And me.

I can't wrench my gaze away. Is his hood a human version of blinders on a horse? Or does he not want people looking in? The rumor mill pegs him as some kind of bad guy, even though what I've seen of him says different. Some part of me sings in his presence, and I don't think I like it. Maybe his bad is my good?

Alex's hood shifts slightly, I catch a glint of his eyes, a hint of a smile. Then he points toward our teacher like he *knows* I'm still staring at him.

Mr LaRue stands behind the big lab table at the head of the room, talking about preservation projects and idly toying with a potted tuft of dune grass. The first day of class, I'd rubbed my thumb along the edge of one long green blade and cut myself to feel the sting. Anything was better than the empty ache ghosting behind me from class to class and screaming Daniel's absence. Now, almost two months since that day, and four months after his fall, the edges of the void are numb – I'm not sure if they've expanded, or shrunk.

One phrase pulls me from my mulling: "joint project."

Groans rise from the class, fluttering and wispy, then die. Eyes roll. Josh straightens in his chair, and tosses a wolfy half-grin at me. Alex's hood edges toward Josh, and Alex's shoulders square.

"And I'll be picking your partners," Mr LaRue says, sending a fresh volley of moans around the room. "Too many groups played on the beach last time instead of working, and I don't want that going on tomorrow."

Josh's hand stabs the air above his head. Papery whispers lift from our teacher's desk as he rifles around. When he looks up, his eyes narrow on the fish-white hand waving above Josh's head. He has the attention of the entire class. Even Asia looks our way after she barks another seal-sounding cough. Mr LaRue heaves a sigh and gives a minute shake of his head.

"No, Josh. No special treatment for members of sports teams…"

Red curls slide from his face as Josh turns and stares over his shoulder. The possessive glance skims my face, before he arches an eyebrow and needles a glare at the side of Alex's hood. Dread uncoils in my gut.

Please don't put me with Josh, I pray silently. *Please don't saddle me with that egotistical, pain in my –*

"Tamara Abernathy," calls our teacher, "and Trevor Ames."

He continues down the alphabetical list he doesn't use for seating, making it a hit list of class partners doomed to epic failures. Two pairings in and Josh Mason realises he won't be harassing me, and lets out a heavy groan. He'll be paired with Shane Lowenstein or Kinnely Minor, both major competition for his prized pitcher's position on the baseball team – and two of his least favorite people.

My mind stumbles down the attendance list, scrambling to figure out who I'll be paired with before the teacher calls out, "Asia Foley and Alex Franks. Then Emma Gentry and Shane Lowenstein."

A horrid retching noise bursts from Asia, sitting in her purgatory of empty seats, like a giant cat bringing up a hairball. Then she leaps from her seat and runs as far as the trash can before puking. A wet, sour smell fills the air, and two people in the front row gag on the stink. Asia slumps to her knees, loops her thin dark arms around the battered can and hurls again. Mr LaRue calmly makes a notation in his list, pulls out a hall pass and hands it to her after her third upchuck.

"Then that makes Alex Franks and Emma Gentry." Josh lets out a hiss of air. Alex inhales, then his profile softens in a smile. He turns his head enough for Josh and I to see into his hood and his grin turns to an "aw, poor you" expression aimed at Josh. When our teacher calls the next pairing, I can't help but giggle. Vicious and short, but it happens. "Shane Lowenstein and Josh Mason."

After that lethal partnership is announced, our teacher ushers Asia out of the room with a hand near her back. Expectancy hovers heavy and foglike in the room. He returns to his list, and announces partners while nudging the garbage can full of vomit into the hall. A pairing, and a screech of metal on linoleum. Splashing sounds and stench. A pairing, and a screech...

By the time the door closes on the offensive can, I'm half sick from the smell and noise. Partners peek at each other from their desks, except for Josh and Shane, who are intensely, seethingly ignoring each other, and me and Alex. Part of me wants to look at him, brush back his hood and see what he's hiding.

The edges of my hollowed heart quiver.

My gaze plummets to my hands, folded over my notebook, a pale heart still marring the summer tan across the back of my hand. I'd worn a broken-heart rub-on tattoo, mourning Daniel all summer, and the sun had burned a negative of the image into my skin.

Thankfully, our teacher wheels a TV stand to the front of the room, presses play on the DVD player, and turns off the lights. An educational video rolls on the screen, the stark beauty of Lake Michigan's dunes, the fragile ecosystem, the erosion destroying them. I recognize the gritty wind, the cutting grasses, and the sunlit sky. I have an intense heartache, and biting guilt now, because some part of me thrilled to the new partnership with Alex like a forgotten instrument singing under a touch.

I shift my eyes to the dune grass sitting in its pot on the black expanse of tabletop. My thumb aches to feel its bite again.

After last hour, the halls fill with the surge and press of bodies. Sounds mix in a cacophony of locker doors banging, and voices trying to be heard over every other. Perfumes have softened, colognes are weaker.

Well, they were until Josh strolls up to my locker reeking of a fresh layer of some knockoff cologne. He leans against Alex's locker. Damned if I don't appreciate the annoyance he represents. At least my heart doesn't want to *feel* when Josh is around. "Your guard dog have some kinda magic?" he asks. "Never saw a more timely spew in my life."

"Really? All eighteen years of it?" I ram my shoulder into my stubborn locker. "Let me get your walker with the tennis balls on the front. You're just stooped over with experience."

"Right after I get you protective gear for when your dog turns against you."

"So says he who's jealous." I glare at my lock, spit a cussword under my breath and spin the combination again.

"Resulting to Yoda Speak, Emma?" He crosses his arms, duffle bag at his feet.

"He might've been a shriveled-up green dude…" My knuckles scream after I punch my locker. "But Yoda was a brilliant Jedi master."

"You are such a geek." Fingers stroke my hair after Josh scoops up his bag and walks behind me. "See ya tomorrow, Gentry."

"Can't seem to get away from you if I tried." I turn and spin the locker combination into my lock. Still nothing. My books drop to the floor, security deposits be damned. I flex my fingers and grab the lock again. Another failed attempt.

Tingles brush across my skin, a whisper of electricity. The weight of a glance presses on my neck a moment before, "Here, let me," comes over my shoulder in a soft tenor voice.

Alex Franks. Dune Eco partner and locker neighbor.

My shoulders slump in defeat. I lift my hand from my lock, catching a glimpse of the white broken heart near my wrist when I do. My gaze lifts to the face hidden in the shadows of Alex's hood as if pulled there by a magnetic force. Bemused expression. Full lips under a slightly crooked nose and hazel eyes. Mismatched hazel, even, one darker than the other with a black freckle in it and…

Alex blinks, and turns to look at my lock. An odd sensation of reeling myself back from some ledge fills me. He taps the dial, spins the numbers from memory and pushes each in, then bumps the door with his hip. The locker eases open like I didn't just punch a dent into its door because it staunchly refused to work for me.

"Thanks," I say. "This is getting to be a habit."

"Happy to help." Alex opens his locker just as quickly, without the extra tweaks. His voice has a tinny edge when he speaks with his head inside it. "You sound like that's a problem, though."

How can I tell him how easily he opens my locker creeps me out? And since Daniel's fall from that balcony, I haven't relied on guys, or let them get close enough to have my locker combination.

"N-not really a problem," I stammer, even though on some level it really is. "Now I feel like I should say I'm sorry." And I hate that word.

I turn and then force myself to organize my books for homework tonight. Shards of hurt grind in the knuckles of my right hand with every movement. Great. Mom will be in a tizzy over this. Probably drag me to the med clinic, too. I hate that place, always crowded, people coughing, and at least one baby screaming.

"No worries," Alex says, spinning his lock once after closing his locker. "And God knows, if Carrot-Top was always hounding me, I think I would want to open that locker and climb in it."

A little snicker sneaks from me. "Josh *is* annoying." And probably hates Alex already

"What's up with him, if I can ask?"

"Long story." I wince when my knuckles throb with heartbeats of their own as I sling my backpack over my shoulder. "Ouch."

Alex's eyebrows furrow. "May I?" he asks at the same time he takes my right hand in his.

The touch is soft, hardly a murmur of contact, but the hair on my arm stands like I'm stroking a plasma globe. Little electric shocks zing from each of his fingers. Speech dries in my throat. I can hardly think when he's touching me, like everything's on short circuit in my brain. Alex turns my hand, tingles following his fingertips as he gently probes my knuckles, already darkening and swelling. His index finger glides across my hand up to the pale broken heart, then back to my knuckles.

"These look broken," he pronounces, and releases my hand. "I can drive you home."

No way. Say it, Emma. I can't spit it out.

"Drive me home?" I turn and walk toward the side door, putting needed distance between us. I don't need to look to know he's following. I feel him over my shoulder. My short question drags him along behind me like bait. "You asked me to save you a seat at lunch, then you don't sit there. If I accept the ride, you'll just leave me hanging."

"What?" he bursts out, a hint of incredulity in his voice. "That doesn't make any sense."

I push open the side door. Clouds litter the sky. Wind gusts rattle the skeletal branches above us. Rich leather scent whisks past me on the wind as Alex shrugs into his jacket he's carried since I walked away from the lockers. Rueful regret fills me, and I long for the sweatshirt Daniel had draped over my shoulders minutes before the accident.

"Makes perfect sense to me." I can't accept a ride from Alex, despite the deepening hurt in my hand or the chill biting at me. Something's off with him. Something's off with me around him. "Besides, I need to go to the library and check out a book for my English Lit class."

"OK, fine. You have homework." He huffs a little breath. "It'll be hard to write with a broken hand."

"What do you think you are?" I shoot him a look over my shoulder and instantly regret it. He's tall, ridiculously handsome with concern softening his features. I jerk my gaze forward. If I stumbled walking and talking at night, I don't want to see what walking and looking at Alex Franks could do to me. "You some kind of doctor now?"

"Nope." He stops walking by the side of the gym, an invisible tether between us pulling me to a halt. "My dad is, though. He took care of me after... after I got hurt this spring."

"Oh. Sorry," I offer out of reflex. A pulse of hurt minces in my knuckles when I push strands of blond from my eyes. "I'll have my mom take me to the clinic when I get home, OK?"

"Then let me give you a ride." His hood slips from his long shaggy hair with the next gust of wind. His left eye pinches a little tighter as he squints against the sunlight. "You'll get your hand taken care of quicker."

"Persistent, aren't you?"

His smile is sudden, and wicked. "I can be."

"I can be, too," I say and motion for him to move along. "It's definitely a no thanks."

A sigh escapes Alex, accompanied by a shake of his head. I can't stop from watching the sunlight slide over his brown hair, and set alight his coppery highlights.

"Y'know, there's not much difference between stubborn and persistent," he says, hooking his hood with a finger and pulling it back up. The motion exposes a scar running from his wrist, down his forearm. I blink, and falter a moment, my mind stuck on the white track in his skin.

"True." Then I shake my head and come back with, "But stubborn sounds so negative, and I don't know you that well. Thanks for the offer, Alex."

The hood slips over his eyebrows and buries his eyes in shade when he gives me a mock bow. "Another time then?"

"Possibly."

"Then I'll see you at your equally stubborn locker tomorrow." He winks. "Bye, Emma."

"Later, Alex."

I slump against the cool brick half-wall running the length of the gymnasium. Alex shouldn't look back – it would be better for both of us – but he casts me a brief glance once he reaches the corner. He lifts his hand in a hesitant wave. I return it and a smile warms the inside of his cowl. The image of his scar slashes through my mind, cutting open veins of questions. What happened? Was that from surgery? Did he do it? Are the rumors right? Why does he do things like Daniel?

Why does he wake up my broken heart?

Chapter Five

Once Alex's car, a black electric/fuel hybrid, pulls into the
flow of traffic fleeing the school, I use my left hand to claw
my cell phone from my backpack pocket. Alex's warning
that something's already broken in my right hand keeps me
from using it. Still, I can't resist compounding the pain, and
give Josh a heartfelt middle finger salute when he roars past
in his ancient Z-28.

Weak sun glints from the display screen as I turn the
phone on and press 1 for Home. One ring, then two. A third
before Mom picks up the other end of the line. Dishes clatter
in the background when she says, "Hello?"

"Hi, Mom." I fight the urge to cry. "Can you come get
me? I hurt my hand today and I think it might be broken."

"Broken?" Her tone rings with surprise. "I'll be right there."

"Right there," ends up being long enough for me to stuff
my phone away, regret not wearing a warmer jacket, and
wish Daniel was here instead of the non-existent jacket.

As Mom's faded gold sedan pulls to the curb, she reaches
through the car and opens the passenger side door for me.
Her face is a frowning, furrowed mask of concern. Inter-
nally I cringe, bracing for the bitch-out I know is coming.

Mom's best vent for worry is yelling, usually at who she's worried about. As expected, when I drop my butt into the front seat she throws a proper fit, wanting to know how it happened, why I wasn't more careful, blah blah blah.

I'm too far gone into the pain, and don't want to admit I punched my locker in frustration. She'd just yell more, tell me I should've seen the counselor when they offered it. And maybe she's right. A lump forms in my throat and tears burn their way over my lashes. Her tizzy fizzles. Underneath the stop light a few blocks from the med clinic, she reaches across the gulf of the empty seat between us and pats my leg.

A wall had appeared between us after Daniel died. I'd hoarded my hurt and loss, and wouldn't let her fix it. I'd slammed my door more times than I ever should've. Mom was always there, waiting, ready to put me back together if I fell apart.

I never crumbled where she could see.

Now, the pain grinds in my knuckles and undercuts my grasp on control. I loosen my crossed arms, and thread my fingers in Mom's. Her gentle Mom sounds bring me to my sniveling weakest. My will disintegrates. The smell of cookies rises from her sleeve when I put my head on her shoulder.

Somehow she knows these tears aren't just over my hand. Mom presses her cheek to the top of my head, silken rustles following the motion as she coddles me.

Wet heat slicks my face, my bottom lip trembles and the hollow in my chest hurts. Yearning aches in me, pushing me to cry on her like I did when I was little. Movement is beyond me. Motion, thought, speech – anything – and I'm going to fall apart. Mom pulls her hand from mine and guides me until she cradles my head in her lap. She whispers over and over, "You're going to be OK."

OK.

It's such a lovely promise.

Promises are like hearts, easily broken.

There, on her lap like I wish I'd been four months ago, the last of my resolve cracks and the sobs finally break free. Guilt roils up and I know I should stop, she doesn't deserve to drown in my misery. How do you close the floodgates once they're open? Mom puts the car in park, leaves the engine running and weathers the storm with me. I'm not Emma anymore, just hurt and loss and anguish in a sack of skin and possibly broken bones. Emotion scores my insides, scrapes them out with the force of a tidal wave.

I cry for Daniel, my heart breaking, my mind bleeding memories I've tried so hard to keep buried. The look of terror, the loss in his eyes... It's gouged into my soul.

I cry for myself, the miserable shell I've been without him here.

I cry for everyone I've hurt by withdrawing from life.

Mom never stops stroking my shoulder, or my hair, a gentle contact anchoring me. I pull in a slow and deep cooling breath and realise the hurt has lessened. I feel scraped and stinging inside, gutted like the jack-o'-lantern sitting on the ground outside the clinic door. Except somewhere in the aching emptiness I see a spark, a flicker of my own, the light Daniel would've wanted me to finally find.

Hope.

Stupid me, I try to push to a sitting position using my right hand, then yelp out a cry of pain. Mom whips her seat belt off so fast the buckle whacks the window. She cradles my hand, barely touching it, with none of the electric tingles that came from Alex's fingers. Sighing, she releases my hand to cup my cheeks, turns me to meet her brown eyes. I'm torn open, exposed as she searches my face, and I imagine her hunting for a glimmer of who I was before.

I see the glow inside. Will she?

A soft curve lifts the wrinkly corners of Mom's mouth. Her nod is subtle. "There's my girl."

My smile looks strained and weak in the rear-view mirror. At least it's real. Hairs shift by my face from her sigh. She wipes at my tears with her thumb, so inadequate to the deluge that wets my cheeks. I think Mom realises it's a losing battle, because she fishes in her purse for a clean tissue, then dries my face.

"You're going to be OK," she repeats.

The solid empty feeling you get after a good cry rocks in my head when I nod. This time, I believe her.

Shoulders sagging, hand aching, I slink behind her through the lengthening afternoon shadows toward the entrance. The pumpkin's candle flickers and dies in the displaced air of the opening door.

Inside the clinic, the smell of carpet cleaner and rubbing alcohol accosts my nose. Off-white walls hem in people. A particularly snot-coated kid wipes his boogers across his sleeve, then smiles with gaps missing between his teeth.

Mom signs my name on the emergency care list, then we take two chairs across from the banks of glass windows separating the wounded and contagious from the caregivers. My backpack slides to the floor, feet away from the door the nurse pops out of to call in patients. Looking at my swollen, bruised writing hand, I can't help but fret over how I'll do my class work, my homework... Heck, how am I going to shower or wash my hair?

My lips part to ask Mom those questions the same moment my cell phone rings.

I think every person behind the divider window glares daggers at me. Heat floods my cheeks and throat, and I contemplate hiding in my hood like Alex Franks does as I yank my phone from the pocket to shut it off.

The flashing name lets me know it's a call from Bree before I stab the power button with my left index finger.

A surly looking nurse steps through the door and calls my name. Mom jumps up, and follows me into the warren of halls and identical rooms. Fear niggles in me, claws up my spine. The doctor will touch, prod, and possibly realign my hand.

I step on the scale. The nurse slides the height guide to the top of my head, then makes note of my height and records my weight, before ushering Mom and me into a little room. Refusing to sit on a table sized for toddlers, I sit in the chair. An exasperated snort escapes my Mom, then the paper lining the table crinkles when she slides onto it. Then she slides off, just as quick.

After a few minutes of hurting and hating my "juvenile themed" room, the door swings open. A tall, stern-looking man with graying hair and wire rim glasses strides in. His dour expression reminds me of a mortician. His white lab coat has no name embroidered, no name tag.

Dr Nobody moves with ease, a fake smile edging into his cheeks. Something about him looks familiar, only my emotionally drained brain refuses to make the connection.

"So," he says, no formal greeting, "hurt your hand, Emma?"

"Yeah." I lift my right hand, putting the purple-blue puffiness in full view. "A guy at school said he thought it was broken."

"Really?" I wish he sounded interested, instead of almost annoyed. Dr Nobody exudes an aura of doing me a huge favor as he sits on the little rolling stool, and scoots closer. He takes my hand, jolts of pain shooting from where he prods and presses in between my knuckles. A wheeze escapes me. "Sorry," he says. "Your friend must be very smart."

Or he saw me punch my locker. "Alex said his dad is a doctor."

"Is that true?" His eyebrows creep up, and his voice drops in timbre.

"Yes, sir."

Suddenly, he goes from a Nobody to a Somebody and I'm wishing we'd gone to the emergency room instead. The doctor's grip tightens on my hand enough to draw another wheeze from me. The thickness of his lenses sharpens his gaze to a scalpel as he scours my face. The pressure increases, knuckles grinding, tears burning in my eyes. Then bones break with a *crunch*. I bite off a strangled cry as my head spins with the fresh pain. Mom steps closer with a sound of alarm.

"Well, Alex must be a lucky boy." Dr Somebody releases me, and jerks upright from the stool fast enough for his lab coat to snap with the motion. He steps closer, actually hovering above me, pinning me with a stare. "We're going to need X-rays. You're not pregnant, are you?"

"Now, just wait a minute," Mom barks, glowering.

"Of course not!" I snap at the same moment. He hurt me and I can't shake the feeling it was intentional. But why?

"Sorry, Mrs Gentry." His voice is slick, quasi-comforting. "It's protocol to ask."

And he sweeps out of the room.

Mom and I stare wide-eyed at each other; neither of us breathe. When she finally exhales, her eyebrows sink, then her color comes up, pinking her cheeks. Then she storms out, on the hunt for Dr Somebody, I'm sure.

The emptiness of the room presses in, threatening to crush me. Indentations of his fingers press into my swollen skin. Ache throbs deep in the joints and just behind, in the bones of my hand. My throat tightens, a lump rises I struggle to swallow.

I've never seen a stranger react so violently to a guy's name. Unless, the doctor's not a stranger to Alex...

Half-formed questions crowd my head. *Who is... Why was he... What's his problem?*

Edgy, ugly pieces are starting to fit together in my head. I rise from the chair, pacing and puzzling. There has to be a connection between Dr Somebody and Alex. Doesn't there?

An orderly pops open the door, and whisks me through the twisty, short maze of halls to the X-ray lab. A cold, dark, unfriendly room as unwilling to give up information on the doctor as my tired, stressed-out brain. The X-ray tech chatters amiably and emptily, using a practiced script of what she's doing rather than engage in real conversation as she arranges my hand, slides films in to the machine, and steps behind the wall to take the picture.

"Hey, um... Tech Girl, do you know which physician ordered the X-rays?"

She mutters something on her side of the wall, then crosses the dimly lit space and pulls the films. Holding them to the light board, she says, "He's a brilliant surgeon. Donates his time here. Ah–" She nods. "Two different sets of breaks. Looks like you're getting an immobiliser."

Two different sets? "Oh, goodie."

Before I can ask her who the psychopath "brilliant surgeon" is who must have given me the second set, she says, "Dr Franks."

The name hits with a sick, sinking kind of weight. I didn't hear her right. I couldn't. At least, part of me does not want to believe it. There must be more Dr Franks in Muskegon County, right?

"Excuse me?" I ask.

"The doctor who ordered your X-ray," she answers. "His name is Dr Franks. He volunteers time here."

The bottom drops out of my gut. I blink at Tech Girl in a numb kind of shock.

That horrid man is Alex's father?

Before I can ask if he has a son, she picks up her work phone, barking orders to someone and guides me back to the room. My feet drag, my brain churns. Disbelief echoes in my damaged core.

Mom's waiting for me. Her eyebrows are mashed together and storm clouds darken her eyes. Her gaze rests on the back of my hand, but the doctor's fingerprints are gone. She reaches out an arm, offering me shelter. The hurt and fear rising inside drives me to her side, a cub to a mother lioness. She's nearly through explaining how she bitched out the ladies behind the desk and then lodged a formal complaint when another doctor opens the door.

This man is young and reedy, with dark hair and watery blue eyes. His embroidered lab coat proclaims him to be a doctor named Jonathan Yates.

A fraction of my tension relaxes, but I can't escape the horrid shock snipping my thoughts short. Mom gives my shoulder a reassuring pat. Dr Yates is gentle and considerate, and he explains everything. He verifies Tech Girl's comment about two different breaks, one close to the knuckles consistent with hitting something, and one's further back in the carpal-somethings, consistent with crushing. He continues with the reason he's the one putting the hard metal brace under my hand and strapping it into a stiff immobiliser.

"I'll be overseeing your visits now." He pauses to rip open the Velcro straps on my new brace. "The surgeon who saw you earlier was called away on an emergency. Dr Franks sends his apologies."

He can send apologies. I don't want them. I don't ever want to see him again.

Chapter Six

By the pinch of Mom's mouth, she's way less than pleased when I ask her to drop me off at the library instead of going home. Her glower is nearly as dark as the clouds lingering on the horizon, choking the late afternoon sun. "No, Emma." She gives me an are-you-joking look. "Your hand is broken. We should be filling your prescription for pain meds and getting you home."

"I've been hurting this long." Lame argument, I know, but it's worth a shot. I take my backpack, and drag it slowly across the seat, giving Mom the opportunity to get serious about denying me. "And you can fill my script while I get my book. Win-win. I have to have it read by the end of the week. I don't want my grade to slip…"

She heaves a tired sigh, knowing she's lost this round of the nurture war. Number one in Mom's world is my health, only slightly less important is my GPA.

"Fine." I know I've won when she turns off of Washington, away from home and toward the library. She turns the car into the library parking lot. "I'll pick up your prescription and be back to get you."

An argument rises in my throat, but it can't struggle

past the rawness tears left behind. I nod and turn from the car.

After Mom pulls away, I lean against the brick façade and watch the dying light. The empty bike rack stands like a frenched rib cage, a suspicious puddle beneath reflecting back the sunset's bloody hues. Daniel always loved this time of day, we watched every sunset possible, from rooftops, beaches, and cemeteries.

The edges of loss gape in my chest. God, I miss Daniel.

I push off the wall and step into the light, forcing myself off the mourning spiral. One-handed, I root around in my backpack, then revive my phone. The screen lights up with notifications of texts and missed calls. Bree's been busy, probably alternating between text and dial, text and dial. Rather than listen to, or read the numerous messages, I press 2 for Bree. And then consider a snicker about her being my Number Two.

The first ring dies a fast death. "Emma, where have you been?" A frantic edge sharpens her voice. "I've called you, like, a hundred times. Jason said Harmony told him that someone saw you holding hands with Alex Franks!"

"Whoa. Breathe, Bree. Breathe." Nothing stirs up the gossipmongers better than a new guy plus depressed girl equation. I lift my right hand, suddenly very aware that the white broken heart has been covered, and tuck the brace into the pocket of my hoodie. "We weren't holding hands. He was just supporting my hand while he–"

"It's TRUE!" she crows at the other end.

"It is *not* true," I snap. Even though he did hold my hand, and brush his finger past my knuckles to what I didn't need him touching. "End of story."

"Oh, no," she says, voice thick with innuendo, "this story's just starting."

"Whatever." I do not need this right now. I heave an exasperated sigh. "Bree?"

"Yes?"

"I love you." I open my backpack, readying it for my phone as I turn back toward the library doors. "But shut up."

"Only for now, girlfriend. I expect a full report later. Bye, Em."

Of course she does. It'll have to be over the phone. She claims actors are professional liars, so she can recognize a fibber when she sees one. Plus, Bree knows when I'm keeping things from her. I can't tell her I felt electricity in his touch – she'd think I was crazy. I think I might be, though. It would be easy to blame the tingles on my oversensitive nerves, but I know better.

And what about his dad?

Like father, like son. Why does it bother me that he might be like his father?

I shut my phone off before entering the library. The glass doors draw in cool air, then swing shut. The smell of captive words, glue and old carpets fills the space. The weight of hundreds of books presses on me. The guy behind the desk points to a sign on the wall beside him demanding all students show their ID cards before proceeding. I sigh, dig it out with no small amount of noise, making a big deal of following his demand with one hand, then wave it at him.

His dyed black hair shifts, thin and greasy, when he shrugs and makes an apologetic noise close to "Sorry."

Evening sun – through the windows of the west wall – falls thick and discolored from the stained glass. Splotches of gold, green, and red splash across the shelves.

I spend a few minutes stroking book spines on my hunt for another gothic fiction novel to compare and contrast with Bram Stoker's *Dracula*. Ghosts, vampires, werewolves, created monsters. After settling on another classic title by one of the Shelley authors – chosen out of desperation by using my school's name as a guide – I carry it to the front desk, check it out, and allow the geek behind the desk to stuff it in my backpack.

Outside, evening shadows have devoured most of the light. Jack-o'-lanterns cast their leering smiles of flame from doorways, splashes of fire in the anemic glow of twilight. Shouldering my backpack, and wishing I had some painkillers in me now, I trudge to the gold sedan waiting for me.

She asks about the book I chose. The cover rasps against my backpack zipper when I pull it out. Mom casts a sideways glance, then nods and says she read it. Her words, the whole trip home, skirt my conscience. On some level I'm here and talking, but my mind is stuck on Daniel. Normally, I would be at the cemetery fence right now, wishing he had a grave.

At home, dinner is a rare take-out event, thanks to my locker-punching and clinic visit. After dinner I make a lame excuse about needing some air, and ease out the front door before Mom can say no. I drift through the neighborhood, drawn by an inexorable pull. Branches creak and groan above me, nearly invisible in the dark before the street lights burn to life.

Leaves rustle and scud along the sidewalk, pushed by my feet and the breeze at my back ushering me toward that familiar stretch of graveyard fence. The gate is not close enough – it's a wrought iron barrier between me and Daniel's memory.

Tonight I don't linger on the border between living and dead. My shoes take me among the headstones as I drift along their stationary parade route toward the mausoleums.

One bone white porch beckons. If I close my eyes, I can see Daniel sitting there, feet propped up on the banister. Here, wandering between the dead, it's impossible for me to think spirits don't live on. I can feel some of them watching a trespasser walk on their resting places.

As every night before, not one headstone has the name I look for. No amount of fantasizing will create a grave for Daniel.

The face of the moon peeks over the trees. My heart stutters, then resumes its pace. It looks the same as that night in June, the last time Daniel and I ever sat here together. He's gone, and I know it, but I wish with everything in me to be able to see him, hold his hand, nestle in his arms again.

Blinking back a tear, I climb the cold railing, my soles squeaking loudly. My backpack settles to the porch with a whisper of nylon and stone. I stand in the spot I'd sat in months ago, with Daniel to my left. Closing my eyes, I wish for a glimmer of his ghost, and slide to my butt with my back against the wall. After all the days spent with his memory, I can picture him to the last tousled dark curl. He would be wearing sneakers, faded jeans, maybe the pair with the hole in the knee. Covering his chest would be a soft white T-shirt, the collar peeking through his blood red zip-up hoodie. The last item I can see in exquisitely painful clarity, because I sleep in it every night.

Daniel. My heart hurts for him.

His smile would almost glow against the tan of his cheeks. A playful, loving light would shine from his hazel eyes.

Would, if he were alive.

I slide my left hand, palm up along the floor beside me, offering it to the phantom I carry in my heart. Nothing but cold touches my skin. When I open my eyes, strange ghostly light lies in a puddle on my palm, and pours down the side of the tomb, a perfect mimic for Daniel's slouch.

I've never let him go, not really. If it is Daniel's spirit, I hope he'll be proud.

Hey, Emergizer Bunny... His voice sounds in my mind, using his favorite nickname for me. *Why so sad?*

"I miss you, Daniel." His whispered name strangles into a sob, and I curl my fingers tighter over the hand that isn't in mine. "It's an ache I can't escape. I've come here so many nights, looking for your name on one of these headstones. But it never is."

Wasn't supposed to end this way, was it? The smile I imagined slides toward a frown on his face. *I'm so sorry I had to leave you.*

The breeze picks up, whispering in the woods beyond the cemetery fence, blowing between my fingers. I peek at the ghost light cupped in my hand, then pinch my eyes closed.

I say, "You never really left." The weight of his memory pushes on my shoulders, drags at the edges of emptiness inside me. "I've carried you in my heart for so long, I don't know anything else."

You shouldn't be here. His voice darkens. When I look at his spectral image, he's the Daniel after his fall, skull cracked, brain and blood in his hair, red trails over his forehead and in his eyes. One red drop slips over the black freckle in his iris. *I'm dead, Em. I don't want you to keep dying inside for me.*

"I don't want it either." Saying goodbye is like losing him all over again. My chest is a mass of hurt. My throat burns, and eyes brim with tears. "Help me let you go. Please, Daniel. I love you, always will, but I have to say goodbye."

He smiles through the red streaming down his face. A

cool breeze blows a kiss on my cheek, damp with my tears. His voice is soft, sad, and resigned. *You just did. Open your eyes…*

His commands were never something I could ignore. My eyelids slide up, my eyes on the light in my hand. The wind picks up, a cloud cutting across the half-moon until it's gone.

And so is Daniel.

Chapter Seven

The first thing I notice is that Wednesday morning dawns cold and clear, despite the weight of storms crowding the air. It's fall in Michigan, after all, crappy autumn weather happens here.

The second thing I notice is the weight of storms pressing on broken bones in my hand.

"Oh my God–" accelerates downhill to much worse words.

"I thought you'd be hurting," Mom says from the shadows of the door. She has the decency not to look like she spent all night worrying about me, even though I'm sure she did.

"Entirely," I agree and push to sitting with my left hand pressed to the snarl of blankets shackling my legs.

"Want help with anything?"

"I think I can manage." I kick my blankets off, and turn so my feet hit the floor. "But I appreciate the offer."

"I'll be downstairs then, getting you a one-handed breakfast."

"Thanks, Mom."

Warm air gushes from the hall, sliding by the closing door. If I were smart, I would've accepted the help – T-shirts and pants aren't easy one-handed, my bra almost impossible.

Stubborn and smart constantly battle for control of me, according to my dad. After levering myself from the bed, I hitch the wedgie of my boxers out of places they shouldn't have crept overnight. Then my closet witnesses my struggle into my favorite yoga pants and a long-sleeved stretchy pink shirt.

A stripe of burgundy catches my eye, then tugs at the new bandage wrapping my heart tattoo. The fleece is soft beneath my fingers when I run them over Daniel's hoodie where it rests on my shelf.

I thought I'd never sleep without the warmth I'd felt in it the night Daniel slid it over my bare shoulders. Last night, I hurt and I wanted it, but Mom helped me into my pajamas and into bed. She would have sighed if I'd asked her to help me put on my dead boyfriend's sweatshirt. Probably would've considered getting me counseling, too. Instead, we choose baggy boxers and an equally baggy shirt. Then she sat by my bed, reading aloud from my library book about the product of a man's hubris coming back to haunt him.

Dark things to fall asleep to, but I did. I blame the painkillers.

Bypassing the reminder of Daniel, I grab a pink camouflage zip-up hoodie to coordinate with my pink shirt. I have to start putting distance between me and his memory, or I'll never get past his death. And I want to get past it, I just don't know how. Regardless, wrestling into today's clothes leaves me ready for a painkiller and a nap.

Downstairs, Dad's bellied up to the breakfast bar, the cap of his salt-and-pepper hair peeking above the local section of the newspaper where his nose is buried, and with a cup of coffee close by. "Good morning, Emma."

The modifier doesn't make sense with the pain grinding in my hand. "Morning."

"Want a ride to school?" He turns the page. Sips his cof
fee. "I have a meeting at the office and need to be in early."

"Thanks. But no." It's a record day – I've turned down both
my parents before 6.45am. "Walking earns me a coffee."

A corner of paper folds down between us, and he gives
me an oddly proud smile. "It's all about the coffee, eh?"

"Runs in the family, doesn't it?"

He's into the local sports section now. His shoulders rise
underneath his charcoal gray suit coat. "Suit yourself, Em."

Mom stands by the door, brown hair frizzing from a loose
bun. A glass of juice sits on the counter next to my morning
dose of pain meds. She holds a bulging tortilla shell in one
hand, my backpack in another. "Breakfast burrito," she says
while I choke down the horse pill and chase it with juice.
"Eggs, sausage, cheese, and tater coins."

In another life, Mom had dreams of running a restaurant.
But then I came along and my parents got married. Guilt is
ugly – a harpy tearing at my guts every time I picture Mom
behind a diner counter spinning a spatula. I take the burrito
and she slides my backpack straps on for me, making sure
not to whack my immobiliser. Then she kisses the top of my
head and whispers, "Be careful today."

Normally I'd say "every day" in retort.

I don't want to lie. Punching my locker wasn't careful.
Neither was letting Alex Franks take my hand in the
crowded hallway. That moment bleeds into this, ink into
white; I see the smile that lit Alex's hood and my hand tingles
with an echo of the electricity that had flowed in his touch.
He'd intentionally touched more than my knuckles. The pale
broken heart on my hand thrums with secrets Alex left there
with a brush of his finger. Why did he have to touch it? His
eyes flash in my mind. Why did he have to touch *me*?

Glittering frost coats the world, sharpens grass and leaves to fragile glass-like weapons. Near a maple tree, I exhale a breath scented with eggs and sausage to watch the sparkle coating melt off a gold leaf.

I know how you feel.

Bright sunshine cuts down, pretty and deceptive. The lawn ornaments, witches and skeletons littering Seventh Street make the neighborhood look like a store full of novelty Halloween decorations. Soon, leaves will darken and wither, temperatures will plummet. Bitter cold will follow, ushering the howl of winter winds down the streets, suffocating the world in white.

I shuffle into the walk-up line at Mugz-n-Chugz, one more uncaffeinated zombie needing a jolt to come to life. I give my immobiliser a baleful glare, even if it is hidden by the kangaroo pocket of my hoodie. There's no way I'm putting on make-up one-handed.

Looking like a Picasso painting is low on my list of priorities.

Scott Morgan, the beefy defensive tackle for Shelley High's football team, stands at the window. He plumbs the depths of his pocket, then dumps crumpled dollar bills out to pay for what Tiny says is a "grandé, half-caff, fat-free skinny vanilla latté." Such a frou-frou drink for "Morgan the Mangler." I choke back my giggle. He cracks his knuckles, then claims the cup from the fleshy hand in the window.

Tiny's window opens, bouncing a flash of sun into my eyes. White spots crowd my vision, and a headache blossoms like a flower of sharp petals on fast forward. By the time I blink the white blots from my eyes, I feel a presence over my shoulder. Another person in line for their morning fix. Tiny clears his throat, drawing my attention.

A greasy film covers his skin and hair, and his uniform shirt looks like he slept in it before coming back to work. My sight zeroes in on a huge zit on his cheek. I want to pull my eyes away. I know I should. It's like a train wreck on his face.

Repulsed comes to mind.

"Hi, Emma." A dopey smile rumples his plump face, temporarily burying the zit.

"Um…" I squash the urge to recoil. "Hey, Tiny."

"The usual?"

His gaze tumbles down the neckline of my T-shirt and I want to smack him for it.

"Yes, please."

"Make that two," comes a familiar tenor from close behind me. "And I'm paying."

A tiny spark dances through my loose hair and I know Alex Franks stands within touching range. His presence brings his father to mind, and his violent, vise-like response to hearing Alex's name. An unconscious wince draws in my shoulders. I turn to face him, expecting to see the relaxed smiling expression of yesterday afternoon. It's vanished.

He wears faded jeans and a midnight blue hoodie, hood up and sleeves all the way down, under his leather jacket. The shocked, bemused expression of yesterday morning widens his eyes, his fingers drop from where they must've brushed the hair stuffed in my hood. The corners of his mouth lift in an enigmatic expression.

He looks like he can't believe I'm really *me*.

So I'll remind him.

"You were right about my hand," I say, and brandish my immobiliser. "Broken in a few places, actually."

He blinks, and whatever spell seeing my face put him

under breaks. The sunlight reaches into his cowl, lighting his face and the mischievous tilt to his lips.

"So, I suppose I'll be on locker duty, as well as buying your breves?"

"No one asked you to do either, y'know. Daniel always bought my coffee." The moment I blurt it out, I want to call it back. I gasp, and cover my mouth with my hand. His eyebrows pinch closer together, the light dies in his slight smile. "Sorry," I whisper and spin around with my face flaming.

"Who is Daniel?"

The quizzical tone in his voice is enough to drive a chill over me. He put it in present tense, as if Daniel's still alive and he should know him. I shrink deeper into the comforting fleece of my sweatshirt. A momentary ache for the cocoon of mourning I existed in before rushes through me, sloshing in the hollow of my chest. I was sad, but safe. Everyone knew. Talking to Alex opens my heart up for numerous "Oh, I didn't know" wounds.

"Was," I say. Tiny's wide girth blocks the light from the depths inside Mugz-n-Chugz. "Tiny's coming. You don't have to pay for my coffee."

"Yes, I do." He steps beside me, burying me in his shadow. "I offered. And... I'm sorry about your friend."

"He was my *boy*friend." I step behind Alex rather than let his closeness rake on my nerves and jolt my heart. "And please don't apologize for something you had nothing to do with." A shake of my head frees strands of blonde to drift in front of my eyes. "I hate it when people say they're sorry."

"Well." Alex draws himself up to his full height – of at least six-foot-two – and pulls his wallet from his pocket. He hoists the fabric shrouding the sides of his face higher. "Didn't realise I was going to push *that* button. People say they're sorry because they feel like they should say something to convey they feel bad."

"I know why people say it. It's just a touchy subject with me." I cast a look across the street and see Bree sitting on a bench, watching us like we're the newest play to hit the stage.

The window never fails to hurl shards of sunlight like a blazing weapon when Tiny opens it. His plump face sags when he sees me behind Alex like some submissive girl-friend. I step forward, plaster on a smile and say, "Thanks," when I take my cup. Before he releases it, he covers my left hand and cup with his other sweaty palm. A small shudder races my spine, darts inward, and curls my stomach. And Alex doesn't miss my reaction.

"S-so, Em," Tiny stammers, "You always rush off before I get a chance to ask you–"

"Tiny," I squeak out through my tightening throat. "Don't do this..."

"But I want you to go out with me this weekend," he whines.

Alex steps forward, slips an arm around my shoulders as casual as can be, and leans toward the window. His voice has a husky, dark tone when he says, "Emma has plans this weekend."

The slimy grip releases from my hand, leaving me feeling weak with relief.

"I always figured," Tiny says, pouting like a kid who dropped his ice cream, "it would be another pretty boy..."

Instinct is to argue. I'm not dating Alex. We hardly know each other. But if a little male posturing by Alex Franks finally stops the awkward moments with Tiny, I'll play along. A one act, one-time performance. Alex's muscles tense, electricity exuding from them like kinetic energy in coiled springs when I lean against his side. Then the tension dissolves, and he settles into his fake role of suitor and slides his arm from my shoulders down to my waist.

Alex pays for our breves, and the dejected Tiny closes his window.

I step away from Alex's side, tearing open a rift between us.

"Thanks for the rescue," I say and sip my coffee as I walk toward the street, and Bree, who is visibly buzzing with questions.

"Anytime," he says, despite the strange hint of loss crossing his face. "Always happy to use my infamy for your…" he flashes me a grin. "I mean my benefit."

"It wasn't your reputation." I match his smile with a puckish one. "Tiny called you pretty."

"Don't remind me."

Alex makes a dramatic, horrified face and winks with his left eye, which highlights the unique quality of his two-tone hazel irises. A true smile flirts across my lips, but a rising sense of something strange keeps it from spreading. Then a shout from the quad across the street tugs Alex's attention away before I can figure out what bugs me about his eyes. Alex waves, then turns back to me and excuses himself, promising to see me at lunch.

Yeah. Right. Lunch, that time when he asked me to save him a seat, then sat with Marin Rhodes. I lift a shoulder, work up a half-grin, and say, "We'll see. Forgive me if I don't get my hopes up."

Shrugging off the irritated feelings I know I shouldn't have, I aim for the school and my best friend waiting to rake me over the coals with burning hot questions like, "Do you like him? Does he like you?"

One step into the street invites the Z-28 and its driver to

barrel down on me. I jump back onto the curb with a yelp and a spat curse. Josh Mason, wearing a black leather jacket, leans out his window, hoots a laugh, then shouts, "I win, Em! You're in your place on the street corner!"

Anger boils in me hotter than my breve. Josh cackles and his car crawls away from me. Alex, halfway into the quad, spins and glares daggers at the redhead. Even at this distance, I can see his fist clench, and the top pops off his coffee cup. Froth runs over his hand like white blood. Alex ignores it.

"And your insults are rustier than your car!" Not my best comeback. I blame the meds.

Alex's attention shifts away once the Z-28 whips around the corner, toward student parking. Cheeks still burning, I schlep across the street to Bree. Might as well get the inquisition over with.

She's all in black, which has the unfortunate side effect of highlighting her dark roots. It also makes her dramatic eyeliner more obvious. Her smile spreads, her lips curling into a catty grin. Then her gaze targets on the immobiliser encasing my right hand. Her eyes widen and all traces of humor leave her face. "OhmyGod! Emma, what happened?"

I lift a shoulder in a shrug. "Stupid finally caught up with me."

"Meaning...?"

"Meaning..." A long swallow of my coffee gives me a moment to decide how much truth to tell. "My locker wouldn't open, I got really pissed and punched it."

She arches a perfectly plucked eyebrow, accompanied by Bree's patented I-know-there's-more expression. "And how'd that work out for you?"

"Depends..." I flick a glance at Alex, his hood up and

blocking most of his face from my view. "I might've broken my writing hand. But Alex Franks held it afterward."

Why did I just say that? My brain/mouth filter must be on the fritz.

"He really did?"

"Yeah. Y'know… to see if my hand was broken. Ask the dozens of witnesses in the main hall…"

"Already did! I just wanted you to confirm the rumors." She slides closer like a co-conspirator in a play, the one who stirs up trouble, and then stage whispers, "What was that at the walk-up window? You two looked really cozy."

I wish I knew. Something is definitely there between me and Alex. Does he notice? Is my heart even ready for another guy? I might have let Daniel go, but I still hurt with every thought of him. I'm not sure I'll ever be over him. Bree squeezes my shoulders, and wiggles her fingers in a friendly little wave when Alex pointedly stares at us.

"That was Alex saving me from Tiny."

She waggles her eyebrows and nudges me with her elbow. "The way he keeps looking over here, I'd say that's not all."

I suck down the rest of my coffee, then sling the cup at the garbage can to hear the empty bang, and think dismally how much I echo its hollow sentiment.

"Can you please just let it rest?" I say and turn on my heel from the storm-heavy air, the eyes of Bree and Alex.

Was that all? It felt like something more.

Do I want it to be more? Am I even ready?

Chapter Eight

Invisible storm shadows cloud the main hall of Shelley High. The normal jostling and joking has a meaner edge. People ebb and flood, jostle and bump.

The tide splashes me from the main surge at my locker. Josh Mason is thankfully not here to harass me. With a droop and twist motion, I shuck my backpack and hook it with my left hand. The traitorous bag has other ideas, and continues its path toward the floor. A long hand catches it before it crashes down.

"I'd say meeting here is getting to be a habit," Alex says, dangling my backpack from his fingers, "But I get the feeling you're not in the mood for joking today."

I blink, and give him my best innocent expression. "Whatever gave you that idea?"

"Basically the feeling you wanna bite my head off."

"Yeah... About that." I toe the front of my locker rather than look into his disconcerting gaze. "Sorry."

"Apology accepted." His voice is softer, his mood more gracious than mine. Then he compounds my guilt by continuing the nice guy thing and says, "Want me to open your locker?"

My shoulders sag in defeat, cue enough for him to hook my backpack over his arm and take up position between me and my frustrating lock. He spins the dial through the numbers, pushing each one in, then nudges it with his hip again. The exact sequence used by Daniel, day after day last year, to open my locker for me. A chill slides down my spine. And the locker pops open.

"No offense, but I hate having you do this." Why is the ugly pouring from me? Alex's dad may have hurt me, but Alex has been almost too kind.

"None taken." He holds my bag out. The surprised expression has disappeared, replaced by a soft smile that reaches his eyes, tugging down a pale, thin scar outside the corner of his left eye. "I'd be frustrated too. Have you talked to the school about it?"

"Numerous times," I huff. Taking my backpack, I turn my focus to getting things ready for class. "The janitor greases stuff, fiddles with other stuff, and it works better for a couple of days."

"Sounds like you need a new locker door."

I jerk my right thumb, the only really mobile part of my hand, in the direction of the office. "Tell it to them."

"I'll keep that in mind."

His long fingers make nimble work of opening his locker, which displays the scar on his wrist. I can't help but wonder, again, if he was responsible for the scars or if they're surgery-related. Fine white lines usually are the result of a surgical procedure. Alex notices my stare, clears his throat, and tugs his sleeves down further. His shadowed expression becomes closed, eyes turn to chips of hazel gemstone, lips a hard straight line, and he shifts his body at an angle, hiding himself in his locker.

Sorry, I think.

The battle for my books is short, lots of metallic bangs and cusswords. When I emerge, flustered and pink-cheeked, Alex stands watching me – like I'm the puzzle he can't figure out, instead of it being the other way around.

I sling my bag over my shoulder. The weight pulls the nylon strap toward the edge of my shoulder. Much to my shock, and to the detriment of my pulse, Alex steps close and eases the strap back into place. His face hovers inches from mine. Then he draws even closer, the scent of his leather jacket filling my nose, as he wordlessly helps me thread my right hand through the other strap.

"See you at lunch?" he asks, his words brushing my cheeks.

"Sure."

What else can I say? My brain is on short circuit, with him severing the rest of the world from existence. It's just me and Alex – and his hazel eyes, my emotional scars, and the visible scars on his wrists. The wretched weight of Shelley High crashes in when he blinks and steps back, and with a wave, disappears into the flow sluicing through the halls.

The next two hours fly by at a high level of awkward. Schoolwork is a huge pain with my writing hand handicapped. Mrs Johnson has a rare moment of auditory clarity and promises to get me online assignments for the next few weeks. And I learn to turn the pages of my Gothic fiction reading assignment by licking my fingertips and pinching the pages between them.

Third hour Group and Individual Sports promises to be its own brand of hell. Sure, I have a broken hand, but asthma didn't stop our gym teacher, aka Drill Sarge, from making Kat VanderVelde run until she passed out last year. Might be part of the No Child Left Behind act, might not. Either way, it's definitely a part of Most Students Pissed Off thing. If we can walk, we have to participate – thankfully Mom notified the school that I'm injured, so I can at least avoid basketball.

On the way across the covered catwalk between the buildings' second stories, guilt rises up, filling my legs with lead. Why did I say yes to Alex's invitation to sit together at lunch? Here, where I met Daniel, the glimmer of hope I shelter feels traitorous and wrong.

I lean against a metal support beam and soak in the heat of the contained sunlight. I've nearly convinced myself there's nothing wrong with making new friends – when the old memories hit. Daniel and I met just across the crimson carpeting, my shadow now long across the textiles, pointing like an accusation at the spot.

His damaged echo demands my attention, skull split open and leaking, the red streaking down his face. Chills sweep my spine when Ghost Daniel walks toward me, solid in the shadows, gone in the sun. Feet away the smell of cinder and death waft from him.

And I can't stand it.

Windows spin around me as I turn and rush the last few yards. My heart hammers at the base of my throat, threatening to strangle me. Once inside the sports complex building with the door slammed shut, I let my muscles relax, and focus on drawing in air. My hand aches, and I cast a look at the ugly immobiliser. The past doesn't want to release me, but I'm not so sure the present is all that safe. Alex may be kind, but his father has the warmth of a grave, and lacks compassion where I, or at the very least, my hand bones are concerned.

Thoughts twist and buzz as I press open the door and step

into the humid funk of the Ugly Room. Cackling girl voices
pierce the air, and Alex Franks is still the topic of conversation. Only now, my name sharpens their tones and sours the
subject.

"Can you believe Alex was talking to *her*?"

"What does he see in Emo Emma anyway?"

"She's nothing but a speed bump. He'll be mine."

The last voice is Marin Rhodes. The snide tone gives her
away – not that she'd want to hide. She'd staked claim on
Alex when she dragged him to the in crowd's table. A short,
hot flash of anger rips through me, and an image of Marin
as a speed bump under the wheels of Alex's hybrid floods
my mind. I'm wearing a dark smile when I walk around the
corner and toward the peach, brown, pukey-salmon tiled
Ugly Room of lockers and nasty attitudes.

The vicious words slither away from my approach, silence
spreading in a wake of downcast eyes in front of me.
Doesn't matter. I know what I heard.

My gym locker is more accommodating than my regular locker. It opens with a few spins of my left hand.
Getting out of regular clothes and into gym clothes is
worth points as a callisthenic workout. By the time I'm
done, there's only a minute left before I'm tardy. Outside
the locker room, the line of students stretches across the
gym, girls to the right, guys to the left. According to our
strutting Drill Sarge and his shiny whistle, today is going
to be a free gym day. Chests sink in a collective, gym-wide
sigh of relief.

I stand with my immobiliser in front of me, my hair loose
because I can't whip it into a ponytail.

"Gentry," Mr Ashford grunts, "I see you're injured."

Pretty obvious, I think with a thick layer of snark. *Plus,*

Mom called the office...

"Yes, sir."

"Walking the track is easy," he suggests.

I nod, and set off at a leisurely pace. Sadly, two laps in, a horde of harpies jogs behind me, their breaths puffing in between their gossip. Marin Rhodes and Nikki Cummings discuss the Halloween Ball between their plodding steps, Nikki ooh-ing like a mindless groupie with every suggestion Marin huffs out.

"We can go as Barbie and Ken," Marin says.

"Cuuute!"

"Or we could go as Zombie Honeymooners."

"Love it!"

"Or Hansel and Gretel."

"Aren't they brother and sister?" Then Nikki surprises me. "I can't picture Alex in lederhosen."

One, lederhosen is a really big word for Nikki. Two, Marin's "we" supposedly includes Alex Franks. Why does that idea set my teeth on edge? We have nothing between us but coffee and that pain-in-my-butt locker. He does look at me like I'm more than new to him, and his touch sends tingles through me, but who is he to me? The guy who unsettles me with eerie similarities to Daniel. The guy with a scary father.

I slow and let the harpy squad jog past, out of hearing range.

The Alex Franks topic continues in the lunch line, Bree included. I roll my eyes and groan. I'm tired of him and I've hardly seen him today. Chewing on my frustrations, I stalk past the entire lunch line into the food service area without a sideways glance. My best friend accuses me of being grumpy and I can't argue.

"Food. Juice. Pain meds," I say. "Then I'll be more social."

"Make it quick," Jason Weller says from the thespian table and holds out his can of soda.

"So self-sacrificing of you, Jason."

He smiles and strikes a ridiculous pose, one hand held aloft in the air. "Leading men know the meaning of self-sacrifice."

I'm too busy negotiating flavorless macaroni and cheese onto my spork to fuss with a retort. The crawl over my skin announces someone watching me. Hopefully my handicapped eating amuses them. My pain meds follow a couple spoons of macaroni, then I take up Jason's offer and chase the pills with lemon-lime pop.

Sudden pain flares across the top of the arch of my foot, driven there by Bree stomping it hard enough to make me wince. Passing Jason's soda back, I glare at her. Drama queen Bree pretends innocence, but gives me a cheeky wink. She inclines her head in the direction of the in crowd tables, where Alex follows Marin to a pair of empty seats. He sinks with his hood pointed at me until a football player draws his attention.

"That girl's had your puppy out of the window twice now."

"Marin can kiss my butt." And like he heard me four rows of tables away, Alex looks at me. "He can, too. I'm tired of them both."

"What! You're joking, right?" Bree's eyes widen to near saucer size. Even Jason lets out a surprised little snort.

Yeah. I don't believe I said it either.

Feedback chews through the intercom speaker before lunch is over. Heads pop up and turn toward the speaker. The announcement chime rings through the large room. Then the main receptionist's voice comes through, "Attention, please. This is a reminder that Mr LaRue's fifth hour Dune Ecology is to meet in the student parking lot immediately after lunch."

"Field trip!" Josh Mason whoops from the sports crowd tables.

"Neanderthal," Jason groans and rolls his eyes.

The bottom drops out of my gut, and I'm suddenly sorry I ate the mac and cheese. Field trip, an entire afternoon spent one-on-one alone, crawling over the dunes with Alex Franks as my partner. If I'm lucky, or unlucky, Josh Mason might follow us, making more of his nasty comments. My mind sticks on time alone with Alex. What will I say, how will he act?

"What?" asks Bree. "Why are you so pale?"

"Well, looks like I'll be stuck with Alex Franks for the next few hours."

"Ooh." Jason's eyes widen. "I'll pray for you. Y'know, I heard he had to leave his fancy prep school due to violence."

"Nuh-uh," argues the dark-haired and dark-eyed Chelsea Reamer. "I heard it was because he spent a year in juvie for accidental manslaughter."

They seem to know the rumors. Do they see that he has mismatched hazel eyes, and scars on his wrist? Or that he opens my locker just like Daniel? They can't know that I am unable to stop thinking about him even though I want to.

A group stands huddled outside the school building, in the parking lot reserved for students. Growing winds push and pull at hair and jackets. And true to the weight of storms I've felt all day, brooding clouds linger in the gray sky, dark as a threat.

Alex remains outside the group, not ignored, but more by choice it seems. Josh Mason's directly across from him, leaning on the hood of his Z-28 and giving him the stink eye. I weave between people until I'm close to Mr LaRue, who's counting heads. He drops a quick look at my immobiliser and arches an eyebrow. I lift a shoulder in a weak shrug, and he responds with a shake of his head. I love silent conversations.

"I'll be taking one minivan," he announces. "Mr Baker will take the other. You can ride with us, or ride separately. Don't get any wise ideas. I will be taking head count at Meinert Park, too."

Josh runs a hand through his carrot curls, then whistles through his teeth and calls, "Yo, Emma!"

I bristle. A disgusted noise issues from the tall hooded guy a couple of feet to my left. I clench my jaw, biting down cusswords. Josh looks at me, expectant, patting his hood and coaxing me like I'm some dumb freshman begging for scraps of attention. Wind whips my hair in my face when I shake my head, then I give Josh the middle finger.

"You wish," he mouths.

If my right hand wasn't in a cast, I'd give him another.

Spinning, I march stubbornly to the school's minivan, half-filled with Dune Eco students, and drop into the seat behind the driver's. Josh climbs into his Camaro, slams the door and guns the engine. A few giggly titters rise from the girls. The guys ignore him, like I'm doing. His project partner Shane Lowenstein, however, climbs in and sits behind me muttering, "I hate that guy."

Me, too. I slouch in my seat, rest my head against the window, and try to doze while Mr LaRue drives the miles of farmland to the lakeshore. The reek of cow crap filters into the minivan's air systems. I bury my nose in my elbow, and close my eyes. Trees litter the dark side of the dunes, scaling up and away from the kidney-shaped parking lot and chipped white bathhouse. A wooden boardwalk clings to the side of the dune, an exposed spine riding over dark flesh, meant to preserve the fragile ground.

The park is a quiet retreat, one Daniel and I often watched the sunsets from.

My heart twinges after I climb from the minivan. One smell of the lake brings memories crawling from the dark where I'd shoved them. The rest of the class climbs from the minivans, and from a few student cars, including one shiny black hybrid, and one rusty Z-28. The trees and dunes have the kind of ageless beauty that makes me feel small and alive at the same time. With memories of Daniel plaguing me, I need that life, and lean against the white vehicle, tip my head back, close my eyes, and just breathe.

A cool shadow cuts into the edge of my consciousness, familiar and strange all at once. Heaving a sigh, I open my eyes and focus on my lab partner standing a couple feet from me. A white notebook and pencil occupy one of Alex's hands. With the sun at his back, I can just make out the lines of his face in the darkness cast by his hood.

"Ready, partner?" He smooth tenor voice is a perfect accompaniment to the breeze whispering in the trees. "I figured I'd bring the supplies, seeing as you're... well, y'know..."

"Handicapped?"

A smile beams from the shadows cloaking his face. "They call it handy-capable, too. We just need to figure out what you're good at."

"What?" I ask, pushing off from the minivan. "Flipping Josh Mason off isn't a skill?

His laugh is rich and sudden. "I think you're making that an art form."

We fall into step behind the stragglers of Mr LaRue's alphabetically partnered teams. Beneath our feet two black rubber tracks gouge the asphalt. Teams break off to do their separate projects as the sun and shadows lurch across the pavement, shoved around by the stiff breeze coming off Lake Michigan. I sink deeper into my hoodie and duck my head. I'm grateful when Alex zips his jacket and shifts to block the wind from hitting me. When I turn my head, nearly everyone has disappeared on the separate trails. Our path is clear in front of us, and so is a disturbance in the leaf litter to the far side of the parking lot.

Unconsciously, I reach out and tug on Alex's sleeve. A hint of a tingle races through my fingertips when he stops and my hand bumps his elbow. I point to the torn dirt near the culvert.

"What," I ask, "do you think that is?"

"No idea."

By the new angle of his steps, we're going to find out.

He treads over sun speckles to the deeper gloom thrown by an overhang of trees, whose tangled roots have broken through the pavement's edge. Water gushes from the entrance of the park, through the gully we walk toward, and then on to the lake. The little ditch's edge is ripped raw, and appears to be bleeding. Red splats of mud cover the mound, and trickle down either edge.

Alex suddenly drops the notebook and pencil and scrambles over the edge.

"Oh my god!" His voice scales up to panic. Wet splashes sound over the muddy rise. "Emma, get help! Get Mr LaRue."

His alarm cuts at my heart, draws me like a magnet. Instead of running or shouting for help, I retrace Alex's steps. The smell of iron hangs heavy in the air over the red mud. The mud sticks to my hands and my clothes as I scramble to the lip of the little creek.

A young whitetail deer lies half in, half out of the shallow creek, rear on the dry dirt, her upper half in the inches of water. The whites of her eyes show in their sockets. Her ribs and side are a torn, bloody mess. White bone protrudes past the skin of her twisted front leg. Only a vehicle could do that kind of damage.

Alex kneels in the muck near the doe's head, his hands crimson and shiny with her blood.

"Get help!" he begs. "Please!"

I've lived in Michigan all my life. I know the mortality rate of a deer after a collision with a car. Alex should, too. The deer needs to be put out of its misery.

"Sorry, Alex. I don't think anyone has a gun."

"A gun?" His eyes are nearly as wide as the doe's. "We can't shoot her. She can't die!"

She's going to. Her eyes, her unsteady breaths, everything says her end is coming. If anything, it makes Alex more agitated. He strokes her neck, looks at me with his eyes wide and beseeching.

Why is he so panicky? His emotions are reaching in, rattling my calm and infecting my nerves with a ghost of his distress.

"I could call the Department of Natural Resources to come get her," I suggest. It's the only logical choice, despite his mad need to save what's already lost. Logic isn't working with Alex's stress screaming in my head. I should get our teacher, but I can't walk away when Alex is so distraught. "The DNR'll take care of her."

"They'll KILL her!"

It's his raw ache, the way he kneels in the filth – as torn by his emotions as the deer by the car – that topples my ability to maintain any distance. With a few steps, I'm in the muddy water, reaching toward Alex. A tear rises in his eye. The hazel is amazingly vibrant. His voice is naked, exposing a wound in him when he begs, "Emma, please. I can't let her die!"

"OK, Alex." *Please let him be OK,* I pray silently, *because I feel as crazy as he sounds.*

I scale the muddy rise, and shout for help. The dune swallows my voice. My second shout reaches farther. Shane Lowenstein's head appears around the corner of the boardwalk.

"Get Mr LaRue!" I shout.

Shane's face is full of questions, but he nods, and disappears toward the glimmer of lake water.

Alex's arms are under her body, the deer's legs lashing weakly, churning the water to burgundy mud when I turn back to the scene of the dying doe. Horrid screams come from her throat, and tighten mine. Before I realise what I'm doing, I'm in the water, inches from her mangled leg and the bubbles in the bloody ruin of her chest. At this angle, a notch in her ear is very visible.

Spots of feverish red stain Alex's cheeks. Foamy deer blood speckles his face. His lips are pursed as he tries to shush and calm the deer.

"What can I do?"

"Get her front." He slides along her spine, easing his arms under her hip. "I'll get her back end."

Heedless to the danger of a wounded animal, I follow Alex's directions. Cooing to the deer, I ease my arms down past the raw meat and exposed bone of her chest and under to the other side. She's a fighter, struggling even now with her life running crimson and wet over Alex and me.

Blood, thick and warm, strains through my hoodie and T-shirt. My stomach rolls violently, and I clamp my jaws against my gag reflex.

Between the two of us we hoist the young deer, her struggles weakening as we carry her out of the creek that could've been her deathbed. People stand in gossiping clumps, Josh Mason is shaking his head, one girl's crying – and none of it rises above the buzz of background noise in my head. Alex, the deer, and her death are crystal cut, high definition. They are real, and ripping my heart to pieces.

Mr LaRue stands a few feet from the tire tracks burned into the pavement. He doesn't ask any questions, doesn't reprimand. "You have the rest of the day," he says. "Do what you can. Just... write me a report about it."

We manage to get the animal to Alex's car. There, feet away from Alex's trunk, the deer stops fighting. Her chest struggles to rise, air gushing in tattered flashes between her ribs. Then she turns one beautiful brown eye on me, and releases her last breath. The tension leaves her body and the light leaves her eye.

"No!" Alex shakes his head. "No. Not after all this. She can't die."

I hang my head, close my eyes and hold her tighter, despite the wetness running down my skin. "She's gone, Alex."

A strangled sob breaks from him. He's shaking, I can feel it even through the deer's still body.

"We need to bring the body to the DNR."

He's quiet, too quiet, face a frozen mask. Then he nods. "OK," he mutters, shoves a bloody hand into his pocket for his keys, then pops the trunk. "You're right."

Finally he's acting more normal, not crazed. It's hard to reconcile the panicked guy in the filthy culvert with the mysterious guy back at school. I want to rewind the afternoon, or maybe push my hair from my face, or clean the blood from his, anything to wipe away the muck and emotion of the past few minutes.

After we jockey the doe's corpse into his pristine trunk, I look at Alex. His face is drained of color and expression. He stares at me, blood smeared across the front of his zipped-up leather jacket.

"You're soaked," he says, as if he only now really realised I was in the filth with him.

I just nod, relieved to have the calm, thoughtful Alex back. "Got any towels in your car? I don't want to ruin your upholstery."

"I don't care about my car." His voice is flat, nearly as dead as the deer in his trunk.

The sound of his jacket zipper is unnaturally loud in the quiet after the doe's death. I watch in a numb state of shock as Alex whips off his jacket, then pulls off his hoodie. Beneath the shirt he's bare. Thin scars run the lengths of his arms, down his chest and the cleft between his stomach muscles. When he offers the dry shirt to me, he exposes lines of white on his neck.

My God. What happened to him? Where did all of those scars come from?

"Put this on."

I can only stare at his marred perfection.

"Emma. Come on. Take the shirt." Shocked, I function on autopilot. My right hand lifts and his gaze goes to my filthy immobiliser. "Crap! Your brace is ruined. Hold still."

My brain is locked on his scars. My senses reel, and I think vaguely I might puke or pass out, then focus on Alex as he unzips my hoodie for me and pulls it gently off. He uses the hood to wipe as much blood from my immobiliser as he can and undoes the Velcro closures. His eyes lock on mine and he whispers, "This might hurt," then removes my brace.

Pain shoots across the back of my hand. I bite my lip while he balls up my sweatshirt and brace, then turns away. Self-preservation, or maybe modesty, regains awareness in my stunned mind and I duck behind the car, closer to the trees, to pull off my T-shirt and sopping bra. I use the back of the shirt, the only dry part, to clean up as much as I can. Alex's hoodie slides over me with a whisper of cotton, the smell of leather and death.

His car door is open, and he's covering his scars and skin with another long sleeved T-shirt.

"You want your brace back on?" he asks, and holds the folded thing out for me.

My stomach clenches. I can't pull my eyes from the shiny, wet interior, like the immobilizer is painted in the deer's death.

"I think I would rather suffer."

He nods. "I'll take you to the clinic so you can get another brace, then I'll take care of the deer."

"OK," sounds limp in light of what's happened, but it's all I can force out.

His seats are covered with sheepskin seat covers. I hesitate a moment, clutching my right hand to my chest.

"Don't worry," Alex promises. "They're washable."

Mutely, I slip into the seat, not at all surprised when he reaches across me and does my seat belt for me. Daniel would've done the same. I scan the inside of his car, and see two black trash bags sitting in the foot wells behind the seats.

"What's in those?"

"Our bloody clothes."

"You travel around with lawn and garden bags in your car?"

"Better safe than sorry," he says, then starts the engine.

I close my eyes and wish I could wash the stink of blood from me. What happened today won't wash away as easily as the seat covers, but I wish it would. I have enough emotional wounds to carry without adding an animal's death and the conundrum of Alex's internal and external scars to them.

Chapter Nine

Death lingers in the dirt and blood clinging to me. Every breath pulls in more of it, coating my throat and turning my stomach. My eyes close and the doe's face dominates my inner vision, pain and life fading from her eye in a repeating loop. Bile rises and I swallow it back. The window rolls down before I push the button, as though Alex knows I'm going to barf.

I inhale huge greedy gulps of fresh air, begging the oxygen to clear my head. I'm not sure anything will wipe that image from my mind – the deer dying, or Alex's reaction to it.

A sick fear digs through me, growing thorns and coiling around my gut.

What if he's like his dad? I'd just let Daniel go, the last thing I want is more drama. An unstable lab partner might as well be filed under the drama heading in the dictionary, especially when his dad is a psycho. It's a double whammy.

"Um, Alex?"

Silence, a white-knuckle grip on the steering wheel and a perfect view of his clean hood pulled up to hide the scars. Otherwise, the only thing he offers is a jerk of his head.

"Alex?" I shift in my seat, facing him as the autumn fields roll past.

He flicks me a pained look at the stop sign at the top of the hill. His eyes are knapped hazel stone and the thin pressed line of his lips screams, "Leave me alone."

I can't. Not after the meltdown I saw back in the ditch.

"What was that back there?"

A brief snort escapes him. His knuckles clench so tight on the steering wheel they crack. Preservation instincts tell me to shut up. Common sense says to leave it alone. Listening was never a strong point of mine. I repeat his name, in a lower tone, more insistent. Then Alex does the last thing I expect. Instead of driving like he's running away from something, he damn near stands on the brakes, steering the shuddering car off the road, next to a field of dry, rattling naked corn stalks.

"You wanna know what happened back there?" His voice breaks into my shocked silence.

His eyes blaze, upper lip curls slightly – his shoulders rise, making him appear larger, a maniac wired on nerves and about to blow. My heart skips a beat. All I see in Alex's expression is his father's face, all I feel in his agitation is his father crushing my hand. I clutch my achy right hand to my chest and inch toward the door. If humans have a fear musk, I must reek.

"You were pretty crazy back there..." My voice quakes and I hate it.

Alex deflates with a long sigh, shrinking back into my Dune Eco partner, not a darker-haired version of Dr Franks. He pushes his hood back, and runs a hand through his shaggy brown hair. A shaky laugh rattles from his chest and dies in the awkward space between us.

"I'm kinda crazy in here, too," he says, and hangs his head.

His left eye twitches when he flicks a look at me, then he scrubs his face with blood-stained hands. A white line traces down his neck, and a knot of white shimmers at his temple.

"I don't do well with death," he says, voice raw like he's forcing the words out. "At all. I just can't handle it."

"But why?"

"Don't you know?" A bitter humor has replaced his sadness. "It's the reason I was gone, the reason I left the prep school to find... Anyway, it's the real reason I missed so much school. I'm not a killer, a juvie hall escapee, or whatever." He folds and unfolds his fists. Then with a resigned glance, he hooks his fingers in the hem of his shirt and pulls it up to expose his stomach and lower ribs. "I died, Emma. Dad insists it was only for a few minutes. We were moving into the manor house, and there was an accident..."

I see every bit of his old fear and pain, pushing beneath the surface of his scars. Inside, Alex Franks is as gouged and wounded as me. My hand lifts as if it has a mind of its own, reaching to touch the pale lines tracing a path down his abdomen. A feather-light touch of my fingertip to his scar and a sizzle of something dances on my skin before he backs away.

"Tickles," he mutters, and pulls his shirt down.

Apologizing for touching him would be a lie.

"Since then, I've been struggling with new fears, new aversions–" and he pins me with a stare so naked and raw it hurts, "new needs."

Suddenly there's not enough air in the car and my heart hammers so loud on my ribs I'm sure he hears it. I think he does, because he leans closer, like he's listening.

Alex's eyes have softened, the stoniness gone. My gaze pores over his features, the slightly crooked nose that might've been broken in the accident that nearly took his life. His lips, parted over the fuller bottom lip to let in his breaths. And his hazel eyes, the puzzle my mind has been trying to master for two days now. A thin line, not much wider than an eyelash, pulls at the corner of his left eye. The ring around the iris is forest green, the hazel color is deeper, and a freckle of black mars the bottom arc.

Just like Daniel's.

Just like Daniel's.

The air leaves me in a rush. The wrong I felt before flares, balefire hot in me and I recoil, pressing against the door. What kind of sick cosmic joke is the universe playing on me? They have the same eye. Might as well be Daniel hiding beneath Alex's left eyebrow. Such amazing similarities, it's like staring into Daniel's eye again. The one I loved because he winked with it, a quirky difference that made me feel special.

The same wink Alex has.

"Take me to the clinic, please," I manage past my shock. "My hand hurts."

"Sure," he says.

He blinks his heterochromic eyes before shifting in his seat to face forward again. The door presses into my side and arm while the fields I want to escape in slide by. I wish the car ran on my heartbeat. We'd be in town already, instead of trapped together with death in the trunk behind me, and a mockery of Daniel's death seemingly hidden beneath Alex's eyelashes.

"Did I say too much?" he asks.

It's my turn to give him silence. Not out of temper. I can't think straight, I can't force words that aren't coming. The deer, Daniel, and Alex have morphed into a hideous single face in my mind. Daniel's eye winks from Alex's socket across the muzzle from the deer's lightless eye.

Alex hits the train tracks on Washington. The memory of the carcass in the trunk is a sick reminder of how awful this day has become. The numbness inside can't scrub the image from behind my eyes, or the hurt from my hand. An errant thought ambles through my head of how upset Mom will be that my brace was ruined. She'll ask what I was thinking, was his panic worth it, yadda yadda. And then it hits me.

It's natural to be where Alex is, regardless of the filth, the death, and the shock of an eye so much like Daniel's. I stare at him, daring him to look, while I sort out my feelings. Alex is there, like he'd cut past my defenses and weaseled into my emotions. Impossible after knowing him a day – implausible, even if I'd known him for years.

I don't think the clinic has anything to fix that. Even though we're parked by the emergency care.

The jack-o'-lantern laughs in flaming giggles, and the door opening for a man in a wheelchair doesn't affect its glow. Its wavering light reminds me of my trip here last night, and the first doctor to treat me.

"Your dad isn't working, is he?"

"What?" The duality of tone isn't lost on me. One part surprise, one part suspicion.

"Is your father working here tonight?" I say in a firmer tone. "He was the first doctor to see me yesterday."

Alex's eyes widen, then narrow, and his brows sink. Serious pressure pinches his lips. "So you're the one," he says.

"Excuse me?" I pop my seat belt loose, and then reach around to open my door.

The locks click shut throughout the car. I spin back to face him, the fabric of his shirt thin defense between us.

"My dad," he says in a self-righteous timbre, "came home ranting about some girl's mother accusing him of hurting his daughter. He said she's threatening him with a lawsuit."

He really believes his father is a good guy. The fractures in my hand say he's not. Anger heats me up, itches over my skin.

"And did he tell you it's well deserved?" I snap. "I mentioned your name, didn't even say your *last name*, and he crushed my hand. I'm glad your dad saved your life, Alex, but he hurt me."

"He's not like that." Alex argues. "How could a surgeon who donates time at a clinic hurt a girl intentionally?"

"You tell me." Muscles along my jaw clench, making my next words clipped. "Mom saw it. Now let me out of this car."

"Fine!"

He flips the locks, and shoots across my lap to yank my door open before I can react. I tumble out, then hardly save myself from cracking my head on the pavement by grabbing the door frame. Alex leaps from the driver's side and scrambles around the hood. Renewed hurt grinds in my knuckles. A sharp cry bursts from my lips, and instinct kicks in, opening my right hand. The world spins, gravity winning, then I land in Alex's arms instead.

"Whatever you think about my dad," he says, inches from my face, "I'm not him."

I bite my lip and nod, trusting the son of the psychopath doctor who hurt me to keep me from experiencing more pain. In a smooth motion, Alex stands and sets my feet on the ground at the same time.

My mouth opens to mumble an apology, anything, to dispel the awkwardness between us. He puts a long finger over his lips, shakes his head, and pulls my things from the back seat. Considerate of my one-handedness, Alex threads the end of the plastic bag through the handle of my backpack. Then before I can thank him, he unzips the front pocket, and pulls out my phone.

"You should call home and let someone know to come get you."

"OK." I set the bundle on the ground and take the phone.

Before anyone at home can answer the phone, Alex climbs into his car and disappears.

My worst fear waits for me outside the nurse's door. Mom's face is pinched as tight as the knot in the back of her hair. She pays the balance due for a second medical device, then steers me to the car with a hard hand on my elbow. Head hanging, blond hair blowing past my eyes, I stand mute while she deposits the black trash bag in the trunk, then my backpack in the back seat. After she opens the passenger's door, I slink into the seat and brace for a chewing out.

"Emma Jane Gentry," she says in a voice that is heated and yet dead even when she slams her door, "do you want to explain why I have to pay a co-pay for a second immobiliser?"

Want to? No.

She doesn't give me enough time to formulate an answer. "Fine. We will talk about this when we get home."

And that's fine by me. A few minutes to think without Alex around to muddle my thoughts is a very good thing.

Mom waits till we're home before venting her anger in little spurts. The garage door opens with a groan and ratcheting sound as the automatic opener chain slips and reengages. "Put those filthy clothes in the washing machine on soak," Mom says in her tight, restrained voice. She takes my backpack from me and steps up the back stairs. "Then get your tail to the dinner table."

She might as well tell an interrogation victim to hurry up to the torture chamber.

"OK."

She's waiting to gang up on me with Dad. They might not talk a lot; in fact, there are days I think they don't talk at all. But they are experts at tag-teaming me around the dining room table and making me feel about as tall as a water glass.

"Guess what Emma did today, Merle." Mom sits across from Dad.

He ladles stew into one of Mom's homemade bread bowls. Then he adds a little hot sauce, dragging out my agony. After a couple squirts of Tabasco and a sip of water, Dad looks at me over the rim of his glasses, then he looks at her. "Something you didn't approve of, Arlene?"

"Our Dune Eco class," I say before Mom can doom me, "had a field trip to Meinert Park. My project partner found a deer, hurt in the ditch, and was really upset. I couldn't just leave him like that..."

"Oh, yes, you could." Mom skewers me with a sharp glance. "And you should've."

Coulda, woulda, shoulda.

Even knowing he scares me, that he gives me sad awful reminders of Daniel, I don't want to do the smart thing around Alex. He *touches* me.

Amazingly, Dad seems more contemplative than pissed. He's the calm to Mom's storm. He regards me with a measured glance. He says, "You haven't mentioned a boy since Daniel died, have you, Emma?"

Whoa. Dad slings an emotional gut check. "No, I haven't."

His gaze sharpens behind the glasses. "So, who is this guy?"

"Well…" With Mom, there's a chance I might bluster my way out of telling the truth. She's a sucker for tears. Dad is not my mother. He's an expert at drama detection, and sifting the truth from the stories I string together. I gave up trying to get anything past Dad shortly after the night I snuck out with Daniel. "He's new to school, yesterday was his first day."

True enough.

"And…?" Dad asks, one eyebrow arching.

"And he's funny and been very nice to me. He helps me with my locker, and bought my coffee today."

"And…?"

My voice shrinks in volume, and my gaze sinks. "And nothing else."

"Oh, no. *Something else*," Mom stresses, shaking her head. "He got you into enough trouble you needed to be dropped off at the clinic in his shirt."

Her voice, the angle of her eyes, and the droop of her lips. I've seen it before, when Mom thought Daniel and I were sleeping together. Indignation bubbles up, seething and ugly, pushing on my spine and straightening it.

"Oh my God, Mom!" I shove back my chair and stand. "We weren't doing anything wrong. The deer was hurt, Alex was upset. I wanted to help. We got muddy. He was man enough to give me the shirt off his back so I had something clean to wear. He insisted I go to the clinic, too."

"He, he, he. Where were you in all this Emma? Willing to do whatever he said?"

"Arlene, please," my dad says in his best diffuse-the-situation voice. "I think this is a good thing. Maybe not this particular boy, but at least Emma's coming out of her… funk…" *since Daniel died* isn't said so much as felt.

"I don't like this." She scoops up Dad's empty water glass and uses it as an excuse to put distance between us. Water splashes in the sink, then the glass. "Not with that boy. Look at her, Merle. She was filthy. She had to get a new brace."

"*That boy* has a name," I huff. I scoop up my plate and utensils. "His name is Alex. And he didn't do anything wrong."

"New brace," Mom ticks off on her fingers, "missing school, and a different shirt."

"Because we were trying to save a wounded animal." Too many emotions today, I'm a raw nerve and Mom's strangling it. I can't just hang my head and clam up. "Forgive me for making a friend. Something you've pushed me to do for months."

Mom doesn't say anything. The flush in her cheeks speaks volumes.

Head held high, I walk from the dining room and carry my plate up to my bedroom where I can eat in peace and not have Mom bitching at me about trying to help Alex. Yelling at me for being friendly with Alex is just stupid.

My door slams behind me with a good shove of my foot. I can always blame it on both hands being occupied, one with dinner, one with a fresh clean immobiliser.

I shove aside my laptop and sit at my desk to eat. It's all mechanical, scoop, chew, and swallow, scoop, chew, and swallow. My taste buds are numb, burned by frustration, or the lengthy exposure to the stink of blood. The last lump of mashed potatoes sits on my spoon when a knock rattles my door.

"I don't feel like talking, Mom."

"It's not Mom," Dad says through the crack, "and I do. Are you decent?"

I heave a sigh, and immediately wish I had Daniel's hoodie on as a barrier between me and Dad. He never comes to my door – never comes into my room. The spoon falls back to the plate, potatoes splatting across the surface.

By the time Dad comes in, I'm on my bed, with a pillow hugged to my chest.

"Emma, I know your mom upset you," he starts.

"Ya think?" OK. It's a smart-ass response, but I'm doubly on edge now.

"You have to understand. We were really worried about you this summer. Things just start looking better and along comes another boy."

"Wait. Stop right there, Dad." I curl my legs into a crossed position. "Alex has just been nice. He's not 'coming along'." I make air quotes with my left hand.

"Mom's just worried you're going to end up broken-hearted again."

I cast my eyes down and away, and follow the seam of the quilt pattern Mom had sewn for me when I was nuts about faeries. Now I hate faeries and don't have the heart to tell her.

"Just be careful, OK, Em?"

"I promise."

"Good." He fishes in his chest pocket, and produces my pain meds. "Mom figured you'd need these."

Even when I'm a jerk, and shout back, Mom's still watching out for me. Guilt fills the place indignation had burned out and I want to cry. I don't, I scrub viciously at the renegade wetness on my cheek. "Thanks. Tell her I said thank you, too, please."

"She figured you'd say that." Dad pats my head like I'm two again, and a pat and a kiss on the cheek would make everything better. "Go soak in a hot bath, kiddo. You'll feel better."

"That's my plan."

I toss the pill into my mouth, swallow some water with it, then stand when Dad walks out. The siren call of Daniel's old comfort is too strong to resist. I gather his sweatshirt into my arms, noticing the contrasting color and fabric of Alex's hoodie encircling it. From there my gaze slips to the blood staining the whorls of my fingerprints. The nurse at the clinic helped me clean up, before putting on a fresh brace, but not all the color came off. Sighing, I grab a pair of flannel pajama pants and tiptoe to the bathroom.

Once upon a time, a hot bath could make everything better.

No amount of hot water will wash away the things I've seen, or purge the thoughts I've had. Things are not right with Alex Franks. And I can't stay away from him.

•

Chapter Ten

Cemeteries, broken and screaming deer and two dead boys haunt my sleep.

Daniel's always out of my reach, drifting between the graves. Mud slips beneath my feet as I run and reach for him, but he passes like mist through my fingers. Eroded mausoleums jut from the ground, compound fractures of granite and stone. A shovel handle trips me, the world lurches up to swallow me, and I land with a wet crunch on a rotten corpse.

Worms wriggle in the snout of the doe, her eyes dilated and fixed on me.

No matter how I struggle, I can't get free of her mangled limbs. My feet break through her ribcage, tangle in her deflated lungs. When I look down, the doe is nothing but ground meat, tufts of hair, and that dead eye watching me.

An enrapt sigh draws my eyes up. Alex stands at the head of the grave, every one of his scars open. Blood vessels dangle from his arm incisions, intestines spill from his abdomen, but his eyes are feverishly bright.

"You're perfect, Emma," he says.

His odd left eye pops from its socket, and blood gushes from his mouth and nose. Laughing, or sobbing, I can't tell, not with the fluids pouring from his throat. Whatever noise he makes, it precedes Alex, the sour stink splashing on me before he buries me with his dying corpse.

I scream myself awake, arms flailing to throw the weight and warmth from my chest. Renfield hisses and bolts from me, a white furbearing missile aimed for the safety of the hallway. He lands in the puddle of light outside my door, spins on his haunches, leveling a scathing, indignant cat glare on me, before tearing a path for the first floor.

Points of ache burn beneath my collarbone, almost at the hollow of my throat, where Renfield used me as a launch pad. Pulling down the neck of my T-shirt displays groups of angry red puncture marks, sticky and shiny with blood.

My parents' bedroom door flies open and Mom hustles into the hall, her hair standing on end and slippers on the wrong feet. Dad's voice issues muffled from their room's darkness, but she waves away his offer to check on me, and ties her robe like she's girding her loins for battle. Her gaze searches my face as she pushes against the wall I built between us. Sniffling, I reach for her, and the wall comes down.

Mom's at my bedside in an instant, arms around me. She's all warmth and flannel and rose linen spray. I slump on her shoulder and inhale deeply.

"Bad dream?"

"The worst." My fingers curl in the folds of her housecoat.

"Do you want to talk about it?"

Why do people always ask that? Talking drags the jagged ugly truth out and tosses it into view of anyone who cares to listen. My silence isn't enough answer for her.

"Daniel again?" Bless her for not sounding annoyed.

"Not really," I hedge. Then I sigh, and give in. "Well, not

just Daniel. There was a cemetery, too. And I couldn't catch him." I inhale a shaky breath and severely edit the rest of the dream. "Then I fell into a grave and was buried alive." My voice breaks on the last words, and I hate it.

"Oh, Emma," she says. "I know losing him was hard. Letting go is hard, too."

If she knew the rest of the dream, would she still pooh-pooh it? Downscale it to a little heartache? This is so much more than Daniel's death and me failing to get past it. Alex was there, alive and dead at the same time. A quiver threatens to run down my back when the image of him flashes behind my eyes. I suppress the shudder, and the urge turns inward, twisting my stomach instead.

"It is hard," I agree. "But I've started."

The cutting sensation lacing through me agrees.

"I know," she says and her embrace tightens. "I'm here to help, if I can."

I nod, not wanting to commit more than that. Missing Daniel is woven into every section of my life, flooding my spine and wrapping my nerves. I'm afraid to share, to show how deep missing him has dug into me. Inviting someone into my empty ache would diminish it, and diminish him.

Mom's hug loosens and she tilts back to look at me, smoothing hair from my face. "It's almost time for me to be up," she says. "Want to help me in the kitchen?"

On a normal nightmare morning, I might have agreed. This morning I sigh and hold up my broken hand.

"OK. Maybe not. I guess I'll let you try to sleep some more."

"Nah." I scoot back and wiggle my legs free of the blankets. "I'm awake now. How about I keep you company in the kitchen?" Anything to wipe the sadness from her eyes.

Mom looks like she lost her best friend, and I don't want her to share my misery.

She tips her head, blinks like she's considering something. "How about we go out for breakfast?"

"Deal."

After another battle with single-handed dressing, Mom and I meet in the kitchen. She's cranked her hair into a bun, gray frizz springing out around her face. Her jeans are dark and look like they've been ironed, and her purse is worn and limp. Total teen embarrassment material. I'm in comfy sweats, Alex's hoodie of yesterday, and my glitter-embroidered gray sweatshirt to counterbalance the guy-ness of the first layer.

I cuddle into Alex's shirt, which Mom either ignored or missed. If I'm being honest, I'm wearing the shirt of a boy I barely know, and he ripped it off himself, exposing more than his scars. In some way, I'm wearing his hurt and hiding in his shadows. The edges of the hollow inside me quiver, feeling a lot like my heart fluttering. I push the impression away and slam the car door to shake the feeling loose.

"Where to?" Mom asks, sitting in the driver's seat and starting the car. "Fast food? The sub place? Mugz-n-Chugz?"

My mom at *the* high school hang out? Everyone will know me. Everyone will see me with my frazzled, uncool parent. She'll mother me, carry my tray, probably send back her breakfast, and want to talk to the chef... But then we would be inside. No Tiny acting heartbroken and weird at the walk-up window. No Alex buying my coffee, sending tingles down my spine, messing up my heart rate.

"Mugz-n-Chugz sounds great," I say, knowing I'm sure to regret it.

I drag my backpack close, and liberate my cell phone. The screen is dark. The thin black cord of Mom's charger snakes from the dashboard, coiled and waiting in the cup of her console.

"Mind if I use your charger?"

"Not at all." She turns into M-n-C's parking lot. "We can go through the drive-through and eat in the car. That way it can charge, and I don't have to worry about you stranded and one-handed."

"Have I told you lately that you're awesome?"

"No." She cranks the wheel, steering the front of the sedan around the back corner of Mugz-n-Chugz and aiming for the drive-through order window. "Given your behavior last night, I thought I was on your most hated list."

Oh God, I groan inwardly. *Do we really have to do this now?*

"I don't hate you, Mom."

"I know." She drops the conversation, rolls down her window and orders a coffee with cream, and a breakfast bagel with bacon, egg, and cheese. I lean toward the center of the car, and order the Pancake-on-a-Stick with Tater Tots, and a breve with a shot of caramel.

"Pancake on a stick?" Mom arches an eyebrow.

"Yeah. A big breakfast sausage the size of a hot dog, dipped in pancake batter and deep fried."

"Sounds awful... and wonderful at the same time."

Mom's gaze shifts faraway after she pays and drives to the pick-up window. I can see her surrounded by ground meat, sausage casings, and batter, trying to improve on the recipe. She could do it, too, add a little cinnamon to the batter, make the sausage a maple sausage... Maybe next time Mom asks me to help in the kitchen, I will. When it comes to food, we seem to think a lot alike.

I wish she agreed with me about guys.

Lydia, Tiny's cousin and daughter of M n C's owner, hands the coffees through the window, and notices me in the passenger seat. "Oh, hi, Emma!" Then she does what I least want. She turns toward the inside of the restaurant and yells, "Hey, Tiny! Your girlfriend's at my window!"

My groan is audible over the car's motor.

Tiny's bulk blocks out the light coming from inside when he waddles to the pick-up window.

"Hi, Em." He takes our food bags from Lydia, and thrusts them through the shade on this side of the building. "You ever want a real man instead of that pretty boy, you know where to find me."

He closes the window with a jerk.

"Do I want to ask?" Mom hands my breakfast sack to me.

"Not really."

She casts a look back as she pulls away from the window. Tiny's still there, watching, his bottom lip sagging in an obvious pout.

Outside, the skies are gunmetal gray and tending toward inevitable downpour. People glide across the quad, burdened with books and hurrying for the doors. Bree isn't in her normal spot, prettying up the place. Then a ray of darkness appears. Tall Alex Franks, hood up, new-looking black leather jacket zipped, and collar popped, with his head down as he walks away from the walk-up window side of the building. The flutter of interest in my chest beats like crows' wings.

Mom doesn't miss my quick little breath, either. She shifts her focus forward quick enough to shake hair loose from her bun. Suddenly the car is too small, the need to escape burns my self-preservation instincts.

"Well, he certainly looks... intimidating..."

"He's actually very nice."

Must be the way I say the word, because Mom's eyes narrow and she watches Alex cross the street, then turn back and scan Mugz-n-Chugz, before shrugging deeper into his coat and standing near the side door. The shadowed face beneath his cowl turns a slow path across the quad, and a silly hope blooms, raw and vulnerable, wondering if he's looking for me. Then his gaze lands on me.

And I *know*.

Mom connects Alex's hidden stare to me, and I almost choke on my mouthful.

"He's the boy who got you into trouble yesterday, isn't he?"

"It wasn't trouble," I argue, unable to wrench my focus from him.

"You were at the med center, filthy, with a fresh brace when I picked you up. I call that trouble."

Trouble sounds so negative when Mom says it that way.

My stomach closes like a trap, any hint of hunger shriveling up in my gut. Even the enticing smell of coffee and caramel, drifting in misty plumes from my cup, has lost its appeal. I'm contemplating making an excuse to exit the car when Josh Mason's rusty Camaro Z-28 guns past.

"Gotta go, Mom. That's Josh Mason's car and he's almost always late."

She pins me with one of her serious looks. "We're going to continue this discussion later."

Of course we are, I groan inwardly. I pull the power cord from my phone and tuck it into my jacket pocket, regardless of the charge.

"Yep. See you tonight."

"This afternoon." Her voice has taken on a hard edge.

"Bree invited me over after school." I brandish my braced right hand. "She's gonna help me with homework."

"Fine." She eases back into her seat. "Make sure you call me when you get there."

"God, Mom. I have a broken hand – I'm not a baby."

"No," she huffs when I climb out of the car. "You're seventeen, still my daughter and I don't like…" and she jabs her half-full cup in Alex's direction, "that guy."

I don't bother arguing "You don't know him." She'll just come back with "And I don't want to." We had that argument once before, right after I brought Daniel home for the first time. Look how that turned out.

Biting cold nips at my face and neck when I shut the door and step away from Mom's car. Storm weight is oppressive, humid, tainting the air. The school looms dark and brooding, waiting for the last of its victims.

A rattletrap beater car putters behind me as I cross the street toward the school, and Alex. Reckless, maybe, but I'm drawn to him. More than I should be.

"Hey," he says when my feet hit the walkway leading to the door.

"Hi."

Surprise and a hint of a smile warm the insides of his hood. The same sense of happiness and disbelief soften his features. I'm his dream come to life, it's written on every line of his face. The world narrows to us, and thought dies. I have the crazy urge to cuddle to his chest and listen to his heart like I did with Daniel. His mismatched hazel eyes fill my vision, the black freckle in the left iris pulling me in, pushing me under. Darkness unfurls in me like a vine, nudging and probing, insisting there's something not right. Then he blinks and the moment's gone.

"Hey." His voice has a husky tone.

"You already said that."

"Oh. Yeah…"

A flash of white shows on his wrist when he pulls a rolled-up paper from his backpack. Alex holds the paper out until I wrap hesitant fingers around it. I look from the white tube to him, one eyebrow lifting in a question.

"Didn't you get my text?"

"My phone was dead." It's an automatic response, like a voicemail feature in my brain. Then what he asks hits me. "What do you mean, *your text*? How'd you get my number?"

"I took advantage of your phone while you were changing into my hoodie." The bemused look is gone, replaced by a smug, teasing expression, made smoky and a tad morbid by new dark shadows under his eyes. "Which looks really good on you, by the way."

"How would you know?" I sneak a peek down at myself. Yep. My jacket is zipped all the way.

"I saw you putting it on yesterday."

Heat floods my face, another automatic response around him. Did he see me wiping blood from my cleavage? No. I have to convince myself he didn't see me half-naked, or my confidence around him will come to a sudden end. If he was getting my number from my phone, I reason, he wouldn't have had time to watch.

Still, I steal a peek at him to gauge the knowledge hidden in his eyes.

The sky chooses now to open and hemorrhage water. People scurry, rats running for dry ground. Alex drags me inside the door frame, thumping me against him, drowning me in the smell of guy, cologne, and leather. Silly goony smiles cover both our faces – I see his and feel mine. Thunder grumbles across the top of the school. Alex turns his face to the sky, a lightning bolt illuminating the pale line down the side of his neck.

"Better get inside," he says.

I nod, grateful for the distance, and follow as he pushes open the side door.

The storm's chaotic energy stirs the people milling in the hall, cussing each other in clipped voices. Catty glances, too sharp, glaring at me walking so close to the new guy. A load of new gossip fills the hall, focusing on me and Alex, his hoodie on me, and where his hands were underneath it. All eyes seem trained on us, peeling, scathing. Alex lifts his head and drinks it in. I bow mine, allowing my blond hair to hang tent-like around my face.

Josh Mason appears in the churn and thrash, his carrot hair dangerously close to my locker. Shifting slightly between me and Josh, Alex splays one hand wide, and moves protectively in front of me. His posture hints at "mine" and "stay away."

And he has no right.

Shaking my head, I sidestep the shielding hand.

"Hey, Rusty," I tease. "Waiting for someone?"

I expect him to say something like "Missed you at the curb this morning." Instead, he shoots Alex a venomous glare, but fails miserably at being intimidating with his pale freckled face.

"Checking to make sure you were OK," he says. "You looked pretty shell-shocked climbing in his car yesterday."

Where's the sniping? The flirting? Where's his annoying arrogance?

"Didn't know you cared," I say, and try to edge past him.

Josh slides directly in my path, tall, familiar, and unwanted. An old anger rattles loose from my heart, banging around like buckshot in the hollow of my chest – when he compounds matters, blocking my path by grabbing my shoulders. We'd been here before and he didn't get what he wanted then. Nothing will change now that Daniel's gone. Beside me, piano-wire tension jerks Alex up to his full height of over six feet. His hand, still open, hangs close and ready to pry Josh off me.

"I *do* care." Josh's grip tightens. "Always have, even when you were with Dan."

He went there. Josh brought Daniel and their muddy relationship up.

"Funny thing," I snap, irritated and wanting this little confrontation over, "when he used to be your best friend."

Josh's hands fall from my shoulders. His expression darkens, his face mimicking the black shade of his shirt. "Age-old story – the girl falls for the wrong guy."

"He was the right guy in every way you never will be."

With that, I shoulder past him, thankful for Alex's ability to slice bladelike between Josh and me. Alex Franks might have dark secrets buried inside, be the stuff of gossip and too many popular girls' interests, but I'd rather have him by me than Josh. A ping in my gut says a wounded Alex is not quite right, but a huge alarm screams in my head that a jealous Josh is not safe to be around. Alex remains a buffer for me right to our lockers. He points to my recalcitrant lock and arches an eyebrow, and when I nod, he adopts Daniel's habit of opening my locker, quirks included.

How can he work my combination like he's done it a thousand times? How can Alex know when to push the lock in, and to nudge the door so it will open?

"Thanks," I say, suppressing the tremor rambling through my insides.

His face peeks from his hood when he nods. "Anytime."

I fumble with my backpack and one hand, tempted to at least hang it from my immobiliser. My heart clenches, squeezing painfully through me, forcing images of Daniel into my mind. Daniel opened my locker every day using the same quirks. The last month of June he used to open the locker without me asking. By the time I force thoughts of Daniel away and have my morning books loaded into the bag, Alex is already done, books in one arm. He stands watching, waiting expectantly.

"Theater's across the school. You're going to be late," I chide him.

"Aren't you going to look at the paper?"

I blink, then memory kicks in and my cheeks heat again. He handed me a paper when he mentioned me in his hoodie. I was so flustered I stuffed it in my backpack without thinking. "Oh, yeah. Sure."

The paper crinkles when I unroll it. The header has "Fifth Hour Dune Ecology" typed directly under Alex Franks and Emma Gentry. Inky letters jumble and ooze under my gaze. Words like "death" and "vehicular accidents" stand out, accompanied by statistics.

My look must be as blank as the circles under his eyes are dark.

"The report Mr LaRue wanted," he says, a hint of laughter in his voice.

"Oh," is all I can manage. He wrote the report for me?

"I had the time last night, and figured you might not."

"That's so sweet."

"Yeah, well – don't tell anyone." He smiles and turns toward the theater and fine arts hall. "Seriously. Don't mention it. I don't want my rep ruined already."

A bark of a laugh escapes me. The burst feels so much better than the tense, awkward sensation usually twisting my heart and nerves around him. I breathe an exaggerated sigh and smile at him before he walks away. Arms crossed, hugging the bag strap to me, my gaze follows after him until he turns the corner. Then my senses catch back up with the faded clock anchored to the wall. Only a few minutes left to get to Trig.

I squash the instinct to run to class, and chase down Alex instead. Tardy happens.

His leather jacket is warm, his flesh firm, and the electric tingle is missing when I touch him. The zing I feel racing my insides is shocking enough. Somehow, he manages to cleave the entire school from existence when he turns and steps closer. I look up, but feel like I'm drowning.

"What's up, Emma?"

"Why are you so nice to me?" Why did I ask that?

He knows the badass rumors floating around the school. He claims to use them to his benefit. So why *is* Alex so kind? Why does he look at me like I'm a gift he never expected to receive?

A short breath sucks between his teeth. Alex's eyes widen, and I get the feeling he's seeing me on a different level when he stares. His pupils dilate, the left a fraction smaller than the right, like a cat with heterochromia. His eyebrows sink, and scrunch closer together, and his gaze changes, as though he's looking inside himself for the answers. A fist clenches at his side, then relaxes.

"I wish I knew," he says, hanging his head in some kind of defeat. "I have to…"

He seems as shocked by that truth as I am.

For a moment he's the wounded, scraped-hollow boy I

saw by the car, a sad jack-o'-lantern covered in deer blood and regret. Ghosts past behind his pupils, then his face closes off, and he grunts, "Gonna be late for class," and stalks off.

I push my hair back with my immobilised right hand, and then stop dead, with my hand before my eyes. A few spots of yesterday's deer blood darkens and crusts the ribbing of his sleeve over my cast, exactly the opposite side of the white broken heart on my wrist.

It's official.

A nightmare beginning to my Thursday is just the start.

Chapter Eleven

If I didn't know the girl the rumors tore apart throughout my morning, I might find humor in her being: clueless and conniving, a slut and whore (there is a difference), a leech and luckiest girl in school, emotionally dead and a cutter.

But, I *am* that girl.

And I would be dead tired if I were all those things – way too much work.

What would those whispering, gossiping girls think of Alex's many scars? He's been cut five ways from Sunday, and I bet they'd find it sexy on him. Have they been close enough to him to feel the electricity in his skin? Something is left of center with Alex, and I don't care – they'd probably run. Would they have ignored his distress and avoided the filth, the blood, and the deer? Would his looks or his money matter if they knew what a psycho his father is?

Marin Rhodes gives me the stink eye the entire third period, and I know it's not because I'm excused from the basketball tourney due to my broken hand. She's staked claim to Alex Franks, and the whispers going around the school have slipped like poison into her ear. I'm no longer an inconvenience, I'm now clearly competition.

If she could've felt the heat in his gaze this morning, she'd know how much.

I sit on the bleachers near to Mr Ashford's usual base of operation, at the corner closest to the locker rooms. My location keeps the basketballs from becoming ballistic weapons, but does not give me any shelter from the bitchy glares or stage-whispered gossip.

Daniel and I used to sit near here for basketball games, and we always sat together at this end for pep rallies, despite his senior and my sophomore status. Now thoughts of Alex cut into my musing, thin but sharp-edged, slicing under my defenses and into the empty ache. He's barged his way into my dreams. He feels familiar and foreign to me at the same time.

I choke back a snicker when Marin's team is cut from the tourney, then suppress a groan when they swarm the bleachers, all long limbs, forked tongues and hard eyes.

When our Drill Sarge blows his whistle, I bolt from the bleachers and hit the lockers. The rest of the girls stream past to the showers. Giggles and hoots and catcalls roll in the steam toward me, and while the joking around tugs at parts of me long gone cold, a bigger part of me wants nothing to do with a nest of vipers. Coiled, waiting to strike, and, lately, I'm their target of choice.

My phone buzzes to life, a short storm in a tea kettle. *Buzz, buzz, bing! Buzz, buzz, bing!* Two texts. Then my factory standard ringtone follows. Undressed to my underthings, I fling my gym clothes over it to muffle the phone.

Somebody's persistent.

Glaring at the wad of rumpled jersey cloth, daring the phone to ring again, I horse my way back into my street clothes, including Alex's hoodie.

"Nice shirt,"Marin says, wrapped in nothing but a white towel.

Averting my eyes, I say, "Thanks."

"Nice for the men's department," she adds, tossing her wet hair over her shoulder.

Don't sink to her level, I tell myself. *Do. Not. Sink...* I can't fight the words rising like bile in my throat. "Funny, because I'm sure that's where it came from."

Marin stops a locker row away, and turns her feral grin on me.

Score one for Marin.

Jerking my focus from her, I hook my backpack over my immobiliser and shove my things into it. My pretty pink cell phone blinks the message-waiting light at me. Just one more thing to avoid as I skulk from the locker room.

I should've kept my mouth shut. Now Marin will either compound the Alex-and-I-got-naked rumor, or start another one saying my mom shops at Goodwill. Not that where my clothes comes from matters. I'm sick and tired of hearing about myself secondhand.

The Ugly Room door closes on the humid, sweet-sour air, shutting in the confirmation my day is getting worse and not better. Flinty glares come from random angles, and cut passing time between gym and lunch into uncomfortable bits. The trophy cases dissect and reflect the faces, distorting them until a multitude of shining faces leer. Another gauntlet to run.

I tip my head down and aim for the stairs to the catwalk.

My footfalls echo in the empty stairwell, tumbling like lead in the cold air. The punctuated silence is balm for my fraying nerves. Tension leeches from my muscles, a fraction at a step, until I can finally relax my shoulders at the second

floor landing. A breeze whistles around the door to the catwalk, an odd sucking and pushing sensation, identical to
how I feel while around Alex and thinking about Daniel.

My heart thumps a sad beat.

And then another.

Wrenching the catwalk door open, I walk a different kind
of gauntlet.

Lightning from the thunderstorm strobes the floor. Daniel's
echo appears by the support bar where we first met. He's the
Daniel after his fall, trail of red leaking from his skull over
his eye. Then a new specter bursts into to life beside him, a
ghost of the Josh that was, all wispy and aspects of fire and
flesh. His body rotates, pulsing with a dark light. Spinning,
smoky limbs whirl around him like flames licking into smoke,
but his stationary face is a savage version of the Josh that is.

"Emergizer bunny," Daniel croons.

I close my eyes and pound across the carpet for the door
into the main building. An itchy kind of fright spirals out
along my nerves. I push the door and the latch catches. I feel
the pressure of Daniel's death, and Josh's destructive tendencies. I push my panic against the door keeping me from
escape. *Please, please,* I beg, *let me out of here!*

I want to get past them.

Please.

The door latch releases with a click and flings me into the
hallway. I stumble into a sea of faces, all of them wiped blank
in a moment of surprise. Numerous gasps precede tittering
and giggles. I'm too relieved at escaping the echoes in the
catwalk to care. Give me gossip. Give me narrowed glances
and bitchy stage whispers. They're nothing compared to seeing the love of my life die before my eyes, and his former best
friend turn to a burning shade.

Maybe I should avoid the catwalk, and the ghosts haunting me there.

Maybe I should seek psychiatric help for seeing what isn't real.

Straightening my backpack, I toss my hair back and am tempted to swipe it from my face with my right hand. The bloody reminder on Alex's cuff flashes in my memory, and I fuss at the fall of blond over my shoulders with my left hand instead.

Voices and lunchtime din sweeps up the stairs, thick and scummy with dirty words and residual gossip. I wade through the noise, plunging deeper into the shallow waters of Shelley High's rumor mill.

I wonder if Alex has had the same kind of day. Has he basked in it? Is it affecting his rep the way he wants?

Why do I feel like a volleyball being whacked back and forth?

Bodies crowd the side hall, the line frayed and snarled enough to look like I feel. In the lunch line, Bree is a dozen people in front of me. Today, I stalk past the whisperers, the zit-faced freshmen, and up to my saved spot in line. Bree's eyes widen, then her eyebrows sink a little, and she reaches out and brushes a hand over the fabric stretched over my brace.

"Didn't get my text?"

"I figured it was your standard, 'I'm saving you a spot'," I say.

"Totally was." She smiles, and winks, flashing her brilliant sparkly blue eyeshadow at me. "So, where's your boyfriend?"

Immediate thoughts rush to Daniel. He's gone. So gone it hurts. Then I realise who she means, and frustration washes through me.

"God, Bree. *Et tu, Brute?*" I quote Shakespeare at her.

She rolls her perfectly lined eyes and hitches one half of her mouth into a smile.

"You know I don't speak French."

"It's Latin," I remind her. We had the same English class in tenth grade, we had the same lesson on Caesar and Shakespeare's version of the fall of his empire.

"Whatever, Em." She glances back the way I came, scanning for someone. Most likely Alex Franks. Between the way he tangles my emotions and the gossipmongers set his name on repeat, I'm fast getting tired of it. When she opens her mouth, I know I'm going to hear it again. Bree says, "I don't speak either of those languages. And what does that have to do with Alex Franks looking for you?"

He's looking for me? Damn my heart for beating quicker.

"Nothing." I wish I could resist looking back, but I can't. He's not anywhere in line.

"Good. Then can we drop the crabby?"

"Sure." I take the tray she hands to me.

By the smell, a mix of Mexican taquería and armpit, it's Chicken Chili Crispito day and my stomach is already rolling up tighter than a fist. Spicy and half-nauseous don't go well together. Once inside the food service room, I aim for the kettle filled with chicken and rice soup, and grab a handful of cracker packets. Bree and I rendezvous at the drink cart. She takes a milk, I grab a water bottle, and we trail past the in crowd for the thespian tables.

I run my tray up the back of Bree's white sweater and nearly dump soup on us both when she stops suddenly. The thin yellow broth slops along the lip of the Styrofoam bowl and splatters the cracker packets.

"What the hell?" I mutter.

"*He*'s the hell," she says, light and surprised, then steps one pace to the left.

At our table, sitting next to Jason Weller, is the reputation spin doctor himself.

Alex smiles under his hood, the only brightness on his face. Dark shadows sag under his eyes. His skin is an off shade of not healthy, like he should be puking, or sweating with fever any minute. *Maybe Asia Foley's flu is catching up to him...* He slides to one side, making room for us. Bree's change is subtle, but I see it, her spine straightens, her shoulders roll back, thereby hoisting her chest and making it look fuller. I shrink in Alex's hoodie, silently cursing myself for the rash decision to wear it.

What was I thinking anyway?

Simple answer? I wasn't.

Like all those months with Daniel, I acted like what's his – in this T-shirt's case, Alex's – is mine.

Bree glides into the seat closest to Alex. The hood turns toward her, a swift snap of motion. Jason makes a sound somewhere between surprise, jealousy, and warning, making eyes at Bree and then shifting them – to tell her to move, not so subtly. She chuffs a breath, lifts her shoulders in a slight shrug, then slides down a place. I feel like an actor delivering a silent soliloquy; for a moment my emotions are unguarded on my face and easily seen by the rest of the table.

Shaking my head, I ease my tray to the table, not the least bit surprised when Alex settles the soup before it spills and then holds a hand out to take my backpack for me. Daniel would've done the same. If he were alive.

Bree arches her eyebrows in a significant manner, flicking her glance between me and Alex stashing my backpack between our feet. She says so much by saying nothing. *See? He likes you. Yep. I called him your boyfriend first. Told you so...* I shake my head at her, eyes wide, telling her to knock it off. Of course with Bree, things don't get better, they get different. And this time, worse.

"So, Alex," she says as she opens her milk carton. "I have a couple questions for you."

"And maybe I have answers," he says, laughter slipping through his tenor.

"How is it a good looking, well-dressed guy like you is single?"

A flash of some emotion moves across his face so quickly, I can't decipher it. He drops his eyes, then worries at the edge of his napkin with his fingers. "I had a girlfriend last year."

"So it's a seasonal thing?" asks Jason. "Cool! Maybe I should try that..."

"No." Alex's hood slips a smidge when he shakes his head. "I mean I had a girlfriend, but when I woke up from surgery I just didn't feel the same anymore. It's like, I don't know..." He rips his napkin in half. "It's like I saw her with different eyes then, and didn't like what I saw."

End of story. Case closed. I can see it in his eyes. Bree wisely moves past it and says, "OK, now that my curiosity is sated, I have one more question. Have any plans this weekend?"

His face is carefully composed to show nothing. "Not sure what you mean."

"Oh, come on. I know you're a smart guy." True to Bree's usual fashion, now she's buttering him up – before whipping out the carving knife and filleting him. "You know... the football game on Friday, and then..."

I want to smile when a flash of recognition flickers in the

depth of his hazel eyes, but he maintains the clueless charade. One shrug, an elegant lift of his shoulder.

"The Halloween Ball on Saturday," she prods.

"Oh... that." He shakes his head. "Nope. No plans."

"You're not going to the dance?" She sounds aghast, one hand fluttering to her chest like the drama queen she is.

"Hadn't planned on it." He lifts the awful Mexican roll he chose and takes a bite, chewing, waiting for Bree to respond. She seems flustered and out of verbal ammo – a rare thing for her. "I have a reputation to keep up, y'know."

I can't help but grin when he turns and winks at me.

Bree doesn't miss the gesture. And she certainly doesn't look flustered anymore. My throat cinches tight around a mouthful of dry, soupless cracker.

"Speaking of..." She leans back a little, eyes bright and focused. "I've heard a lot of chatter about you and Emma lately. You know she's going to the dance, right? Perfect opportunity to perpetuate the gossip."

Or stop it completely.

My calf muscle convulses with the sudden desire to kick her under the table. Instead, I sputter and glare at her.

"You never said Emma was going," he says to Bree, but holds me with a lingering gaze. Damn my heart for trembling. Then he kills the thrill by saying, "Rep maintenance is good."

"Oh, no, new boy," I say, and hold up my spoon. "Worry about your reputation. Leave mine out of it." Mine's taken a nosedive into depths I don't know if I can plumb to pull it back up.

I expect him to be flip, to tease or toy with me.

Alex turns, fixing me with his shadowed gaze. His raw darkness pulls me in, shuts out the rest of the thespians, the crowds, the world. I sit limply, the wrongness in him repelling me but the honesty and sweet open need in his eyes drawing me. My right hand is out of view on my lap, Alex reaches a finger closer, runs it over the Velcro straps cinching the brace closed. His other fingers settle on the immobiliser, his index finger resting where the hollow heart is in my skin.

"It won't be worth it if you're not there, Emma."

Maybe it's the honesty in his voice. Maybe it's the way he exposes himself from the inside out.

"Fine." I blow out a long-suffering sigh. "I'll go."

His smile goes all the way to his eyes, disturbing the dark shadows beneath them. If anything, his skin pales to a greenish hue, and he lifts his hand from my cast to wipe at beads of sweat on his forehead.

"You feeling OK, Alex?" I ask.

"Not really," he answers. "I'm feeling kinda tapped out."

"Low blood sugar? Asia's flu?"

"No. I've been dealing with this since I woke up from the accident." He scoops up the backpack and deposits it on the seat where his butt was minutes ago. "Can you turn in the report to Mr LaRue? I think I need to go home."

"Sure." The word sounds more hesitant than it should. Worry unfurls in me, a dark, bitter blossom I haven't tended over a boy in a long time. "You wrote it. The least I can do is turn it in."

He teeters a little where he stands, all bravado and attitude gone. More color drains from his face, and the bags under his eyes turn almost black.

"Want help to the office?" Who am I kidding? I'm a borderline gimp at the moment.

"No." The shake of his head is a weak jerk. "I'll make it. Just gonna call my dad."

His dad.

Of course he'd call his dad. The man's eyes, pinching nearly as tight as his grip on my hand. The brusque way he brushed off my pain. How could he be so loving and dedicated to saving his son?

Guilt roots me to the spot. I should help him. A strong urge burns in me to slip under his arm and walk with him to the office, to be there even if he doesn't need me. I know he would be there for me. Instead, I sit numbly and watch Alex go, his back straight and head bowed.

"Poor guy," Bree says. "Got the flu that's going around."

It's not the flu. I'm not sure how I know, other than we have a connection we forged over the dying deer, or that deeper note that trembles in the hollow inside me. What's left-of-center in Alex is sapping his energy. His naked chest flashes in my mind, all the careful scars shining in the sunlight.

What really happened when his father brought him back?

What price does he have to pay now?

Chapter Twelve

"You really slid your arms under that deer?" Bree asks. A delicate tremor rides the length of her spine as she spreads our homework over her polished wood dining room table.

"I really did." I nod.

Her blood ran into my cleavage, I think. *I watched the light die in her eye.*

I push away the flashes of sunlight and death, and pick at the blood in the cuff of Alex's hoodie. Bree and I'd already discussed the garment and its ownership – she accepted me stripping my shirt and bra off while standing in the parking lot, with a boy a few feet away, and wearing his shirt home. She smiled and danced her eyebrows even. What she can't adjust to is me wading into a muddy culvert and helping Alex lift the wounded deer.

"Why would you *do* that?" Her eyes are wide, the blue eyeshadow almost gone.

"I don't know." I poke at paper in front of me. Why did I do it? I've mulled it over. The only answer I can come to is the way Alex bared his soul to me in his panic. "Alex was so upset about the deer... I couldn't just leave him there."

"Wow." She drags out the "o", staring at me like I've

grown a second head. "You two must have *some* connection," she says. Then she walks to the door to the kitchen, smoothing her skirt and not touching the wood trim of the doorway. "Want a Diet Coke?"

"Gross. How about coffee?"

"Gross," she mimics, couching a hand on her hip. "I don't know crap about making it and I am not touching Mom's fancyass brewer. We've got instant in the cupboard."

Dear God, kill me now.

"Do you have pop that isn't diet?" I ask.

She nods, dark roots showing in her hair with the motion, as she stalks into the kitchen. The fridge creaks, two metallic clinks sound through the door. Cupboards rattle, crinkling sounds issue from the door, some cusswords follow.

I gaze around the fussy room, deep beige walls, white trim around the windows and doors, the furniture all cherry-stained wood. Gilded picture frames and marble sculptures are artfully and intentionally arranged. Despite the rich color scheme, it feels… sterile. The rest of Bree's house is the same: beige, white, cherry, gilt and stone. Classy, but no real personality. The living room feels like a museum; I half expect to be charged admission fees and see ropes cordoning off big abstract art and the statues in niches.

Bree returns through the door butt-first, shoulders rolled forward under the weight of something. She turns, displays a tray heavy with pop cans, one diet and one not, assorted junk food, fruit, and string cheese.

"So, do you?" she asks, holding out the can of regular cola.

"Did I miss something?" I take the pop and try to wash out the taste of confusion slicking the back of my throat. "Do we *what*?"

"Have a connection." She stresses the last word like I'm silly for not noticing, that it's already a foregone conclusion for her and I'm just here to testify.

"That's not possible." It comes out too fast, and too crabby. "I mean... One, connections are in nervous systems and electrical things. Two, I hardly know him."

Kind. Funny. Emotionally raw, and way too much like Daniel sometimes.

"I think you do." The last word comes out sing-song, her point proven by me hedging the question. "And it doesn't stop him from looking at you like you're Juliet and he's Romeo come back to life."

"Bad theatrical reference, B." I drag a homework sheet closer. "They both died."

"OK, fine. Whatever." She throws up her hands, then drops into the chair across from me. "So death is bad in romance."

"Ya think?"

I start scanning the trig problems. Multiple choice. This is going to give me a worse headache than Bree's inquisition. And make my hand hurt, too. Sure, I can check the appropriate boxes, but I still have to do the math.

Bree says, "You have to admit you guys have major chemistry."

I know what she's talking about, I feel it in the tunneling, tumbling sensation, in the way he can cut the world away with a turn of his body, in how he makes my heart beat again.

"We have Dune Ecology." I don't want to admit anything. "That's my only science class."

"Are you this difficult in your dead quiet neighborhood?"

Leave it to Bree to bring up Memorial Gardens Cemetery, my dirty little secret.

I retort, "You know what pirates say: 'dead men tell no tales.' The dead also don't drive me crazy."

"Nope. That's my job." She opens her Diet Coke, pulls a big swig off it, then grabs a handful of potato chips from the open bag on the serving tray. "You can deny it all you like, Em. But there's chemistry between you two and I think the entire school's noticed."

Think? The school *has* noticed. I've noticed. It has a ring of the unreal to it. When I close my eyes, I have the feeling I've known Alex for years. Then I see him, his scars, and the brief flashes of raw honesty and horrid secrets, and I think I don't know him at all. And I can't stay away. Those moments of open ache from him caught my heart, promised it a wounded companion.

"Yeah. Rumors abound."

"Kernel of truth," she says, then drops her focus to the books and papers.

One thing about Bree. She eventually figures out when to drop the subject. This one is now officially dropped.

I stick a pencil in my right hand, wedging it under the thumbhole of my immobiliser, and free some notebook paper to do the problems longhand. Bree expresses how stupid she thinks my Trig teacher must be to give me a sheet like that. I tell her my teachers are setting up online work and should have it ready tomorrow. After, we sit in companionable not-talking-about-Alex almost quiet, focusing on schoolwork with a sprinkle of gossip – who's dating who, who's hating who – rather than the other way around. Bree takes dictation, writing my paragraph essays in her pretty loopy script. My writing was always hard to read, all peaks and skinny letters, and half the time my brain is too far in front of my hand.

Close to dinnertime, and a no-show from her parents, I'd asked Bree back to my house for the company, but she swore she was going to order pizza on her parents' tab, then watch a horror movie marathon. With homework finished, Bree stuffs everything in my backpack. My phone slips from the front pocket, as if straining for the light. She scoops it up, and I hope she'll mindlessly ease it back into the pocket like I would've done.

No such luck.

"You know you have messages?" she asks, eyeing the blinking light.

"Yeah. Most likely you."

"Let's see, shall we?" Bree slides open the phone, deftly turning out of my path when I lunge for it. The texts are from Bree. A few anyway. Three are from Alex. "Midnight," she says, "awfully late to text someone you have no chemistry with."

"Stop harping on our chemistry, would ya?"

My jaw snaps shut when she clicks on the message and it opens. She reads it and then tips my phone for me to read.

Thank you for holding me together when I fell apart at the dunes.

Bree lets out an airy "Aw," and then skips to the next, sent two minutes later.

I wrote the report for Mr LaRue. Hope it makes up for getting dirty to help me.

The third and last one is from this morning, roughly during passing time after first hour.

Saving you a seat at lunch. Not sure what I meant when I said I don't know.

"What's that last one about?" Bree asks.

Of course she'd pick the most awkward one for me to explain and still keep my snarled emotions to myself.

"Well." I shoulder my backpack and edge toward the door. "I asked him why he was so kind to me. Then he said he didn't know."

"Duh. Because he likes you."

Like a boy being mean, and someone saying he did it because he likes you and doesn't know how to show it? I try for a reassuring, you-answered-it smile, but fall short. Bree opens her mouth, I'm sure to coddle me, tell me how she's right, and I'll just see. Mom's car horn beeps into the quiet and saves me dealing with or denying anything else.

Bree says, "Say hi to your mom for me."

"Sure thing." I string my left arm around her shoulders and hug her tight. She uses the position to replace my phone. "Thanks for helping me."

"Homework's no biggie."

"Not just that," I say, then go silent around a lump tightening my throat. Bree's my best friend. She stood by me when most of the school turned away after Daniel's death. She occasionally encouraged me to get out of my funk, but never pushed, never got bitchy.

"What are friends for? Better get moving before your mom toots again."

"Two toots and a grounding." It was always one of Mom's favorite punishments.

"That was when we were kids," Bree says, then pulls from my arm. "See ya in the morning."

"Definitely."

My last task, after assuring Mom all my homework was done, and that I hadn't talked to "that boy at school" since lunchtime, was to text him back.

I curl under the cover of my blankets, with the power

cord to my cell phone snaking between my sheets like a thick black vein, and stare at the text thread from Alex. Hiding to text him seems even more surreal surrounded by the screen's anemic blue glow. I read his messages again and again, knowing I should reply. Then I type:

Thanks for writing that report. Don't apologize. I don't know what you meant, either, but I won't let you fall apart alone.

Those last words are as raw as he is beneath his scars. I should delete them. I really shouldn't make promises I'm not sure I can keep. My finger drifts from Delete to Send, and then I push the button. Once the text is gone, I turn the phone off, knowing I'll have to deal with the consequences tomorrow at school.

As it turns out, Friday dawns cool and bright. The storm scoured the dingy autumn hues to a brilliant wet shine, like fresh skin beneath a burn. After checking my phone for messages, and pouting because there weren't any, I stuff Alex's freshly laundered hoodie into my bag, climb into clean clothes, and fail miserably at leaving my closet without touching Daniel's sweatshirt. The aching loss is still there, quivering and hollow in my chest. The miracle of the morning is it's smaller.

Flooring passes beneath my feet in a blur when I launch from the stairs. Mom has another breakfast burrito ready for me in our lived-in kitchen, shakes her head and natters about me getting up earlier. She launches on another nagfest, and then helps me into my backpack straps.

I've gotten into the habit of tucking my right hand in the open zipper of my sweatshirt. I wedge it there while I inhale my breakfast burrito and take in the late October morning.

Sunlight bleeds through the sheer clouds, softening the edges of the world. The creepy atmosphere of my late-night walks is gone, the jack-o'-lanterns are only grinning, not ghoulish, no presence dancing on my nerves.

An odd sense of hope rises in me. And, I refuse to believe it's because of Alex Franks.

He's nothing but trouble in a kind, brooding conundrum.

The line for the walk-up side of Mugz-n-Chugz is long. I join the queue, raking at my hair with a brush while I wait to order my breve. Eyeliner is so not happening this morning. One person from the window and my Friday hits the skids. Tiny sees me and his eyes narrow in a glower. I sink further into my hoodie, and flirt with wishing for Alex to play my boyfriend again. The only other time Tiny left me alone was when I dated Daniel.

The coffee is as hot as the needling glances from Tiny when I walk away from the window. I suppose I deserve them for pretending to like another guy. Pausing at the curb, I look left and right, not so much for safety but to avoid a pedestrian/vehicle collision with Josh Mason's Camaro. The rumbling rust-bucket of a Z-28 is conspicuously absent this morning and I'm running late as normal.

Has the universe shifted? Tiny hates me. Josh isn't here to harass me. Alex Franks is invading my life...

Bree's on the bench closest to the side door. She's in black from her head band to her suede boots. How she makes a kicky little skirt and military issue boots look good together is beyond me. I definitely lack the put-together gene that Bree Ransom has in abundance.

"Morning!" she sings. She tips her sunglasses down, eyes me and her expression turns sympathetic. I'm sure she's thinking about whipping out her make-up bag.

"Hey." I slump to the bench beside her and take a big drag off the sweet, creamy coffee.

"So, did you talk to your boyfriend last night?"

"Haven't we already had this discussion?"

"Yep." She stands and holds out a hand for my coffee so I can use my left to stand. "And I believe if you think about something hard enough, it will be true."

"Why are you getting all metaphysical beliefy on me?"

"Because I think he'd be good to you. And you need a good guy."

I arch an eyebrow at her. "Really? All the stuff going around about him and you think he'd be good to me?"

"Call it intuition," she says, shaking the wrinkles from her skirt at the same time. "Call it whatever. Other than Daniel, I've never seen a guy look at a girl the way Alex looks at you."

Me neither. He replaces the planet, makes my heartbeat faster, and God, I can't believe it, I think he makes the ache a little less lonely. I scan the quad one last time. Still no Alex. Is he sick with Asia's flu? He never replied to my text last night. Did I scare him off with that stupid promise? What was I thinking when I sent it?

The entire day passes without a sight of or any answer from Alex.

His absence whips the gossip hounds into a frenzy. According to Marin Rhodes and her harpies, and anybody else with an opinion, Alex Franks is done with me. Word has it I gave him what he wanted and he didn't come to school because I flipped out when he told me. According to the all-knowing "they", I should be on suicide watch.

The words dig in like barbed wire, but I'm tired of letting them hurt me.

At lunch I check my phone, and then again after school. Still no reply. The little bubble of hope I'd felt this morning has faded. At this point, the graveyard fence holds more attraction than Bree's museum dining room, or any non-existent text from the guy who is definitely not my boyfriend. With help from the janitor, I gain access to my locker after school, fumble with my books, then load my bag and head for Memorial Gardens.

The wrought iron gate looms into view, black rotted teeth ripping through the grass edging.

A whisper of fear flits through me.

What if Daniel is the scary corpse I've seen the past two times? Where will my broken heart find sanctuary then?

My phone buzzes to life in my bag. I linger at the corner of the cemetery, eyes on the distant mausoleum drenched in afternoon shadows. Torn between backsliding into hanging on the fence and wishing for a grave that will never be, and allowing whatever text it is to delay it, I sigh and give in. The backpack straps whisper over my shoulder.

My pink phone flashes a red message light.

Sliding it open, I see the sender's name. The fear crashes. *Alex Franks.*

I click on the text and open it.

Been home sick. Will be back to life tomorrow. Save me a dance?

I feel the smile come without forcing it. The pumpkin across the street echoes my expression. I type into the text field, *Of course! Feel better soon.*

I know one little text from him has that effect on me.

Chapter Thirteen

Yards and yards of fabric and I still feel naked. Not for the first time I wonder why I let Bree talk me into these costumes and this dance.

Tank tops don't show as much skin between my cleavage and chin as this dress does.

Skirts flare when I spin and pin Bree with a half-hearted glare.

"Oh, come on, Emma!" she huffs, and glitter whisks from her exposed skin. "Admit it. We look amazing!"

Her gown floats above the floor when she glides to stand next to me in the full-length mirror backstage of Shelley High's auditorium. She's dressed nearly identically to me, and seems to have blossomed in the gown, where I feel like pulling on the garment bag the dress came in. Layered skirts of ivory silk, while bodices embroidered in gold or silver are pushing up our boobs. Filmy sleeves off our shoulders and our blond hair curled, pinned, and dangling. The best Twins costumes she's ever created.

"OK. I admit it."

"Yes!" She pumps her fist in the air. "I finally win one! You've never agreed with me before."

"Don't rub it in." I'm tempted to cross my arms.

Jason Weller emerges from the dressing room to our right. A giggle escapes me, shattering whatever regal image Bree created.

"A monk?"

He smiles broadly, his hood flopping over to cover his face when he bows. I pick at the scratchy brown fabric of Jason's robe when he rises.

"What else would I be?" He eyes our exposed boob-tops, scrunches his eyebrows together, and then brandishes his Bible like an offensive weapon. "Every royal family should have their own clergy to steer them from the paths of wickedness."

"Whatever." Bree gives him an eye roll and sigh combination, then links her arm in mine and gestures vaguely toward the door. "Then lead on, holy man."

Jason produces a lighter from his robes, then lights an incense cone inside the ornate metal globe hanging from a chain. Then he smooths his cowl, adjusts his huge wooden cross pendant, and puts his best monk face on. Striding slowly, chanting some complete nonsense, he walks from the backstage area and into the side hall, leading us as if we really were two fairytale princesses.

"I was thinking about killing you," I whisper to Bree. "But I've reconsidered."

"You'll be thanking me when Alex Franks sees you."

"And now I'm thinking maybe I should smack you."

"That would not be ladylike," Jason sings into his mock monk chant.

"Plus your hand is in a brace," Bree says, parroting his tone.

I say, "Only one of them."

Voices and laughter, thin and jumbled, wash over us once we turn into the main hall. The normal lunch line has turned into a costume parade. slutty angels and trampy faeries, fantasy and horror characters, sports heroes and more. Marin Rhodes shows most of her skin in a Playboy Bunny outfit complete with tail and ears. She turns a catty bitch glare on me, way too predatory for her bunny outfit.

Flutters come to life, battering my insides. I've made myself practically invisible since Daniel died. Now here I am, dressed as a princess with most of my cleavage standing out, without my jeans and sweatshirts to hide in. Probably not the best idea with all the gossip flying around since the Dune Eco trip.

The rest of Bree's friends cluster at the end of the hall. They are a welcome buffer of familiarity, even if the thespians look like refugees from the Ren Faire. The guys are in tights and puffy pants, with pompous-looking jackets and feathered hats. The girls wear long skirts and bodices, similar to mine and Bree's, but no other costumes beat ours in elegance.

"Wow, Bree!" says Amber Miller, a curly-haired girl with freckles. "You two rock the princess look."

"*Totally* rock it," agrees her brother Michael, who is not surprisingly dressed like a court jester.

As one big group, we join the queue, a knot in the line edging and bumping along toward the open double doors.

Inside, the walls are lined in paper cut-outs of tombstones and crypts, skeletons and ghosts. Crepe streamers drape from the ceiling, white crinkles catching and diffusing the few lights that shine. A sad attempt at a graveyard under moonlight, but it makes me yearn for the fence of Memorial Gardens for a moment. I'm not an artist, but I could've done a better cemetery landscape on familiarity alone.

People cluster in the same crowds, the ins and the sports, the outs, and the thespians. A wolf whistle rises above the mid-tempo music. Bree and I turn in a cloud of silky skirts toward the shrill noise. Prince Charming the Carrot-Top slouches casually by the entrance to the food service bay. He's a cheap knock-off of Bree's designer brilliance: pleather knee-high boots, a limp cape, a gold chain over his chest. The drama club is obviously as shocked as I am at his attempt at coordinating clothing.

Then he staggers toward us, swaying like a pirate on the high seas.

Bree's tight grip shows off her chunk of costume jewelry on her finger, and keeps me from slinking into the shadows. Instead, I try to match her stance, head high, back straight. A smell ghosts in front of him. Worse than spilled whiskey, more like whiskey and beer mixed together. Add the stagger to the booze stink and there's only one conclusion: Josh Mason is drunk.

"Emma." He nearly trips over his feet. "'Bout damn time you showed some skin!"

He stops a couple of feet from us, his gaze snags on my hips before jerking to my chest and the curves thrust up by the bodice. I want to rip his tongue out when he licks his lips. Bobbing in place, Josh squints into the line trickling in the doors. His eyes widen to ridiculously huge, then he shoves a hand through his hair.

"Shit," Josh mutters. "Of course. Of course *he*'d be here."

Sending a dark greedy look at me, he staggers back the way he came and disappears into the food room. Hopefully he's finding something to eat that will soak up the alcohol.

An air of "what the hell?" hangs over the thespians. As one, they turn toward the door and the source of Josh's ire. A couple shrugs and a "harrumph" and someone mutters, "There's no competition for the Best Costume Contest." Most break away toward the dance floor, or the snacks, leaving me and Bree.

I can't move.

I see the real source of Josh's anger. I smile involuntarily as I watch the tall, black-clad villain at the ticket table. He turns toward me, locking me in his mismatched gaze, shadowing the rest of the world, filling the air around me. Even Bree melts from existence.

Alex Franks' black clothes fit like they were tailored for him – given his father's money, I'm sure they were. His knee-high boots look dashing, not ridiculous; his gloves go up to his elbows over billowed sleeves. A black bandana covers his hair, tied back by the mask around his eyes, but leaves the silly drawn-on mustache and his full lips completely visible. A smile crooks his mouth, reaches under the mask and touches his eyes.

"Ooh-ooh-OK then," Bree says from a thousand miles away. "I think that's my cue to leave."

I might nod... I'm not sure. All I see is Alex. All I hear clearly is my heartbeat filling up the emptiness.

He comes toward me; any hint of him being sick is gone. There's a spring, a purpose to his stride. When he draws close, the energy of a couple days ago has returned, crackling in the space between us. The awe and wonder have returned to his eyes, too – I'm something so much more than common to him.

Alex's gaze trails slow and easy from the hem of my gown, over the bodice ties. It strays on my lips, before brushing my freckles and settling on my eyes.

"Milady," he says, bowing at the waist.

"Good sir." My voice is wispy and foreign. I drop a tight curtsy, wishing I had left my clunky brace at home.

The DJ – Jason's cousin, Adam – leans toward his mic. The beak of his giant Raven mascot costume comes danger-ously close to whacking the microphone when he says, "And now we're going to slow things down. Couples, this set is for you."

Guys and girls pair off, blurry in my Alex-focused vision. Devils and angels in short skirts, sports stars and cheerleaders. Alex slides closer, the scent of leather and cologne wafting in my nose. Inside, I'm alive and tingly, excited to see him again. On another level, though, blooms a strange familiarity. How can this guy I barely know feel like a boyfriend already? On some intimate, emotional level, he feels so much like Daniel.

"Want to dance?" he says, extending a gloved hand.

I can't resist teasing him. "With you?"

"I don't see anyone else here."

"Then I guess you'll do."

His laugh is rich, and pulls a bigger smile from me. I take his gloved hand, expecting an electric shock but only feel a tingle. Disappointment sparks in my chest, replacing the charge I'd hoped our connection would ignite – intangible but so real, and part of what makes Alex who he is. A buzz hums beneath his leather glove, almost a tease in compari-son to his raw electricity.

Thoughts jumble with feelings, clogging in my chest. Ten-drils of hair tickle on my neck as I follow him, weaving deep into the heart of the dancers. I should be more hesitant. Marin Rhodes is out here, and Josh, too, and both of them glaring daggers.

The shyness fights to come free of where I stuffed it. It's just impossible to feel bad around Alex.

He lights me up like a current through a light bulb.

"Great costume," Alex says, voice husky as he draws me

close. One gloved hand rests on the back of my hip. I surrender and brace my immobiliser on his shoulder. "Really, Emma. You are beautiful."

"Yeah?" My cheeks flame and I tuck one against his shoulder where he won't see. "Except the stupid brace."

"It does fracture the illusion." His velvet tenor sends chills racing over my skin.

"What illusion?"

Alex's grip tightens, hugging me to him, squeezing the air from between us. When I look up, I see his eyes smoldering behind his mask. He leans closer, the ties of his shirt brushing my bare skin when he whispers, "That you're a dream come to life."

I giggle. What else can I do after a compliment like that?

Then the truth of his words sinks in. Warmth fills me, rushing into the gulf left behind after Daniel's death. Alex is admitting to what I've wondered from the moment we met. The marvel, the disbelief in his expression every morning... He really thinks I'm fantasy become real. Like when he pulled off his shirt for me and exposed so much more than the scars lining his flesh. He's baring his soul, despite the easy way he tore himself open.

A heavy sigh escapes me, and if he wasn't holding me so close, I might melt and pour from this dress.

Alex clings to me like I may honestly be a fairytale princess and when he lets go, I'm going to disappear. He pulls off one glove, tingles following his bare hand as it glides over the curve of my back, up my neck to tangle in the curls that Bree had spent so long setting for me. He guides my head to his chest. Thunder rumbles in his heartbeat, and his electric surge slicks over my skin like warm oil.

Neither of us speak. Words have less meaning than time in his arms.

"There's so much I want to say," he whispers in my ear. I press my fingers to his lips. My heart jolts when Alex kisses them. Then he curls them in his gloved hand and holds my hand pressed above his heart. "Feel that? It doesn't beat for me, Emma."

Then the lighting changes and the reality of the Halloween Ball crashes back in. Spangles of strobe lights stab the comfortable shadows. An upbeat rap song blasts through the speakers after the last slow song dies. Faces appear and multiply, too many and unwanted right now, driving a knife in our embrace, prying Alex and I apart. He ignores Shelley High, looking only at me. Those hazel eyes pull me in, pull me under, the black freckle in the left iris identical to Daniel's.

It doesn't beat for me, Emma. What did he mean?

"Can I get you some punch?" he asks, derailing my thoughts by trailing his bare hand down my arm, cupping my right hand and the brace in a gentle touch.

"I'd love some."

And I need some room, some air to breathe, some time to think.

It doesn't beat for me.

Alex compounds the emotions surging in me. He lifts my right hand to his lips and kisses my fingers where they peep from the brace. Each kiss gives a tiny shock, and by the time he reaches my pinky, my hand is tingly alive and numb at the same time.

I follow him, mute and blinking, to the edge of the dance floor.

Jason Weller chooses the worst time to reprise his role of protector of princessly virtue. He strides up, chant as fast as his steps, and bats at Alex, shooing him away with, "Begone, and cease your wooing deviltry!"

Playing along, Alex throws up his hands, takes a step back, the picture of black-clad innocence for a moment. Then, with a rakish grin and a sweep of his cape, he turns toward the food service galley.

"Thanks a lot!" I tell Jason at the same time Bree appears and says, "What the hell?"

Shaking his head, he thrusts his Bible at me, and claims we wayward women need to study it more, before he hikes his robes and wades through people toward the restroom.

"So-o-o...?" Bree says, eyebrows arched over her know-it-all grin when she thumbs in Alex's direction.

"So what?"

"You two were all like..." she twines her fingers and then twists her wrists until her hands turn sideways, "wrapped up in each other."

"Tell me about it."

"Do you like him? Because he so-o-o likes you."

"You keep saying that." I fan my face and neck with Jason's Bible. Sacrilegious, maybe, but it's convenient and I'm a little flushed. "I don't know Alex enough to say I like him. I definitely have strong feelings for him, but I'm not sure what they are."

"You said 'feelings'!" she teases, then elbows me.

Alex's black bandana and mask appear near the edge of the crowd, two cups of punch in his hands. Josh Mason, true to his hit-and-run tendencies, cuts across his path and sticks a foot out. Without spilling a drop, Alex boots his foot away. Foul glares drift after him, and if Josh isn't muttering a cussword, he's saying something out loud and I can't hear it. Whatever it is, it isn't nice.

"Ladies," Alex says and lifts the cups, holy chalices filled with precious wine by the way he offers them to me and my princess twin.

Bree puts on her best flirty smile, and arches her back to squeeze a little more boob out of her dress, then takes the cup. He shifts his masked gaze to me and winks with his left eye when I take the second cup. The majority of the drama club members sift from the dance floor. Alex discusses the upcoming production with them, at ease, although a wall surrounds him – the one created to both draw people in and keep them at a distance. By the third fast song, he's standing beside me, brushing my hand with his gloved one.

The fourth song is a popular one, bluesy and still dance-able. Half of our number splits off for the sea of strobe lights. Alex's foot taps as he stands next to me.

"Why don't you and Emma go dance?" Bree asks.

"I don't dance." His answer is immediate, with a ring of practice to it.

"Uh, riiight. You were dancing with Emma."

He takes a step to the side, slides an arm around my shoulders and guides me until I'm in front of him. My pulse quickens – we're curve and plane, breath and skin. He slips his arms around my shoulders, hands resting atop my collarbones. It feels so familiar and right, I ease back against him.

"That's different," he says, words as evasive as his outfit is dark.

"So you only slow dance?" she prods.

"Something like that."

Alex Franks, proud owner of a cloudy reputation, stands behind me, using me like a shield through the last of the fast dance set. When Adam Weller announces another slow dance coming, I'm sure Alex is going to wash my world away again.

Instead, he releases me, smiles a caught-in-the-cookie-jar grin and says, "Lady Bree, may I have this dance?"

She gasps, then tosses an apologetic look at me. I roll my eyes, knowing inside she's dying because she wants to dance with him.

"Gotta make friends with the friends," he says, and extends his gloved hand to Bree.

"Go on," I say. *He's not my boyfriend,* I think.

Jealousy digs in claws, regardless. How could I not be disappointed when Alex succeeded in making me feel like there was no other person on the planet but us? And the way he was acting a few minutes before... Assumptions are bad, but I made one anyway. I assumed he'd dance with me again. Only me. Watching Bree and Alex, though, I see plenty of space between them, furtive glances my way from both, and Bree almost gloating when she looks my way.

Does she feel the same tingle I do? I wonder.

A thorny, dragging weight pulls at me, someone behind me and wanting attention.

Josh, I think, and then cringe. The beery miasma confirms it.

"Keepin' his options open," he slurs.

"His choice," I say, trying for unaffected and failing. Seeing another girl with Alex rattles nerves that it shouldn't. "I didn't see you slow dance with anyone."

"'Cause you're the only girl I wanna dance with." My skin crawls when he thumps an arm over my shoulders.

"Josh..." I start and try to shrug off his arm. He interrupts with, "Now you're gonna give me a chance, 'cause Prince Charming always gets his girl."

He's so far from charming right now I have the urge to punch him. Josh squeezes my shoulder to the point of pain, and herds me toward the dancing couples. He reeks of booze, and clenches harder when I try to turn away.

"Let me go!"

"You're gonna gimme a chance," he insists.

"Dammit, Josh." Gut instinct says this is going to go very badly. This isn't the teasing, insult-game Josh. This is a drunk, grabby, jealous Josh. Fear suddenly rushes my veins. I struggle more, feel his hand continue to tighten, a vise digging into my bones. "You're hurting me!" I yell. "Let me go!"

Heads pop up and swivel in our direction. Bree's face is horrified. Shockingly, it looks like sympathy on Marin's face. Alex turns Bree enough to see past her upswept hair. His jaw clenches, eyes tighten. He whispers to Bree and she pushes him toward us.

Josh paws at me with his free hand, misses my other shoulder and grabs a handful of my hair. Using my bun, he forces me deeper onto the dance floor. Hurt flashes across my scalp, throbs in my shoulder.

Tears burn my eyes, and a panicky tightness grasps my chest. I cry, "ALEX!"

Then Alex is there, a solid wall blocking my body from moving further.

He says, "Let her go, man."

"Screw you," Josh says, and releases my hair in favor of trying to shove Alex away.

Alex edges closer, putting himself between me and the drunk crushing my shoulder. Stymied, Josh releases my shoulder and helps gravity along by pushing me toward the floor. Alex catches my elbow before the linoleum rushes up at my face. With a dizzying spin, he uses my elbow to steer me behind him.

"Don't touch me." Warning thickens Alex's voice to a

threat. Tension fills his body, everything in his stance promising pain. "And don't ever touch Emma again."

Josh shouts, "I'll touch who I want!" With a grunt, he
slams both hands on Alex's chest and pushes him into me.

After a little stumble, Alex regains his footing, raises his
fists, and remains between me and Josh. The strain tightens
in him, piano-wire tight.

"Oh, yeah?" The redhead's eyes narrow to a glassy stare.
"You wanna go?"

Alex says, "No," but every inch of him screams, "Yes."

Not satisfied – and acting half-crazed, just like he did the
night Daniel fell – Josh pushes Alex hard. The tension snaps
in Alex, his black mask can't disguise the anger flashing
across his face, then he shoves back. Josh topples to his butt
in a flail of limbs and flutter of cape.

Alex's fists are up when he says, "Enough. Go home and
sleep it off."

Ugly spots of red blot Josh's cheeks. Saliva peppers his chin
as he sputters that no one tells him what to do, then scrambles
to his feet. The drunken bully drops his hands, pretends he's
going to walk away. I watch Alex's shoulders sink, and his
hands follow, then Josh spins and sucker-punches him. Alex's
answering blow is swift, wrapped in leather and slung like a
pro fighter. Josh's curly head rocks back.

Blood comes away on Josh's glove when he wipes at the
lip Alex punched. He throws a looping punch, one Alex easily bats away. My protector circles to Josh's right, forcing
him to back away from me.

Josh lunges, hurling a punch into Alex's stomach. Alex
crumples a little, folding around Josh's hand, and I worry that
he's hurt. Then the redhead pitches off balance, lurching toward and back, as Alex uses the fist he caught to manipulate

Josh. Their bodies collide with the floor, Josh underneath and Alex sliding sideways. Rolling to his side, Josh kicks and misses, then smacks Alex in the face.

Red blossoms at the corner of Alex's mouth. He drives a knee into Josh's gut, catches the counter punch, too, wrenching the forearm across Josh's throat. Kneeling on one arm, Alex pins the captured fist with one hand. "Don't you hurt her again!" A savage punch to the jaw and Josh's body goes noodle limp.

Adults swarm Alex, yanking him off the guy on the ground. One teacher pins his arms behind him.

Alex stands there, chest heaving, his eyes locked on mine. The teacher's grip tightens when Alex struggles, calling my name. His expression, the emotion in his voice… it's like the deer in the culvert. I can't resist him. I'm drawn forward, only to be pulled back by Bree.

An empty ache tugs in my chest as the teacher drags Alex away. Someone somewhere mutters about calling 9-1-1. A hand brushes my arm, and Bree envelops me in a hug. I don't know I'm shaking until she tells me. Her hand skims my shoulder and pain throbs there. She leads me past Josh and I barely control the urge to kick him, too. I wish the teacher hadn't pulled Alex away.

Josh once called Alex my guard dog.

I hope the bastard regrets it now.

Chapter Fourteen

People linger a few feet back, a shadowy costume store of blank-faced mannequins. The only face I see with clarity is Alex's. Lip cut and bleeding, cheekbone and temple blackening, the faint scar on the left side not affecting the wild light in his eyes.

Words jam in my mouth. Emotions tear at my insides. He's hurt because of me. Acting on an impulse I shouldn't have yet, I lift a napkin toward his chin to dab the blood there. Alex pushes my hand away.

"Don't worry about me," he says.

I do. He's wormed his way beyond my defenses, taken up residence like he's always been in my heart.

Leather and bloody knuckle scents catch in the back of my throat and itch like tears when he cups my face in his hands. My lip trembles and I think the tears might be real. But are they for me, or Alex? His eyes pore over my face; he slides his fingers over my scalp, then across my bare skin to my shoulder. His eyes darken. The corners of his lips pull down at the shadowy bruises rising beneath his touch.

"Josh hurt you." His tenor is nearly a growl.

"Not really."

I feel a completely separate anger snapping in the electric charge in Alex's touch. Hair stands on my arms, and up the back of my neck.

An icy weight touches my palm, as Bree appears at my side and presses a bag of ice into my hand. Her thumb brushes my cheek, and comes away wet. I guess the tears are real. She jerks her head toward Alex, mouths, "Take care of him," then steps back toward the crowd hemming us in. Her arms lift, her sleeves creating a white curtain as she herds them back, giving us room.

My heart patters, while my skin tingles from his touch. With a hesitant smile, I dodge his next blocking motion and pull the black silk kerchief from the pocket of Alex's costume. He sits mutely, watching me wrap the frigid bag in it and lift it toward his face. Then he stops it, a firm grip on my wrist as it hovers inches from his skin.

"I didn't intend the night to end like this," he says.

"Me neither."

With a sigh a lot like defeat, he releases my hand. I glance down to the lack of distance between us, my white skirts twined in the black of his costume. Ice crunches in the pack when I press it to his jaw. "Where'd you learn to fight like that?"

An elegant shrug ripples his cape, like what he did was nothing special. "Martial arts classes at Sadony Academy."

"Pretty impressive." The deep ugly red outside of his eye puffs up, too. I stop myself mid-thought of *I bet he's sexy with a black–* "You're going to have quite a shiner."

"Don't care." He winces when I shift the pack closer to his eye socket. "It was worth it."

"To perpetuate your violent reputation?" I know differently, but have to pry.

Hurt flashes over his face. "To protect you." His fingers brush mine, where they peek from the brace. "And to punish him."

The raw honesty in his voice and face leaves me speechless. It's like a hit to my chest, collapsing the hollowness inside. Or is it filling again? I'm not sure, but in one week Alex has changed me. He's chased away the loneliness and loosened my grip on Daniel's memory. My throat tightens. Instead of talk, which would lead to crying in front of him, I dab at the blood on his lip with a napkin from the nearby table.

"You didn't have to."

"Yes, I did," he argues, voice gone soft, almost like he's talking to himself. "I was driven. I've never been that angry. I didn't just want to stop him. I wanted to hurt him so bad it *hurt* me." He unfurls his hands, runs a glance across his palms and up one arm. "So bad it burned."

"Because you're a good guy," I reason, "and he was hurting me."

"It started because of that, Emma. But then it became something... I don't know. It felt like so much..." he pauses, clenches a fist, "so much more than that."

Alex opens his mouth to say more, I cut him off asking, "What did you mean by 'it doesn't beat for me'?"

An electric caress warms my hand when he threads his fingers through mine and pulls the ice pack away. By the look on his face, his answer may cut us both. He smiles, hesitantly, but it doesn't make it to his eyes. A different light glows there. He inhales; he pulls his bandana and mask off with his free hand, exposing the scars on his neck. His other fingers tighten on mine.

Then the principal arrives, all angry expressions and flapping coat, to lay down the law.

Alex detaches his grip on my hand and moves away like he may contaminate me.

It's too late for that, I think. I'm poisoned. Bree was right, Alex and I are connected – deeply – and I don't know how it happened. Days ago, I wished for a graveside to mourn Daniel, today I fret over Alex's hurts, the external damage from Josh and the ones beneath the scars I've seen. He's tried to perpetuate the rumors, but I know some of the truths Alex Franks hides.

The vice principal, and the head of Shelley High's PTA group, separate Alex and Josh, leading them to separate sections of the side hallway. Both guys watch me when the principal leads me down the hall, past Josh, to his office near my locker.

Inside, it smells like old carpet and new cigars. He turns his narrow rat-like face to me and says, "Have a seat, Emma."

I try to dislodge my heart from my throat and sink to the leather chair opposite his desk. Why do I feel guilty? I didn't do anything wrong. Josh started it all.

"I never expected to see you in this office," the principal says, that patented tone of disappointment in full effect.

"Wasn't in my plans," I mutter, after a hard swallow loosens the knot in my throat.

"Being flip won't save you," he says.

No. Alex did.

I sigh, hang my head, and let the principal think I'm properly admonished. He rapid fires questions at me in a mildly accusatory tone. Alex and what he might have answered to "it doesn't beat for me" are foremost in my mind, but I answer the chief inquisitor's questions honestly. I stress repeatedly that Josh is drunk, and I did not in any way aggravate or come on to him. I recount the fight, from Josh starting it by pushing first. After making me repeat it all, the principal makes some notes on a scratch pad and sends me to the backstage dressing rooms – with the warning that my parents have been notified and asked to pick me up.

My stomach constricts into a nauseous, achy knot.

My mom already thinks nothing but bad of Alex – her "jump to judgment habit" as Dad calls it. She's going to hate Alex now. Helping with a deer in the mud is one thing, but being the reason two guys fought is something totally different.

Backstage is blessedly vacant, except for Bree, when I arrive. Wordlessly, she helps me out of the medieval torture device of a bodice, and the rest of the costume before leaving. Once free of the dress, I pull on my pants, then work my way back into my bra and pull Alex's hoodie from my backpack. It doesn't smell like him anymore, and the blood is out of the cuff. I want something of him with me when Mom blasts me for being "in trouble with that boy again."

Josh sits in the hall, the sickly sweet smell of alcohol tainted with the metallic tang of his blood. An ice pack covers part of his face when I reach the intersection of the hall. The ice doesn't deflect the heated glare he sends my way.

Alex didn't beat you enough, I think.

I turn away, casting a glance through the frosted pane of the principal's office door. The tall shadow on the other side freezes, and I imagine Alex's head turning toward me. Knowing the upcoming conversation won't be pretty, I hurry out the side door and to the incensed woman sitting behind the wheel of the sedan idling at the curb.

My ears sting, my cheeks burn. Mom was as angry and narrow-minded as I thought she'd be, bitching at me from the school curb to our garage, calling Alex "out to ruin me", "a troublemaker", bitch, bitch, bitch.

"He's on a downward spiral and just going to pull you down with him, Emma," she says when I shove the car door open. "I'd rather have you alone–"

"And what?" I snap. "Alone and pining for my dead boyfriend who I can never have back and won't ever come between you and me again?"

Her mouth pops open; her brown eyes bug a little in obvious disbelief.

Yeah. I can't believe I said it either.

Using her silence to make my getaway, I slam the car door – then open and slam the garage door, too. Scooping up Renfield, I ignore his indignant cat glare and cradle him to my chest as I storm through the house toward the stairs. Dad stands in the basement doorway, a chunk of wood in one hand, a file in the other and confusion over his face.

"What in the hell is going on, Emma Jane?"

"Ask her!" I growl, and jerk my head in the direction of the garage door.

Clutching the cat, I weasel past Dad and pound up the stairs to my bedroom. With the door slammed and locked behind me, I collapse to the bed. Renfield launches from my arms, and scurries under the bed like he usually does when there's a storm outside.

This time, the storm is inside.

Putting distance between us should help. It doesn't. I'm mad, sad, and everything in between. All I want is to rewind time to the moment in Alex's arms.

Heated voices clamor through the floorboards. Mom's voice sharp, Dad's loud enough to match hers. The tension and sound match my thoughts. Not so much thoughts either, it's boiled down to images, and feelings. Alex and that warm familiarity we shouldn't have. Mom and her stupid hasty opinion. She never gives anyone a chance, just automatically doesn't like someone she thinks isn't good enough. She shouts loudly below me. *Good*, I think, *you can be angry, too.*

My cell phone buzzes, sounding like bees and chicken bones as it rattles against the pencils in the front pocket of my backpack.

Rolling to my stomach, I drag my backpack close and dig out my cell phone with my right hand because I want to feel the pain. It's hot and cutting and mine, something Mom can't control or keep from me.

Alex Franks, the display screen reads.

I catch my breath, not wanting to feel the hope that blossoms. *It doesn't beat for me*, he said.

Maybe he'll tell me now. I slide the phone open and click through to his text message.

I still have so much to say. It'll have to wait. The principal suspended me for a week for fighting. I'd do it again... (1/2)

My dad is pissed. I'm grounded the rest of the weekend, no phone after this text. Can I walk you home on Monday? (2/2)

He has to ask?

I type back, *How can I say no?* My fingers hover over the keys, the truth pressing against all of my nerves. Then I finish, *Bree thinks we have some kind of connection. I can't say no to her either.*

Closing my eyes, I click Send.

I know I'm dreaming, and I can't wrench myself out of it.

Moonlight splashes whitely over the cemetery. The gown from the Halloween Ball floats around me as I trail after a tall hooded guy. *Alex.* My heart pounds. *Alex!* Like before,

I can't catch him. Crumbling headstones snag and tear my skirts. Bony hands claw my legs until they bleed.

Then suddenly, he turns around.

I skid to a stop, chest seizing in shock.

He's Alex and Daniel. Curly hair and straight hair war in a wild shock on his head, one hazel eye isn't just similar to Daniel's, it *is* Daniel's. His eyes are fixed on me, wonder in Alex's, knowing in Daniel's. His clothes are a mix of the villain costume and the clothes that Daniel wore the day he fell to his death. The black and red patchwork shirt hangs open, exposing his pale chest. Seeping incisions line his skin and a red hole gapes beneath his breast bone.

He extends a gloved hand. His heart thumps on his palm, blood drips between his fingers and stains my dress.

Both voices come from one mouth. "It doesn't beat for me, Emma."

I jerk awake, Renfield crouching at the end of my bed watching me with wide eyes. A bitter feeling burns in me. I place my hand on my pounding chest. I can't tell which hurts worse, the air rasping up and down my throat or my slamming heart.

Groaning, I collapse on my pillows and look at my clock. *3.03am.* Moonlight pours through my curtains, soft and white, not chopped and poisonous like in my dream.

Renfield creeps across the bed, a cautious shifting of weight from one end to the other. His paws touch my arm first, then he crawls atop me, eyes luminous while he watches me, probably questioning his safety and my sanity. I stroke his ears, head, and neck until he purrs and my heart rate calms.

"These boys are gonna be the death of me, Renfield."

He sneezes. A perfect response.

Chapter Fifteen

Mom's answer to my "outburst" is grounding me – for Sunday. She bangs on my door at a rudely early hour, demands my cell phone, and informs me I'm going "nowhere."

My answer? Rolling over, pulling the pillow over my head. She pads into my room, mumbling the entire time. "I swear, Emma Jane Gentry, if you were awake…" She unplugs my cell phone, then stands by my bed. "That boy is going to bring you nothing but trouble…" I clench my fingers, hand curling to fist in my faery print quilt, but don't acknowledge her. "Mark my words, young lady. I knew boys like that at your age, and they were…"

Hypocrite, I think.

Mom wants to punish me for doing nothing wrong? Fine. I'll punish her right back.

I refuse to speak to her the rest of the day. If I'm lucky, I can avoid her Monday morning, too. Hours into the morning, and three-fourths done with my Gothic novel reading, Dad mutters something about sulking from his side of my door. He can call it what he wants. It's effective – Mom hates it. Dad's always in the basement tinkering with something. It will be just Mom, her soap operas, and her romance novels all day.

After the back door slams and her car roars to life, I creep downstairs, grab food and a couple of water bottles. The scent of sawed wood and dust drift under the basement door, the ghost-colored air curling around my toes when I sneak past, arms loaded with munchies. I retreat up the steps and leave the cat behind on the way to my room. He follows, grumbling at me, then leaps onto the bed and eyes me from his spot on the end.

Bleak November sky greets me when I pull open my curtains. I can't help thinking it's one less barrier between me and Alex. Dressed in his hoodie, my flannel PJ pants, and cushy socks, I prop the door open a crack for Renfield, then take my laptop to the bed.

My thoughts drift to Alex and the emotions I wonder if he only shows to me.

Sunday afternoon swills down the drain of researching Alex Franks on the Internet. A little stalkerish, sure, but things about him aren't adding up to anything normal. The odd tingle in his touch, Daniel's eye looking out of his face, all of his scars... Beyond the physical, and way more disturbing, the way he feels so familiar to me. How can I feel like I've known him for years? How can he open that damn locker just like Daniel?

What answers I find apply to few of my questions. He's eighteen, a senior, was on the martial arts team and long distance track team at Sadony Academy before a horrendous accident. According to an article in *The Visionary*, Sadony Academy's school paper, Alex's grades had him on the fast track to any Ivy League college of his choice, where his potential was limitless, though most expected him to study medicine and become a doctor like his father.

So what's he really doing at Shelley High, a public school

with nothing more special than AP courses? And why does he seem so caught up in me?

Hell, why am I so caught up in him?

I don't know him, even if my heart insists I always have. *It doesn't beat for me.*

Sitting back, I can see how last night's nightmare makes a sick kind of sense. I've been missing Daniel so badly, for so long, that when someone came along the least bit like him I squashed Daniel and Alex into one person.

Alex is a rebound.

Even while logic wants to grab that thought, expand on it, and absorb every bit of sense it makes, my heart recoils.

Of course it would. Why would I want to believe I'm feeling displaced affection for Alex?

A hot nip behind my ribs spreads until I feel queasy all over, frustrated and suddenly sick and tired of thinking about Alex Franks. Knowing Mom will check all of my social pages on the Internet, I close down the web browser without updating any statuses or sending Bree any emails. No need to add fuel to the Emma's-in-trouble fire. Then I open up my media player, bring up a sufficiently creepy playlist and place the laptop back on my desk.

Renfield slinks across the top of my faery quilt, putting all his unnerving feline grace into action, and curls in my lap. Stroking his ears, I fight my mind's instinct to bring all the pretty bits of Alex out to daydream on. Reaching for the nightstand, I grab my library book and spend the evening immersed in a Gothic novel, and dreaming about a romance that isn't, and won't ever be.

Monday morning is the kind of hollow I don't want to see again. It feels like the darkness I'd slipped into after Daniel died. Life twists into a frigid, otherworldly version of itself. The cold air grows fangs, biting and sharp. Buttery sunlight lays bare every naked skeletal tree and rotting jack-o'-lantern as I walk the neighborhood to school.

Every long shadow, or pulled-up hood, sparks the hope that Alex is shirking his suspension to see me.

Despite the hunger twisting my stomach from sneaking out the front door to avoid Mom, and drowsiness pulling on me, I bypass Mugz-n-Chugz. Without Alex helping me, I'm going to need every extra second to open my stubborn locker.

Bree meets me at our normal bench. For a moment, I pause and watch the knots of people unfurl, or break away in clots drifting toward the doors.

"So…?" says Bree, her bright voice at odds with her moody gray and black outfit.

My shoulders sink. I can't play this game today. "You were right."

A smile spreads, slow pretty poison across her face. "Right about what exactly?"

"Alex and I being connected." A heavy sigh drags my shoulders further. "But I don't want it."

"Don't want it?" she repeats, her voice scaling up, making my confession sound crazy. By her shocked expression, I have to think that was Bree's intention. "How can you not want it? He's smart, he's good-looking, and totally into you. Plus, he got into a fight. *For you*."

"I know." I start toward the side door, dreading the surging halls and cutting glares. "It's just…" How can I tell Bree about his similarities to Daniel? She'll think I'm crazy, creating excuses or something. I finish lamely, "It's all happening so fast."

"What's happening? Him driving you to the clinic for a new brace? 'Cause that's just crazy to do when a guy hardly knows a girl. You two dancing? 'Cause you didn't look like you were complaining..." She steps in front of me. "Help me out here, Em. You guys seemed totally into each other on Saturday, and now you're all 'I don't know' about him?"

"I *do* know about him," I huff, and edge past her. My heart knows, and it scares me. "I know I like him. A lot. And I know I don't want to."

Warm air blasts my face when I jerk the door open. Inside, the hallway constricts, narrowing as I watch, like something out of a horror movie. Or does knowing Alex won't be here drain the life from my Monday?

Bree's going on about how I need to wake up and let go of the dream I had and see what's right in front of me and... and... But I'm not hearing her. For once, I zone out when she starts to compare my life to dramatic plot lines, rather than buck her attempts at making me a character in one of her productions. A commotion in front of my locker accompanies a metallic smell and screech, and wrenches my attention completely from her.

"See you at lunch, B," I mutter and walk away.

"Damn right you will," she says, no vehemence in her tone.

A few students cluster in a loose ring around my locker, an arc of whispers and bent heads. The slightly battered slab of a metal door leans against Alex's locker, the heart Daniel had scratched into the inside reflecting the harsh lights. The internal mechanism hangs exposed like entrails of a locker disembowelment. In its place stands a spotless, brand-new door. No chipped paint. No heart.

Instinctively, I reach for the pale broken heart under my brace. Another aspect of Daniel unceremoniously ripped from my life. I hardly notice the man in the coveralls stand-ing by my locker.

"You Emma Gentry?" he asks, voice sounding like a two-pack-a-day habit.

"Yes?" I'm not questioning my identity, more why he's asking about it.

He thrusts a piece of paper at me, full of barcodes and price info.

"Hold on." I raise my immobilised right hand. "I can't pay for that. I didn't order it."

"No charge. He already took care of it," he rasps. "This here is the work order, with your new combination on it."

"Oh," is all I manage as I pluck the sheet from his fingers. "Who ordered this? Shouldn't the office get these papers?"

"Private job." He grabs the paper back, finds what he's looking for and turns it around, one dirty digit indicating the billing info. "Apparently, money talks. Guy's name is Alexander Franks."

Alex did this? Damn my heart for flip-flopping in my chest. My cheeks burn, the heat rising and pulling a stupid smile with it. The man gives me a curt nod, then heads to the main office, three locker doors and a few feet of plaster wall down from where I stand.

I scan the information again. His full name, home address, and phone number, and the last four digits of a credit card are in the billing box. Then handwriting in the notes section grabs my attention.

Emma,
I can't be there to open the old door for you, so I got you a new one.
See you after school.
Alex

The warmth in my cheeks flushes through, dribbling into the empty part of me.

It remains sloshing inside, keeping me company. The Ugly Room's nasty chatter hardly touches my good mood. Which, I notice, Marin Rhodes' voice is entirely absent from. Jealousy still scrunches her face into something less Cheerleader Barbie and closer to Cheerleader Harpy, but her glossy mouth twists a little when I catch her eyes. The soft heat resurges at lunch when the thespian crowd recounts Alex's valor of Saturday night. Jason Weller blows up the tale till Alex sounds like a hero laying his life down for me, rather than the villain he was dressed as, or the gossip made him out to be.

"It's a shame he got kicked out," says Amber Miller. Her brother adds, "Someone shoulda given him a medal."

Despite Asia Foley's return to fifth hour, Dune Eco lays limp and wounded in Mr LaRue's room, nearly gutted by the absence of Josh and Alex shooting venomous glares back and forth. Discussions of upcoming projects bounce around, grazing the inside of my skull. The only thing sticking is the blood on my thumb – a purposeful cut from the blade of dune grass – and the fact that the lab partnerships will remain till semester's end.

My last two classes pass in a blur. The pressure of anticipation builds in my chest. The clock hands drag, lethargic and mocking me. Taking notes fills my time, and bypasses my brain. Then finally the end-of-day bell rings.

I dive into the rush of bodies, fighting the surge to get to the stairs and down to my locker. The stairwell winds in a squared spiral to the first floor, closest to the main office. It's also the least used. My footsteps ricochet in the relative silence until I hit the second floor, close to the doors to the catwalk between this building and the gym complex. I cast a glance at the doors, a ghost of Daniel resting like a beautiful lie over my heart.

Shaking it off, I launch down the last section of steps and surrender to the main hall flow. A few jostling steps and I pull free of the tide, and find my locker.

A bright white piece of paper flutters from the vents, and smells like leather when I pull it free.

Waiting on the Bree Bench. Want a breve for the walk home?

The new combination is ridiculously easy. And with each number I click in, I snip a thread connecting me to the memory of Daniel opening the old locker.

In minutes, I burst from the side door, and into the weak light of a gray afternoon. Heavy fall haze thickens the air. People move in dark ghostlike blurs. My gaze flies to the Bree Bench, as Alex called it, where Bree usually waits for me in the mornings. The painful anticipation uncoils and I can't beat back the smile. Rebound or not, Alex Franks has that effect on me. His profile is paler than the vibrant, healthy color of Saturday, his hood is up, his shoulders curled against the cold.

Wonder and joy show on his face, brief but still very *there.*

"Hey," Alex says, voice husky as he stands.

"Hi." At this angle the watery sun halos him, his mismatched hazel eyes framed in the dark hood. His grin tugs at the thin scar at the corner of his eye. Words crowd my mouth and die. He tugs on the zipper of my jacket, pulling it down a couple teeth and loosening my voice a lot.

"Thanks," I say, "for the new locker door."

"You're welcome. It's the least I could do, seeing as I got myself suspended for a week."

"You're *not*," I stress, "required to open my locker for me, y'know."

He pauses, cold light hitting the planes of his face. "You're right. I'm not. But I feel like I should be."

"Helping a damsel in distress?" I tease.

"Don't talk like that!" His smile turns devilish, and he winks. "It makes me think about your dress and..." he leans whisper-close and says in a husky voice, "villainous things."

Heat floods up my throat and cheeks. A tingle sparks along my nerves. Any smart remark I might have burns off and turns to ash on my tongue. I snap my mouth shut on the soot of my emotions: embarrassment and excitement.

"Speechless?"

I smack him with my left hand and mutter, "Shut up, Alex."

"Shutting up." Of course, the promised silence doesn't last long. Alex points across the street. "Want that coffee for the walk home?"

I look across the quad towards student parking. "What about your car?"

"Cars..." He shrugs. "They're so hasty."

"True... And if I came home too early my mom would get suspicious." We step off the curb and cross the street. Instead of queuing in the walk-up line at Tiny's window, we walk inside, where there's only two other people in line. "Heck," I add, "if I show up later than she thinks I should, I'll get texted to death, too."

"What's up with your mom? She overprotective?"

"Only all the time."

Conversation dies as we step to the counter. Before I can answer the new girl's question, "What can I get ya?" Alex orders for us.

"Two breves with caramel, and two vanilla biscotti."

How did he know how I take my coffee? Or that I only like the vanilla biscotti?

Alex must sense – because he doesn't see – me grab for my backpack to get money. He reaches behind him, catches my elbow with his fingers – sending a little tingle through to my skin – and says, "I offered, Em, I'm buying."

Daniel said that so many times that hearing it again is like a punch in the chest. I huff a breath and stare wide-eyed at the back of his hood. He pays for our order, hands me the cookies wrapped in wax paper and leads me away from the counter. Instinct screams to say something, to not stand in front of Alex and stare like a goober, but my brain feels like it's swimming in toxic waste. Any thought big enough to grab, stings.

"You OK?" he asks, eyebrows sinking toward the bend in his nose. "You look like you've seen a ghost."

Heard one's more like it. "I'm fine," I lie.

"So," Alex says, and pushes the doors open. "Where's home?"

Oh, a couple blocks from the Memorial Gardens Cemetery, where I used to lean against the fence and wish someone was buried there.

"On Seventh Street."

"Oh, yeah?" His voice takes an odd, hesitant tone. "I know the neighborhood."

"Really?"

The scraped-raw expression returns to his face. Even his lips twitch and turn down. "My mom's buried in Memorial Gardens. I visit there every now and then."

Oh God. With my luck, his mother is interred in the mausoleum where Daniel and I used to loiter, cracking jokes and drinking filched whiskey. A chill slides through me.

"My condolences," I say.

"Thanks." He elbows through the main door and out into the late afternoon shadows. "She's been gone a few years now."

He's quiet for a few blocks, sipping his coffee and sneaking peeks at me. I catch him looking and smile. The hush grows between us and I don't prod it with any personal questions. I know I'm lucky to have both my parents, still together after twenty years. I won't ask him about his mother, but I can ask him other questions.

"So…" I ask, "what brought you to Shelley High? I know it isn't the level of education you're used to."

"It wasn't the school…" He holds my eyes, a long searching glance that seems to sting us both. "When I woke up, I just knew I couldn't go to Sadony anymore. After fighting with my dad, threatening to grow my hair, quit school, and join a hippy commune, he let me win."

"Quite persuasive of you."

"Dad can be a jerk sometimes, but I know how to manipulate him."

"Is that what happened with your ex-girlfriend, too?"

"Not quite." He shrugs deeper into his coat. "Hailey's really tenacious, and took more convincing."

"*Is* tenacious?" I ask. Jealousy is ugly, but I flirt with it anyway. "That's present tense. I thought you said she was an *ex*, as in past tense."

"She is." His hard tone says he doesn't want to discuss her anymore. And neither do I. Thinking about Alex with any other girl abrades new, tender nerves. I've dragged my past around, nursing my loss and mourning Daniel, and that hasn't turned out so well.

I take another sip of my coffee, lose track of what my feet are doing and nearly trip over the fire hydrant on the corner of Seventh and Sycamore. Alex catches my elbow before the ground can catch my face.

"Careful," he cautions before releasing me.

I heave a sigh and smooth my hair. "Mom says I'm clumsy. Dad says I have decreased situational awareness."

"Neither sound very nice."

"The truth isn't always pretty," I say. He snorts a short laugh, and nods. Lifting my immobilised right hand, I point at our gray two-story with black trim, white cat body stretched in the front window. "There's home."

"Nice house," he says. "Think we can sit on the porch and dunk the biscotti? This walk got over awfully fast."

"Dunking biscotti with Alex Franks on my front steps," I say. "Sounds kinda naughty."

I'm as shocked I said it as Alex seems to be. He chokes on his breve. Funny, I've only known him a week and I can recognize the angle of his jaw in a smile. Color creeps into his pale cheeks. A cough unsettles the fluid in his throat, then he swallows noisily.

Touché, I think. *Touch my zipper and I'll make you choke on your coffee.*

We sit side by side on the bottom step, where no one will see us from inside unless they actively look. Knowing Mom, the active looking will come soon enough. Alex pries the lids off our coffees, then we dunk and munch in companionable silence for a while. He leans back against the second step, leans his head back, and says, "Cat lover, huh?"

"Oh, I don't know. I think Renfield and I have a love/hate relationship."

"Renfield?" His eyebrows arch, and his full lips pucker like he's trying not to laugh.

"Yeah." I give him an eye roll. "I love *Dracula.*"

"Me, too. We should do a movie night."

Did he just suggest a date? Like a "him and me and no one else" kind of date?

"Sounds good," I say. "I can't stand Keanu Reeves as Jonathan Harker, and I still watch it every chance I get."

"It's a date," he pronounces.

I'm about to tease him, ask him if it's a reading party date, or a movie date, when my cell phone comes to life in my backpack, the annoying *buzz-buzz-buzz* I have set to Mom's cell phone number.

"Mom," I groan quietly. Alex puts down the empty cup and unzips the front pocket for me. I fish the pink thing out and the display screen confirms my suspicion. I tilt toward Alex. "See?"

"Better answer it then," he advises and slouches as low against the stairs as possible. I don't want to tell him that the angle would give anyone looking out the window a perfect view of his long legs and the fly of his jeans. I wrench my eyes away from what I don't want my Mom to see outside her door, and slide open the phone.

Where are you? Standard Mom message when she has expectations I'm not meeting.

I type back: *Close to home.*

Alex nods and mouths, "Very close."

Her reply is my last sip of breve away. *You're late, Emma Jane.*

Great. She's using my middle name. She's mad.

I know, I type. *I got caught up talking. I'll be there in a minute.*

Alex and I both count while we wait for her response. "One... two... three... four..."

Buzz-buzz-buzz!

If you're going to be talking with someone, I'd prefer you just do it here.

Alex lets out a snort. I'm sure Mom has no idea we're on the front steps. If she had even a ghost of that thought she'd be out here with a broom to bat Alex away. However, I can almost hear the tone she typed it in, and it isn't pretty.

"I have to go in," I say, ceding defeat. "You want to meet my mom?"

"Test of manhood," he says.

"It might be more than that." I stand and stack our coffee cups. "Last chance. You want to run, I won't blame you."

"Nope," he says, slides his hood off and stands. "If I plan on seeing you with any frequency, I need to weather this storm sooner or later."

"Seeing me?" Why do I sound shocked? If I'm honest with the feelings building up inside me, I want to see him more.

"You're the only one here besides me." He glances at the white face floating in the shadows above the sofa as the cat watches us through the living room window. "And seeing of any serious sort can't happen without parental approval."

"Batten down the hatches," I use his seagoing metaphor.

"Aye, aye, Cap'n!"

Just before I open the door, he brushes his fingertips through my hair, pushing it aside to whisper, "I'd weather any storm to be with you."

Is that what he meant by *it doesn't beat for me*?

Chapter Sixteen

Renfield beats Mom to the door, and winds around my ankles. She's standing there, a few feet back, arms crossed, foot tapping, and white frilly apron detracting from her mean mom demeanor. I give her a pleading please-be-nice look and bend to scoop up the cat. Renfield twists like living, clawed silk in my arms and pins me with an indignant look before settling into the crook of my arm.

"Come in," I tell Alex, then step to the side, closer to the sofa, leaving room for him to make an escape if things turn ugly. Which, knowing my mom, they probably will.

"So you were texting me from *the porch*?" she asks.

At this rate, ugly is going to happen before the dinner I smell in the kitchen.

"Yes," I say. I have a flimsy excuse brewing, but don't give it. Alex reaches a hand forward and says, "Hi, Mrs Gentry. I'm Alex Franks. I walked Emma home and she was just thanking me before coming in."

Smooth, I think. *I could learn to like this guy.* He tries to get me out of trouble and is not afraid to stretch the truth to my mom to do it.

Mom eyes his hand like she'd just as soon push it away

than shake it. Tension builds, the energy of a storm blowing off Lake Michigan. Then she takes it, and gives his hand one swift shake.

"Nice to meet you," Alex tells her.

"Mm-hmm," she says. "You, too."

Her expression sours, but he remains close to me, an easy smile firmly in place on his lips. Knowing Alex like I'm beginning to, I don't think she could claw it off. As if to prove he could fit in here, Alex lifts his hand higher to pet Renfield, who'd been watching the icy exchange between him and Mom with feline disinterest.

"Watch out," I warn. "He hates everybody but me."

That's not true, though. Renfield always loved Daniel. He should have. Daniel brought him to me as a kitten. We'd watched *Bram Stoker's Dracula* that night and named him after the poor crazed man under Doctor Jack's care.

Renfield lies in my arms now, eyeing Alex's approaching fingers and all I can think of is: *Great. My cat's going to give him more scars.* Mom watches with cool interest, too. She knows how awful the cat can be – his passionate dislike of pretty much every other human is legendary. Maybe she's hoping he'll roust Alex out for her. Instead, the cat bonks his head against Alex's fingers, then lets Alex pet him. A rare purr rumbles in the feline throat.

"Making a liar out of me?" I ask the cat in a whisper.

"Alex Franks," Mom says slowly. I look up and see a horrible light dawning in her eyes. "The doctor's son?"

He stiffens slightly. "Yes, ma'am."

"And you're the boy," her eyes narrow, "who dropped Emma off at the clinic, filthy and needing a new brace because of helping you?"

"I am."

If anything, instead of shrinking under her scathing gaze and uncompromising questions, he stands taller and moves closer to me. Dad appears in the dining room door, chipped coffee mug in hand. His eyes skim over me, and land on Alex. Dad dusts sawdust from his salt-and-pepper hair, and peers through his glasses. "Emma, who's your friend?"

Relief washes through me. Dad's always the diffuser in the Mom-Emma-Dad concoction.

"Dad, this is Alex Franks."

Alex offers his hand, and Dad shakes it hard enough to dribble coffee out the chip at the top. "So, you're the boy involved in the fight on Saturday?"

Bless him for having a hint of a grin.

"Yes, sir."

"I heard you broke Josh's nose." A ghost of a smile dances across Dad's face. "And cracked a couple of his ribs."

A flash of something – pride? – in Alex's eyes. "I've heard that, too."

"Well, for protecting my daughter," Dad says, "I'm willing to give you a chance. There's something to be said for a man willing to risk hurt to defend our Emma."

"Thank you, Mr Gentry."

Mom visibly deflates. She gives my dad a mutinous look, and I'm sure a cold night on the sofa is in his very near future – like tonight. She turns toward the kitchen as he aims for the basement door.

"Not a big chance," she warns.

Two shocks right in a row. First, Renfield doesn't hate Alex; instead the cat acts like they're old friends. Second, Mom didn't kick Alex out and tell him never to speak to me again, which is what I dreaded she'd do.

Of course, the afternoon isn't over yet.

"So, One-Armed Warrior... have any homework I can help with?" asks Alex.

"Yeah. Homework is a pain with this brace," I say at the same time as Mom barks from the kitchen, "Not upstairs, you don't! Bring your laptop down here."

"Dining room table, then?" Alex suggests.

I lead the way, with Renfield peeking over my shoulder, watching Alex with his lamp-like eyes. The cat flinches, back claws flexing when Dad starts up the power tools in his workshop. Like any other day, the sounds of a saw and the smell of cut wood drift beneath the basement door. Normally, it's comforting in an odd way. With Alex Franks standing in the dining room, I tend closer to chagrin than to cozy.

"What's he doing down there?" Alex asks.

"Not sure. He's always building something. Chairs, picture frames, puzzle boxes..."

"That's cool." He sounds honestly impressed. "My dad's always locked away in his lab, muttering over formulas and studying any advancement in surgical procedures. The only thing he made," he pauses, then looks at his chest, where I know scars crisscross his skin, "is me live."

"Then I like his handiwork," I whisper.

When Alex sets my backpack on the table, the cat launches from my arms, using his back claws for traction. He might not have fangs, but he has some vampire qualities. Renfield lands on Alex's chest. Lightning quick, Alex wraps his arm around the slinky white cat, and says, "Hey, kitty. You don't look like a crazy character."

The cat screws his face up, sneezes at Alex and twists out of his arms. His paws glance off the tabletop, enough to change his angle and shoot for the stairs.

"Well," I deadpan, "the honeymoon's over."

"Odd cat."

"I'm shocked he liked you at all." OK, so I'm teasing him.

"Thanks," he says, mocking pain by the scrunched look on his face and the hand over his heart.

Immediately my nightmare flashes behind my eyes. The still-beating heart, blood dripping between the fingers... *It doesn't beat for me.* Alex holding my hand over his heart and saying those words. I can't ask him about it now, with Mom one room away and banging pots and pans to let me know she's very close and can most likely hear every uttered word.

After excusing myself, I dash up stairs for my laptop. One handed hunt and peck typing in front of Alex will damage my ego, but it's easier than doing it longhand.

Unlike Bree, who wrote my essay problems for me those first days, Alex takes the computer over completely, positions scratch papers between us and patiently takes dictation for every class. He even writes out the trig problems for me, and helps on the few I struggle with. Mom scuttles out of the kitchen a few minutes before 5 o'clock, eyes serious, mouth set in a thin line.

"We'll be having dinner soon, Alex." Though the look on her face says anything but, she adds, "You're welcome to stay."

His face brightens, pale as it is. "I'd appreciate that."

"Emma Jane," Mom says. "You two can clear off the table.

I heave a sigh and get an elbow to the ribs for it. Soft, not like the vicious hits Alex gave Josh, but the point is made. Together Alex and I reload my backpack, and return my laptop upstairs. Silently, we help set the table, putting out Mom's linen placemats and good china. Funny she'd bring that out when she acts like she hates him. Then Mom opens the basement door and yells, "Merle! Dinner!"

Cop in an apron directing traffic.

"Merle sits at the head of the table. I sit here. Alex, you there—" She points to a seat by the window, then points across to the opposite side, saying, "And Emma, you there."

Divide and conquer.

Alex obliges silently, despite the empty seat beside the one I'm supposed to sit in. Dad comes up the steps, sawdust whitening his clothes and clinging to his glasses. He eyes the seating arrangement, then my mom, before sitting where he normally does with a slight shrug of his shoulders. Once I'm seated, Mom brings out the chowder and rolls.

"I hope you're not allergic to shellfish, Alex," she says innocently. "We're having clam chowder."

"Actually, I love seafood," he says.

If he's foiled her plot to run him off, she doesn't show it. Mom ladles the chowder for us, and then passes the rolls and butter. Dad pops up, dusting off sawdust, and walks toward the kitchen. He points at Alex before disappearing through the door. "Like hot sauce? I prefer my chowder with a little kick."

"Love some."

He's trying too hard, I think.

The bottle of red poison – I hate spicy stuff – passes from Dad to Alex. He adds a liberal amount to his bowl. No hot sauce virgin could get away with that much without making some kind of face. The entire table watches his first bite, and the aftermath.

Nothing.

"So," Dad says after a spoonful. "Have any plans after high school?"

"I'm not sure, Mr Gentry. I was thinking about going to med school."

"And become a doctor like your father?" Mom asks. Her tone is conversational, but I know her. I see the tightening around the eyes.

"Now, Arlene..." Dad says in that soothing voice of his.

"Don't 'now Arlene' me." She shoves part of a roll into her chowder, drowning it with force. "That boy's father hurt Emma's hand. On purpose."

Alex's eyes widen, and he swallows his mouthful. The temperature drops in the room, a cold front emanating from Mom's expression. She could probably crack nuts with her eyebrows with how hard they're pinched together.

"I know what you think of my father," Alex says. I'm not sure if it's recklessness, or bravery in action. "And I'm terribly sorry Emma was hurt."

"But...?" she prods.

"No but. He taught me not to argue with adults." OK, so he's not reckless.

A harrumph escapes Mom, who then eats her soggy roll. Tension shifts and swirls around the table. Dad holds her in an even stare, giving one slight shake of his head before saying, "So, how are you liking Shelley High?"

Alex chews, swallows, then swiftly glances at Mom. She's busy tearing another roll to crumbs. He turns back to my dad. "It's taking some getting used to. Shelley High is smaller than Sadony, and people weren't very welcoming."

Mom doesn't say anything. Guilt maybe? She hasn't been very welcoming either. Whatever her problem, Mom keeps it to herself, eating the chowder and monitoring every little look that passes between me and Alex. Dad seems uncomfortable, either from the awkward silence, or the fact there's a boy at his table.

"How," he asks, "did you meet our Emma?"

Alex turns to me, gaze soft enough to be a caress. Heat spills through me and I wish we weren't at the dinner table with my parents. I'd cuddle my face into his chest and breathe him in. "She was standing outside with Bree Ransom, drinking coffee. We said 'hi'. Then I helped her open her locker."

"After he chased off Josh Mason." I add.

"The boy he got into a fight with," Mom points out, jabbing her spoon in Dad's direction.

"We've already established that, Mom."

A sharp whack in the shin under the table can only come from Alex. He doesn't argue with adults, and obviously I'm not supposed to either, or back-sass as Mom would call it. She's definitely stabbing me with the look that says she does not appreciate my lip.

"If that boy was hurting her, then Alex did the right thing," Dad says.

"Would you like to see the bruises?" I offer, needling Mom with a sarcastic glare.

"He bruised you?" Dad and Alex say at once, sharp notes of shock, mingled with sour notes of anger in both voices.

An unpleasant shade of red creeps into Alex's cheeks. Mom's cheeks have blanched, like someone siphoned the blood from her face.

"Yeah." I stab at a clam with my spoon, wishing it would pop, bleed, anything to dispel the tension in the room. "It would've been worse if Alex hadn't stopped him."

A solemn nod from Alex. He adds, "Josh *was* drunk. I tried to talk to him, but he wasn't having it."

It's impossible to miss Dad arching his eyebrows, as if saying, "See, Arlene?"

Quiet descends, except for the scrape of spoons. The only

conversation is Mom and Dad, giving each other Significant Glances. Apparently, Dad wins. Mom stands, wipes her hands on her apron and says, "Well, Alex, it was..." I want to rail at her for pausing, before she continues, "a pleasure meeting you."

The frosty dismissal is unmistakable. Alex stands, gathers his dirty dishes, and says, "It was nice to meet you both." He gestures to my bowl. "Are you done, Em?" When I nod, he piles my dishes into his and carries them into the kitchen. Mom watches wide-eyed, but her eyes narrow when he walks to stand beside me, and close to her. "I understand my father has destroyed your faith in him. Please give me a chance to prove I may be my father's son, but I care about Emma and would never hurt her."

Dad inhales, and I think the entire house does, too.

"I'll try," she says. Then adds, "But if you're going to be seeing Emma, in any capacity, it will be here."

A smile lights up his face, tugging at the pale scar lines. "Thank you, Mrs Gentry." Then he turns, and holds his hand out to my dad. "Mr Gentry."

The guys shake hands, and Dad adds, "Nice meeting you."

At least Dad sounds honest about it. With Mom, it had all the tones of "Get out of my house."

The drab gray walls are even more morose with Alex walking away from them. I don't look at my parents as I follow him to the front door. When he pauses, the rest of the house could fall away into black, the world with it. Alex fills my vision, the resigned expression from dealing with my uptight mother melting into the expression just after the amazement I see every morning. One part tender, one part joy, all of it mine. He laces his fingers in mine, and pulls me closer. Then closer still. Kissing distance. With a motion of his chin he tucks my head to his shoulder and slides both arms around me.

I melt into him, breathing in the warmth of his skin. I can taste the smell of leather on my tongue. If he kissed me now, I wouldn't mind. One arm loosens, then he slides his hand up my sleeve, across my shoulder to my chin. With gentle pressure, Alex guides my face toward his.

The look on his face is more intimate than any kiss.

"Have sweet dreams tonight, Emma."

They will be now.

He releases me, takes hold of the doorknob, wishes my parents a good evening and then steps onto the porch. Renfield reappears, leaps onto the back of the sofa and watches out the living room window, his tail swishing gently. Alex lifts his hood, then without a backward glance, steps out of the dingy yellow light and the night swallows him whole.

A shudder runs down my spine when Renfield yowls plaintively. He made the same noise the night Daniel died. So did I.

What connection do we all share? Daniel, Renfield, me, and Alex?

I flick off the porch light, and turn to face my parents. Dad gives me a little smile, then scoops his coffee cup from the table and retreats to the basement. Mom has the same look on her face that she had the day that Daniel left after he'd given me his class ring to wear. She's losing me, she thinks, it's penned on every line of her face. Her lips turn down, her frustration and sadness cutting at me and filling the void between us.

I want to say something, make it better somehow.

"Well," she says, "he's not so... intimidating up close. Seems mannerly, too."

"He is, Mom." Might be grabbing at straws with her, but I'll take what I can get.

"Don't get too comfortable," she says, but the angry edge has left her. "Jury's still out on Alex Franks."

Tell me about it.

Does he like me? Is he just a rebound? Where did the sense of history come from I feel whenever he's near?

Despite the questions, I can't wipe the image of his face from my mind. In that moment by the door, he looked like he had kissed me a thousand times, and yet never. He looked like he wanted to, and wanted to prolong the wait.

He looked like he already knew I was his.

Chapter Seventeen

Mom's crabby mood filters through the house after dinner, washing up the stairs, cresting at the second floor. Renfield and I seek escape in my room, where moonlight and shadow dance on my carpet. Faeries flit darkly across my quilt when I plug my cell phone into the power outlet. It's becoming a habit to forget to charge it.

I stand by the window and the boxed-in safety ladder disguised as an old radiator box, and stare down Seventh Street. Mr and Mrs Jones are outside, with a ladder, a flashlight, and I'm sure, plenty of cussing. He's on the ladder propped against the tree, she has the flashlight pointed at him, rather than the witch-in-a-tree he seems to be trying to liberate from its oak-bound position. Mrs Peterson, further down, is stuffing the rotting jack-o'-lanterns into her garbage can. No more leering pumpkins seeing their echo in me.

Autumn is over. Novembers are fickle, but the constant chill in the air tells me the dying is done. Now comes the frigid death of a Michigan winter - bitter winds and suffocating snow.

My cell phone display screen lights up like the Fourth of July when the battery finally gets enough juice to take calls.

The notification tones set the pink bit of electronics stagger-ing across my desk. One look confirms my suspicions:

Bree Ransom.

Bree Ransom.

Bree Ransom.

And then one I secretly hope for:

Alex Franks.

I click through the texts from Bree: *Hey. Call me.* Next is, *Hellooo? Did you forget to charge your phone again??* And then finally, *I heard that Alex Franks walked you home. You two going out yet?* I know there isn't sugar in Diet Coke, but there is caffeine. I wonder just how many cans she had be-tween text one and text three? I hit Reply and type: *He did walk me home. Stayed for dinner too. Mom hates him, of course. No, we aren't going out.* Then I click Send.

Next, I click on Alex's text: *Why can't I get you out of my head? You're my dream, Emma, and I don't ever want to wake up.*

How on earth do I respond to that? I can't tell him he has the starring role in the worst nightmares I've ever had. Do I tell him he isn't a dream for me, but a memory I've almost forgotten? Emotions tumble around loose inside me, rattling against my bones, bruising my heart. There's definitely a wrong way to respond, but is there a right way?

I press Reply, then type: *I've wondered the same thing. I'll hold back the dawn as long as I can.* Thinking maybe I shouldn't, I click Send.

Like the last time I made some silly, poetic promise, I ag-onize over what I just did. Will he roll his eyes?

My cell's standard notification tone chirps in my hand.

Alex Franks.

I click through to the message.

I'll hold you to that. I don't want to do this alone.

Do what? Regardless, my fingers act on their own agenda, and type: *You are not alone. See you after school tomorrow?*

The wait is short.

I'll be waiting.

A dreamless sleep leads me to a weak gray dawn leaking through my curtains. After my nightmares, dreamless sleep is a blessing. However, I wake to Alex's face behind my eyes, and his voice whispering in my mind. "It doesn't beat for me," he'd said. Then last night he'd texted, *You're my dream, Emma, and I don't ever want to wake up.*

School is my new nightmare, the crush devoid of Alex. I sleepwalk through the day to get to the afternoon and sweeter dreams.

Glancing at the pristine inside of my new locker, I wonder for a minute if I should etch something on the inside in honor of Alex. The metal stretches unspoiled from top to bottom, the locking mechanism in perfect working order. I think I like the image the blank slate gives – limitless potential.

Bree, well aware I won't be at her house for homework, waves and makes rude kissy faces at me from the performing arts hall. Alex is going to help me. He's out there waiting, and the knowledge fills me with an aching kind of longing. I can't get out of the building fast enough.

Alex lounges on the Bree Bench, reminding me of how he seems to shun and attract attention. Hands stuffed in his pockets, normal thin hoodie traded for an ivory knit one that's heavier weight. His face is framed in the pale ivory, shadowed beneath by the rich cocoa color of a new leather jacket that makes his hazels really pop – just like that color combo always did for Daniel.

The familiar feeling swells and ripples through me, like going home after a long, stressful trip. My heart flutters. The same look of wonder crosses his face, then his visage softens into that tender expression. His shadow covers me when he stands.

"Hey," he says.

Questions crowd my mind and force my mouth into automatic response mode.

"Hi."

He holds out his hand, empty with his palm up, offering, not asking. I lift mine to his, hovering it there, feeling the muted tickle of electricity dancing in the air between our skin. His smile grows, tugging at his faint scars, and I think, *Alex knows what I feel.* He's trying to tell me something, show me, without saying anything.

Warmth builds, energy pulses when I settle my hand on his, palm to palm. How can he steal my breath just by knitting our fingers together and turning our hands?

"Aw. How cute!" comes nasty and hateful from the street, issuing from the approaching Camaro Z-28. Crimson glows from the traffic light at the intersection, trapping Josh. Stationary, he's a still life painting of the losing guy in a fight: a black eye discoloring his face, and white tape over his lumpy nose. "Asshole!" he shouts and shakes a fist out the window.

Sometimes, the best responses are silent. Alex pulls me close and then gives Josh a middle finger salute – a move I loosely translate as, "She's mine, so screw you!"

Livid, ugly red flushes what isn't black-and-blue on Josh's face. The light above him turns green, and sour blasts peal from the car horn behind him. A stream of cussing louder than the exhaust system pours from the windows when the car backfires and then moves sluggishly forward.

Then it hits me. Josh looks like someone beat the crap out of him. I shift my gaze to Alex's face - over his cheeks, his lips, his eyes. Nothing but the surgical scars. No black eye. No scab on his bottom lip. It's as if he never got into that fight at the dance.

My long stare becomes obvious. Alex's expression hardens slightly, he fidgets and nearly lets go of my hand. I tighten my fingers around his.

"What?" he asks, eyebrows and lips tilted down.

I can't ply him with questions here. Instead, I lift a shoulder in a half-shrug, and try for nonchalant.

"I thought I wouldn't see Josh this week," I huff.

"Suspensions are supposed to work that way," Alex intones with a heavy note of sarcasm. "Not allowed on school property, or within a hundred feet of it, or something like that."

"Look how well that works for you." I squeeze his hand.

"I'm a ghost," he says, and rubs his thumb along my finger in reply. "No one sees me."

"Oh, yes, they do." Oh, yes, *I do*.

He's there every time I close my eyes, haunting my thoughts. And from his text last night, I must frequent his, too.

People retreating from November's chill fill Mugz-n-Chugz, the ins, the outs, the sports – heck, even the thespians like Amber and Michael Miller. Normal chatter stutters, then dies. All eyes are on our clasped hands. *This*, I think, *is how the rumors really start*. And they do. Words whisk up, breezing from cluster to cluster, division between the various crowds momentarily forgotten.

"Heartless."

"Tramp."

"I knew she was easy."

Vicious, nasty words, taking on lives of their own.

Let them gossip. The gentle pressure of Alex's hand, and the hum coming through his touch are worth it.

"Hiya." Lydia's behind the counter and mercifully doesn't bring Tiny's attention our way. "Breve with caramel for Emma..."

"Make that two, please." Then he looks at me. "Biscotti? Cookies?"

"Just the coffees, Lydia," I say.

"Coming right up." Her long black braid swings like a whip when she turns to fill our order.

"You're going to spoil me, y'know."

He smiles, manipulating our hands till he pins my arm behind me, and my curves to his hard lines. Tingles race up and down my body. The smell of Alex and leather glaze my throat. Alex's words are warm on my lips when he locks eyes with me and says, "That's not the worst thing I can do..."

A blush stains my face. His slow smile radiates a palpable heat. "Your freckles are so cute when you blush."

"Ahem." Lydia clears her throat.

Alex steps back, leaving me feeling weak and noodley, and oddly wanting to smack him for making me that way. He pays the bill, then stuffs our cups into insulated cup collars and a carrier before weaving through the growing crowd to the door. Suddenly, all playfulness drops, his spine stiffens, and he ducks further into his hood.

"What is it?" I ask.

He scans the street through the fingerprint-covered window sporting the Mugz-n-Chugz logo.

"I thought I saw something."

"We're in a coffee shop across from a high school. I'm sure you saw a lot of somethings."

Chill whisks in, claws prickling my skin as he pushes the door open. Instead of walking in the normal direction of home, he cuts through the parking lot, past the line of feet-shuffling, arm-whacking coffee freaks at the walk-up window.

"Not just anything," he says over his shoulder in the back alley. "Something I don't want to see, or be seen by."

Wait a minute. What? The old Converse rubber soles of my tennis shoes squeak when I dig in my heels, something he seems bent on ignoring. Tension pulls in my left hand and arm when he tugs. "Mind telling me what's going on?"

"Can we get out of here first?" Alex shoots a glance past me, at the driveway feeding into the main street. "Please?"

The "please" does it. He's the raw guy in the culvert again, calling my name like I'm the only one who can help him. Resisting Alex when he's like this goes against everything in me. I might as well tell my own cutting ache "no".

"Fine," I mutter.

Surprise zips through me, set alight by Alex. He reaches behind my head, and frees my hair from the messy bun Bree'd twisted it into this morning. Brusquely he stuffs the elastic band into the front pocket of my jeans. Damn my hopes for piquing an interest in the proximity of his hand to my body. Then he grabs my hand again and hikes down the back alley in a vaguely homeward direction. Alex sends protracted looks down each direction at every cross street, weaving a bumblebee path to my house like he's running to it and away from something.

Once inside, Mom casts a half-hearted glare at us and he blanches. He stares blankly, the hand on mine loosening, while the hand around the coffee cups tightens.

A swift elbow to the ribs where Mom can't see breaks him out of it.

"Hello, Mrs Gentry." A slight strain tugs at his voice.

"Mom, do you mind if Alex helps me with homework again?"

I can't send him out there to face whatever he's fleeing.

"Your homework needs to be done, and he seems as good as any *friend*." She stresses the "friend" like that's all she'll allow him to be by the sheer force of her will. "I suppose you'll be staying for dinner again?"

Pleading bleeds from every line of his face despite his neutral expression. "I would love to, if you're offering."

"It's the least I can do to pay you back for helping Emma."

"I'm happy to do it."

A heavy sigh drags her shoulders down. "So I've noticed."

She strides over the basement door, shouts down to Dad that "Emma and *that boy*" are in the dining room, and she's going to pick up pizzas. Grabbing her battered purse, she eyes me from the back door.

"I'll be back in a while" never sounded like more "Behave or you'll regret it."

The door swings shut and I turn on Alex. "Look. I don't mind taking the scenic route home, but either you tell me what that..." and I jab a finger at the living room window and direction we'd just come, "was all about or we won't be walking together again."

A puppet with cut strings, Alex sinks to the chair he sat in last night while I did homework. His gaze falls, as if the dark carpet holds the world's secrets, and shakes his head. "Sorry about putting you through that, Em. I just didn't want him ruining things."

"Him who?" Was he talking about Josh? I would've heard his loud engine inside the coffee shop.

"My dad."

His father? That horrid man who squeezed my hand hard enough to break bones? The will to stand leaves my legs, and I drop to the seat next to him. Memory throbs in my hand, sharp and hot. Unconsciously, I lift my left hand to rub the brace on my right and Alex doesn't miss it.

"Exactly," he says. His tone, his face... Alex's ceding defeat.

"Why would he be following you?" My voice sounds faraway, muffled by the waves of shock and fear.

"Your mom and him have a lot in common." I watch while he opens my backpack, and pulls out the homework for me. The jittery motion in his hands says he needs an activity to focus on. "Overprotective."

"So what?" A defensive, cornered feeling rises in me. "He doesn't like you making friends?"

Maybe it's the last word, or the vehemence I pack into it. Alex hits me with a wounded look, asking "That's all we are?" without saying a thing.

"Since the accident..." he slides his hood off and shoves a hand through his longish brown hair. "Since I woke up, Dad hasn't liked anything, or anyone, that takes me away."

"I'm taking you away?"

"According to him, I'm throwing myself away on any girl in high school."

Why does that statement sting?

"Am I just 'any girl'?"

"No!" Anger sharpens his word. "You're..." he pauses, glances around, then looks at me. The grind and scream of power tools cuts off in the basement, and the door to my dad's workshop creaks open. Alex says, voice barely above a whisper, "You're everything, and he knows it."

Once Dad reaches the top of the stairs, any personal talk dries up to a shriveled husk of "So what else happened at school?" My heart and head chatter back and forth debating his words, *You're everything, and he knows it,* and what he meant.

I slink up to my room, heart and mind whirring, then return to the dining room with my laptop. We do my homework like the night before, with him brushing his sock toes on my feet. When Mom comes in, arms laden with carryout boxes, Alex beats my dad to the kitchen to help her. Her thank-you is only mildly disgruntled – progress. After dinner, Mom doesn't dismiss Alex, and Dad invites him into the living room to watch some game.

Alex and I start out side by side on the sofa. The polite Mom-is-watching one-full-cushion distance between us is maddening, as is the quiet. There's so much to talk about. Eventually, I realise Mom isn't moving and Alex is trying his best to fit in. Stuffing away the questions plaguing my mind, I slide to the floor and lean back against his shins.

Mom peeks up occasionally, not missing a thing happening across the carpeting from her chair. Her eyebrows go up when I wriggle between Alex's legs and rest my head on his lap. A tickle of energy zips along my scalp as he strokes my hair. I close my eyes and float in the odd new/old connection we have. By the end of whatever game they're watching, I'm more than half asleep, with one arm looped around Alex's calf, and my head resting on his inner thigh.

"Wake up, sleepyhead," he says, nudging me. "Game's over."

"Yes," Mom agrees, using her finger for a bookmark in some paperback with lusty cover models on the front. "And you have school tomorrow, Emma Jane."

Warm and heavy with drowsiness, I drift to the door with Alex's fingers twined in mine. Then his hand is on the doorknob, and with chilly air rushing through the cracked-open gap, he says, "See you tomorrow, Em."

He compounds the heat and comfy feeling, wrapping me in a hug. His heart beats a steady rhythm, one I feel an echo of in my chest when he presses my head to him. "Sweet dreams, Alex."

"I'm holding mine," he whispers, then places a light kiss on my forehead.

Tingles dance across the skin beneath his lips.

After the door closes, and I lean my back against the wooden panel, I sort through hazy thoughts to the one too bright and impossible to ignore. I know what he meant when he said his heart didn't beat for him. I don't think my heart belongs to me either.

Clouds smother Wednesday's sky, leeching the sunlight and heat. The world outside my house has drifted into an alternate horror-movie state. Chilly haze muffles, mutilates or devours sounds. The color of trees and cars and houses – everything – has bled off into the faint black smudges of shadow beneath them. I watch for Alex all the way to school, and flinch whenever fancy cars roll past.

Anticipation threatens to suffocate my heart when I open the side door after school. The empty Bree Bench all but kills the emotion. I scan the quad, people tucking tighter into their winter jackets, leaves scraping and whispering over the pavement. No Alex. No hybrid in the student parking lot either. One block past the gym complex, though, a black SUV drives across the intersection and away from my neighborhood, followed directly by Josh Mason.

As if today didn't suck enough already...

He pulls to a stop at the curb, throws his Camaro into

park in a posted No Parking Zone, and then climbs out. Maybe I'm used to staring at Alex now. Josh looks awful, stringy thin, his hair seems even redder, his skin paler. And a haunted look fills the creases made by the swelling from his fight with Alex. I can't muster enough snark to play our old insult game.

"Hell-bent on annoying me?" I ask.

"Not fair, Em. Not fair." Josh casts looks up and down the street, fidgets with his jacket cuff. When he shifts his gaze back to me, I know he's not playing games either. "You need to stay away from Alex Franks. You have no idea the trouble you're walking into."

"What? And you do?" I tip my weight back on one hip and away from him. "Wait." I peer closely at the tape over his broken nose. "I guess you do know."

"You have no idea." Another glance down the way he came. "You can't date him."

"Excuse me? Who died and made you judge of who I can date?"

"Daniel did."

My response is immediate. I whip a hand out and slap his face, the purpled bruised side. Josh covers his cheek with his hand. He doesn't have the decency to look remorseful, just resigned and angry.

"How dare you?" I growl. "You were best friends! You were right there on the balcony when Daniel fell. How the hell can you make a mockery of his death?"

"You don't understand!" Josh shouts, and clutches his hands in his hair. "If you had any idea what I've done to be with you!"

"I don't." I put every bit of venom and anger I can fit into my words. "And I don't want to."

I leave him there, fingers knotted in his wiry carrot curls, eyes wide, haunted by ghosts of the accident that stole Daniel from us. Hell with that, from *me*. Josh doesn't miss him, doesn't mourn him like I do. Swearing under my breath and wishing desperately for Alex, I stomp across the street. Houses drift past my heavy-footed march on a side street parallel to the alley Alex had half-dragged me down yesterday.

Where does Josh get off saying what he said? Daniel died and left him to judge who I'm supposed to date? And what in the world could he have possibly done to be with me? He lost out on that one long ago. Daniel beat him to it.

I'm so busy mentally bitching, the guy standing beside the old livery barn on the alley edge goes unnoticed until he wraps his arms around me. Instinct kicks in, flooding me with adrenaline and forcing a shout up my throat. A hand settles over my mouth and cuts short my yelp of surprise. The smell of leather fills my nose.

Alex.

I sag against him, then blindly turn and bury my face in his chest. I yearn for him to chase away the darkness eating like acid at my day.

"Where were you?" I say over his heart. "I looked all over for you."

"Sorry, Em. I didn't want my dad to see us together." His fingers leave no tingle when they slide under my hair, but it feels wonderful anyway. Safe and comforted and cared for, despite what Josh said about me walking into trouble. When I look up, the shadows have returned under Alex's eyes. His skin seems paler.

"Hey," he says and gives me a wan smile.

"Hi." I smile back. Yes, a warning alarm rings in my gut,

screaming be careful, that something's not right with Alex. But I've known that. If Alex Franks is trouble, I want it.

"Come on." He knits our fingers together, then says, "I know a place we can go for a while. His shift at the clinic starts soon."

I follow Alex down familiar side streets vacant of jack-o'-lanterns to a chain link fence that I've cut my finger on four times since June.

"Memorial Gardens Cemetery?" Surprise drags my voice up a couple notches.

"Yeah. My dad can't stand to come near Mom's grave." The metal screeches in protest when he lifts the lever and pushes open the gate. "He didn't even go to her funeral. It's like if he denies it long enough, she'll just come back home."

It isn't until he's inside the graveyard that he notices I'm not with him.

My heart clenched the moment my fingers touched that cool metal. The rift, cobbled closed with moments with Alex, cracks and opens, visions of me and Alex tumbling into the dark that Daniel left behind in me. This is *my* place. This is where I've mourned Daniel for months. Being here with Alex feels wrong. Memories, faulty and empty as they are, stand strong as the rusted fence between me and the guy beyond.

"Emma?" Alex's voice sounds miles away. "You OK?"

In a vicious flash, the dead-and-rotted Daniel from my nightmares is Alex, blood flowing over his hazel eyes, then he's gone. Still, I recoil when Alex's hand reaches for me.

"Hey," he says, voice soft and soothing like he's coaxing a feral animal. "Come on, Em, you're freaking me out here."

"S-sorry," I stammer. "It's just that… well, I…"

"It's OK," he says, and takes my hand again. "We don't have to stay."

"It's just that I used to stay here." I gesture my braced right hand toward the section of fencing I leaned on, mourning Daniel for weeks. "I came here every day."

"Why?" His mismatched eyes widen, the scar tugging at his left eye. The black freckle in that pool of hazel only makes me think of Daniel more.

I sigh, and for once in four months, I breach the barrier between the living and the dead. A shudder ripples up my spine, coats my skin in goosebumps. *I'm cheating on Daniel's memory,* I think.

Once inside, my gaze plummets to the crushed gravel path leading off into the shadows by the trees. We walk together, but we're worlds apart. Inside, I see all the times Daniel and I came here: the urn he knocked over and we straightened, the pothole on the little drive that popped his dirt bike tire, and God, the mausoleum where we sat so many evenings.

"Emma," Alex prods gently, "why did you come here?"

"Because…" Old sadness cinches my throat, making my eyes itch. The gulf in my chest threatens to go full-blown and devour every little happiness I'd found with Alex. "Because this is where I came with Daniel. This was our place. Then, after he died…"

The lump in my throat rises, and I can't swallow it down. Alex steps off the path and sits on a mossy bench, dragging me down beside him. The angel I'd often stared at regards me with a look close to pity. Late afternoon light sits on the curves of her cheekbones like tears. Alex waits, patient and silent, giving me time. It only makes me want to cry more. Here I am mourning the boy I lost with the guy who seems willing to do anything to be with me.

"Anyway," I force past the tightness and swallow again. "After Daniel died, his parents donated…" I lose the battle with the tears, and somehow it galvanizes me to finish my tale. "They donated his body to science. They cremated his remains, what was left, and keep them in their house in a stupid shiny urn Daniel would be ashamed to be in. I can't see them because his parents blame me. He would've never gone to that party if we weren't dating."

I wipe at my wet cheeks. Alex catches my hands, and dries my face with the sleeve of his hoodie. He says all the right things, "It wasn't my fault, his parents aren't being fair," but they don't sink in.

"Daniel was everything to me, then he was just gone. Fell from my life like a comet shoved out of orbit. I didn't have anywhere to mourn him, so I've been coming here since June."

"God, Em." Alex says. "I had no idea. I'm so sorr–"

"Don't apologize. You're not responsible for his death."

If I'm honest, here where Daniel should be buried, I can admit the darkest part of my heart believes somehow Josh is responsible. He couldn't drop the damn beer and grab Daniel's hand fast enough when he fell. I reached the railing too late to save him, but with plenty of time to see him fall and hit the pavement below.

"It's not an apology," Alex says, that soothing tone still in his voice. "I was going to say I'm sorry you're still hurting."

"But I'm not," I blurt out. "Not as bad since you came to school."

His features twist with an expression that seems surprise tempered with sadness. It radiates from his eyes. The black freckle in his left eye more pronounced the way the sunlight hits his face.

"Y'know… You kind of remind me of him."

When I look down, he's inched away. Or have I?

"What?" Shock twists that one word, making it ugly and stunted.

I would be shocked. But I'm too far gone to notice if he wants to hear it, like I've opened a vein for bloodletting and can't stop spilling the truth.

"Not in looks. Other than your eyes." The left is slightly more dilated, when I look. "It's what you do. How you wink the same. How you opened my locker just like Daniel. The same push to the numbers, the same nudge with your hip." Alex extends a long hand across the space between us, despite me comparing him to my dead boyfriend, and I have to think I'm the one moving away. "How did you know to do that, Alex?"

"I don't know," he says slowly, taking his hand back, curling it into a fist and looking at it as if it's untrustworthy. The shaft of air widens between us, his hand falling just short of mine, and his expression darkens. "I just did. It… felt right." He prods his chest. "It felt right *here*."

It doesn't beat for me.

Alex's head pops up, ear tilted like he heard my thought. With a shaky inhalation, he jerks upright suddenly, nothing muscular or fluid about it. Daylight has slipped from the angel's face. Still, she watches us, like we are Romeo and Juliet about to drink the poison and raise the blade.

I shrink in on myself, suddenly wishing I were anywhere in the world but here. Why did I say those things? Alex didn't really want to know. Guys never want to know the truth. They just ask to make girls feel better.

Alex's expression doesn't help. It makes me feel worse.

He's waking from the dream.

His gaze trails from my face to my hands to his chest. It follows the length of his arms to his hands, open with the palms up and full of the late afternoon sun. When he speaks, I don't think it's for me. "Why do I do things like he did?" He shakes his head, paces, mashing the sleeping grass beneath his feet. "Coincidence," he mutters. "Just coincidence."

"Daniel said there are no coincidences."

We both recoil, my words sharp and double-sided.

"When did you say he died?" Alex asks. "How did it happen?"

Why would he ask? I already said how Daniel died. My heart stutters, teetering on the yawning rift inside. When I look up, I expect to see Daniel's echo sitting on the mausoleum's porch. He's not there. Alex stands in front of me, with the cloud-laden sky turning to blood and bruises when the sun slips beyond the cloud line.

"It was right at the end of the string of disappearances in June." Somehow I've gone cold and hollow, and the facts roll out. "We were at a graduation party. He and Josh argued. Next thing I know, Daniel's screaming my name and falling. His skull cracked." My voice catches, and Alex stretches a hand toward me, then to his head pushing his hair from his forehead. "The hospital couldn't save him, and his parents agreed to donate his body."

"That must've been awful," he says, voice sounding oddly empty. His expression is closed off, like he's seeing something inside rather than out. A sharp kind of clarity lingers there.

"I think I should get you home," Alex says suddenly. "I'm surprised your mom hasn't texted you."

Mom? Home?

The concepts are foreign. There's only me, Alex, and the story of Daniel between us.

"OK," I say.

Standing, my toe catches in the crack on the path, the brittle grass rushes at my face. And Alex doesn't catch me. I lay for a second, renewed hurt pulsing in my hand and my heart aching. The smell of dry earth coats my nose when I inhale. Not caring about my dignity, I scrabble to my hands and knees and see Alex staring at the mausoleum porch like he's seen the ghost that's haunted me since June.

"You used to sit there," he says, face in shadow, voice quaking. "You sat on the tomb's porch, laughing…" his empty hand flexes at his side, holding nothing in a white-knuckle grip, "and drinking."

Does he see us, echoes of the Daniel and Emma that were? Shock and wrongness war inside me. The moment has taken life, and doesn't listen.

"How did you know?" I ask, voice hardly above a whisper.

"I'm not sure. Good guess, I suppose…" A half-hearted shrug. Then Alex runs his hand over his hair, rubs the back of his head and pulls me to standing. "Let's get you home."

His hood slides up, and casts his face into deeper shadows. *He knows.* I saw it in his eyes. He *knows* we sat there.

I follow behind him, mind reeling in disbelief, hands brushing off the grass and dirt he was too busy staring at the mausoleum to notice. Silent tears fall, blurring my vision, adding to the aching haze my day has become. How could I say all that and expect him to just be OK with it? He doesn't see me backhand moisture off my face before we step into the ring of the porch light either.

A faraway look darkens his eyes. Alex stands on the middle step, and I stand on the creaking porch floorboards.

"Em…" he says, voice soft. He's wearing all his hurts in his eyes again, his scars only pulling the skin tight over the gouged-out boy. Resisting his open palm-up hand is impossible. I can't resist Alex like this – I can't resist Alex at all. My toes on the edge, Alex envelops me in his arms, burying his face against my chest.

"Alex?"

"Shhh." He cinches his arms around me tighter. "I'm listening to your heart."

"It doesn't beat for me," I tell him.

"I know."

I slide his hood from his hair, just skin on skin when I run my fingers under the long brown strands. Hidden scars reveal themselves to my fingers. He shudders as I touch them, touch him like he's mine. I curl my head down until my cheek brushes his hair. We stand like that until I can't measure time anymore. Eventually, Dad opens the porch door and says, "Almost dinner time."

"I should get going," Alex mutters, suddenly gone tense and his muscles tight beneath my fingers. "Dad will know if I don't show up soon."

Alex's fingers tighten on me, like his body refuses to do what his mind commands. Reluctance exudes from him, heavy as his rich leather scent. Alex's arms release me in little increments. The shadows under his eyes almost engulf the heterochromic hazels. When he walks away, with no promises of tomorrow, I wonder if Alex Franks really knows that my heart beats for him.

Chapter Eighteen

After dinner, Renfield trails behind me, mewing for attention rather than skewering me with a disdainful glare. Darkness squats in the kitchen, Mom's not there, no prep sounds for tomorrow's cooking. Perhaps I've stumbled into an alternate universe. Fine with me. I have no appetite, hardly even nibbled dinner. My stomach pitched over the edge and abandoned me along with my heart. Sure, it's there, beating behind my ribs, but in a very real sense Alex took it with him when he left.

"Everything OK?" Dad asks from the armchair by the TV.

I should lie, slink past and climb the stairs. It's close to bedtime and my cell phone is almost dead. Maybe there's a text from Alex. Instead…

"I'm not sure," I say and perch on the edge of the sofa.

"Want to talk about it?"

With my dad? Oh God, no. The vein I cut open in the cemetery is still spurting truths, though, and I can't stop now that I've started talking. "I think I committed a major dating sin."

"Oh, really?" An eyebrow arches above his glasses.

"I talked about my old boyfriend with my current." Then I realise what I said – Daniel as my old and Alex Franks as my new – and add, "Not that Alex *is* my boyfriend. We're just friends."

"Oh. Of course you are." I hate that parental father-knows-best timbre in his voice. The expression on his face is a physical echo of the you-are-more-than-friends tone. "Look, Em. Daniel was a big part of your life. Any guy interested in you has a pretty big shadow to fill. If they can't understand that, then they aren't worth your time."

In some ways, Alex overshadows Daniel.

"Thanks, Dad."

I stand up and yawn as an excuse to retreat to my bedroom. Dad doesn't know the depth of what's going on, though I love that he can give me his angle on this. *I don't* even know the depth of what's going on. The line between Alex and Daniel has become so blurred, the question of who he is and why he's so much like Daniel, I'm not sure there's any separating the two.

Renfield remains behind me, a sleek white shadow. I bend to gather him into my arms, but apparently it's not dignified to be carried like a baby. He uses his back claws in readjusting to an upright position in my arms. The sadistic beast is bent on making me bleed. The hot scratches in my arm are welcome, though, real physical sensations to draw attention from the tumult of emotions rattling like buckshot in my head and heart. I cradle the cat, stroke his ears and listen to his purr as I climb the stairs.

I wish he could talk and explain why he likes Alex the way he liked Daniel. Maybe then I'd know, too.

Light lies in a puddle beneath my parents' bedroom door, and I know Mom's in there reading. I pause outside the door, then knock and open it. Sure enough, Mom's leaning against the pillows, blankets pulled up, and her finger marking her place in her romance novel. A frown and a smile war on her lips, then she settles for one of her blank tired expressions.

"You didn't answer my texts," she says.

"Phone's dead again. I think I need a new battery." I poke my toe at the doorjamb, worried that she's madder than she seems. Things need to be better between us. Especially with whatever's going on with me and Alex. "I'm sorry–" *for worrying you*, I don't finish.

"It's OK." She fluffs her blankets. "I noticed you didn't eat anything for dinner. You just pushed things around on your plate like you used to. You aren't getting sick, are you?"

"I don't think so." Not physically anyway. Heartsick maybe, not knowing how Alex feels. "I just wasn't hungry…"

"Well, I hope that's all it is." Her tone implies she thinks it's more, but won't say it. "I would hate to have you missing school so close to Thanksgiving break."

"Me, too. Good night, Mom."

"Night, Emma."

Things aren't perfect between us, but at least they are fixable. Mom's one of the few constants in my life, and I want it to stay that way.

My bedroom is a study in shadow and texture, dark and moonlight, hard and soft. I leave the light off. Once inside the bedroom door, Renfield leaps for the bed, paces circles on my pillow, then drops down. He regards me through slitted eyes while I plug in my cell phone, debate firing up my computer, and then grab pajamas instead. By the time I've made it back from the shower, the notification light is bleeding red light into the shadows over my desk.

One text.

Alex Franks.

My hands tremble as I open the message. He held me on

the porch as if he needed me, and still fear burns in my veins, thinking I'd said too much, he had time to think, and this is the brush-off text. The letters hang innocuous and black on the screen, and my mind struggles to fight free of the thorny emotions of this evening and read. The first time through they are just letters, then I focus on what they say:

When you said those words, I realised it isn't just me. I want to ask you something tomorrow. See you after school.

I check the time stamp. Alex sent it minutes ago. How could he send that and think tomorrow would ever be good enough?

No, I type, *it isn't just you.* Then I hit Send.

And follow that text with: *Tomorrow?* I type. *Ask me what?*

The cat gives me a surly I-was-here-first meow when I sit on the bed by my pillow. "Deal with it," I tell him. "I'm bigger than you."

He stands, lifts his tail to an arrogant angle and struts to the end of the bed where he usually sleeps. My cell phone vibrates in my hand. I have it open before the buzzing is finished.

Patience, Emma. This isn't something to say over text.

OK. He knows how to push my buttons at a distance.

Being patient is overrated. Give me a hint.

I can almost see the smile on his face. It would slide over his cheek bones and tug at the thin surgical scars. The message appears silently, since I never closed out of the conversation.

Your persistence is showing. ;) Trust me. You'll agree it isn't a phone thing.

There's no question if I trust him. Despite the niggling sense there is something wrong with Alex, I can't dig him out of my soul. His pain, his hollowed hurt, his tenderness have etched Alex on my heart. How can I doubt part of myself?

How can I not, when the calendar says I've only known him for barely two weeks?

Fine, I type back, *see you after school.*

I shut the phone, then turn it off. The poor thing is never going to get a full charge if I'm typing with it all night. Carpeting whispers under my feet as I ford the shadows to my desk and put the phone back on the charger. I pull my curtains mostly to, leaving them open enough to see the moon hanging low and white outside my window. Maybe Alex is looking up, too.

The pillow is still warm from Renfield when I settle into bed. Sleep comes quick, stealing into my head on soft wings and painting everything black.

The dream drags me back to the cemetery.

Broken gravestones, graves, and something I never wanted to see again. The fraternity house where Daniel died stands where the mausoleum should. White cats sit everywhere when I walk in: on a bookcase, on the chair, two on the sofa, even one on the keg. The moment they see me, they scurry away.

I don't want to be here. Never wanted to be here again. Then a Renfield peeks from under the chair next to me. He dashes for the sofa in the middle of the room, and pointedly stares at me.

Follow, his eyes tell me before he disappears again.

The bookcase Renfield appears, streaks toward the stairs, and my heart hammers at me to hurry. Another white face snaps into being halfway up the steps.

Up, I think, *I have to go up.*

I follow the feline guides and touch the stairs. Breath catches in my throat. I climb and sob, the need to be upstairs heaving in me like a living thing.

Renfields dot the top floor, too, ghostly flashes of white leading down the hall to that hated room. Moonlight fills the rec room. Two familiar male figures stand bathed in white light at the edge of the balcony. They fight as I run through the hall, one cat or another winking in and out in front of my feet. One of them falls, and I ram into the railing, knowing I've missed my chance to save Daniel again.

Josh stands on the deck, beer in one hand, looking at his empty other hand.

Daniel and Alex lay on the ground beneath us, with identical wounds and the same dying light in their eyes.

"I couldn't catch 'em," Josh slurs. Then he combusts into the whirling devil I saw on the catwalk the last time I saw Daniel. He plants his hands in my chest and shoves...

I wake when my head makes contact with the floor. Dawn shines at a crazy angle through my room. Sheets tangle around my body, and Renfield's perched on the footboard of my bed with his back arched and fur standing straight up from his head to his tail. Mom's voice joins the cat's hissing. "Emma Jane! You're going to be late for school!"

"Oh God," I groan.

Swearing worse than anything coming out of the boys' locker room, I fight my way from the sheets, and then lunge for my closet. On instinct, I grab clothes, struggle into them despite my brace, snag my phone from the charger and rush down the stairs.

Mom's there, in her normal place, acting as if life is back to normal. A homemade version of a pancake-on-a-stick occupies one hand, my backpack in the other, and a to-go cup of coffee sits on the counter. She helps me into my backpack, slips my cell phone in, then tells me while she loads me with coffee and food that she ordered me a new battery for my phone, and they will be home tonight, and Alex is welcome for dinner, and on and on. She shouts, "Run a comb through your hair," as I dash out the door.

Thinking and walking and breakfast do not successfully add up for me. I sacrifice thought for food. My stomach opens into a snarling pit once the smell of the cinnamon-spiced batter hits my nose. The roads pass unnoticed, vehicles and houses, too. The last swallow of coffee swills through the lid as I reach the school.

Bree, in denim and faux fur, sits on the Bree Bench, waving her big-tooth comb at me like a teacher might have brandished a ruler at a naughty student.

"Good Lord," she says, "did you fall out of bed and run to school?"

"Pretty much," I say. Why lie?

"Well, walk slow and careful and I'll comb that mess for you. I'm sure Lover Boy's going to be here after school and I don't want you scaring him away." I'm sure she's searching through her mental Rolodex for a play that might fit that moment while she rakes at my head. I walk as carefully as possible toward the side door.

"So…" she says. Rake. Rake. "Tell me all about him."

I don't even bother playing the "Him who?" game. "He's sweet, and funny, and caring. Listened to me cry about Daniel, even."

"You went there?" Rake and snag. Comb, comb. "You actually brought up your old boyfriend?"

"Yeah. It just kinda came up while we were in the cemetery."

"Wait." She stops and the raking stops, too. "Lover Boy is as freaky as you?"

"At least as far as cemeteries goes…"

Her brown eyes widen. She blows out a low whistle. "You two are perfect for each other."

I don't argue.

"It feels like forever since we talked," she chides, working a loose braid into my hair.

"We talk every day."

"More than at school." She twists a rubber band at the end of my braid. "Just make sure Lover Boy knows he's supposed to share."

"I'll make sure to tell him. Not that we're dating or anything…"

She shakes her head, giving me a visual check. "You deny too much."

"Well, it's true…"

We part ways at the corner of the main and creative arts halls. School becomes the hurdle I have to leap to make it to the afternoon. I text Alex at lunch while the actor members of the drama club discuss their upcoming performance and the Winter Formal. Alex responds to my pestering with promising I'll know soon enough. The afternoon is both a pain and a blur. I can't focus on anything, and I don't want to. I stare at clocks, willing the hands to move faster.

The bone white note stuffed into my locker vents – like a blade between ribs – stops me in my tracks. Did he decide not to come after all? Rather than let my mind flounder in the quagmire of what-ifs, I snatch the note down, and open it.

Em,

Waiting at your house.

Yours,

Alex

Mine? He signed it. Is it his way of saying it without actually speaking?

Mine. I like the sound of that.

One word erases all the possible ways I could've pouted from Alex's note. Instead, I almost skip out the doors. The empty Bree Bench doesn't bother me, or waiting for the traffic to clear. A shiny black SUV, a couple rattletrap boxes on wheels, but no Josh Mason. Even the November chill can't taint the sweet anticipation climbing higher in me.

The sight of Alex slouching like a male model against my porch pillar slaughters every sad thought and bad dream of the past couple days. His scruffy casual clothes are way too high-end to be anything but designer. Black jeans and knit hoodie, brown leather jacket and sneakers. The only time he might have looked hotter is the night of the Halloween dance, all in black, with a bruise under one eye and a trickle of blood on his lip.

"Hey," he says, voice all husky and making it sound personal.

"Hi." Fluttery and light, probably matches the beat of my heart.

"You going to invite me in?" he asks, eyes bright despite the dark shadows beneath them.

"I don't know." I waggle a braced hand at him. "You gonna say what you came to say?"

"Nope." He pretends to shiver. "Not outside in the cold. Invite me in…"

"Fine," I huff and throw up my hands in mock defeat.

I tromp across the porch to the front door, and grab the doorknob. There, with the knob turning under my hand, I spin and face Alex. Unsuspecting, he bumps into me, denim on denim in close to inappropriate places. Color flushes his face, heat floods mine, but he doesn't move back. Instead, Alex loops an arm around my back and adjusts my angle to better fit against him. His eyes say a thousand things when he leans close.

"Tell me," I whisper.

"No." His lips are close enough to brush mine. And I want them to.

Then Alex turns the knob and our weight against the door does the rest. I stumble backwards and away from him. Recovering my footing is less than graceful, colored with a choice swear word, too. Flinging back my braid, I cast a pouty glance at him. He stands rooted to the sill, so when my mom's head pops from the kitchen we're both pink-cheeked, but not in a position he'd be kicked out for.

"Getting cold out there," she grumps. "Shut the door."

"Sorry, Mrs Gentry."

"Have homework?" Mom asks.

Before I can answer, Alex says, "We'll get right to it."

"Thanks, Alex."

Where's the rabbit hole, I wonder, because I'm sure I've fallen down it now.

"Thanks, Alex?" I mouth while he deftly strips me of my backpack, and runs up the stairs. When he returns with my laptop, he pulls out a chair for me. Pushing out an exasperated sigh, I sit down on the seat, not the least bit surprised when he pushes it in for me. He follows suit, sliding his chair up to the table. The wail of a power tool cutting through wood fills the room. Using the cover of its sound, I beg Alex, "Tell me."

"You have any idea how persistent you are?"

"Totally." I bat my eyelashes. "I could've warned you about that if you'd asked."

"Never thought I'd have to." He sounds so serious, but he's smiling.

Mom passes in and out of the kitchen, never giving me a good chance to question Alex again. Chicken stew in home-made bread bowls soon cover the table, dragged out unmercifully long by torturous small talk between Mom and Dad about his company's Thanksgiving party. Alex and Dad clear the table, and Mom suggests we watch a movie while she goes upstairs to read. Thankfully, I'm not facing her and she can't see my smile.

"Planning on any certain movie?" Dad sounds intrigued.

"*Dracula*," Alex says.

"Oh." A minute shrug and polish of his glasses. "We've seen that quite a few times. You two won't mind if I go back to the workshop, then?"

Dad doesn't wait for an answer, just fills his chipped mug with decaf coffee and heads for the basement. For a moment, the lack of immediate parental supervision feels odd. I poke a toe at the table leg. Alex tugs at the zipper of his jacket. Our eyes meet, we inhale in sync, and drop gazes just as quickly.

"I don't have the DVD anymore." I say, sure that he expects me, the super fan with a cat named Renfield, to have a copy. "Bree spilled nail polish on it."

"No worries." Alex pulls the DVD from the inside pocket of his leather jacket. "I came prepared."

His smile is cute, and a little annoying. He must think he's successfully derailed me from pestering him. "You have shin and elbow guards in there, too?"

"No." The querulous tone in his voice feels like a small victory. "Should I?"

"Yeah. I'm going to sic Renfield on you if you don't break the suspense soon."

"Who?" he asks all sweet and innocent, and collects the white cat circling his feet. "This kitty?"

The damned traitorous cat purrs, and lifts his chin to be scratched. I flex my fingers, and buff the nails of my left hand against his hoodie, which I'm wearing because I grabbed it when I ran on autopilot this morning. "I have claws too."

"Ooh," he teases. "You're a big threat with just one hand."

"Brat." I whip a pillow at him, dislodge the cat, and nearly knock the DVD from his grip.

"By the way…" He skirts my throwing arm and edges for the TV. "Nice shirt. I wondered where it got to."

"Oh yeah? Want it back?"

"Depends…" He waggles his eyebrows. "You gonna take it off now?"

A blush permeates my cheeks, and I busy myself piling throw pillows in the corner of the sofa, and dragging a couple of blankets from the closet. Alex fishes the remote from Dad's armchair, and works our TV like a pro. In minutes, he has the movie started and has nestled in the corner like I'd cozied it up just for him. He pats the cushion next to him.

Heaving a sigh, I sink down onto the red sofa and lean back. Not long into the movie, Alex sits up, pulls my braid free from being trapped behind me, takes off the binder and unweaves the plait.

"I love your hair," he says, voice just above a whisper. "Com'ere."

The way he slides the words together is a definite West Michigan thing, and with his husky tenor it's definitely enticing. How can I refuse?

He takes my shoulder, guiding me to the edge of the cushion while he slides a leg behind me, and pulls me back against his chest. Warm tingles pour across my scalp, following the light touch of his fingers running through my hair.

"Now that I have you where I want you," he says, "we have something to discuss."

"We do?" I feign surprise.

"Yes." Shivers spread over my skin as Alex slides his fingers across my neck, pouring my hair over one shoulder. Twisting a little, he nestles me in the crook of his arm. The tunneling sensation flares, narrowing the house to this sofa, and the world to this moment.

"Two weeks of knowing you isn't enough, Em. Two weeks of being friends isn't enough either."

"What are you saying?" Suddenly, I can't get enough air and I feel like I'm melting into him.

"I want you to be mine."

The falling sensation becomes intense. I slide my hand up his chest, my fingers brushing his cheek below the scar. "I already am."

Smiling the tender expression I know is just mine, he cups my hand against his face a moment, leaning into my fingers, and my heart dances. Then he releases my hand and places his fingers under my chin. Moving slowly, giving me plenty of time to say "no" to the kiss I know is coming, Alex tips his face to mine. My eyes slip closed when he whispers, "Com'ere."

Alex's lips brush mine, a feather-light first contact. I melt into him, whispering his name. He sucks in a breath, stealing mine – and I don't care. The couch spins, only Alex holding me to it when his mouth touches mine again, firmer this time, more confident. I don't know where to put my hands, and my hip is driving into his thigh. He must like it all twisted up and awkward. Alex crushes me to him, kissing me like he's waited a thousand years for this moment.

Too soon it's over, and the stairs creak under Mom's feet. I quickly adjust so I'm leaning against him, and he manages to shove a pillow between us before Mom appears.

Her gaze hits us. No anger, just a resigned acceptance framed in brown and gray hair. "Want anything from the kitchen?" she asks. "I'm getting a pop."

"No, thanks," we say in stereo, his velvet tenor a little husky, my soprano a little squeaky.

After Mom rummages in the fridge, then makes a return trip up the steps, I shift in his arms, ready for another kiss. He's so pale, the shadows gone purple-black under his eyes, I can't manage another kiss and I don't think he can either. He kisses the end of my nose, instead.

"Not feeling well?" I ask.

"Better than I've felt since I woke up in recovery." Alex hugs me to his chest, tucking my head under his chin. "But I'm going to need another treatment tomorrow."

"Another?" *What treatment?*

"Once a week my dad gives me an immunity booster and vitamin shot." His grin is so sweet it hurts to see. "It helps me to heal quickly."

"That's why you don't look like Josh." I pretend to punch him.

"Exactly." He laughs out loud. "Plus, I'm just better looking."

"Damn right you are."

I curl my fingers in the neckline of his shirt. He sits very still, eyes slipping closed when I brush a kiss on his jaw. A shudder ripples through him when I move my lips to his neck, beneath his chin. Then I pull his neckline down and kiss the intersection of scars below the hollow of his throat.

"God... You're killing me," he sighs. "And I like it."

I cuddle into him after that, only half watching the movie. I've seen it so many times I can recite every line. Somewhere around the time Dracula turns Mina into a vampire, things start to get fuzzy, and my eyelids droop.

"Hey." Alex jostles me. "I think it's bedtime for you."

"I'm not tired," I argue, even though I am.

"Your body heats up when you're tired, so don't try to lie."

I want to argue, ask him how he knows that. Instead, a yawn comes out.

"See?" Alex teases. "I'm feeling pretty whipped, too."

He stops the DVD and retrieves it while I stand yawning, with my eyes watering. I can't fight the pout when he pulls on his jacket. "Don't worry," he promises. "You'll see me soon."

At the door, Alex cups my face in both hands and his gaze pores over me.

"What does this make us?" I blurt.

The stairs creak, and Mom says, "Time for your boyfriend to go home."

"There's your answer," he says, all soft. "You're mine."

"I like that."

One more light kiss, and he says, "Me, too. Sweet dreams, Emma."

Chapter Nineteen

Mine. The word winds through my mind, wrapping sweet tendrils around it. The way he said it, the way I feel it, on a level deeper than easy emotions. It cuts to the heart, and through. Things haven't been easy from the first day to this. Bring on trouble. Bring on the rumors.

"Never invite trouble," as my mom likes to say.

Standing outside Mugz-n-Chugz on a chilly Friday morning, I can understand why. The rumors once flocking around Alex swoop in on me, blacker and sharper-clawed than the crows who murdered him with gossip. Tiny's walk-up line has morphed from zombies to wide-eyed whisperers. Nikki Cummings and Faith Lewis take on the task of trying to humiliate me with a special zeal.

"OhmyGod," Nikki says in a whisper meant to be heard, "Can you believe how fast she moved on to Alex Franks?"

Of course she can't, because the hypocritical harpy squad wasn't all over him the first day. Nikki wasn't drooling over him, and her friend Marin wasn't claiming him. They mock and throw stones when I'm mourning Daniel, but I move on and they crucify me.

"I know," Faith agrees, skewering me with a bitchy

glance. "Daniel must not've meant anything if she's hooking up with Alex already."

Some sophomore acolyte of the harpies even pipes in with, "Pretty pathetic."

The words hurt, as biting and mean as they're meant to be. I might not know why Alex has so many of Daniel's traits, but I do know he's mine, and whispering isn't going to change it.

"Pathetic?" I stalk up to them. "You wanna know what's really pathetic? Your lives are so damn empty you have to fill them up with what's happening in mine."

A dual volley of "You bitch," and "How dare you?" shoots from them. But, right now, I'm beyond them hurting me anymore. I've given them that too many times. Instead, I give them a bright, wide smile when they walk away. Tiny must've heard it all. His normally happy demeanor is flat and stale as day-old coffee. He doesn't flirt, suggest, or hint, just takes my order and delivers the drinks.

Bree's on the bench and waiting for me. The pink of her jacket matches the pink in her cheeks and nose from the cold. Few things can warm her up quicker than what I'm carrying, both in the Mugz-n-Chugz cup, and in my heart. I drop on one knee, holding the cup up like Alex had offered the drinks at the dance, a holy chalice.

"Is that chai latte?" She blinks, her pink glitter eyeshadow winking light back at me.

"Extra whipping cream and cinnamon," I add.

"Gimme that." Chai sloshes in the paper cup when she grabs it. Steam curls through the hole, reaching her nose, and she inhales. The sniff is followed by a long sip. "Oh, yummy." Then she lifts a perfectly penciled eyebrow. "What has you in a chai-buying mood?"

"Oh, you know, plenty of sleep, Mom made me an awesome breakfast..."

Another sip. "And...?"

"And I may have a boyfriend." I wish I could keep the smile off my face. It would be easier to joke around if I didn't look like a total fool for Alex. And it's easier to be excited when I don't think about Daniel.

"Yes!" She thrusts a fist into the air and jumps up. Heads swivel our way, and a light goes on in Bree's eyes. The mischief kind of light I know is bringing a public embarrassment my way. Her skirt flips up and shows way too much thigh before gravity yanks it back down when she jumps up onto the Bree Bench.

"What are you doing?" I flick a quick glance around the quad. "Get down before someone thinks I'm worshipping you."

"Honey, you already do," she teases. Then she stands straight, cupping one hand by her mouth, and shouts, "Attention, Shelley High Ravens! Alex Franks is off limits! My friend Emma –"

I yank the chai cup from her hand.

"What the hell?" she huffs, then jumps down to the walkway again. "If it's official, then the whole school should know."

"Maybe he wants to perpetuate gossip," I suggest. God knows it's flying around.

"Whatever." Bree snatches the cup and guzzles her tea. "That boy's been into you since day one."

"So you've said." Grabbing her by the elbow brings no complaint. She's too busy sucking down the sugary sweet tea. I drag her toward the door. Before stepping inside, I chuck my coffee cup into the garbage.

"What are you lovebirds up to tonight?"

"Um…" Does she know about the accident? His injuries? It's not my place to tell her about Alex's weekly treatments. Heck, I've just learned about them myself. "He's fighting a relapse of whatever he had last week. His dad's keeping him home tonight."

"Bummer."

Tell me about it.

The morning passes in a long slow drag of painful clarity. Days of skating by and daydreaming and worrying about Alex have me way behind. Fighting hand cramps, I type notes into my laptop one finger at a time, ask questions, fight to get caught up. The Ugly Room and my gym class are a welcome break from the thinking marathon. Nothing the harpy squad says can touch me – they already tried. The haunting echoes on the catwalk still scrape my nerves raw, but in minutes I'm past them.

I check my cell phone at lunch, hoping for a text from Alex. Nothing. Does the booster and shot make him too sick to text? Does it knock him out completely? Whatever the case is, I don't hear from Alex the rest of the day. Somehow, being his girlfriend seems tainted, being at school without him.

"What's up for you tonight?" Bree asks me at my locker. "Nice door, by the way – is that new?"

"Nothing," I say, stuffing my backpack one-handed. "And yes."

"Care to clarify that?"

"Nothing's up tonight, and yes, it is a new locker door. Alex ordered it for me."

"Wow." Bree drags out the "ohhh," and I know something sassy is coming next. "Most guys just give their girlfriends their class rings. Maybe a necklace. Yours gets you a new locker door. How romantic."

"Actually, the note accompanying it was very romantic." I hunt on my top shelf and can't find it. It's not in the clutter in the main section either. "He had the new door installed Monday morning because he couldn't be here to open the old locker for me." I struggle into my backpack one-handed. "I thought it was very sweet."

"It is when you say it like that." Bree's phone warbles some Top Forty tune in her purse. She pulls it out, flips it open and has a really short conversation. "OK. That was Jason. We're going to DarkHouse tomorrow night. You're bringing Lover Boy."

DarkHouse. The busiest teen hot spot in the West Michigan area. Also the place with the worst reputation. Drug raids in the parking lot. A stabbing. One guy was mugged. Another went missing. I'd have to lie to my parents – there's no way they'd let me go to the scene where one of the guys disappeared from last spring.

"Well, thanks for informing me." I roll my eyes, and check my phone again. Still no text. "I'm not sure Alex'll be up to it."

"He'll just have to be. He looked great on Saturday after being sick on Friday."

"OK, OK. You're so bossy!" Her curtain of hair swishes, and she stumbles a little when I nudge her from behind.

"What was that for?" Bree snaps, brown eyes wide when she whips around.

"I don't know... You're being so pushy I figured it was OK to push you too."

She shakes her head, mouths, "Good one," then flags down

her mom's car. "Wanna spend the weekend at my house? Then you wouldn't have to try sneaking out on Saturday..."

Bree knows my mother well. The lure of DarkHouse, with Alex, is huge. Not just because most of Shelley High goes there. Because I want to be wrapped in his arms, buried in darkness and drenched in rhythm. DarkHouse is a cement square, with blacked-out windows and horrid, rancid green neon signs outside. Inside it's all black, floors, walls, chairs – everything – and lit with black light so anything light, white, or acid-washed glows. And Bree's hair. Something about the bleach she uses does it.

"What they don't know won't hurt them..." she urges.

Sneaking, lying by omission, and drowning in Alex...

"OK, fine. You win!"

"About time you just cave and let me have my way."

"Where's the fun in that?" I wink and wave to her mom when she pulls up to the curb. "I have to keep my arguing skills sharp."

"It wouldn't hurt you to just be agreeable every now and then." She opens the passenger side door and sits. "See you tonight! Bring clothes for two days."

I wave, then watch them pull away from the curb. Bree's the best, but I can't believe how easily she railroads me. Alex knows how to push my buttons at a distance, Bree knows how to push them and wring a tune from me. Yes, yes, yes, and suddenly I'm roped into going to the biggest nightclub in White River with my new boyfriend.

Hopefully, he's up to the challenge.

The factory setting ringtone on my phone wakes me in the middle of the night. I roll off Bree's trundle bed, wade on hands and knees through a deluge of clothes and shoes and accessories toward the outlet. My right hand aches, I'm so fuzzy from sleep it takes a moment for my brain to catch up and realise it hurts because it's broken and I'm crawling on it. I grab the phone, snap it open and whisper harshly, "Hello?"

The alarm clock above me reads 1.00am. My foggy brain and dead-weight body agree.

"Hey!" Surprise kicks Alex's voice up a notch. His voice has the same effect on my heart rate. "Um... You caught me off guard. I thought your phone would be off and I was going to leave you a voicemail for the morning."

"Aw. That's so sweet." Waking and hearing Alex's voice... It is very sweet now and would've been a wonderful surprise. Bree's snores choke off and I shoot a glance at her bed. She rolls over, her teddy bear in a stranglehold, and mumbling in her sleep. "I'm glad you called."

"You are?" I'm sure the scar is tugging his left eye from the smile I hear in his voice. "Me, too, I... missed seeing you today."

"Technically it's tomorrow now."

His laughter is as warm and cozy as the quilts I was under. "You are picky and persistent. OK, so I missed you yesterday."

"Then let's not let that happen today. Bree and Jason want us to go out with them tonight."

"Where?" A quizzical and mistrusting tone darkens his voice. "DarkHouse."

"Really?" The mistrust plummets to dislike. "I'm not fond of the nightclub scene, Emma. Bad things happened there." He's silent a moment, and makes a decision. "I'll go. Someone has to be your bodyguard."

"Mm. Guarding my body – I like the sound of that. I'll text you when I know more, OK?"

"Definitely."

"Sweet dreams, Alex."

"They're always about you." And he disconnects the phone. Alex has been the lead character in every dream I've had since I met him. Mine have all been nightmares. Just once I'd like to look at Alex and see him the way he sees me, a waking dream, the person you hoped for, but never believed was real or alive.

Shutting off the phone this time, I crawl back through the remnants of Bree's Pick Emma's Outfit marathon, and then climb under the blankets. Looking down, I see the empty spot at the end of the bed where Renfield would be sleeping if I were at home. Sure, he can be rotten – I still miss him.

Despite Bree's snores and the lump in the mattress from the support bar underneath, I fall back to sleep. Dreamless. No graveyards, no dead boyfriends, and no white cats.

A line of people stretches at least a third of the way down the city block. Faces turn toward the building, hands coming up to shield profiles that might be seen in the glare of headlights. The reaction affects at least half of them, twitching and turning every time a car drives past. Which, being in the downtown district, is quite often. How many kids are here without their parents' permission, dreading the sight of a familiar car? How many are waiting in line, saving a spot for their significant other?

That would be me.

"Where is he?" Bree asks, her jaw chattering in the cold. Jason Weller unzips his neon green hoodie and invites Bree inside with him. A flash of a genuine emotion crosses her face, and it's obvious that she *likes him,* likes him. She backs into Jason's jacket and shivers in his arms. "You told Lover Boy 9 o'clock, right?"

"For the third time, Bree. Yes, I told him to meet us here at 9pm."

"Maybe he doesn't know how to get here," Jason suggests.

"Everybody knows how to get to DarkHouse," Bree says, then executes a spin inside the jacket and buries her face in his neck.

"Jeezus, woman!" Poor Jason's eyes go wide as coffee mugs. "You're freezing."

"Duh." Bree squirms closer, and Jason wraps his arms around her. The emotion on his face isn't a flash, but a slow build to something deep, and much warmer than the West Michigan night.

"If she'd just wear something bigger," I nag, "than that miniskirt and flimsy blouse..."

Sure, the black skirt and tank top with the white lace overlay will look amazing under black light... I missed out on the style versus substance gene. Chilly air bites into my face and hands, but only nibbles elsewhere. My jeans, tank top, and clingy white thermal hoodie might not be sexy, but I'm not freezing my butt off either.

"Well, look who it is," Jason says, inclining his head behind me.

I spin. Alex saunters up along the line of people fading into obscurity around the corner. Tall, unbelievably gorgeous in jeans, a black T-shirt and a white knit hoodie – hood up, sleeves down. His eyes reach me, and the same flicker of amazement washes his features, then the smile tugs at his scars. Girls up and down the line turn to him, their boobs lifting and tracking, like indicators on radar.

"Hey, Jason," Alex says, with a guy-to-guy nod; then adds, "Hi, Bree."

"Hi," comes in stereo, one part clear and strong, the other muffled like a voice in a fog.

With pleasantries over, Alex focuses on me.

"Hey," he says. He steps close, electricity dancing across my skin, streaking through me. His skin is a healthy, vital shade, his eyes bright hazel and almost glowing. A gravitational pull hits me when he opens his arms, and invites, "Com'ere."

I slide into his embrace, the last puzzle piece clicking home. I'm vaguely aware of a dozen crestfallen girls, and Bree turning around inside Jason's hoodie again. When Alex slips two fingers under my chin and tilts my face toward his, we could be the only two people on earth.

Taking the invitation, I pop up on my toes and press my lips to his. His little gasp of surprise is a sweet reward. Then things slip past sweet and into intense when he deepens the kiss, parts my lips with his and slides his arms around my back. People watch and I don't care. I slide my left hand into his hood to touch his hair. Alex smiles against my mouth, and kisses me one more time.

"Yep," says Bree. "It's official."

"You guys really only known each other a couple weeks?" Jason asks.

"Yeah." Alex winks, and says, "We're just getting started."

He twirls me around and tucks me back-to-front in his arms. The chilly, breezy night takes on a magical air as if nothing can touch us. We walk as one group in the long line, and finally meet the doorman. He's as tall and wide as a door, with brutally short hair and a bull ring in his nose.

"IDs," he grunts.

The four of us are proclaimed LightBringers, and given white wristbands. DarkBringers are the twenty-one-and-over crowd and get black wristbands. Once past the doors, DarkHouse earns its name. When the interior is black, and lit with black light, everything loses dimension. Only the bar, the sunken poolroom in the far corner and the bathrooms on the opposite wall are lit with normal light. The bar's lighting is recessed, hidden behind the bottles of alcohol or tucked into overhead lights.

Music pumps from speakers, the bass deep and reaching into my chest. Alex pulls me tighter to him, no air left between us, taking his bodyguard duty very seriously, as we follow Jason deeper into DarkHouse. The guys find us a table close to the pool tables, then leave to hunt down a waitress or fight the crowd at the bar for drinks.

"He is so into you!" Bree shouts over the music.

"Amazing, isn't it?" I yell back.

"Blazing?" she yells back, misunderstanding me. "He is hot…"

I shake my head and shout, "Never mind."

She gives me a smile and a thumbs-up. No one wants to think in DarkHouse – too much dimly lit eye candy to entertain heavy thought. Beyond the edge of our table, DarkHouse becomes a churning cauldron of light and shadow. Shirts. Shoes. Occasionally, gloves. Acid-washed jeans. Alex looms into view, the shadows within his hood making him look like a ghoul as he glides through the crowd. Jason's annoyingly green hoodie isn't far behind.

They tuck into the seats, both smelling of hot skin, warm cologne, and the incense pumped into the air system. Added to Alex's smell of leather, it's… exciting.

The guys lean over the table, talking loudly. Jason shoots me a quick look, then pats Alex on the shoulder. Even I can hear Jason say, "Awesome, man!"

Alex sinks to the seat beside me, trailing his fingers along my arms. I don't know if he's aware of the tingles he's causing, but I feel like a wind-up toy being cranked, and cranked again. When he pushes my hair from my ear, his breath sends hot shivers down me. "He asked what was going on. I told him you were off the market."

I love the sound of it, but have to tease. "Staking claim, huh?"

"Wait till Monday," he says.

The hot shivers spread inward when he kisses my neck, just below my ear, and traces lingering kisses down to the neckline of my shirt. I'm going to go nuclear soon, bounce off the walls and land in his lap.

Eventually, the DJ has mercy and plays a slow set. Alex weaves with innate grace through the empty spaces toward center floor. I surrender to the pull between us, and wrap my arms around him. Heat builds, dancing with the electricity he puts off like a Tesla coil. One hand plants firmly on my hip, the other strokes my hair. His skin is warm, heartbeat drumming in my ear. I could live forever in this dance. But eventually the set ends, and the tempo picks up again.

Back at the tables, Jason motions for Alex to meet him over the table, then shouts loud enough I can hear him anyway. "Wanna shoot some pool?"

Alex replies, "Sure!"

"The girls can try, too. We'll play doubles."

Try? The girls *can try*? Daniel and I spent almost every weekend at the bowling alley just to play pool. His cousin Gavin worked at Starlight Lanes and let us play for free. Jason saying I can try to play was like saying a cat can try to scratch you. Jason takes Bree's hand and that same flash of real emotion touches her face.

I'm sure when Alex laces his fingers in mine, I have the same look.

We follow behind the guys and down into the normally lit poolroom. Half-walls cordon it off from the rest of the club, and baffles come down from the ceiling, leaving four-foot window-like openings into DarkHouse. The separating affect also cancels some of the noise and makes conversation possible.

"You need help picking a cue?" Jason asks.

"No." OK, so it came out a little snotty. He doesn't know who he's patronizing. With Bree's help, we twist my hair into a swift, messy bun – knowing full-well Alex will just pull it out, but when I get serious, the hair has to go up. I walk to the rack of pool sticks, test a few, and choose one with decent balance and weight to it. "Who's breaking?"

"Depends on who's racking," Alex says.

"You rack 'em, we crack 'em." Jason cavalierly takes a cue from the wall and stands by Bree.

Alex drops quarters into the table, then puts the colored balls on the green felt top. My brace hinders making a tight rack. He helps me align them in the triangle, then slides behind me, running his fingers down my arms to my hands. Every muscle in my body tenses, and I think my heart rate races past healthy levels. The rocking motion he uses brings flames to my cheeks.

"Helping because of the brace," he says, but the warmth from his legs against mine says he's willing to help with a lot more.

Jason's break is sloppy, the white cue ball eventually knocking in a solid and a stripe. "Choose," he says and points at me. Bree watches me pace the table perimeter, knowing my game and how much trouble they're in. The smile on her face when I choose solids says she's good with it, too. Ball after ball smacks the back of the pocket and drops into the tracks underneath. Jason starts fidgeting. Alex leans back against a post.

With only one solid ball left, I miss a pocket.

"Jeezus," Jason groans. "You didn't tell me you're a pool shark."

"Oh, yeah!" comes an annoying, familiar voice from the steps. "Emma's got skills when it comes to playing with balls."

Josh Mason strides up to the table. He's wearing a sad attempt at Alex's style of clothes, only all in shades of ugly: dark jeans, red shirt, off-white hoodie – hood down, cuffs up and the neckline showing his ugly red chest hair. Alex bristles, fingers tightening around the pool cue. Alex is around the table in an instant and standing beside me.

"Apologize," Alex says in a growl.

"It's OK," I say, sliding closer to my "guard dog" as Josh had called him. "Josh is just jealous because I'm playing with you, and he's used to me busting his balls."

Josh's cheeks flush with angry spots of red. "You are such a bitch, Emma. I don't know why I bothered."

"Why you bothered to what?" I retort. Alex strong-arms me, pushing me behind himself. Trying to move him is like fighting with an oak tree. "Why you didn't bother to be decent? Didn't bother to respect me? Didn't bother to catch your best friend when he fell?"

"Screw you, Gentry!" he barks and stomps closer. He's chest-to-chest with Alex now and pushing to get past him. Josh pokes a callused finger at my face. "You have no idea what I did that day!"

"You two fought. I went for help. I came back just as

Daniel fell." I drop my voice, acidly spewing the truth I'd kept bottled for months. "And you let him."

Josh's hand pops up, nearly smacking Alex. Alex's muscles tense in front of me and I know he's going to do something, use one of his martial arts moves on Josh. The redhead stumbles back a step when Alex shoves him and Alex adjusts his stance. I step aside, watching Josh warily. He's a contained storm, ready to destroy.

"You let him fall, too," Josh says, spittle flying from his lips.

It's too much. *How dare he?* The barb hits my heart as Josh intended. I snake around Alex, and slam my braced right hand into Josh's face. I feel the crack, and hear it too. White-hot pain flares in my hand and I know I've rebroken it. Josh slams into the pool table behind him, eyes glazed and mouth dangling open. He recovers quickly, focusing a scathing glare on me.

I add, "Go to hell, Josh Mason."

"I'm already there. Been there since the day I met you!"

Moving my fingers in the brace rekindles all the hell I'd put there two weeks ago. I wince, and draw my hand to my chest. Josh lunges forward and Alex reacts. He grabs a fistful of Josh's hoodie, and sweeps his feet out from under him. The jerk drops hard on his rear, spitting cusswords and dribbling blood from the lip I split open again.

Bree swears, calling Josh every horrid name possible. Jason has her hand and pulls her back.

Bouncers pour down the stairs. The biggest one hauls Josh up from the floor and traps him in a bear hug. Josh, struggling and shouting nasty cusswords, digs in his heels as the bouncer drags him backward toward the rear exit. Foul words fly from Bree, Jason restraining her while two other burly guys step between us. I stand still in shock. Josh said *I* let Daniel fall. He was already over the railing, I couldn't have helped him, but God – the pain and guilt geyser up anyway.

The bull ring guy from the door crosses his arms and says in a solemn, seen-it-too-many-times voice, "You four are gonna have to leave."

Bouncers flank our exit from DarkHouse, and a waitress hands a bag of ice to me for my hand. On the way to the parking lot, Jason mutters, "That guy likes to ruin nights."

"And ruin lives," I huff.

The pain is undercutting my usual attitude, cleaving away my calm and manners. I cling to Alex and fight tears. Josh's hateful words keep repeating through my mind, and I know if he was here, I'd punch him again, then kick him when he was down.

At Jason's beat-up Ford Bronco, Alex releases my hair from the bun, pulling his fingers through the blond strands, before pressing a kiss to my lips. The sight of Alex's car and knowing he's leaving somehow scrapes me raw. How could I have come to need him so quickly, just like my hand needs the brace to keep it steady? "Go to the clinic," he says, "and get your hand taken care of."

"Yessir," I pout. The last thing I want after sneaking out, and lying by omission to do it, is to call my mom. Telling her I rebroke my hand – by punching Daniel's former best friend in the nightclub I wasn't supposed to visit – is going to send her over the deep end. I'm not even sure what punishment she'll mete out – it's sure to be big, nasty and thorny.

"Monday will be better," he promises.

"I'm going to hold you to that."

Chapter Twenty

"A plaster cast?" Bree asks, eyeing the new decoration on my right arm with pity.

"Yeah." I glance at the hot pink plaster encasing my right hand, then across the quad. Scudding clouds cast choppy darkness on the ground. People kept to the shadows beneath the catwalk, faces turned skyward, waiting. "Apparently, re-breaking your hand while it's in an immobiliser is a bad thing."

"Considering the silence since we dropped you off," she says and sips her chai, "I'm guessing you're grounded?"

"Totally." A far-off rumble promises to deliver on the thunderstorm the weatherman forecast this morning. "Within an inch of my life, as my mom put it. No cell phone, no overnights, no homework at your house. Just school and home until Thanksgiving."

A delicate shudder ruffles Bree's denim and white outfit. "Harsh."

"More like slow murder."

"She didn't take into consideration that Josh is a Class A asshole and deserved to get punched?"

"Oddly enough…" I pause and let out a sigh when I see

Alex at the walk-up window of Mugz-n-Chugz. "The cast and me punching Josh isn't why I'm grounded. Alex showed up at the clinic and explained how horrid Josh was. Mom's pissed because we went to DarkHouse."

"There goes next weekend's plans." She gives me a wink. We both knew there was a high possibility of me getting grounded – we went anyway. Next weekend was never an option. "So they're OK with the new boyfriend, and the fact that he was there at DarkHouse, too?"

"Thanks to Alex…" I wave when he leaves Tiny's walk-up window. "My parents think he was there to protect me."

"Oh, sure." An Olympic eye-roll flashes silvery eyeshadow at me. "That slow dance, with his hands all up in your hair and grazing your butt was for protection…"

"Of course it was," Alex agrees, appearing from Mugz-n-Chugz, his long fingers holding out a cup I know has breve in it. Thanking him silently, I take a long sip. "Best way to guard her body," he continues with a devilish wink, "was to keep a firm grip on it. Look what happened when I let go of her for a couple of minutes. She slugs Joshhole."

Bree bursts into giggles at the combination of Josh's name with the way he was behaving. I don't get a chance to giggle. Alex takes my coffee, hands it to Bree, slips an arm behind my back, and drags me to him.

"There are rules about PDAs," Bree warns.

Public displays of affection have earned suspensions at Shelley High before. Alex chuffs a breath between a laugh and a snort, like silly school rules don't affect him, and lifts me off my feet. Bright pink cast trapped between us and my shoes brushing he tops of his, Alex back-walks to the curb where he steps down into the street. The slide down his body and back onto my feet is slow, his eyes locked on mine.

Tingles course my skin, and tickle my lips when he tips his face within kissing distance.

My cast is wedged between our hearts, and I don't mind. Close isn't enough with Alex. I lean up, a jolt of energy coursing through me when I press my mouth to his and nip his bottom lip. Pressure squeezes the air from my lungs when a sound between a sigh and a groan escapes Alex, and he crushes me to him.

Then my good mood chokes and dies on the fog of car exhaust.

A roaring engine precedes Josh's slur about whores and payment. Alex breaks our kiss, sends a glare in Josh's direction, and whispers, "Best revenge is a better boyfriend."

"Then I'm getting the best revenge of all."

Standing close to Alex, I know electrical energy when I feel it. When the hair on my arms and neck stands up, I know it's seconds before the storm hits. Then lightning rips down into the quad, and a clap of thunder resounds in the gray skies.

"We need to go in," I say. "We'll get soaked."

And the rain starts. By the time we've made it to the shelter of the side door, the sky tears open and rain sheets down in earnest. Alex opens the door and ushers me in. The halls teem, people pushing, jostling and shouting. Then life grinds to a halt, and I can feel all eyes on us as we walk into the main hall, hand-in-hand. Alex eats it up, looping an arm over my shoulders and pulling me to his side. He nods at guys too busy staring to nod back, and ignores the petulant lip-puffing pouts from the girls.

"By the way," he says, "my dad called the school and insisted my schedule get changed."

"What?" I hate the note of panic in my voice. "Why?"

"He didn't feel classes with Josh," his tone is a perfect mockery of his dad's, "would be good for my academic career."

"Oh," is all I manage around the sinking feeling in my gut. Will we have lunch together? What about Dune Eco? I'll be alone with Josh in that class. My jaw clenches, and my fingers wiggle – then the fresh hell in my hand reminds me not to punch people... for a while.

"Nice locker," Alex says, a hint of teasing elevating his voice.

"You should know – you bought it. Did you also set the combination for the date we met?"

The white scar near his eye flexes when he bats his eyelashes and makes an innocent face. "Who? Me?"

"Yes," I poke him with the index finger not trapped in a cast. "You."

"Are you always so persistent?"

"Yep."

"Well, Ms Persistence." He unclips the barrette holding my hair back, then runs his long fingers through the blond strands. "I'll see you at lunch."

"Sounds great."

Mrs Johnson's Trig class is more of a pain than last week. Shockingly, people want to sign my hot pink cast, and Mrs Johnson seems to have caved and purchased hearing aids. She narrows her eyes at my cast, *tsks* through her teeth. Her shoulder blades move sharply under her thick sweater, while she covers the white board with ridiculously tough equations.

Fifteen problems on the board later and the first cell phone goes off.

"Sayer Thomas," she says without turning around, "put that phone on my desk."

A collective gasp runs around the room, followed by furtive movements and sounds. Lots of people looking in their laps, none of them smiling, all of them turning off their phones. The rest of the class passes in a stunned, well-behaved silence. Second hour is taken up with more thunder, rain lashing the windows and a movie to round out our study of Gothic literature. How many times can I stand to watch *Dracula* in a week? The flickering light reflects from the surface of my cast and eventually lulls me to a doze. Mr Hansen wakes me near the end, nudging me.

"Painkillers can make you drowsy," he says, then pats me on the back.

The entire building's lights flicker when I hit the second-floor hall on my way to the catwalk between the main building and the gym complex. I brace myself for a run-in with Daniel's ghost, or Josh's fiery other who haunted my dream. Instead I see Alex, standing halfway between the catwalk doors and the stairs, an obvious debate raging in him by his tense expression.

"Hey," I say, hurrying up to him.

What's wrong with him? The graveyard and deer are the only times I've seen him so unsettled.

"That's my line," he says, voice husky, but eyes not quite in the moment.

"What's the matter?" The urge to touch him burns in me. His crossed arms hint it wouldn't be welcome. "Lost?"

"Not really. I know where I need to go, I just don't like the options to get there."

"Where's your next class?"

"I have weight training." He casts a nervous glance at the doors. "I just... don't like the idea of that walkway."

"Don't be silly." I offer my left hand. "I walk it every day, and it's way better than getting soaked in the downpour."

Everything in him tilts off-center, away from the lightning flashing outside. Then he threads his fingers through mine, and nods.

"Do you have a fear of heights or something?" I ask. Valid question, seeing as I'm dating him now.

"I never did before..." The doors wheeze inward, opening onto the catwalk, a tunnel through the storm. Wind and water rage on either side. "But this doesn't feel right."

Tension heightens through his fingers where they wrap around my hand. Storm winds buffet the tunnel, and the floor shimmies a little under our feet. At each end, the flexible buffer zones give with the force of the gust. The tension in Alex's fingers increase to something closer to vise-grip than human. He stops moving and I have to pull to make him take a step.

"Come on, Alex," I huff and tug again. "What's the matter with you?"

"I'm OK," he whispers.

No, he's not. I can see the raw, damaged boy surfacing in him, pressing under his scars. We walk past a panel of glass, rain streaming down, and the sense of wrong often whispering from him turns to a shout.

"Oh my God, Em." Alex stops dead, voice gone guttural and grip gone way too tight.

"What?"

"Something's wrong..." Alex's face is ashen, his hand paws at his chest. What's the matter with him? His gaze locks on the plummeting water. His hand fists in his hoodie, right over his heart, like he's trying to stop it. "Emma, help me."

"I'm right here." I stroke his arm with my fingers. "You're fine."

"No, I'm not." Wind gusts shove against the glass walkway, and the catwalk shakes once. Alex's muscles clench, then his arms fly out like he's fighting for balance. "Oh God! I'm gonna fall!"

I catch his hand, and he jerks it away. His infectious panic claws at my chest, clenches around my throat. Alex sends a confused, terrified glance at me, but seeing me makes it worse. His eyebrows shoot up, his mouth stretches in a silent scream and Alex staggers backward, arms flailing.

Daniel's last moments flash in my mind. If it wasn't for the location and the physical differences between Alex and him, I'd swear I was watching Daniel fall to his death again.

My heart rate ratchets up. Tears tighten my throat.

How can this be happening? I shake my head, letting the tears fall. It's a losing battle when I'm trying to keep two people's sanity. If I were alone, I'd fall apart. I reach for Alex again, his flinch only making my chest ache worse.

"God. Don't look at me!" He throws a hand over his eyes and rams his back into the brace between panes of glass. "I'm falling and all I see is your face!"

"You are not." Memories run in a loop behind my eyes, twisting my heart until I think it's going to break. Still, I run to his side and peel the fingers from his eyes. "Listen to me. You're on the catwalk, having a panic attack or delusion or something."

"It's real!" he shouts. "It's REAL! I'm falling and dying and I see your face."

His words are a pure echo of the hell I'm feeling inside. My heart cracks, the ache shooting through me when he curls into a fetal position. His entire body jerks, a grunt escapes him like it was driven from his lungs in a collision. The door at the far side opens. I don't look away from Alex. Even a glance to the side rips at my heart, and there's so little left. When voices bounce our way, I scream for help.

"Falling and dying and I see your face."

"You are *not*, Alex." My voice breaks. But Daniel did. And his eyes stayed riveted on me until he struck the cement below.

"Red in my eyes when the lights went out." He scrubs at his face with his sweater, like he's trying to wipe something from his eyes, and the zipper scratches his forehead.

The moment cuts like a double-edged knife; it hurts to see him reduced this way, hurts hearing what I hear and knowing what I saw once already. I shake my head, my cast pushing back against the ache in my chest. This can't be happening.

Carpet tugs at my knees when I kneel in front of him. I'm struggling to hold on – he pitched over the edge and fell, too far gone to reach now. Touch is reassuring, I've heard, and I need it as much as he does. I rest a hand on his arm. His fingers search for mine, clench around them.

"You were wearing your favorite white tank top." He shakes his head. "And my red hoodie."

He might as well rip my heart out and throw it on the carpet. Only three people would remember what I wore that night, I think wildly. One is dead, the other isn't here.

"I'm wearing your blue hoodie."

"I know," he moans.

He's calming down, totally confused still, but I think the worst is over. I wish it was for me. The full force of what he went through slams into me. My throat hurts enough to have screamed Daniel's name again, my heart hurts enough to have lost him again. Because, in a horridly impossible way, I think I just did.

Footsteps pound and bounce around us when the paramedic and school nurse rush up. They crouch to either side of us, hands hovering.

"You have to let him go, hon," the medic says, her voice calm and so out of place.

Alex's fingers convulse around mine, and I wince. He isn't letting go.

"Son, you've got to loosen up." She pries his fingers from mine and a piteous wail comes out of him. "Emergizer!" he whimpers when they force him to stretch out on the floor. "Emergizer, don't leave!"

The words are a sledgehammer to my chest. How does he know that name? Only one person ever called me that. *Only one.* My throat cinches tight on a wail of my own. Mind reeling, I scoot out of his reach.

Questions rocket around from the emergency responders and bounce off Alex and me. Neither of us can muster a response.

"What happened?"

"What caused this?"

"Did he fall?"

I cover my mouth and ease back, afraid of the answers. They don't need to know he's delusional. He'd have to be to see Daniel's death through Daniel's eyes. And those words... that nickname...

They were Daniel's last words to me before he fell and died.

I slump to the window and watch in a numb state of shock as the medic runs the list of questions on a confused Alex. He glances at me, tears glistening in his Daniel eye, and a cut on his forehead exactly where Daniel's skull had split. Time bleeds into nothing, movements blurring in the catwalk and in my head. The paramedic coaxes Alex to his feet, and the nurse pulls me to mine.

When the medic and Alex pass the doors, my heart fractures, and the tears come.

"What happened back there?" the nurse asks.

"I'm not sure," I mutter. "I think he has a fear of falling…"

A lie is so much better than the truth.

Alex Franks relived Daniel's death.

Chapter Twenty-One

"No, I'm not fine," I grumble at the nurse. "And, no I do not want you calling my mom. I just want see if Alex is OK."

"You can't right now." Her dark curly hair swishes when she packs away some gauze in the white cabinet on the wall.

"Can't as in not capable?" So I'm cranky. I'm emotionally fried potato chip crisp and don't want someone crushing what's left of me. "Because I can walk just fine."

"No. *Can't*," she stresses, "because his father is with him and insisted on no visitors."

Oh God. "His father?" I echo. My stomach knots into a nauseous tangle. He broke bones in my hand just at the mention of Alex being my friend. If he knows I was with Alex, that we've been together the past week... what will he do? "Please tell me my name is being kept out of it."

"Well." She fidgets at her desk. "I'm not sure."

"Can you check? Please?" She casts a concerned look at me. I don't say anything, don't move, but I let my focus fall to my cast. Her eyes widen, then she picks up the school phone and dials a number. She walks to the far side of her office, behind a privacy screen. The conversation is hushed and short. "Yes, Emma," she confirms when she comes back. "Your name has been kept out. Now, what's this all about?"

"Two weeks ago, I punched my locker and hurt my hand. Alex told me to go to the doctor. His father was the attending physician at the clinic, only I didn't know who he was. When I mentioned Alex was my friend, he crushed my hand, breaking the hairline fractures." She sucks in a little gasp. "My mom filed a complaint, and threatened a lawsuit."

"Are you afraid he'll hurt you again because of this?"

"I don't ever have to see him again. I'm worried what he might do to Alex if he thinks I'm involved."

Her curls slide when she nods brusquely. She strides out of the office completely, dialing the phone as she goes. Left alone, I worry the paper on the examining table to confetti, and agonize about Alex. What *happened* to him up on the catwalk? Why is he channeling Daniel's behaviors, his words, and his death? My heart clenches in my chest, and hurt sucks the air from my lungs. My brain is running on a treadmill of razorblades, every thought and question as cutting and painful as the next.

Will I ever be free of this pain?

The nurse returns, an all-business expression on her square face.

"Alex will be going home," she says. "And seeing as you are refusing treatment, and me calling your parents, I'm sending you back to class."

The bell for the end of fourth hour rings. After stopping at my locker for my afternoon books, I head up to the sciences wing and Mr LaRue's Dune Ecology class.

Josh Mason sits in his normal seat when I walk in. He stiffens, and gazes snap from him to me and back. Seems the gossip chain has been working just fine, and in my favor for once. Everyone knows I broke my hand on Josh's puffy black-and-blue face. The flickering light of the storm outside splashes on the dune grass blades in the pot at the end of Mr LaRue's big lab table. I stand there, even after the bell rings, then deliberately run the pad of my thumb of my right hand down the blade.

Heat flares across my skin, red appears in the cut. I pinch my finger over it, trapping the blood. Rather than sit in my usual seat, I walk to the far side of the room, and take the seat behind Asia Foley. There, beneath the privacy of my desk, I guide the fat drops to my pink cast, and draw a heart in blood, over where the broken heart lives in the skin of my wrist.

I blot the remaining blood, and then organize my books and papers. Asia turns around during roll call, and says in a conspiratorial whisper, "Next time you punch that jerk, take a video."

"Not a bad idea," I say. Actually it's an awful idea, but she's being nice.

"I heard about the catwalk," she says. "Alex going to be OK?"

Her pretty brown face softens in lines of concern, long curly eyelashes sweeping over light brown eyes when she blinks.

"I hope so."

Mr LaRue closes the attendance book, and digs around in his desk. I take the opportunity to ask Asia if she has any clear nail polish. She nods, rummages around in her bag, and then slides a bottle of polish over my Dune Eco book.

Only half-watching Mr LaRue, I shake the bottle and paint over the bloody heart on my cast. When he passes out paperwork on dune erosion, the bottle makes a return trip to its owner.

After our teacher calls the class to order, I zone out, batting around pieces of the Daniel-Alex puzzle until my head hurts. The puzzle pieces don't fit together, or make anything pretty. None of it makes sense. Not in the real world. It's almost like Daniel's haunting me through Alex. Or he's attacking me for liking Alex, and using Alex as the weapon of my heart's destruction.

Mrs Ransom offers me a ride home, rather than let me walk alone in the late fall storm. I droop against the back seat, left hand on my head, pushing back against the ache pounding there. Bree's not sitting safety-belt safe in her seat while we idle curbside. She's turned sideways looking at me with sad eyes, and downturned lips.

"I heard about the catwalk," she says.

"You and the rest of Shelley High." I rub one temple.

"He'll be OK, Em." She reaches into the back seat and pats my leg and then fastens her seatbelt. "Who knows what kind of accident he had. Maybe this is just a residual effect..."

I think she's grasping at straws. Her mother seems to think it's a fun game.

"What accident?" her mom asks. She's dressed in a smart business suit, and is as well put-together as Bree. "What boy?"

"Alex Franks," Bree answers.

"The boy from your kindergarten class?"

"Yeah."

"I heard at church that he was nearly crushed to death in an accident in his father's lab. Lots of internal damage. If it weren't for his father, he would've died."

He did die, I think, *for a few minutes.*

"See," Bree says. "He's survived worse."

"And I suppose," her mom continues, "head trauma – or lack of oxygen – might cause lingering effects."

Somehow, it's not as comforting as the Ransom women think. I "mm-hm" politely, try for a smile and fall short. I let the false expression bleed off and return to mulling over what happened on the catwalk until Mrs Ransom pulls into our driveway.

"Thank you for the ride, Mrs Ransom."

"Anytime, Em."

"See ya tomorrow, B." I pull my jacket up over Alex's hoodie, pray for my backpack to stay dry and then hurtle for the porch door. The house already smells like roast beef when I burst in.

"Wipe your shoes," Mom calls from the kitchen – then adds, "Hi, Alex."

"He's not here, Mom."

Silence. I struggle out of my backpack, and shake the water from it like I wish I could shake today from me. Drops of water hit Renfield, and he growls and stabs me with one of his cat glares. Mom peeks from the kitchen doorway. "He's not here?"

"No. He's… not feeling well."

"Well," she says, "That's a shame. Need help with homework?"

"No. Mostly reading today. Just a few trig problems online."

Doesn't matter. I can't focus. I try, but I can't wipe the images of my two boyfriends out of my mind. Daniel fell out of life. Alex fell in his mind. He'd gone past the raw, hollowed-out guy to someplace I couldn't understand or begin to follow. Chills run up my spine, tighten my scalp. How can someone living experience the death of someone else? There's no doubt in my mind Alex lived Daniel's death. He called me by Daniel's nickname, using the exact words Daniel had moments before he died. He mentioned me wearing my favorite white tank top under Daniel's red hoodie.

And possibly the worst thing – red trails in his eyes when the light died. Like the doe two weeks ago, Daniel died with his eyes open and fixed on me. Only Daniel's blood flowed over his eyes, one red streak over his left iris.

Mom breaks through my musing with dinner after hours of me pecking away at the keys of my laptop with my left hand.

My appetite died on the catwalk with Alex's breakdown. Still, I scoop the roast, beans, and potatoes and gravy onto my plate. Dad pokes at his slab of beef, grabs the salt and pepper, and then decides for hot sauce instead.

"So, where'd you say Alex is?" he asks. I know by the slight elevation in his eyebrows he's prodding. But nicely. Mom would've used her filet knife, or maybe her meat cleaver.

"I didn't."

"Oh. Well… He was becoming a fixture around here."

"Maybe tomorrow, Dad." I stab my roast, twisting the fork to watch the tines shred the muscle fibers. My left hand isn't as skilled at random roast destruction, though, and my fork skids and screams across my plate. "Alex wasn't feeling well this afternoon."

I'm not feeling well either. The few forkfuls I manage to chew and swallow slop and stew in my stomach. My head still pounds. And, God help me, there's a weight on my chest I can't get off. I can't breathe with it and I want to cry.

Mom eyes me, a long careful glance. "You aren't catching what he has, are you?"

"I don't know. Maybe." Is crazy catching? I can't think he's completely sane if he's channeling someone else's habits and death.

"And you've hardly eaten your dinner," Mom points out. I nod, and feel the weight of the motion dragging on my face, rocking my head. "Maybe you should have one of your pain pills and go to bed early."

Hopefully painkillers stop heartache. "Maybe you're right."

Mom hops up, and hurries into the kitchen. Beneath Dad's normal layer of silt-fine sawdust, he looks concerned. It's the same expression he had shortly after Daniel died, when they realised I wasn't going to "just get over it". I give him a weak smile, which he returns. When Mom comes back, she has a fat pill on one palm, and a warm cup of milk with vanilla and cinnamon to wash it down.

The pill catches in my throat, not surprising with all the tears I've been fighting today. The sweet creamy milk chases it down and soothes the tightness.

"Thanks, Mom."

"Just get some good rest."

"I'll try."

Renfield races in front of me, a white moving obstacle all the way up the stairs. The crazy cat nearly knitted himself to me, now he looks like he's contemplating it again. *Is it that bad?* I wonder. I refuse to look in a mirror for proof, though. Instead, I indulge in a long, hot bath, then pull on some flannel pajama pants, and a warm hoodie. I don't need to worry about plugging in my cell phone – Mom has it. Street light trickles between the crack in my curtains, and I open them wide before crawling under my fairy quilt.

I'm not sure of the hour when I close my eyes.

I am sure I won't sleep well.

Constant *plink-plink, plink-plink*s sift me little by little out of a heavy sleep. Thoughts are fractured bits of fuzz. I blink as I try to drag the fragments together and become coherent.

I turn toward the window, wondering foggily if bugs are committing suicide on the glass panes before I realise it's November. *Plink-plink!* Where I sit now, it's clear the little noises issue from pebbles hitting my windows. *What the heck?* My muscles feel like sandbags when I stand and shuffle to the windowsill. *Who is throwing rocks at this hour?* Then another thought comes. *What time is it? Are my parents awake?*

Just after midnight according to my clock radio.

The snoring across the hall says my parents are both sleeping.

One story down is Alex Franks. My heart leaps into a sprint, and tears tighten my throat. He's really here, and he's fine. Pebbles from Mom's well-tended flower beds fill one hand. The other hand is raised, wrist cocked back to launch more stones. When he sees me, the wonder lights his face and pulls his full lips into a smile. The hand with the stones waves me to come down.

The horror of earlier today undermines my joy of seeing Alex. I grab a sweatshirt from my closet, then creep down the stairs with Renfield on my heels. Silent dark fills the first floor, eerie in the street light coming through the windows. Suppressing a shudder, I slip on a pair of Dad's slippers and step onto the porch.

Alex climbs the stairs, my heart pounding harder with each step. I want to launch into his arms and trust him to

never let me fall. His breakdown in the catwalk roots me to
the porch floorboards.

"Emma," he says my name with all the reverence of a
prayer. "I'm so sorry about today."

"You really freaked me out."

"I freaked myself out."

The distance between us must be too much for him. Energy tickles over my skin when Alex slides his arms around
me and lifts me into a hug. For a moment, I stiffen, but my
heart needs him like I need air. I soften, and droop against
him, burying my face in the collar of his jacket. He smells
like warmth and Alex. Tingles spill across my face when he
kisses my cheek.

I nuzzle deeper into his collar and whisper, "What happened to you today?"

Muscles stiffen beneath my hands. His embrace tightens
like he's afraid he's going to lose me.

"Red hoodie," he says, an almost absentminded tone
weakening his tenor. "You were wearing this sweatshirt in
my... vision."

"But that's not possible." I was there when it happened.
How could he know anything of that moment?

"I know what I saw, Em." His arms loosen and he places
me back on my feet. "And I know what I felt." He runs his
fingers over my hair where it pours in a blond fall over my
shoulder. "What I still feel."

"What did you see?"

He turns, paces in the weak glow of the porch light. The
light plays on his hair when he takes his hood down and
pushes a hand through the long strands. A new scar, healing
skin and not a scab, cuts across his forehead.

"I've seen you in my dreams since I woke up from surgery,"

he says. "And in a recurring nightmare. I thought that's all they were, until I came to school and saw you. *I saw you*. Can you imagine? God, my heart started thumping, Em, thumping like it knew you. But I didn't. I had no clue who you were.

"The dreams come every night, then I see you every day – and the amazement is still there." He catches his breath, clenches his fists, then continues. "Then today, something happened, and the nightmare came back. Only I was awake through it and you were there, in my head and right in front of me."

His bottom lip trembles and his eyes shine with moisture.

I know before I ask. I need to hear his answer. "What's your nightmare?"

"I'm on the edge of something," he says in a faraway voice, and steps to the edge of the porch. He spins to face me and I'm not sure if he sees me now, or then. "I don't feel right. Like drunk, or something, and mad. Then someone pushes me. I lose my balance as you come running, screaming my name. My last thought is 'I love you' and then I hit bottom. Pain explodes, and is snuffed when blood streaks over my eyes and the lights go out."

"That's… impossible," I whisper. "You don't know what you're saying."

"I do!" He paces back and forth. "Details are so clear. Your hair is down, blowing in the warm breeze. The white lace edge of your tank top peeks out above the zipper of my sweatshirt." He grabs the sleeve of Daniel's hoodie I'd picked from the closet on instinct. "This sweatshirt!"

Alex's hand falls from the sleeve, then flies to his mouth and he shakes his head. A tear rolls down his face. "I told you not to wear that tank top because–"

"I'd be too cold when the sun went down," I finish. Where

is this knowledge coming from? Alex wasn't there, those words weren't his. "But, you didn't say that. Daniel did."

"Daniel?" Disbelief colors his tone, darkens his eyes.

"Yes. You just described – except his thoughts and someone pushing him – the night he died."

"But it's my nightmare," Alex says, hand hitting his chest. "My dreams, and my feelings. They are in *me*."

"That was Daniel's death," I insist. Damn his sad face for making me feel guilty for knowing the truth.

"It's mine. I see it in here." Alex places a finger atop the scar on his temple. "And I feel things here," he says, taking my hand and putting it over his heart. "It doesn't beat for me, Emma. It was never mine. This heart has always been yours."

Tears threaten, moisture filling my nose. I sniff, and swallow against the lump in my throat. "What are you saying?"

He exhales a strangled sob. He releases my hand, and unfurls both of his like he's begging me for something. "That I love you, Emma Gentry. I have since I woke up."

"You can't," I argue. He looks at me like I slapped him. "You hardly know me."

"But I feel like I've known you forever."

"You can't," I repeat, desperate to put distance between me and the beautiful lie Alex Franks turned out to be. He was supposed to be new, and different, and capture my heart all on his own, but he's tainted. He's got Daniel's death in his left eye, Daniel's dying emotions in his heart. I step back until my hand finds the doorknob. "And I can't."

"Emma, please," he begs.

"Go home, Alex. I need to think and I can't do it if you're here reminding me of Daniel."

"Emma!"

I turn the knob, stumble in, and shut the door.

Leave, please. Leave and take Daniel with you.

The door holds me up while I fall apart. I muffle my sobs in the sleeve of my hoodie, until I see the color and remember the night I got it. I rip the zipper down, peel off the red sweatshirt and fling it into the closet. I grab Mom's ratty old gardening jacket and bury my face in it, instead. It smells like roses and tears as I cry.

Why did I have to fall in love with a boy so broken?

Chapter Twenty-Two

There's no relief. I can't outpace the heartache and disbelief haunting my steps, my silent miserable companions in this house of shadows.

I thought I'd escaped the agony of losing Daniel. It just found a new way to break my heart. How will I ever be free of the hurt if Alex is somehow reliving his death? My chest aches and my breath shortens thinking about the look of confusion and pain in Alex's eyes when I told him those memories weren't his. He *believes*.

Alex can't have them. He can't know what Daniel said, or what I wore that night. They're pieces of my private pain.

But he does.

And it's impossible.

Holding Daniel's hoodie out at my side, I wrap my arms over my chest to keep from flying apart, and climb the stairs. My room is filled with stuff, and empty as a tomb. I feel equally desolate without Alex. It's only been weeks, and I need him to hold on to, I want him to shelter me from this storm. Maybe the connection to Daniel is what wove us so tightly together – now it's tearing us apart.

A short tearless sob breaks free. Renfield regards me from

his spot at the foot of my bed, eyes saying he thinks I'm crazy. I think he's right.

"I'm losing it, Renfield." Because I believe Alex.

"Alex is losing it, too." Because he believes Daniel's death is his.

The cat in his wisdom stands, and fluffs my faeries with his paws. Then Renfield moves in a circle, trampling them when he settles in the same spot, facing the other way. He has an excellent point.

I punch up my pillows, pull Alex's sleeves down , and then climb into bed. The quiet is deafening, thundering in my ears. Or is it the drumming of my heart? Funny that it keeps beating after what happened to Daniel and how his death happened to Alex.

"Things are so messed up," I tell Renfield.

He snores at me.

I curl on my side. My mind runs over the same ground, never finding answers, and I'm so tired. I feel like my body is in the mattress, not on it. Eventually, exhaustion wins.

Morning hits like a freight train. Mom's yelling my name from the kitchen and Renfield's looking down at me where I lay on the floor. My brain has turned to rocks rubbing against each other. Sheets cocoon my legs - carpet nap stings my face where it's ground into my wet cheeks.

After my last nightmare, I fear it's blood. A cautious test with a fingertip proves it's just tears.

"Emma Jane!" Mom yells, her voice whacking into my head.

My mouth tastes like metal and cotton. I feel weighed down when I try to move. Standing unsettles everything, my brain clunks in my head, my body feels like it's still on the floor. *OK*, I think. *No more painkillers for me. I'd rather hurt than feel like this.*

Hangers rattle in my closet as I whip off my pajama pants and Alex's hoodie. I dig to the bottom of my pants pile and pull on my camouflage pants with all the pockets, a snug thermal shirt, and then a lightweight black hoodie, sleeves down, hood up. I don't have scars to hide, but I like the security of it.

Mom holds out my backpack; beside her on the counter sits a big pretzel and a steaming to-go cup of coffee. She doesn't question my choice of clothes – she does comment on my hot pink cast clashing with the woodland camo, however. I try to joke about sneaking into the library to return my overdue Gothic novel, but my heart isn't in it. She shakes her head, slides my backpack on for me, then hooks the pretzel over my right thumb, despite the cast, and nestles the coffee in my other hand.

"A pretzel?"

"Bacon cheddar pretzel," she says. "I thought it would pair well with the maple coffee."

"Have I said lately that you're awesome?"

"No." She opens the door and nudges me out. "But I'm sure you've thought it often."

Mom's right, as usual: the thinking she's awesome, and the savory pretzel and sweet coffee being a perfect ambulatory breakfast. I wish I could stop thinking about Daniel and Alex and enjoy the food, the fresh cool air, and scrubbed-clean look of the neighborhood after the storm. I can't. I eat because I know I need to.

The sight of Bree on the Bree Bench tugs at my aching heart, and chips at my desire to keep everything bottled up.

"Hey you," she says, "what's up? You look awful."

"Thanks." I sling the coffee cup in the trash and relish the *bang*.

Josh Mason's rusted Camaro announces his approach before anyone can see his car. Everything in me clenches, and after the dream I had, I know I can't handle school today.

"Bree, I need to get out of here."

"What?" She blinks, scans the quad. "You mean ditch?"

"Yeah." I cast a scathing glare at the battered car's hood when it turns the corner.

"God, I thought you'd never ask!"

"You don't need to come." My best friend doesn't deserve to be a passenger on my trip to Crazy Town.

"Are you kidding? Let my best friend incur the wrath of parents alone?"

She hops up, straightens her jacket, hooks her elbow in mine and then casually saunters toward teacher parking. We put the Z-28 and its driver behind us, and the student parking lot, where I'm betting by the gravitational pull I feel that Alex is parking his zippy hybrid car.

"So what's the plan?" she asks.

"No clue. I can't do school today…"

"Yesterday still bugging you?"

"You have no idea."

"Well," she says, digging her phone out of her purse, "I know the perfect place to go, and you can give me an idea, seeing as I'm lacking in that department." She presses number 1 on her speed dial. "Hey, baby. Girl emergency. Emma and I need your truck. The keys still hidden under the bumper?"

A voice sounding a lot like Jason Weller comes through the teeny speaker.

"Thanks!" She says, then loses her phone. "I promise I'll make it up to you."

"Baby? You called Jason 'baby'?"

"Yeah. We both have boyfriends now." She winks and gives me a big smile before leading the way down the row of sensible teacher-type cars to Jason's Ford Bronco. Once there, Bree feels around under the bumper. "Got it," she mutters.

"When did this become official?"

"Since you've been grounded."

I clamber into the passenger seat, and look at Bree, right at home in Jason's big beater of a vehicle. Conversation isn't an option once the Bronco starts. I tuck my hand and cast into the kangaroo pocket of my hoodie and stare blankly out the window as first Shelley High fades and then White River follows. She hits the highway, and then takes the East Sternberg Road exit. A tangle of asphalt and a jumble of cement buildings loom off to the right of the overpass.

The mall. People overload, and no place to talk seriously.

"Shopping?"

"Hell no," she says. "The West Shore Café has the best peanut caramel sundaes. Nothing better to cure what ails you. Except maybe a cheeseburger... And I wouldn't mind hitting Statham's pre-Christmas sale."

"It isn't even Thanksgiving yet."

"Exactly."

Outside the mall is boring, makes no structural sense, with stores sticking out like cancerous growths from a bone white lump. Curving arches stand one store down from a squared-off entrance. Despite the industrial carpet and vaulted ceiling, the inside is crazier yet. Signs for pre-Christmas sales accost us from the second we walk in the door. Even the sundaes Bree wants are discounted through the month of November.

"So…" She waves at girls walking in the opposite direction across the fountain in the middle of the mall. "I'm guessing this is about Lover Boy…"

"You're right. And please don't call him that."

"Ah-ha. Then there's trouble in new love paradise?"

"New love," I echo when we walk into the West Shore Café, and skirt the stained glass dune divider behind the waitress station. "It doesn't feel new at all."

At the table, with sundaes and pops in front of us, Bree twirls a stringer of caramel above her dish. "What's going on? I thought you and Alex were totally into each other."

"That's the problem."

"What?" She licks the caramel off the spoon. "How is dating a guy like Alex Franks a problem?"

"Because something's not right with him." His visions of death, his similarities to Daniel. God, the way he makes me feel alive…

"Care to elaborate? Because I'm not currently picking up what you're trying to put down."

"It's hard to explain." I tug on my sleeves. "I'm not sure what's going on. Let me put it this way: Do you believe in ghosts? Because I'm not sure I do."

"Sure." She eyes me, arches one eyebrow. "Do you believe in hate?"

Where did that come from? "Yeah."

"Do you believe in love, then?"

"Of course." *It's currently killing me, one heartbeat at a time.*

"Ghosts are like that." She smiles triumphantly and slurps a big spoon of ice cream. It's my turn to arch eyebrows and give her a quizzical look. She sighs, and then says, "I see you're not understanding. Love and hate are real, even if you don't see them."

"But it isn't like that..." I heave a sigh, wondering if choosing my metaphysical-leaning girlfriend was the right person to confide in. I've started now, though, and Bree is the most tenacious person I know – except my mother. I lean across the table and tell her everything: Alex winking and opening my locker like Daniel; his breakdown on the catwalk; his confessions last night. I finish with, "He was even talking like Daniel, called me by Daniel's nickname, said exactly what Daniel said the night he died."

"Wo-o-ow. OK. One, *weird*. And I stress the weird part. And, two, it's just like I was saying. True love is like ghosts... it's a famous quote by some old guy."

My dubious expression prods Bree to explain. She says, "You see love in someone, right? And you see hate in them, too. Somehow, you're seeing Daniel in Alex."

"But why?"

"You're going to have to figure that one out for yourself. That was my moment of brilliance. One flash and it's gone."

I've seen Daniel's ghost. I've talked to his echo. They were separate, outside of Alex.

"Don't you think it's crazy, though?" I ask, "They didn't know each other... And, God, Bree it was awful. Alex was so confused, totally convinced it was part of him."

She makes a dismissive gesture with her spoon. "What about you? How do you feel?"

I lean back in the booth, and cross my arms. "I don't know what I think."

"I didn't ask what you *think*. I asked what you *feel*."

What do I feel? I close my eyes, try to shut down the screaming denials in my rational brain. I picture Alex, his long brown hair shot through with copper highlights and his mismatched hazel eyes. The look of wonder every time he sees me. The way I felt with him. My heart races, and a melancholy kind of yearning flashes through me.

"The sad smile on your face says enough." Bree slurps her melted sundae. "I think you need to talk to him now. And don't worry..." She tips her dish and drinks what's left. "I won't tell a soul. This is crazier than you hanging out at the cemetery."

"So... Statham's, eh?" I spoon my sloppy ice cream to watch the peanuts swirl and drown. "You buying lingerie for your boyfriend?"

A blush reddens her cheeks. She drops her gaze to her hands, and meddles with things in her purse. "Boys don't wear lingerie," she says. "Besides, I like their perfume."

After not eating my sundae, and hours' worth of my butt going numb on various benches throughout the mall while Bree shopped for everything but perfume, we finally climb back into Jason's Bronco.

"You and Jason, huh?" I tease.

"You and Alex, huh?" she shoots back.

"Well played, my friend. Well played."

Key in the ignition, she says, "Home then?"

I nod, then settle into the seat when the engine roars to life. The Ford shimmies a little as Bree drives along the snaking two-lane road circling the mall; it gives access to restaurants, a hearing aid clinic, and a pie shop Mom once wanted to buy.

At the traffic light, Bree splutters above the engine growl, "Shit! You're going to be late. School must be out."

The evidence passes under the light in front of us. Josh Mason in his crappy, rusted Camaro.

"Where do you think he's going?" she asks.

"No clue. I'm already late. Let's follow him and find out."

Stalkerish, sure, but Josh hates the mall and all those "prissy stores on Sternberg." His being out here is suspicious enough to warrant a nosy reaction.

Once the light changes, Bree enters the flow of traffic a few cars behind the Z-28. He sticks to back roads away from the mall, toward the Spring Lake Industrial Park.

"Think Josh got a job?" Bree asks over the Bronco's idling at a corner.

"Doubtful."

Then Josh turns down a dirt service road and jounces toward a little building with a big sign reading ASCENSION EXPERIMENTAL LABS.

"Hey!" I say, sit up straight and fling an arm across Bree. "Slow down. I recognize that SUV."

Bree backs off on the gas, the beast of a vehicle shuddering as she turns down a side drive – so Josh and the owner of the shiny black Suburban won't see or hear us. I crane my neck to watch as Josh steps out of the Camaro, then I lose sight of him. An antsy energy builds in me as Bree turns behind the building and creeps up behind the dumpster. We ease open the doors and sneak to the corner of the reeking garbage bin.

Choking on the stink, I crouch to watch. They are too far away to hear clearly. But when the SUV's driver steps out, my heart leaps into my throat.

"Who's that?" Bree asks.

I have to swallow my heart back down before I can answer. "Alex's dad."

"What!" she hisses.

"My thoughts exactly."

What are those two doing together? Why would Alex's dad have anything to do with Josh?

If we leave the cover of the dumpster, they'll see us. I strain to hear anything more than the creak of Josh's trunk. Then I slap a hand over my mouth to stop the gasp – when he lifts the stiff body of a dog from the shadows of the vehicle's rear. Disdain is evident on the haughty face of Dr Franks when he opens the tailgate of his SUV.

Josh puts the body on the plastic sheeting lining the cargo area, then grabs a towel from the trunk and wipes red smears of animal blood down its length.

Dr Franks produces a wallet from his suit coat, and pulls money out. After the cash changes hands, things get stranger.

Josh says something, stabs a finger toward town, then waves his arms. He's all fire, even at this distance. Alex's dad is the opposite. He's cold and unflappable in the face of Josh's fit. He takes a step toward Josh, towering above him. His face darkens, and he jabs a finger repeatedly into Josh's chest. Then – seemingly for emphasis – he flips Josh under the chin with his wallet.

For a moment Josh stands defiant, fists balled at his sides. Then the fire bleeds off. He hangs his head and walks away.

"Now that," Bree whispers, "was the height of weird."

"Yeah."

One more messed-up piece in the puzzle that's becoming the Franks men. The brilliant surgeon and jealous loser are in cahoots to the point of money exchanging hands is strange. Fragments of my old boyfriend's ghost inhabiting my new boyfriend is the kind of weird I'm not sure I can handle, though.

Chapter Twenty-Three

Mom stands at the front door, hands on her hips, her hair clip sliding toward its certain demise on the floor. Her position and pressed-tight lips indicate that she's not on the same planet as pleased, and has punishments waiting and ready for me. She watches Bree turn the corner in Jason's Bronco.

"With Bree?" Mom asks. Her tone says she already knows the answer.

"Yeah." Why lie?

"I think I liked it better when Alex was coming over every day. At least he got you home on time."

I liked it better, too. "Sorry, Mom."

"That's a word that loses its magic after a while," she warns. "Please don't wear it out."

"I won't."

Thanks to class syllabuses, I have all my assignments. I try to pretend it's any other day and I'm just late – and not late after having ditched, too. Mom watches, arms crossed while I put my books out, and open my laptop, fumbling with my pink cast. She lets me get everything settled, then walks to the kitchen, saying, "School called, by the way, reporting that you were absent. I told them you had a doctor's appointment in Grand Rapids about your hand."

She knows.

I can't even meet her over-the-shoulder look.

"Welcome to being grounded until Christmas, Emma Jane."

That's fair, considering the shame spiral I've been on.

"And Alex called."

My heart slams so hard at the mention of his name I have to catch my breath. I miss him so bad already that it hurts.

"What did you tell him?"

"The same thing. And that you were grounded."

My "how my mom is awesome" comment of this morning comes to mind. I think awesome could be upgraded to amazing – except for the crazy overprotective streak.

I spend the rest of my night doing schoolwork, getting a bath, and thinking over what's happened in the past two days. The jittery sense of wrongness rattles around my bones, twisting my thoughts and emotions into a sick snarl. I yearn to see Alex, to hear his voice, to feel his fingers stroking my hair. I feel as strongly for him as I had for Daniel. Maybe more. After seeing his episode on the catwalk and hearing what he said last night, I think the intensity stems from his odd connection to Daniel. Regardless of Bree's reasoning, it still feels so impossible.

By nightfall, I'm a heartsick mess. It doesn't matter if Alex Franks is all kinds of wrong, I still want to be with him.

Wednesday disappears in a sucking black hole of misery. Alex and I can't keep our eyes from each other. I want to run to him, throw every aching thing at his feet and beg him to still love me. I can't take that first step. Neither can he, it seems like.

Thursday morning, all of my intentions to talk to Alex jam in my throat and leave me speechless. Instead of striding to the Bree Bench, wrapping me in his arms and kissing me, Alex pauses a few feet away and meets my gaze.

He's become raw again, his eyes are darkly circled, like bruised flesh, and his cheeks look sunken. Still, the wonder on his face hurts to see and reminds me of why it's there. Some of Daniel's thoughts are now Alex's dreams. Did I hurt him too badly when I told him I needed to think? Or did I hurt him when he said he loved me and I couldn't even think enough to say it back? Can he see the regret in my eyes?

My lip quivers. Tears burn past my defenses. Alex gives me a melancholy nod, hangs his head, and walks away while new whispers take life.

"Emma and Alex broke up."

"She saw him flip out on the catwalk and dumped him."

On and on.

A rumored-over, super-short relationship with the high school emotional wreck and Alex is back to being talked about like an outsider. Lips press into flat lines, faces take on looks ranging from pity to totally closed off to him. Jason Weller, however, claps him on the back and leads him toward the doors of Shelley High's dingy halls.

Every girl daring enough to talk to me wants to know what happened. Oddly enough, Marin Rhodes verbally defends me in third hour. After escaping the Ugly Room, I stand in the stuffy air of the empty catwalk and watch Alex walk beneath. The wind plays with his hood, pushing it off and exposing his face and scars to the light. He's not perfect, damage and hurt lie just beneath his scars, and he's still the most beautiful guy I've seen.

As if he feels the weight of my stare, Alex looks up. Our eyes meet. Our connection hits with the force of a Mack truck, my chest tightens, a sad smile curls my lips, and tears blur my sight. I press my hand to the glass, fingers spread in a pleading gesture. His lips turn down, then rise to mirror my sad smile.

I can't stand this anymore. Daniel's echo and Josh's fiery other are conspicuously absent when I run across the red carpet. I ram the door with my shoulder, burst into the hall and charge down the stairs. Anticipation builds, pressing in my heart and limbs. The lunch queue is long, Bree in her normal spot at the head of the line, but Alex is nowhere to be seen. Hushed voices follow, snaking person to person, as I hurry to my best friend. Her lips turn down immediately, and she drags me into a hug.

"The poor boy isn't right," she whispers. "I didn't say anything, but he just looks broken."

"Where is he?" Alex couldn't have disappeared already. I just saw him minutes ago.

"I haven't seen him since first hour."

"I need to talk to him." I hate the panicky edge to my voice.

"He'll be around. Give him a while. He probably feels rejected."

I didn't reject him. Sure, I sent him home, and told him I needed to think, but how can he blame me?

After a trip through the food service room and choosing a bland lunch I know I'm not going to eat, Bree and I sit at the thespian crowd's lunch table. Seeing Jason and Bree so wrapped in each other cuts me in a way I never thought it would. My best friend's happiness only makes me want the ignorant bliss Alex and I had a few days ago; I could've lived with the similarities and been happy. Can I ever be happy, knowing they come from memories he shouldn't have?

The rest of the afternoon drags by like a wounded animal. I stand at the door to Dune Ecology, dreading another hour trapped in a room with Josh.

I saw what he did Tuesday. I kept my mouth shut yesterday – the truth boils in me, hot and acidic over the icy loss I feel without Alex.

The last thing I want to do is talk to Josh.

"Hey, Gentry," he calls when I enter the room. "Can I talk to you?"

"Depends on the topic." Distance spreads between us as I walk across the room to the seat by Asia. "Are you wanting to discuss your douchebaggery of late, or what you were doing Tuesday after school?"

His eyes widen to saucer size and his face blanches. Not a good look on an honest to-goodness redhead. The color drains from his neck, making his chest hair redder where it peeks from the neck of his Alex-wanna-be hoodie

I lean back on my hip, putting distance between us and readying a thornier question. Mr LaRue puts an end to it though, calling the class to order.

Josh glares from across the room. Asia eventually squirms under the weight of it. I refuse to satisfy him with a response. He is a creep and a liar, and he doesn't intimidate me. The next time I catch him staring, I lift my cast in a slow, obvious motion, and then rub my chin in the same spot I'd punched him and dropped him to the pool table at DarkHouse.

At the end of the hour, Josh storms up to me. "Whatever you think you saw, you're clueless. And trust me, you aren't going to like what happens if you keep on seeing Alex Franks."

"You once warned me off from Daniel, too. Look how that turned out."

"Exactly," he growls and slams his books onto the desk by me.

I refuse to cower. He can't hold my gaze. With a snarled expletive, Josh snatches up his books and stomps out.

"He's such an ass," Asia whispers.

Enough to make you sick, I'm tempted to say. Then I consider who I'm speaking to. Asia, sick, and fifth hour isn't a pretty combination. "Total ass," I agree.

My next hour lags behind the slow clock hands. Opening books is the closest I get to paying attention. Alex is my only thought.

Surely he'll be at our lockers after school. He always is.

I think my heart stops when I see Alex standing at his locker, watching me walk down the main hall. My mind shuts down, and I let my need for him rule me. The other students can't move fast enough. My body thrums with an echo of the energy his touch holds.

Neither of us speak. I drop my books to the floor, security deposit be damned, run the last few feet, and launch into his arms. Biting thoughts die, doubt shrivels, and for a moment everything is *right*. I bury my face in his chest, mine hitching in silent sobs. Tingles spill across my skin like warm oil when he loosens the braid Mom did for me, and buries his face in my hair.

"God, Emma," he whispers against my neck.

His heart thunders in his chest, and I can't stop the memory from rising. *It doesn't beat for me, Emma... This heart has always been yours.* Can I ever hear that sound again and not remember? Will Daniel always haunt me through Alex?

"What is it?" he asks, his grip loosening. "Is it what I said?"

"It's just..." I turn away from the hurt in his eyes and open my locker. "Well... God, Alex, it's a lot for me to process."

"A lot for *you* to process?" A sharp, edgy note sours his velvet tenor. "What about *me*? Do you have any idea what it's like?"

"Do you have any idea what it's like for me?"

"I *know* what you went through, Em," he says in a defeated tone. Crashing and banging of books in his locker echo in mine. "I can't believe it, but it's here inside me, and I hate that I'm causing you more pain."

With that, he slams his locker and plunges into the tide of bodies surging through the doors before I can gather my wits. I stand, numb and blinking, staring after Alex's disappearing form.

What just happened? How did it all go wrong so fast?

Why do I feel worse? Like a selfish, whiney brat...

Then I realise, since Daniel died, it's all been about me. My loss. My hurt. My inability to get over him. Finally someone comes along who makes my heart sing, and when things get dark and difficult, I whine about myself again.

Heart dragging behind me, I drift home for another lonely night thinking about Alex and Daniel, and all the twisted ways I suddenly feel awful. Renfield greets me at the door, and doesn't complain when I bury my face in his fur and cry. Mom doesn't bother me either. She brings dinner to my room, and a towel for me to dry my cat. I wish she had a towel for my soul.

• • • •

Friday is a special hell.

No Alex – surely at home, getting his weekly booster. And a massive two-hour pep assembly takes up most of the afternoon. The Shelley High Ravens football team is going to the championship game and everyone has something to say about it, from the coach to the principal to the local news channel. Then we're released early.

Long shadows of a November afternoon stretch across the quad. The Bree Bench is empty, and the quiet walk home gives me time to formulate a plan.

Probably not the smartest plan, but I can't stand the distance between me and Alex.

Saturday, Mom and Dad leave for one of his plentiful job conferences. Before walking out, Mom suggests I stay home and get some rest, "for good behavior," she says, then adds, "don't waste the opportunity to build some trust back."

Rest is the last thing on my mind.

I pick up the house phone and the phone book, and call the local hospitals to ask if Dr Franks is working. After dealing with minutes of the automated answer crap, a very friendly receptionist at Mercy Hospital suggests calling the local clinic. Rather than have our house number show up on their caller ID, I dig out my cell phone from the drawer in the kitchen and turn it on. Buzz after buzz tells me I have text messages. When it's finally silent, I use my cell to call the clinic and find Dr Franks scheduled to work the afternoon shift. When the lady on the phone asks, "What is this call concerning?" I hang up.

Establishing a window of opportunity for a possible breaking and entering is never a good answer to give an adult.

The texts are all from Alex. Temptation burns in me to

read them. But I'd rather hear what he has to say face to face. I select to Delete All and click to confirm.

In my room, I riffle through my desk and find the receipt for the new locker door with Alex's information. With the ghosts of boyfriends – both the dead and the living – hanging in my closet, I change into my camouflage pants, tight thermal knit top, and black fleece hoodie again. Then I tie my hair into a ponytail, the kind Alex would pull free if he could.

I plan on giving him a chance – to play with my hair and to listen to me apologize.

No matter what has happened, I can't get past missing him.

I just hope he feels the same.

Mom's car sits, sullen and somehow attentive, like a ghost of her is in there watching me. Dad's Buick is gone. Bree doesn't have a car, and Jason's Bronco is too loud for anything stealthy. Heaving a sigh, I set off for a hike toward the snooty neighborhoods by the lake, in the gated community where you need passcodes to drive on the road.

Clouds scud in, darkening the sky to match my mood. Shadows on the ground stretch and warp the farther I get from home. Near Lost Valley, the straight orderly streets turn and twist, rolling up and down small hills. Bent Pine Drive gives onto Black Oak Lane, and the gate that's supposed to keep interlopers like me away. Well, ones that drive cars, anyway. I'm on foot, and find trespassing here too easy. I trail the fieldstone fence back into the woods a couple yards, and slip through the gap between the stone and the wire fencing.

Black Oak Drive leads downhill towards the swamp and the only home on the street. Estate is more fitting, a large stretch of property, completely enclosed by a high fieldstone wall. Showing above the barrier spins an old windmill, the dull blades chopping the air. *Looks like a prison*, I think. It's not a place to welcome things in, more a place to keep them out.

Big black wrought iron gates stand at the mouth of the drive. Backing the iron scrollwork are boards stained black, completely obscuring any view inside the property.

Everything about the Franks' property screams GET OUT.

A chill crawls up my spine, like sharp claws puckering my skin. Somewhere inside the fence, an animal cries. Maybe it's the damp lake air, or the unsteady rhythm of my heart, but the animal cry doesn't sound natural. *It's just your nerves, Emma,* I chide myself.

Do I really want to go in there?

When Alex needed to talk, he came to my house. I need to talk to him, apologize and make him understand how much I care. I pull my cell phone from my pocket and open up the messaging program. I scroll through contacts to Alex's name, select it, then send him a text, telling him I'm at the gates. Waiting only makes the creepy feeling worming its way through my guts worse. The breeze rattles the leaves and the sky looks like it could open and pour at any minute.

I send him another text:

If you don't come out, I'm coming in…

Chapter Twenty-Four

Anxiety scrapes my nerves raw. I check my phone, make sure it's getting a signal.

Three bars glow in the service indicator. Alex just isn't answering.

The clouds darken to storm warnings above me, and wind wails in the tall white pines close to the big lake. Sandy soil gives under my Converse soles when I sneak up to the gates. Testing them is as futile as trying to escape what Alex has done to my heart. Black. Imposing. Unmoving. Giving up on patience, I pace the fence to the left, then right, until I find a gnarled oak tree leaning on the fieldstone, its trunk wide enough for me to straddle and scooch up.

Halfway to the top of the fence, another spine-chilling wail freezes me in place. I catch a breath and clutch the trunk. Focusing on small, quiet movements, I wriggle further. Finally, in the lower branches, I can see the estate beyond the barrier.

The property spreads toward the dunes of Lake Michigan in the distance. Green grass rolls within the fences, studded here and there with trees or shrubs. Small white-sided outbuildings huddle near the main house, probably storage sheds, though one looks like a garage, with the driveway feeding into it. Behind the big manor house, the property turns nightmarish; a small creek cuts through the estate with a dark grove of trees beyond its bank.

Alex's house is ridiculously big, easily two of our old Victorians on Seventh Street. Windows and fieldstone walls make up most of the ground floor. Narrow white siding and arched windows cover the top floors, and hold up the many gables of the forest green roof. Very pretty, but in an Alex-on-first-day kind of way, designed to attract and shun attention at the same time.

Bark scratches raspy complaints against my pants as I inch across the top of the fence on a large branch. Do I really want to do this? How can I walk away now? My gut hurts with the amount of wrongness on this side of the fence, and Alex is inside the house somewhere. Denying my instincts to flee the way I came, I drop to the ground and tiptoe into the shadows of the pine a few yards from the fence.

A pale yellow glow shows through the downstairs windows, on the side of the house closest to me. A tall shadow passes between the lights and the glass before moving deeper into the room.

Alex, I think.

My heart pounds, a sweet wanting kind of ache, even though my stomach tightens and threatens to roll with nerves. I edge along the fence toward the driveway. Maybe to look a little less like a creeper who climbs fences, I'm not sure, but I feel better with gravel beneath my shoes than damp grass.

The driveway meanders between trees, and on the first bend I hear movement off to the side. I pause, gazing in all directions. Despite not seeing anything, I catch a whiff of something awful. A little late to think about it now, but what if they have guard dogs? My gut clenches, and a sweaty chill rides my spine. I don't have an exit strategy… What am I going to do if I need to leave in a hurry? The rustles sound too haphazard, and I don't see any guard dog charging in to rip me to shreds.

Pushing against the sense of wrong fouling the air, I walk on. Then the source of the rustling noise and stink comes into view.

My jaw falls. Daylight outside, a possible storm brewing, and a young deer shambling along the grassy patch beside the gravel? Whitetails bed down during the day, and rarely get this close to humans. A doe, by the lack of antlers, with an injured front leg by the way she's limping.

Dread fills me. Deer catch diseases and this animal isn't acting normal. No flight instinct, no fear of humans. I can't stay here, waiting for her to disappear. Walking softly to not startle her, I draw even with her wandering gait.

Then my stomach rolls into a knot and punches up into my throat.

The doe's ears flick, turning in my direction. *Wrong!* My instincts scream, *wrong!* A thick, rotten tang scent wafts from her. At this angle, the wrongness I felt blares in silent accusation from her chest. Her rib cage is a ruin of stitched flesh and open wounds. A scum of milky film covers her eyes and a hole cuts through her ear, like someone shot at her and missed.

"Oh my God," I gasp.

Denial shrieks in me. Recognition clamps me in a fist of misery. She was dead! That doe died in my arms less than a month ago. Alex and I had tried to rescue her from death in the culvert at Meinert State Park, only to have her fade from life on the way to his car. He said he was going to take care of her...

How can she be here, wandering the Franks' estate?

Those filmy eyes find mine, and horror rips through me. Everything in me recoils, sneakers kicking up stones as I backpeddle on the gravel drive. She lets out a pitiful wail, unnatural and somehow so like a human infant. Her wreck of a front leg has been pieced back together with metal rods and screws. The hardware flashes in the weak daylight while she staggers toward me, crying like a baby for its mother.

I want to run. I want to scream. Shock silences me, and a tree trunk cuts off my escape.

Trapped, and choking on my heart, I hold out a hand between me and the undead thing stumbling my way. *Click-clack-click* rises from her hooves on the crushed stone. The cries weaken with each repetition, and a yellow fluid leaks from the open wounds on her chest. Her nose touches my hand. It's cold, slimy, and she trembles when she tries to cry and nothing comes out.

I don't realise I'm crying until moisture slides over the corner of my mouth.

"Shhh," I tell her.

Do the dead hear? She must. She can limp and wail. Shudders rack her body, and her legs give out. The doe crumples to the ground, muzzle at my feet, eyes open and watching me through the white haze.

Gravel crunches beneath my feet when I sidle along the tree until I'm past it, hand still held out. *Please stay down,* I think. *Please.*

Walking backward, keeping my eye on the doe, I hurry, and go round the bend. Once she's out of sight, my stomach sends a gush of bile up my throat. I can't stop it, my jaw muscles convulse, and I drop to my knees and throw up everything but my memories at the side of the drive.

How in the hell do the dead walk?

It's not natural. Death is the barrier we can't cross.

My empty stomach reacts again, but nothing comes up. I sit back on my heels and swipe a sleeve over my forehead. Every breath draws in the smell of my vomit and the ever-present stink of something other. Across the field, near one of the small outer buildings, is a rack of garbage cans, while rattling in the sticks underneath them is another creature. What other horrors can this estate hold?

Rising on rubbery legs, I try to ignore my impulse to stare, to investigate the accident.

The drive arches toward the building, and when I draw closer, I see a rake and a shovel leaned against the siding. Beneath the trash cans, whatever is moving scrabbles to the surface of the refuse. An ordinary raccoon. Another animal not normally out in the daylight on a populated estate? Disbelief seems absurd after what I've seen. Then it swings its mangled head toward me and I know the Franks' estate has only begun to reveal its sins.

Half of the raccoon's head is compressed meat and shattered bone. The jaw hangs broken, sharp yellow teeth dangling. Something like a hiss issues from what's left of its mouth.

A yelp of shock bursts from my lips, and I give in to my instinct to run.

Up a grassy incline, and that impulse puts me in close proximity to the manor house. Stink hits me in waves, flooding from a dog lying at the foot of the porch steps. The coat is a chaos of mange rot and matted fur; both eyes are open, one of them opaque and fixed, the other burst into a slop of tissue and jelly in its socket. Hand over my mouth to keep in the screams, I try to sneak past the sightless dog.

Its muzzle lifts, the cracked nose twitching, before the head swings toward me. I'm close enough to hear the air rattling in the dog's throat and lungs, and read the name tag: Pam.

"Stay," I whisper. "Stay, Pam."

Rotted zombie dog Pam doesn't stay. Her body rises in a trembling motion, then the joints in her legs give way, and she drops to the grass again.

This isn't real, I tell myself. *This can't be real.*

I was willing to believe maybe Alex was haunted by Daniel's ghost. But this? *This?*

The undead wander the Franks' estate like it's a game pre-serve in hell. My mind runs in the same screaming loops: *How is this possible? Why here? Who did this to them?*

Then shouting snaps me back into a self-preservation mode and I flatten against the wall.

"What did you *do*, Dad?"

Alex? Shouting at his father? Oh God, the last man on earth I ever wanted to see again.

"I did what was necessary to bring you back." Such a calm, unaffected voice.

Bring him back from what? What are they arguing about?

My ridiculous urge to delve deeper into the blackness hid-den behind the gates wins. I drop to the level of the rotted dog, pinching my nose shut to avoid the stench, and crawl along the wall toward the windows emitting light. Movement at the windows stops me short of the yellow square on the grass. I arch my neck till I can see Alex. The sight of him jump-starts my heart. He's dressed differently in his house – no hiding in hoods and sleeves. His snug short-sleeved shirt shows muscles I'd run my fingers over, and displays the white scars marking his skin. A wild light blazes in his eyes. His skin is vibrant, like he's just home from vacation.

"Necessary?" Alex locks gazes with his father. "There are punishments for what you've done."

"No one can touch me." The arrogance on his father's face sets my jaw on edge. Whatever's going on, he fully believes he was in the right, apparently. "After all I've given you, you should be thanking me, not whining."

"Thanking you for making me a monster?" Alex shouts. "You should've let me die!"

"Let you die?" His father's voice is ice to Alex's righteous fire. He crosses his arms. "I will never let you die. You are *my son!*"

"What about Daniel?" Alex stands nose to nose with his father now. "He was someone's son. He had friends. He had a girlfriend."

"Inconsequential," his father scoffs, stepping behind the desk. "He had the proper blood type. He was the ideal match for a tissue donor."

"That's all he was to you? Pieces and parts? He was a person! A thinking feeling person!"

"Rubbish," his dad says. "Unsubstantiated metaphysical hokum. He was vessels, tissues, and brain matter that I needed to bring you back. Nothing more."

The relentless unrepentance in his father's voice only angers Alex more. "What about the consequences, Dad? Did you think about those? Did this end justify your means?"

"There were bound to be complications from such an extensive procedure."

"Complications?" Alex roars. He bangs his chest, above his heart. "You call having a dead guy's memories and emotions a *complication*?"

"The formula was meant to preserve viability." His dad steps away, arranges things on the desktop beside him. "I didn't have enough subjects to test it on."

My chest tightens. I didn't think I could feel more horror, but this place reveals layer after layer.

"What did you do?" Alex repeats, voice as icy as his father's and heavy with threat.

"The details are unimportant, and will only hamper the healing process."

"It's not the physical I'm worried about!" Alex strides to the phone on the desk, and grabs it from the base. "There has to be someone to tell. Someone who wants to know what happened to their son."

"Fine." His father sniffs, smooths back his hair, and then yanks open a file cabinet. He reaches in, chooses a file, and tosses it on the desk between him and his son. He drops into the chair, and props his feet on the desk. "Since you're so keen to know the miracle I worked to bring you back to life... It's all in there. Charts, blood types, formulas."

A doubtful look clouds Alex's face. He pulls the fat manila folder to him; breath clogs my throat while I watch his face. He pages through his father's documents, scanning some, reading snippets of others. His expression shifts from denial to anger, then from depression to a sick acceptance.

"So, you had him drugged." Alex shakes the folder at his father. "Had him pushed off the deck. Took what made him Daniel and shoved it in me. And you didn't think there wouldn't be any side effects?"

Shock and pure horror slam into my chest.

My boyfriend, the person I loved most in the world, was murdered for his "donated to science" organs. And then Alex's father gutted him and used his parts to revive Alex?

Oh my God. The guy I loved was murdered, in order to make the guy I've come to love return to life.

"I bargained," Dr Franks says. "And my son *lives*. Perhaps the residual memories and emotions left in the flesh will fade. The studies are hypothetical at best…" He starts to ramble, the nauseating sound of his voice rolling in my head. "Theories suggest there is a soul, and it can reside in the flesh. I must admit, with the brain matter, and him not entirely dead when I took it, that concerned me…"

The words "not entirely dead" finally break me out of the paralysis of emotional shock. Murdered. Gutted. Repurposed. Revived. Tainted. It's not just Daniel's ghost in Alex, it's parts of Daniel *in* Alex. A strangled sob breaks free of my chest.

The argument dies inside the house. My shattered heart jolts to terrified life. If he had Daniel murdered for his organs, what will he do to me?

Blind terror fuels my limbs, and I hurtle through the theme park of undead monsters, scramble over the fence and am on the road before I hear a garage door open. Black Oak Lane rises to the intersection with Bent Pine Drive. Chest heaving, I skid down the far side of Bent Pine, and huddle in the dune grass.

Tears leak over my hands, my chest burns with pent sobs. If I had something left in my stomach, I would puke it.

That man had my boyfriend killed to harvest Daniel's body so he could revive his son.

Then clarity strikes.

Daniel didn't fall. He was pushed.

Everything I believed was a lie.

And so is my relationship with Alex.

Chapter Twenty-Five

The gates of the Franks' estate open with a squeal of metal. Dirt rushes at me as I drop to my belly in the grass. Above, the Suburban growls out of the property. It stops at the intersection, the idling engine feet away and sounding irritated, ready to run me down.

Cowering in the shadow of the slope, I follow the instinct to hide. They had to see me. Dr Franks has to know it was me, and what I overheard. Breaking my hand means nothing in comparison to him drugging Daniel and using his organs to rebuild his own son. What will he do to me? He's already broken the laws of man and nature.

If he can make one death look like an accident…

The pieces of my broken heart beat, as undead as the doe Dr Franks ruined. I wish it would stop and give me some relief. It's all too horrible to believe. Daniel murdered. His body parts put into Alex. Alex adopting Daniel's ways because, in a way, isn't he also Daniel now?

My brain refuses to grasp it.

Somehow, that madman pulled off the impossible.

After what seems like an eternity, the SUV turns the way I came and rolls down Bent Pine Drive. I lay in the dirt, chest aching, air whistling down my tight throat.

The clouds thicken above, darkening and seeming to sink toward me. Cars pass by until I lose count. All this time and no noise from the estate. I haul myself up, and peer down Black Oak Drive. The gates remain closed, backed with black-stained boards and locked to hide the horrors inside.

My head hurts too badly to think clearly. I act on instinct, moving on autopilot through the neighborhood. Flashes of the sins Dr Franks committed disturb my mind. Daniel. The deer. Alex. A horrid sadness cuts through me, tearing open a new gulf of misery. The loss of a love more intense than what I shared with Daniel carves me out.

How can Alex really love me, if he has so much of Daniel in him? Where does one guy stop and the other start?

And how can I love Alex, knowing he's alive because Daniel isn't?

Of course his heart doesn't beat for him. It isn't his at all. It's stolen.

Seventh Street appears, soothing me like a balm on my soul. Home. Renfield. My parents. Then I see a big black vehicle creeping down my street, with an evil gargoyle face behind the wheel and leering at my house. Branches tear at my hair when I dive into the bushes two houses down, and pray my camouflage will conceal me.

Dr Franks drives slowly down our street, his face turned toward our house. He turns the corner, and then drives down the alley dividing our block. He stares at our house, our garage, then guns the engine, throwing stones from the tires when he roars away.

That monster of monsters knows where I live. What does he want here? My mom for the lawsuit she never started?

Me for owning the heart he put into his son? Or me for knowing he did it?

I wriggle free of the bushes and dash across the last two yards to home. The dove gray walls seem so flimsy after Alex's father staring holes through them. I open the door, tuck myself hurriedly inside, and slam it shut behind me. Renfield pokes his head out from the kitchen where Mom keeps his food bowl. He watches me like I've lost my mind when I run through the house and lock the back door, too. Then I check the shadow box frame Dad made that hangs in the living room. The handgun is still there.

The cat follows me up the stairs, his mouth open as he smells the dirt and funk of the Franks' property on me.

I strip down, shove my clothes into the hamper, and then climb into the shower, cast in a plastic bread bag and shoved outside the curtain. No amount of hot water or soap will wash away what I've seen and what I know.

Mom and Dad return home as the hot water runs out. Dr Franks' sins have dirtied my soul and I don't know how to remove them. Shivering, I towel off and then pick clothes that never belonged to either guy.

Nerves on overdrive, I flinch when the garage door rattles. I mentally count steps to the gun from the bottom of the stairs while I creep to the first floor. If an intruder breaks in, I'll still be able to reach the gun before they can grab me. The door opens, and I brace to run.

Mom enters first, her frumpy purse bumping the door-knob when she comes in. Dad pushes in behind her, arms loaded with pizza boxes. Grateful for a bit of normalcy, I grab paper plates and napkins from the kitchen. But nor-malcy is a pipe dream. We sit down in our regular places, but nothing feels right anymore. How do I act, knowing what I

know? Will my parents figure out something is really wrong?
I bite and chew mechanically, swallow, and try to respond to
appropriate comments about the conference.

A knock echoes through the house, and I cringe.

"My goodness, Emma," Mom says. "Are you all right?"

"If it's Alex, please tell him I'm not here."

"Emma Jane…"

"Please. I don't want to talk to him."

Dad balls up his napkin, and pushes back his chair. The
knock comes again, louder this time. I shift in my seat, ready
to run for the stairs if it's Alex, or the gun if it's his father.
Dad opens the door, and a whiff of leather whisks through
to my nose and spear through to my heart.

Alex.

"Good evening, Mr Gentry." His voice is edgy. "May I
talk to Emma?"

"I'm sorry, Alex. Emma said she doesn't want to see you."

His leather jacket rustles, I hear his sneakers shift on the
porch floor. "Please, sir. Just a few minutes?"

"Whatever this is…" The hinges creak as my dad pushes
the door nearly closed. "You'll have to wait till she's ready."

I feel rather than see him lean around my dad. Raw emotion twists his voice. "Emma, please…"

How can I look at him? Who will I see? Alex, or Daniel?
I shake my head and look away.

"Time to go, son," my dad says, and then closes the door.

Mom doesn't let the silence last very long. "You want to
tell me what that's all about?"

No, I don't want to. My mom is one of the last people
who would begin to understand what happened with Alex
and Daniel. She'd close her ears and just refuse. "Can I just
say Alex isn't the guy I thought he was, and leave it at that?"

"For now." She pushes at the hair clip slipping from her hair. When she focuses on me, her expression is one big frown. "But when you've had a chance to think about it, I expect to hear more."

"OK."

I clear my dishes and climb the narrow stairs. The cat is curled on my pillow, weak moonlight spilling through my curtains and softening his white into something ethereal. Tonight I do not want to see the moon, or know who's looking at it. I yank the curtains closed, change into pajamas and slide into bed behind Renfield. He gazes at me, yellow eyes glowing in the thin blade of moonlight cutting between the curtains.

"I know why you like Alex," I tell him.

He blinks, rises and stretches, then pads to my chest and curls into a ball by my heart.

"Exactly."

My sleep is broken with flashes of Alex and Daniel, and the undead creatures on the Franks' property all sutured into one grotesque monster. The proud voice of Alex's dad calls it his greatest creation. The vision runs in a jagged loop, like a chainsaw in my mind, cutting through the entire night.

That morning, I drag myself down the stairs, mumble a good morning to Mom, who's cleaning up from her morning tradition of making amazing breakfasts. She pours me a large cup of coffee and I pick up one of her breakfast burritos. With the burrito balanced on my cast, and coffee in my left hand, I take breakfast back to my room, and fire up my laptop. I may be grounded, but this is more important. She can ground me forever, and throw the computer away if I can find the information I'm looking for.

The screen throws artificial blue light into my dimly lit room. My desktop wallpaper seems a mockery of truth I know now. The cemetery scene speaks of the peace after death; of having a place to mourn. Dr Franks has ruined all that.

I pull up a webpage, go to a search engine and then type in Dr Franks' name. Hit after hit fill my results screen and I follow each one. A few similar articles in medical journals discuss his studies on electrical impulses and the varied effects on living and dead tissue. More recent articles talk about his attempts at regenerating dead tissues with a combination of chemical formulas and electricity.

That explains the undead animals on their property. And what he did to Daniel and Alex. They were the end results of his lifetime of research. But something as exquisite as Alex's regeneration must've taken more practice. I know about Daniel. Where did the others come from? And, who helped him?

Daniel's death was the last in a line of suspicious accidents over the summer…

I do another search for "Alex Franks" cross-referenced with "injury", and find his old school's article about his injury in early May. After opening another tab, I research the local news sites, and find a list of boys missing or dead in the rash of mysterious incidents. Shortly after Alex's accident, the first boy went missing in the White Lake area. His body was never found. Another boy had a motorcycle accident. One boy drowned. Two fell. The last one was Daniel.

Alex's dad did it. He did it all.

But he wasn't there the night Daniel fell. We were at a fraternity house party. The place teemed with people, all of them teens.

Dr Franks orchestrated Daniel's fall; used a puppet to do his dirty work.

Feet on the stairs alert me to someone approaching. I stab the power button and rush the darkened laptop back to my desk. I'm not sure I could stomach much more, anyway.

A knock on the door, and then Mom walks in.

"I'm not sure what's going on, Em. But I'm getting really worried about you."

"I don't know what to say." I heave a sigh. She'd think I was crazy, or she'd believe me, snatch up the phone, call the police, and report Dr Franks. I should turn Dr Franks in, I know that. His crimes would have him jailed. But how can I do that knowing it would affect Alex? If his father's arrested, what happens to Alex? What will they do to him? Poke, prod, take samples...

Why would the authorities even believe me?

"Then don't say anything. Just listen." She comes over, and sits on the end of my bed, across from Renfield. "There's help available anytime you want it. Your dad's work has a counseling service. And you know you can talk to Dad and me anytime. I just don't want things to get worse. You're lying, skipping school, sneaking out, getting into fights."

"It won't get worse, Mom. I promise." Anything to make her go away.

"Please don't let it. And talk to that boy. I don't know what's going on between you two – you act like you've been dating for years, not weeks. And he is genuinely hurt."

I think, *You have no idea.* I say, "I'll talk to him at school, OK?"

"At school, over the phone, wherever."

"Phone? Are you giving it back to me?"

"No, I am not. But I will bring the house phone to you if he calls."

"Sounds good."

Even though I doubt he'll call. What's happened between us isn't something we can talk about through text or over the phone. And definitely not at school. The rumor mill has almost broken with all the shifting gears they've gone through, trying to keep up with me and Alex. One whisper of Alex and Daniel and the madman who combined them, and the school will go insane.

I'm surprised I haven't lost my mind yet.

Chapter Twenty-Six

The next morning, the horrors of the weekend haven't dimmed. I've compartmentalised them so they are easier to deal with. The boxes are all jagged-edged, jostling and stabbing in my heart and mind. At least it's not overwhelming me.

I stand in my closet, yoga pants and T-shirt on, debating what else to wear. My tendency is to grab Alex's shirt. A lingering whisper drifts through my soul to wear Daniel's. Maybe I should wear them together – Alex's father ruined them both. Ruined me, too. And I can't tell Bree about what I overhead on Saturday. She would demand action, want his father turned in – anything other than me heartsick and frozen. She would be right, too. In a way, I kicked a hornet's nest over on Saturday, and stingers are everywhere I turn.

The neighborhood stretches quiet and sleepy in front of me while I walk to school. Thin sunlight dribbles down. The cold empty feel of November settles like a blanket, West Michigan waiting for winter to barrel in and bury it. Even the line at the Mugz-n-Chugz walk-up window is quiet. Sure, there's the usual stamping of feet and rubbing of arms to keep the blood flowing and get warm. But chatting? Dead. Flirting? Dead.

Kind of how I feel inside – when I'm not hurting.

Bree is waiting on her bench by the side door, with Jason standing behind her, sheltering her from the wind. I know in my gut that I won't see Alex today. Josh Mason turns the corner in his Z-28, a damning omen appearing at the same time I think of Alex.

Josh rolls down his window, and flips me the middle finger.

One look at my breve and I think, *caffeine is overrated.* I hurl the cup at his windshield and smile when the lid pops off and creamy coffee splatters the hood. A string of expletives fouler than his car's exhaust pours out his window. I add insult to injury by shrugging and walking away.

"Wow," Bree says when I join her at the bench. "Quite a show already this morning. Who rattled your cage?"

Dr Franks, I think.

"Long story," I say, and stuff my hands in the kangaroo pocket of my sweatshirt.

"Oh oh…" Her eyebrows arch. "Like the story you told me last week?"

"Worse."

"Holy shit." Her eyes widen, stress-testing her eyeliner.

"There was nothing holy about it."

She arches an eyebrow, and I shake my head. A slight lift of her shoulder, and a droop of mine. A silent conversation of her asking if I want to talk and me refusing. I glance around the quad, looking for Alex, looking for the source of the many rumors that had flown around the campus.

"He's not coming," Jason says.

"What?"

"Alex." Damn Jason for sounding sympathetic. Damn me for wanting him to. "I recognize that look, Em. He sent me a text, told me his dad insists on him being home schooled after 'the trouble here'," Jason does air quotation marks, "and he won't go back to Sadony Academy."

Alex's dad won't let him come back to school because of me. The bottom drops out of my hopes. "Home schooled?"

"Yeah. Alex's pissed, too. Said he will get back to you. Then this morning he asked me to ask you not to give up on him."

I nod, feeling more hollow and alone than I did the day I met Alex.

That emptiness haunts me, tearing me up inside, ripping out pieces with every moment that passes without him. By the end of the week, I've withdrawn into the shell I lived in while mourning Daniel. Though even that's tainted for me now. How can I mourn him when parts of him live on in Alex?

The first day of Thanksgiving vacation, I glare at the snow clouds thickening the sky and nestle deeper in my new fleece-lined hoodie, my hood up and sleeves down. Chill from the metal creeps through my jacket as I lean on the fence. The cloudy afternoon devours both sun and shadow, casting the headstones and angels into a strange muted light. Memorial Gardens has a surreal quality, everything sharper and duller at the same time.

Wind moans in the trees behind the mausoleum and whistles in the fence links. How many times had I come here over the summer, missing Daniel, wishing he had a grave for me to mourn beside? Now I stand here, and all I can think of is Alex.

The gate creaks when I push it open, the crushed stone path leading my feet through the cemetery. I wander past headstones and urns overturned for the winter. An ache pulls at my core, guiding me deeper into Memorial Gardens.

I tug at the loose hair tie cinching my hair back, and let it fall around my shoulders. When I look up, I see exactly where my longing has brought me. The mausoleum where Daniel and I used to sit and drink his father's whiskey.

I climb the marble railing on the far side, and place my left hand against the cool stone building. My eyes slip closed, and I tip my head back, smelling the air. Damp grass, the raw earth of a new grave, and the sweet smell of whiskey.

Daniel?

I walk to the corner and see a long pair of legs propped against the railing. Flutters dance in my chest, before my mind catches up with the clues that it's not him. The pricey sneakers, the sanded jeans. I round the corner in slow steps, revealing more of the source of my heartache. Leather jacket, cuffs peeking out, one hand holding a pint bottle of whiskey. The last step shows me all of Alex Franks.

And I can't muster up the surprise I should feel.

He is, in some very essential ways, Daniel.

"Hey," he says, and tips his eyes up. The tell-tale sign of tears redden his eyes, contrasting with his mismatched hazel irises. "Want a drink?"

"Alex," is all I can manage. Heartache catches in my chest.

Alex repeats, "Hey." He flaps a hand, waving me down to the cold stone beside him.

I sink to the mausoleum porch, a shallow column of air between us. "You already said that."

"I know." He slides until our shoulders touch, then leans his head on mine. The top-shelf bourbon smells sweet and strong on his breath. "Are we ever going to be OK, Energizer?"

God, that name. It's like a punch in the chest.

"I don't know."

"I don't either." He places his hand upside down, offering

it to me. Will I be touching Alex, or Daniel? Closing my eyes, I place my hand in his, the electric charge zipping over my skin. "Things are so messed up," he says. "I'm messed up inside, and it's killing me."

"Me, too," I whisper.

"I know you heard what my father said." He tips up the bottle of whiskey, and takes a swig. "I read the papers. It's real."

I can't say anything. My throat goes tight; tears burn the backs of my eyes.

"And you know what's worse? I love you, Emergizer. I really do."

"Please don't use that name," I whisper. "Daniel used it all the time."

"It's just so natural," he says, voice thick with alcohol. "It's in my head. Automatic."

"Then how do you know *you* love me?" I can't believe I say it – that thought has burrowed so deep in me I didn't think it would be anything but a secret. "What if it's just Daniel's heart telling you to?

"It's *in* me." He bangs his chest, amber liquor sloshing with the motion. Then he tips the bottle and takes a deep pull.

"Give me that," I tell him. And I know he'll obey me – Daniel would've. Alex hands me the whiskey without complaint. "And the cap."

"Don't have it," he slurs. "Didn't plan on needing it again."

"That much alcohol can't be good for you... with all the surgery you've had." I jerk up to my knees and dump the rest into the grass.

"That's alcohol abuse," he pouts. Such a cute expression.

"Tough."

"Emma." He takes my hand, tugs it till I look at him. The lines of his face have softened; he looks more like a young lovesick boy than a guy who's suffered so much heartache and pain. "I said I love you. Can't you say it back?"

God help me, I want to because it's true..

I loosen my fingers from his tight grip. The truth presses on me so hard, it feels like it's grown claws.

"I do." I stifle a sob and then ease my fingers from his. "I love you. And I don't know if I'm loving you, or the you that is wrapped up with so much of Daniel." Free of his grip, I stand and kick the railing. "This is so screwed up! It has to be Daniel's influence. And how can I live with that? Every time I brush one of your scars, it's silent evidence of Daniel's murder."

Alex recoils like my words are a slap in the face. *Truth hurts,* I think miserably. I scrub furiously at the tears on my cheeks. He lets his own fall.

"I'm alive," he says, voice empty of emotion, "at the cost of his life."

"Yes." I shove my hands in my pockets. "It hurts and confuses the hell out of me."

He's unsteady on his feet when he rises, and instinct guides me to grab his jacket to keep him upright. Alex reaches out, running his fingers through my hair, before offering me his hand again. "Com'ere…"

I shake my head. His lips turn down, he won't withdraw his hand. I give into the pull between us, allowing it to draw me into his arms. Alex tangles a hand in my hair, wrapping an arm around me.

He frowns, then says, "Can't love be enough?"

"When it's this broken?"

There's no right answer. He doesn't have one, and neither do I. It feels so perfect when he presses his mouth to mine instead. The tingle surges from my lips to my heart, surging in my veins, melting me.

He groans when I loosen my hold, and squeezes me tighter. "No. Don't let me go yet."

"We need to get home," I coax. "They're forecasting a snowstorm for tonight."

"Uh-uh." He shakes his head, keeping one arm around me. "Tell me we can make this work. Please. It's Thanksgiving – I don't want to sit alone with my heart breaking."

"Neither do I." My voice cracks, echoing the pain in my chest.

"Can I walk you home?"

"Yeah." I try for a smile and fail. "Then I'm calling you a taxi because you're not driving home drunk."

He clings to my hand, as if he's drowning and I'm the only thing between him and death. How can we have anything, when my heart just breaks over and over?

"Are your parents home?" he asks. "I'd like to wish them a happy Thanksgiving."

"Actually, they are at my dad's company's Thanksgiving party." The first flakes begin to dance in the sky. Pretty and light, and entirely the opposite of how I feel.

"You're alone tonight?"

"I'll be fine, Alex." I pull my fingers from his when we reach my porch. "I didn't want to go with them. And I'm sure your dad doesn't want you with me."

He can't argue. Alex doesn't say anything, other than calling for a taxi. The sofa arm holds him up when he droops there. His gaze rests on me, the waking dream expression in his eyes. When I pace along the sofa, he grabs my sleeve and reels me in.

I should fight him. Everything I'd shoved into a mental box to deal with later has sprung free, and the only thing that makes the thoughts stop is Alex's arms around me. I nuzzle his neck. His skin tingles with energy; his muscles relaxed with whiskey in his veins.

When the cabbie honks the horn, Alex starts as if he was sleeping with me in his arms, and reaches into the inside pocket of his jacket. I step back, still close enough to feel his breath on my lips, and taste a hint of the whiskey. Alex pulls out an old velvet-covered jewelry box. Everything in me tenses.

"I know we're in no place to be making promises, but I know what I feel." The hinges complain, then the box yawns open to display a pearl ring nestled in the black velvet inside. "My heart only beats for you."

I stand frozen, my mind and heart warring.

"Please," he says, sounding so sober and serious. "It was my mother's."

My hair slides forward when I nod, and I let him slip the ring onto my left hand. Lost so long in the shadows of loss, only to be shoved headlong into unnatural horror and heartache, I can't turn him away. He's a kindred soul. Broken, remade, and my perfect match.

Chapter Twenty-Seven

The oven timer dings, signaling my Thanksgiving dinner-for-one is done. I grab a towel, fold it in half and plop Mom's special turkey pot pie on it. The single-serve casserole dish is heaped with a pie crust, over turkey and vegetables in gravy, then topped with piped garlic mashed potatoes. A homey dish, and with all the stress lately, it's all I want.

I cradle the hot dish in the towel and carry it through the quiet house. Mom apologized a hundred times for leaving me home alone – I reminded her one hundred and one times that it was my choice.

I hardly know who I am anymore. I'm in no mood for a flashy party filled with loud people. Last year, Daniel and I had eaten dinner with his family. What are they doing this year? I can't imagine a holiday meal with ashes in an urn one room away. And Alex? How can he eat a meal with the monster who murdered to make his son live again? What kind of a holiday can Alex have, knowing Daniel will never have another because of him?

For a few minutes I stand and watch the snow falling, heavy and wet, casting the world into melancholy tones. The newscasters had been breaking into my holiday programming to report road closings and traffic delays. And the white stuff keeps falling.

The snow softens the world's edges, buries its sins under a powdery blanket. Too bad it can't work the same with life.

Renfield curls next to me on the sofa. His eyes track my spoon. Up and down. He makes a sound somewhere between a purr and a meow. Up and down. Heat throbs in my fingertips, and the pearl ring shimmers in the light when I pluck a piece of white meat from the casserole dish for him and blow it off. Then the cat has the nerve to glare at it like it's not an acceptable offering – before he begrudgingly takes it.

"You're a wonderful dinner companion," I tell him.

He yawns, flashing all his teeth, stretches, then pads around in a circle and lays down again.

With dinner done, I check the weather channel. Beneath the ticker constantly scrolling with road closings, another announcement runs, saying the main highways are now closed to all traffic. The full list of roads includes the two main roads my parents need to come back home. The excited weatherman claims it's the biggest significant November snowfall in recent West Michigan history.

Minutes later, the shrill ring of the house phone stabs into the relative calm.

"Emma," Dad says after I answer. "We're snowed in and your mother's having a fit. We're trying to find a way home to you."

"Don't worry about me." I pace to the front door and lock it. "I'll batten down the hatches, hunker down, and all those other weather-the-storm sayings. You guys just stay where you're safe."

"Safe and trapped with your mother aren't necessarily the same thing." A muffled thump broadcasts clearly over the phone connection – Mom whacking him with her purse, most likely. He covers the mouthpiece and I can still hear him arguing with her. "Your mom said we'll keep our ears open and come home if we can."

"No rush. Renfield will keep me company."

"OK, Arlene, I'll tell her," Dad snaps. "Your mother says don't burn any candles and make sure the emergency pack is loaded."

"Fine. If she'll stop nagging you."

"Not sure that will ever happen. See you soon, Emma."

"Love you, Dad."

After hanging up the phone, I pull the Holy Grail of Preparedness from the closet. A military surplus backpack Mom keeps loaded with whatever the TV says to: blanket, medicines, dried food, cat food (due to my insistence), water bottles, flashlight and batteries. I stuff a couple of granola bars into the front pouch, and then leave it on the counter. It'll make her feel good to see it when she comes home, and maybe save me some lectures.

With the pack checked and a long night ahead of me, I put Alex's *Dracula* DVD in, pile pillows in the sofa corner, then get comfy. Between my stomach full of food, a warm cozy corner and the familiar movie, I doze off before Vlad and Mina ever meet.

Around 10pm, I wake up to a darkened room, the windows full of the weird directionless light of a blizzard. The DVD player shut itself off, and the TV's talking to itself. One click on the remote shuts it off, then I pad around the house and turn lights off, too. The cat races me up the stairs, where I skip the shower and head directly to my bedroom. I pull on warm flannel pajama pants, followed by Alex's hoodie first, then Daniel's. It makes me feel closer to both of them, and on a very sensible level, as my room is the coldest in the house.

I might've convinced my dad I was fine, but being alone in this drafty old house with a blizzard raging outside scares me. It's easy for the awful things I've seen to come flooding back. Is the doe freezing? Are reanimated animals affected by the cold? Every creak or house groan sends chills skittering up my spine.

Renfield needles me with a frosty glare when I displace him from my pillows. Tail up and flashing his butt at me, he paces around the end of my bed before coiling his sinuous body into a knot by my chest.

Blankets shift away from my face when I loop an arm around my cat. Muttering against the cold, and wishing for Alex to keep me warm, I pull up both hoods. The snow driving outside my window obliterates any light through my curtains, I stare until my eyes slip closed.

Sleep is elusive, teasing as I dip in and out before crashing into the black.

I awake with a violent start to a choking smell. Blinking, I wipe sweat from my forehead and try to piece it together.

Only one thing makes any sense.

Fire.

Panic floods me. I lurch up, then the cat uses my stomach as a launch pad and then runs for the shadows of my closet.

"Renfield!" I scream.

He never listens to me on a good day. Why would he listen now?

I run to the door. Touching it only tells me how close the flames are. And the roar outside my bedroom is now worse.

A sound pulses in the din. I can't risk trying to hear it.

I rip the faery quilt from my bed and cram it in the crack underneath the door. My heart hammers in my ears and panicky terror turns my legs to rubber. *I have to get out of here,* I think, *get my cat and escape.*

A shuddering groan rocks the house, then a boom follows. Probably the flammable liquids in Dad's workshop catching fire an exploding. My floor shakes, and the heat builds. Sweat runs down my back, collects in the hollows of my body. Pale icy light taunts me from the window, a hollow promise. More air will only feed the flames. The sound repeats in the din, closer.

"Renfield, you stupid cat!" I shout. "Come here!"

I run into the closet and grab my own emergency pack, loosely stuffed with random necessities I never thought I would need. The repeating noise grows closer when I drop to my knees and sob my cat's name. I can't lose Renfield, he's my link to Daniel.

Every breath of air brings the taste of smoke. My lungs itch. My eyes burn.

My bedroom door explodes inward, the panel slamming against the wall, and the voice yells my name again. Another slam punctuates the fire's noise.

"Renfield!" I croak, at the same time someone screams, "EMMA!"

"HERE!" I cry, my voice no match for the roar, hand still reaching for Renfield.

A hand touches my back, grabs Daniel's hoodie and hauls me upright. I struggle. I want my cat. "Emma," he says, "Hey."

Those two words are all it takes. The fight leaves me, and I sob, "Alex!"

"Is there anyone else here?"

I don't answer. My brain is reeling. How is *he* here? What the hell is happening to my house?

"Is there anyone else here?" He demands. "Where are your parents? I couldn't find them!"

"They're not here," I shout. "Just me."

Alex wrests the backpack from my hand and drags me toward the door.

"No," I plead. "Get my cat!"

I breathe shallowly, smoke tainting my breaths, as he pushes me against the outside wall, the coolest place, farthest from the fire devouring my house. My backpack hits the floor, then Alex pulls off his leather jacket, flings it at the cat, then bundles Renfield in it. Another groan rocks the house; I grab my emergency pack and fling myself at Alex, trusting him to keep us safe.

Smoke is everywhere. Down my throat, in my eyes. I squint out the window when Alex pulls me to it. Outside the snow wails past the window, heaven compared to the hell we're in.

Alex steps toward the door, warping in the heat, then flings his arms up to protect his face.

"Too hot!" Desperation rings in his vice. "We're trapped!"

The fire must be on the other side of the door – in-between us and escape.

He casts a wild look around the room. Then his gaze falls on the box affixed to my wall that Dad made to look like an old-fashioned radiator box. Inside is the answer. A safety ladder mother insisted he install in every upstairs room. Chain and rungs, just a rickety ladder between us and freedom. Oh God. My heart threatens to choke what the smoke hasn't. I fling a look back into the black roiling in my room. A wild thought rambles through my mind. *Mom's kitchen is gone.*

And we're going to be next.

Not wasting time fighting with the stubborn lock and screwed-tight storm windows, Alex smashes the panes with the legs of my chair. Cold air rushes in, snowflakes swirl past and expire in the heat as he yanks the top off the box and flings the ladder out the window. Glass crunches beneath my feet, scattered across the carpet.

"You ready?" Alex shouts and hurls the emergency pack to the snow.

"No!"

"Too bad! You first."

Terrified, I fumbled my way out the window and down the chain ladder. Wind tug at me, melted snow makes the rung treacherous. Butt first, I land in the snow, sucking frigid air in my lungs, watching Alex make his way down one-handed, clutching the leather-cocooned Renfield to him.

Outside, the blizzard still rages. The world is an odd mix of frozen white and savage red. Horrified, we watch from the ground as a massive explosion jolts through what's left of my house. A rain of fire begins as the upper floor disinte-grates. Alex flings us downward, skidding through the mushy snow until we ram into the porch.

Dully, I'm aware of sirens wailing in the distance. The house wall gives way, Alex lunges, wrapping his arm around me and dragging us toward the front walk. We land in a tangle of stinking, smoky limbs. Smoke curls into the neighborhood, gray and nearly obscuring the red wash of escaping tail lights.

"You saved me!" I fling my arms around him, sandwich-ing the writhing cat between us.

"Of course I did." He kisses my hair, then grabs a handful of snow and washes my face. His eyes are amazingly bright when he says, "I love you."

He tips his chin closer, giving me a chance to refuse. I meet him halfway, heedless of the sirens, the emergency vehicles screaming to a stop, or the growl of a familiar engine a few houses down. All that matters is I'm alive, and I'm with Alex.

He kisses me as if he's never kissed me, and as if he's kissed me a thousand times and knows how to make me dizzy. I surrender, trusting him to hold me as my home falls down in a ruin of flame.

Chapter Twenty-Eight

I stand, freezing outside and numb inside, watching the fire-fighters put out the remnants of the blaze that devastated my house. Snow swirls around black timbers stabbing up through the wreckage. Sooty water, thick with slush, gushes past us. It's gone – my stuff, Mom's pictures and kitchen, Dad's handmade furniture. Destroyed. And I'm all cried out.

Alex's arms circle me, he whispers promises that it will be OK.

Such an ugly lie.

OK was home. OK was Alex before we discovered the sins his father committed.

OK vanished.

According to the first responders, the authorities suspect arson. First piece of evidence is where the fire started. The second is the gasoline can and book of matches found in the trash can by the remains of our garage. Someone set that fire on purpose. Someone wanted to hurt me, and my family.

"Yes, sir," the paramedic says into his cell phone. "Your daughter's cognizant, answering questions, and refusing treatment." He pauses, eyes me and Alex, and the cat carrier

Mrs Peterson carried over for Renfield. "I need your permission to release her."

A minor ruckus comes through the earpiece; Mom, I'm sure, arguing that I should go to the hospital, or they come back, despite the half-dozen accidents reports I'd heard over the paramedics' squalling radio. I can't say "come home", because there isn't one.

Then the paramedic nods, and says, "Yes, Mr Gentry."

He snaps the phone closed and says, "OK, you're free to go. Keep an eye on her, Mr Franks."

"I will," Alex vows and pulls me closer.

After signing papers saying we refused treatment by the paramedics, Alex takes Renfield's carrier and my emergency backpack, and carries them to his car, with me ghosting sock-footed behind in his wake. Memories leap out when he pops the trunk, and I can't help seeing the doe. He'd placed her there once. Her death has been trivialised by the atrocities Alex's father committed to reanimate her.

It seems small with my house – *my house* – a smoking steaming mess.

The backpack displaces the echo of the doe's carcass when he puts it in the trunk. Warmth rolls from the inside of the car when Alex opens the door and wedges the cat carrier in the back seat.

"Come on," he says, and points to the passenger seat.

I sat there before and ended up at the clinic. It's stupid to recoil, but I feel like I'm devolving to gut reactions whenever numbness isn't a good enough buffer. "Where are we going?"

"Just trust me, OK?"

Fate leaves me with few choices: throw myself on the mercy of the paramedics and their needles and facemasks, or trust the boy whose life hurts my heart with every stolen heartbeat.

"Fine," I mutter, slump to the seat, and burrow deeper in my sweatshirt.

The car jiggles a little when Alex climbs in behind the steering wheel and shuts the door. Renfield lets out a low growl-yowl, plainly saying he's had enough stress for one lifetime and further upset, of any kind, isn't appreciated. He's named after a crazed man in a Gothic novel – but right now, I have to agree.

I wish my brain and mouth could come to a compromise and not make things worse.

"I should be dead right now," I say, my voice as hollow as I feel. "How'd you know to come?"

He exhales a breath, blowing the smell of smoke around the car. His knuckles whiten on the steering wheel. I think Alex is going to talk when he flicks me a quick look, but then he sputters a cussword, clutches the steering and steers out of a skid. Drama and blizzards don't mix.

Underneath a stop light on the way out of town, he turns to me, face as serious as the death he cheated. "I couldn't let my father hurt you."

"Your father?" How can I feel stunned when I've been slammed so many times? "Why would he…?" I can't even finish the question.

"We argued," he says, driving white-knuckled through the blizzard. "He kept throwing you – and my 'unhealthy infatuation with you' – in my face. When he stormed out, I followed. I knew he was going to do something bad."

"Like what he does in his lab?" Now that I've roughed up the wound, I jab him in a tender spot.

"You saw the animals?" He lays on the horn and narrowly

avoids a car sliding out of its lane. A drunk, probably. It's the busiest bar night of the year and close to closing time.

"And I overheard your argument last weekend," I remind him, then add, "and I've done some research on my own."

"Research?"

"Internet, Alex," I say and tighten my seat belt. "After you were hurt, a string of suspicious accidents and missing person reports hit the news. All guys. Daniel was the last one. Considering nothing as perfect as you happens by accident..."

A smile flirts with his lips before he pulls them into a frown. "You think my dad killed them all," he finishes for me.

I nod, though I'm not sure he sees it with his defensive winter driving skills being taxed.

"I'm not sure what he's capable of anymore," Alex continues, turning onto a snow-choked country highway. The world has turned to white – he must be driving by instinct now. "I always thought the animals were his way of giving me back what was broken."

"Broken isn't dead." If it is, my heart would be hanging limp in my chest.

"I know." He scrapes at the frost on the windshield, then guides the car off the road and into a seeming field of nothing. A sea of white spreads in front of us. Headlights hit a stand of trees acres back and an old farmhouse. The house looks empty, but too well-taken care of to be abandoned, when the wheels churn to a halt in the driveway. "We're here."

"Where's here?" I leave the seat belt buckled.

"The only safe place I could think of." The car shudders a little when he puts it in park, and then kills the engine. "My grandparents' house."

"Are you crazy?" My voice gets sharp. He's feeding me to the wolves. "You brought me to your grandparents' house?"

"No, and yes."

Infuriatingly, Alex unhooks his seat belt, and climbs out. Discussion over. The trunk opens, then closes and Alex appears at my door with two bags in his hand. My brain is locked on the fact that he's driven us out into the middle of nowhere where his crazy father can come and murder me in my sleep. "That's it," I tell Renfield. "We're going to die."

The cat doesn't respond.

I lock gazes with Alex when he opens my door. His lips curl down, mismatched eyes radiating hurt that I don't trust him. I can't help it; too much bad stuff has happened. Even though he came to my rescue, his dad tried to end my life. A tickle follows his fingers across my stomach when he unhooks my seat belt. "You'll freeze to death out here."

Huffing a sigh, I climb out into knee-high snow. Bone deep chill burns my sock-covered feet and sopping wet legs. I yank up my hood to ward off the blizzard winds. The farmhouse watches us through dead, curtain-covered windows. I put on my emergency pack and take the handles of a leather carry-on sized suitcase, while he ducks into the back seat and coos to Renfield as he lifts the carrier out.

"Back door," Alex says into the biting wind, then forges a path for us.

At the rear of the house, he stands on tiptoe and wedges a small window open a couple inches. A metallic flicker stabs through the snowfall when he pulls a key from the windowsill. I huddle closer when he slides the key in the lock and opens the door.

A short set of stairs rises in front of us, and a longer set plunges off to the left into the gloom of a cellar or basement below. The braided rug swishes under our feet on the landing. The utter difference of my life hits me when I watch

Alex climb the short back steps with the cat carrier in front
of him. I have nowhere to go, except to a friend that I don't
want to bring trouble on. I follow Alex.

He opens another door at the top of the stairs and steps
into a kitchen.

Everything is sunny yellow paint and white wood, and
covered in doilies.

"Where are your grandparents?" *And how can you think
this is safe?*

"They're in Florida," he says, and flicks on the lights.
"They're my mom's parents, by the way," he adds, "and my
dad hates them. He hasn't been near here since she died."

He walks to a thermostat on the wall, and jacks up the heat,
then walks further in the house and turns on more lights.

Safe, I think. Actually safe, with no fire or madman chas-
ing me.

All the tension keeping my spine straight and legs moving
snaps – like a wire stretched to its limits – and coils back inside me. Standing doesn't work anymore, and I slowly
crumple. Tears rush over my cheeks, and a racking sob hurts
my throat. I'm vaguely aware of Renfield mewing in the crate
over the snotting, sobbing wreck I've become.

The awkward tension leaves me when Alex takes the
backpack from my shoulders and bag from my hand. Then
he crouches and gathers me into his arms.

"You're OK," he says. "I'll make sure of it."

I fling my arms around him, nuzzle close to his neck. I
crave the leather and Alex smell. Instead, there's nothing but
smoke.

"You stink."

"Well, thanks." Rich laughter rolls from him. "You don't
smell so good either."

The world tilts and then centers on Alex as he stands. He takes my good hand and hauls me upright. Upstairs in the sunshine house – the yellow and white theme is everywhere – he leads me into a small bedroom with more lace than a sewing store. White ruffley embroidery dissects the squares of a pastel calico quilt on the bed; the doll leaning against the pillows wears ivory and lace; and the curtains are lace.

"Gran," he tells me in a voice both soft and reverent, "said this was my mom's room. They redecorated, but kept her things."

He disappears in the closet, then comes back dragging a large cedar trunk. The scent of lavender and mint whoosh off piles of folded denim, flannel and jersey when he lifts the lid.

"Find something clean," he says. "And we'll wash our clothes."

"Oh. Um…" I didn't think there was room left for awkward in my overload of stress. "I feel really funny wearing your mom's clothes." *His dead mom's clothes.*

"Please don't. I'm sure she would've wanted my girlfriend taken care of."

Girlfriend. The word makes my heart want to soar. I drop a glance to the pearl ring on my left hand. Of course he'd call me that – even if I have doubts, Alex doesn't. I heave a sigh, and slide closer, hesitant to touch the chest full of memories. He nudges me, knee in the curve of my butt, and the folds of material tip toward my face.

"Hey!" I catch the edge, and swing my cast at him.

"Just helping," he says, ducking the pink cudgel. "I have a spare pair of clothes in my bag downstairs." Then he's gone.

Resigned, I carefully sift through the clothing in the chest. Simple jeans, flannel shirts and pajamas, team jerseys from the different sports his mother played. The sizes are all wrong. Alex's mother was taller than me, and curvier in the areas I wish I were. Thinking I lost the wardrobe lottery, I settle on a pair of pink flannel pajama pants (legs cuffed), a baseball jersey, and a pair of socks.

Alex stands in the hallway, leather bag in hand. "The bathroom's through there. I'll shower first and give the hot water time to heat up for you."

"Aw. You don't have to freeze for me, Alex."

"Haven't you figured it out?" he says. "I'd do anything for you."

A dozen things jumble in my mouth and die. I smile, and know it goes all the way to my eyes.

"By the way..." He ducks into the bathroom. His voice comes muffled from the other side of the door. "There's cat food under the sink in the kitchen for Renfield. Gran has a litter pan somewhere, too. And here..." the door opens and I see a long vertical flash of skin when his clothes fly into the hall. "I'll wash our clothes once you've showered."

Blush saturates my cheeks, flows past into my forehead and throat. Atop the pile of smelly clothes lies a pair of boxer shorts. Toeing his underwear under his shirt, I gather his clothes and then return to the sunshine kitchen. The cat supplies are in the cabinet under the sink, neat and tidy – until I get Renfield taken care of and released from the plastic crate. The desperate cat uses the litter right away, even in a stranger's home. Then I ferret Alex's cell phone from his jacket, and call my parents.

Mom's a wreck, Dad's not much better, and they're more concerned about me than losing everything. I don't tell them the darkest part – Alex's dad is most likely the culprit and trying to kill me. The story I give them is a big string of false-hoods, from Alex coming over to watch movies, to him being snowed in and sleeping on the couch. Him rescuing me from upstairs is totally true.

They aren't happy with not knowing the address of where we are, either.

"It's kinda hard," I say, "to read street signs in the middle of the night in a blizzard, Dad."

He says, "Well, keep in touch, and we will, too. We're just so thankful that you're all right."

"Don't worry so much. I'll see you tomorrow."

"Goodbye, Emma."

I push End Call, and close Alex's phone.

The glory of the sunshine kitchen presses in on me. Welcoming, pretty, happy, and so foreign. I feel like a filthy intruder fouling the beauty here.

I pace the downstairs, drifting from room to room. Pictures are everywhere, from black-and-white and old, to more recent times. There's no rhyme or reason like my mom would've made with them; elementary here, junior high there, high school in the living room. A young girl in pigtails and a gingham dress shares a shelf with a young woman cradling a brown-haired baby. In another room is a framed older couple – the setting sun at their side – and an elementary school Alex. I find one of him in the kitchen, probably last year, wearing an apron with a jar of preserves in his hand.

He has a whole different life with his grandparents. He had a different life before he woke up wanting me. The stairs creak, and I feel him coming back to me, like a song rising in my blood. The electric tickle courses my skin.

"That's my favorite picture," Alex says behind me. "Gran

and I picked the berries and canned them that day."

How do I tell him I'm glad he had a normal influence in his life, other than his psychopath father? When I turn, the thought flees. Alex wears a dark pair of jeans, and a forest green short-sleeved shirt. The color makes the green in his hazels really glow, and it somehow highlights his scars. How could I have ever thought he was anything other than beautiful?

"OK," he says, and winks with his left eye, "now that I'm clean, you smell really bad."

"Thanks a lot." I roll my eyes, and he herds me to the stairs.

A big claw-foot tub commands my attention the minute I peek in the bathroom. A bright yellow checkered curtain encircles it, inviting me to scrub away the stink of disaster. Still, it takes washing my hair three times with the citrus-scented shampoo to get the smell out.

Hair pulled back loosely, and a stranger's clothes on, I walk out to find Alex waiting in the hall. Renfield sits at his feet, and the leather bag hangs from Alex's hand.

"Emma." A somber expression clouds his eyes. "I have to show you something."

I follow him down the hall to another bedroom. This one is paneled in blond wood, with white trim on the doors and windows. An old patchwork quilt of sunlight colors mixed with denim patches covers the bed, and matches the rag rug on the floor. Guy stuff sits around the room – a martial arts trophy, an autographed baseball, a collection of well-worn fantasy novels.

"My room," he says, answering the question I would've asked. "I've spent at least one week a summer with them every year. The bastard that my dad is," he runs his fingers over the dresser, "he wouldn't tell my grandparents they couldn't see me."

"It's hard to picture him being kind."

"Things were fine, as long as they went his way. For the most part they did."

"And then you woke up…"

"And then you woke me up."

He smiles, steps closer and runs a fingertip along my neckline to my bun. I knew it wouldn't last long. With a little tug, the strands spill loose and fall damply down my back.

He says, "I dreamed about you before I regained consciousness."

How can I respond to that?

"Sit down," he tells me, pointing at his bed. "You'll probably want to anyway."

I perch on the edge of the bed, near the pillows. My cat runs up, and pads across the pillows, making himself at home, as long as he's close to me. Alex drags his leather bag to the other end of the bed and sits, too.

"Before I left my house, I took the file my father showed me." He pulls out the manila folder and puts it between us. He returns his hand to the bag's unzipped mouth, and pulls out at least a dozen plastic vials of a red liquid. "This is the serum my father has been injecting me with and telling me it's a vitamin booster. It isn't. My survival depends on weekly injections of that combined with a modulated electric treatment."

Alex places the formula on the folder, and pushes them to me, then watches me. The red liquid is the color of rubies, and has a thickness and sparkle to it in the overhead lights. He suffers injections of this every week? Alex is still paying for his father's sins. Tied to a drug and electrical current to keep him alive.

"My life is in your hands," he says. Then Alex grabs the

hem of his T-shirt and pulls it off. His scars are a map of life and death and the laws broken to revert them. "I know what my dad took from you. I've seen it. I've felt it. And I swear I will never take another dose of that medicine if letting the heart in my chest stop beating will end your pain."

The shock of his words stabs into me. An unbidden image flashes behind my eyes: Alex, pale, lifeless in a coffin. My heart catches, and the pain flares. The thought of losing Alex hurts worse than any ache I ever suffered. The truth he's insisted on – since we discovered the crimes his dad stitched into his body – finally hits me. Daniel's heart *is* Alex's; his memories are, too. It doesn't matter who the guys were before. Alex is alive and loves me. And I love him.

"Oh God, no, Alex." I push the folder and formula back into the bag and shove it to the floor. "I don't want to live without you."

"I mean it, Emma." He pulls me to him, eyes searching my face. "My heart is yours. I am yours."

I brush my fingers over his cheek, and into his hair. "And I'm yours," I whisper.

I feel his groan when he hooks an arm around me and crushes me to him. The electricity races along my nerves to my heart.

"We'll have to turn my dad in," he whispers. "It's the only way to be safe. I'm sure my grandparents will let me stay here."

"I want to be with you." The weeks at school without him echo like a hollow ache. I don't ever want to live like that again.

"You are," he says, voice husky. "And I'm not letting you go. Ever."

I don't want him to let go. I want to live forever in this

moment. A nervous kind of anticipation floods me when he guides my knees and presses me back on the pillows. Renfield sniffs indignantly and pads to the other end of the bed. Energy teases my skin in waves when Alex kisses me. Not hesitant or awkward. Firm, claiming me, claiming us.

He gasps a little when I nip his bottom lip and then press his mouth open. A quiver having nothing to do with the blizzard's cold rides the length of his body.

I slide my hand between us. Light shines on his lean muscles and his scars, both an invitation and a pathway to learn who Alex has become. I trail my fingers down the lines in his neck, following the feather-light strokes with kisses, then across his chest to cover his pounding heart. I place my palm there, thinking, *it beats for me.*

"My turn," he whispers.

Shivers chase the tingles over my skin when he brushes his fingertips along the hem of the baseball jersey. The tingles turn to surges of heat when his fingers brush my ribs and his lips find my neck. His fingers stray further, sweeping curves where my bra should be. Breath hitches in my throat, and escapes in a sigh.

"Want me to stop?" he asks, his words warm on the skin of my collarbone where he's tugged my neckline down.

It's my turn to groan. "No."

The warmth he's brought to my body – and back to my soul – spreads when he slides his fingertips down my stomach, and glides them along the waist of my borrowed flannel pants. His mouth leaves a tingly path down my stomach. I melt beneath his lips when they brush the skin below my belly button.

"Did you mean what you said?" His lips brush over my

bare skin. "Are you mine?"

"Yes."

Words die. I drown in Alex's touch. He places kisses everywhere, with our clothing hitting the floor as he goes along. I'm amazed he thought to bring protection, then conscious thoughts go the way of words. His touch is electric, his kisses like fire. I'm more alive in his arms than any moment in my life. Being with Alex is all sensation and emotion, building and building, taking everything fractured between us and burning it into something pure and singular.

"I love you," I whisper, before pulling on his T-shirt and then the blankets.

"Always yours," he promises, his jeans rubbing my legs when he curls against my back, after shutting off the lights.

Chapter Twenty-Nine

The bed lurches, and the motion wrenches me awake. I reach for Alex, and find only empty sheets. Wrongness abrades my drowsy nerves, fills the air and smells like fancy cologne. Blinking, I try to scrub sleep from my eyes. The light is all wrong, choppy and moving as shapes twist and writhe.

Worry seizes me.

"Alex?" Where is he?

"Emma, run!"

Run? What is he talking about? I pray for my sleep-fogged brain to wake up.

"Hold still, damn you," a familiar voice growls.

"No!" shouts Alex, and then, "Stay away from her, you asshole!"

Who needs to stay away from me?

Another blink, and I scrub my eyes until my vision clears. I turn to the front of the bed, where a scuffle breaks up the light in the room. Alex's father and Alex are all tangled up and wrestling by the window. The father has his son in a headlock. Panic screams from every line of Alex's body. Alex jerks and writhes. He rams his head backward into his father's jaw with little effect.

"Let me go!"

"Oh, no, son." His father's voice drips icy sarcasm. I gasp when he pulls a syringe from his pocket, jabs it into the vein in Alex's neck and depresses the plunger. "I did let you go, and look where it got me." He wrenches Alex around so he's pointed at me. "I gave you the perfect life, the perfect future wife. But, no, you're so blindly in love with that pathetic girl you can't see straight. You want to be with her so badly, fine. I'll make it permanent."

"No," Alex mouths. A pull batters my insides when his hands reach for me.

The fight leaves Alex. His eyes widen, and tears shine above his lashes. One fat drop rolls down his cheek. Gravity claims his hands and then Alex hangs like a rag doll from his father's arm. Dr Franks bends at the waist and opens his arms, letting his son's body drop to the floor. Alex's eyes stay fixed on me until he can't keep them open anymore.

The boy I'd given my heart, and myself to, lays silent on the floor.

My pain finds a voice. "You killed him!"

"Don't be stupid," the arrogant man scoffs. "After everything I did to make him live again? You're not worth that much. Now," his father says, gesturing to me with a gloved hand. "Take care of that, will you?"

Take care of me?

Motion behind sends chills rocketing up my spine. I spin, yanking the quilt back up around my bare legs. He's there, lurking at the foot of the bed like a monster in a horror flick. Ugly red hair and a twisted grin.

"Josh?"

"I guess all my cracks about you being a whore weren't far off…"

Stars explode in my vision when he lunges forward and backhands me. Pain flares in my jaw and the side of my head.

"Really," Dr Franks sniffs. "I'm not paying you to beat her."

"Call it creative license," Josh says, then pounces up on the bed.

I drive my knee up, hitting his thigh instead of what I'm aiming for. Josh shakes his head, starts to *tsk* through his teeth, and I stop his mocking noise by clawing his face with my left hand. His eyebrows slam together over his nose, matching the speed of red welling in the scratch marks. I notice the shiny color right before Josh smacks me again.

The hit drives the pain from my jaw into my head. Ringing pierces my ears, and the bed spins in a dizzy fashion. I slump to my elbows, head bobbing and blood wetting my lips.

"Shoulda done that a long time ago," he says, his words doubling like echoes in my ears.

"You should," Alex's father says, "do what I hired you for. Inject her."

"Happy to."

Then Josh straddles me, pinning my arms down with his knees. He takes a loaded syringe from his pocket, then pulls off the cap.

"It didn't have to be like this," Josh says in a ridiculously conversational tone. A sharp jab in my neck leads to a burning pressure. "If you could've just learned to like me. But, no…"

The heat in my neck spreads, into my head to muddle the pain, through my shoulders and into my body, singeing my veins. I want to fight, want to throw Josh off me, but my limbs are full of warm sand. My breathing slows, and panic flutters in my chest, but the drug slows that down too.

"What didya give them?" Josh asks.

"Fentanyl, which I had the lab alter to my purposes." The doctor crosses his arms and watches me with clinical interest. "A narcotic a hundred times stronger than morphine."

"Sounds like fun…"

"It's not recreational."

Before my eyes slip closed, Josh leans over me, close enough for me to smell the toothpaste and coffee on his breath. My eyes struggle to focus. Hate seethes so hot for him it might gag me. Glaring back doesn't work, my eyelids are so heavy.

"I didn't just let Daniel fall, bitch. I pushed him."

Monster! I shriek in my mind.

Then my eyes sag closed. My hearing is the last to go.

"Tie them up," Dr Franks orders. "And we'll take them back to the lab."

I can't scream, can't move, can't fight them at all, and then the black finally wins…

The room spins, or I'm spinning. I'm not sure. Light comes from every angle, highlighting the veins in my eyelids, making the vertigo worse. Sharp medicinal smells fill the chilly air. Where am I? I'd been in bed with Alex, then his father and Josh drugged us…

I'm still lying down. But now hard planes beneath me deny movement, and I know instinctively Alex is not beside me. Edgy panic causes my racing heart to speed blood through my body. Fear tastes sour in the back of my throat. My eyelids drag like sandpaper when I force them up. Ceiling, walls, floors – everything is white or metal. Wires and tubes, lights and machines everywhere.

An operating room.

Oh my God. Fight-or-flight reactions kick in, jerking me

up against pain and bonds I can't yet see. I'm trapped. Tied atop a narrow, rickety operating table with my arms cranked down and below the edge. I cannot lift my hands – someone must've tied them underneath this table.

I can't move enough to gauge where I am, or what's going on. I catch a shadow of something, or someone past me where I'm able to turn my head. Then my heart skips a beat. Alex, pale as death, lies on another table a few feet away. *Oh, Alex, no!* He's unconscious, a mask over his face, electrodes taped to his temples, chest barely rising and falling, monitor leads and IVs in his arm. Ugly yellow-brown iodine covers his chest.

"Alex!" I scream.

No response.

I wrench against the ropes on my wrists. Heat saws into my skin, the knot gives a little.

"You're probably wondering where you are," comes the infuriatingly calm voice of Dr Franks from over my shoulder. He strides into view, wearing surgical scrubs and gloves and wheeling a cart loaded with wicked-looking instruments. "What do those signs say? 'Trespassers will be prosecuted'? Well, consider this your punishment for weaseling your way into our lives."

Punishment? This isn't my fault. He brought this on us all when he got in the way of Daniel's love for me. Twisting my left hand around, I get a grip on the cords tying my hands. If I could just keep him talking, I can untie myself.

"Why are you doing this?" Damn my voice for shaking like I'm terrified.

"Why?" His eyebrow hardly arches. A sneer curls his upper lip. "To get my son back, to restore him to the life I planned for him. Med school, a brilliant wife, eventually his own practice."

He runs his fingers over the tray of tools, and eyes me critically. The rope gives a little. I need so much more time.

"What are you going to do with me?"

"Conscious donors are so chatty." Then he says, like we're old friends, "What am I going to do? I'm going to eliminate the one thing standing in the way of all that."

Conscious donor? The fear sharpens, turning nauseous and sour in my gut. Loops in the knot loosen, but I can't get my fingers hooked in to pull it. My heartbeat echoes in my ears when the psychopath walks the few steps to his son. *Don't hurt him*, I plead, *kill me, just please God, don't hurt Alex anymore.*

"Since Alex woke up, he hasn't been right. Wanting nothing to do with the girl I picked for him, more obstinate, more opinionated…"

"Sounds just like Daniel," I retort at Alex's dad, and work at the ropes on my hands.

"And *obsessed*." His jaw clenches, any friendliness gone. "Going on and on about some girl in his dreams."

"Daniel loved me," I say, exploiting his weak spot, and working a loop of the knot loose. "Bet you didn't expect that."

The jibe works, his face darkens as he paces back and forth. And I pry another section of the knot free.

"Love," he says, "is not science. It's not measurable. Not real." And then he turns to me, face impassive again. "But it *is* symbolic. I'm going to take the biggest symbol possible. I'm going to take your heart, Emma Gentry, and give it to my son. Then Alex'll stop pining after you."

"He'll hate you!" My voice is steady despite the fear poisoning me. If my emotions – and my soul – reside in my flesh, Alex will hate his father forever.

My fingers slip and I lose my grip on the ropes briefly. Despair threatens me. Then a fire sparks – I lost myself to that

darkness once. I won't do it again, not as long as there's a
chance at hope and Alex is alive. I track Dr Franks' movements as he fills a syringe with Alex's formula, then injects
it into Alex's vein. Humming tunelessly, he types a code on
a tablet computer wired into the bank of machines, and flips
a switch.

Dr Franks turns scanning the read outs of the machines
attached to Alex, then presses a button and speaks into the
camera eye of the little computer, "We're about to start.
Meet me in the lab."

A girl's voice replies, "Yes sir. I'm turning on to Frituvale
Drive. I'll be there shortly."

His smile is as chilly and clinical as the room when he
turns back to me.

"What son doesn't hate his father? *That*," he stresses as he
reprises our conversation, "is real. And perfectly natural."

"Nothing in this place is natural." My voice is level, my
mind filling with images of the reanimated animals and the
crimes this man committed, against people and nature.

"Maybe not to you," he says, then rolls the cart closer. "I
don't expect you to understand." Then he grabs my chin,
and forces me to look at Alex, flat on the table. "He is my
greatest achievement. I cheated death for him and I will not
let some girl, and the emotions of her dead boyfriend, take
that away from me."

Alex isn't a son, he's a trophy. There's no love from his
father, only possession. I love Alex. Every bit of my heart
confirms it. And I will do anything to be with him.

One last bend in the rope. I work it with careful fingers,
while Dr Franks selects a pair of shears off the table. His
expression becomes analytical. The metal is cold as he cuts
my shirt up the middle, exposing most of my chest and

stomach to the uncaring lights. All business, he reaches for a jar and swab, and then a stack of blue paper sheets on the supply cart.

My hopes plummet – the end of the cord is so long to feed through the last loop, I may not get free in time.

The cold in his eyes and the antiseptic both sink into my gut as he swabs my skin, then frames my chest in the blue paper sheets.

"Have to prevent contamination," he says. His voice has a sing-song tone, like he's teaching a beginner's course for psycho surgeons. Anger would be better, anger can be affected – detachment is so much scarier. My fingers tire from worrying the knot, the cord feeding through a teeny bit at a time.

Then Dr Franks places a stainless steel pan beside me, ice in the bottom and a sealed sterile bag atop the ice. Humming to himself, he sets a pair of shears next to it – to cut open the bag, then stuff my heart into the germ-free insides, I'm sure. Terror drives my heart against my ribs, and I wonder if he'll be displeased with a bruised organ.

The loop shrinks in my hand. *Almost there...* It slips, slips, slips toward the floor. Then the doctor picks up a scalpel and faces me again.

"No," I beg. "Please, no."

"Bargaining is one of the stages of grief," he says matter-of-factly. "It may dismay you to know, I found on using your boyfriend Daniel's organs, the more conscious the donor is, the better success of the transplant. So, I apologize if this hurts..."

The blade is frigid, the burning pain when it cuts into the skin between my breasts is unbelievable. A gasp sucks cold air into my lungs that I let out in a high whine.

And then the cord falls free from my hands.

Surprise widens Dr Franks' eyes when I ram my cast into his throat. One hand clenches on my shoulder, his other opens and the scalpel falls to the floor in a spray of red. Air whistles in his windpipe and it's not enough. He's still standing between me and Alex. I claw at his hand, then Dr Franks shifts his grip and clamps both hands around my throat.

The panic I felt morphs into anger.

Blood courses down my skin when I twist, and bring my cast around. Heat floods my face, blood trapped by the surgeon's hands. Then I swing the cast down like a sledgehammer, crashing it into his thin wrists. Something cracks on impact, and Dr Franks lets out a yelp. Hurt flares in my hand again, but I'm used to it. His chokehold springs open and he stares at his wrist. I must've broken bones in him, too.

I swing the cast one more time, up and out, hitting his chin and driving him backward. The focus goes out of his eyes, then they cross and he pitches forward to the floor.

"Weren't expecting that either. Were you?" I say.

I wedge a pad of gauze into the cut oozing blood from my chest. Then I untie my feet.

Chill from the floor spreads across the soles of my feet when I slide from the surgical table. I grab a sheet smelling faintly of bleach and wrap it around me. All I can think is to reach Alex, wake him up, and escape this hell house.

"Alex," I sob, stumbling over his father's outstretched hand. "Alex, wake up."

Nothing.

Medicinal scents waft from the mask when I rip it from his face. I gaze uselessly at the monitors. The numbers and squiggly lines make no goddamn sense. He could be dying and I wouldn't know what to do. His shoulders are limp;

his arms are loose when I shake him. Pink flares on his white cheek when I give into desperation and slap him.

Still nothing.

A sob of fear and a growl of frustration merge in my throat.

Think, I tell myself. *Calm down and think.*

His father filled a needle with the formula Alex has to have once a week, and then typed something into the tablet computer.

Feet slapping the floor, I step back to the thin tablet and press Execute on the touch screen.

An immense power draw dims the lights, and buzzes in the air, crawling over my skin like bees. Alex's body arches like a bow from the surgical table. The monitors squeal, needles bury in the black, every one of his joints lock, every muscle a cord of steel standing beneath his skin.

I can't help it. I scream his name and drop to my knees.

The lights return to normal, and the monitors begin a comforting rhythmic beeping.

"Please, be OK," I whisper.

The gauze falls from my chest and blood trickles down my skin when I stand. High color flags his pink cheeks; his muscles visibly relax, joints loosen. I thread the fingers of my left hand in one of his.

"Wake up, Alex," I plead, then kiss his lips. "Wake up and say you love me."

Chapter Thirty

Alex draws a breath through his nose, then a smile crooks his lips. This close, the energy I just poured into him crackles in the air between us. His mismatched, beautiful hazel eyes open and fix on me with the wonder and amazement I've grown to cherish.

"I love you," he says, giving me what I begged for, then follows it with, "What happened?"

Tears of relief burn past my defenses. I don't know where, or how to hug him with all the wires and tubes, but I want in the worst way to bury my face in the crook of his neck and smell his skin.

"Your dad wanted to rip out my heart and trade it for yours." I'm not going to lie. His father's on the floor, my shirt's cut, I'm bleeding, and Alex is vital and tingly to my senses. "I wasn't going to let that happen."

My hands flutter over him, one club-like weapon, one aching and tired. Alex pulls the electrodes from his temples, and then the IVs and tubes out as he sits up. He flexes his arms, stretches his spine, rolls his neck and shoulders. He looks as healthy as the night of the dance, and as beautifully uncovered with his scarred perfection, as he did last night. His gaze falls to his father, prone on the floor.

"I'm not sure I want to know how you managed that," he says in a neutral voice.

I waggle my hot pink cast between us. "I figured he broke my bones, I could use the cast to break a couple of his."

"Karma." A bitter laugh escapes him as he slings his legs over the side of the table. "There are scrubs in the end cabinet," he says, eyes gliding down my body before flicking a gaze at the far wall. "We don't want you to freeze."

"You're not exactly fully clothed..."

I'm so bent on leaving, I didn't even think about the snow. At least he still has his jeans on.

I step over his father, heading toward the cabinets. The counter is stocked with vials of Alex's necessary formula, plastic-wrapped packets of tools, bundles of gauze, and other stuff I don't recognize. I can't leave Alex's life on the shelf, and I scoop up as many bottles as I can in my left hand and take them with on my hunt for clothing.

The cabinet is tall as a broom cupboard, and full of tops, pants, lab coats, and boxes of gloves, masks, and paper booties. I take a lab coat, and stuff the vials in a pocket, then pull on a pair of baby blue scrubs. Blood seeps from the cut in my chest and stains the front of the shirt immediately. *Grab another one*, I tell myself. The vials clink and jostle in the pocket when I wrap the jacket around them. One slips to the floor, and when I bend to retrieve it, I see motion in the middle of the room.

No. It isn't even a thought. It's a violent gut reaction.

"Alex," I shout before I can get my head around the cupboard door.

Lightning cracks in the side of my head, slammed there

by the cabinet door. Once, twice, three times. I drop to the floor, a jumble of hurt flesh.

"Dad!" Alex bellows. "Leave her alone!"

"I will not!" Dr Franks shoves me over onto my back, plants a foot in my chest, pressing on the cut. A squeaking wheeze rushes from me. "She's ruined everything. Med school. Hailey. I had it all planned!"

Life freezes, and I see three things at once: His father raises his foot, about to kick me. Alex vaults the surgical table. And the precious vials roll away, free of the lab coat.

Then life jumps into high gear. Airborne, Alex slams into his father. The younger Franks wraps his arms around his dad's as the force drives them both into cabinet shelves. Medical paraphernalia flies from the shelves, hitting me and them as they tussle. Throwing my arms over my head, I cower away from the vicious barrage of punches.

Alex slams Dr Franks spine-first into the cart of tools. Blades and things go skidding in all directions. Alex's dad wrenches a hand free and grabs for a needle full of a clear fluid – just like the Fentanyl they used on us at his grand-parents' house. A guttural sound rips from Alex, and he spins them both until he can slam his father's hand against a bank of machines and shake the syringe free.

The monitors all flicker.

Spitting a cussword, I lunge for the tablet computer his father had used and yank it from the cart. Then the rest of the electronics in the room go black and silent. Grunts and half-sputtered curses fill the silence.

"I will not let you hurt her," Alex vows.

His father laughs, a manic sound.

They go down again, Alex sweeping his father's feet from under him. Vials crack, and sparkling red spills over the white tile floor. Alex's father scoops up a pair of surgical shears before he buries it in his son's shoulder. A howl of pain blasts the room. Rearing back, Alex lets go long enough to yank the scissors free, and then spins them in his palm and drives it home in his father's ribs. The older man gasps, staring at the injury his son gave him.

"That's right." Alex nods. "I'm not yours anymore."

He steps back, crushing one of the medicine vials.

The room centers on his father, and the air burbling around the handle jutting out of his chest. His hand shakes when he pulls it out and flings it to the floor.

"Let us go, Dad," Alex demands.

"Let you go?" his father snaps. I keep him in my sights as I gather the last couple formula bottles. The man rises, then slams his hand against a red button. An alarm sirens in the house. "I will never let you go. I made you. I own you!"

Snarling, Alex scoops up the tablet, and slams it into the side of his father's head.

"Like hell you do."

Worrying about the valuable information in it, I grab the little computer as Dr Franks staggers backward, and collapses on the damaged monitor bank. He grabs for it, and rips it down with him when he falls. Instruments clatter beneath him as Alex's father tries to stand. Alex extends a hand to me, and leads me to the door.

"We can't risk this happening to anyone else," he says.

This hell shouldn't have happened to us – we can't leave any possibility of his father doing it again. I nod, and watch him kick over a big industrial-sized bottle marked FLAM-MABLE.

A staircase climbs in front of us. Red light suffuses the main floor in pulses, synced with a screeching alarm.

Stopping at the bottom stair, I cast a look over the room I could've died in. Behind us, the flammable liquid spreads across the floor, washing away the blood, the formula and when it hits the shower of sparks and catches fire, possibly Dr Franks' sins.

Flames spread in every direction, turning the lab into a cauldron of fire. One good kick slams the door shut, then Alex drags me halfway up the stairs before the first explosion. Stairs shake beneath us, working loose a vial from the pocket I shoved them in. Alex clutches the handrail and me, riding the bucking stairs till they settle. I curse the clumsiness of my cast, trying to juggle the tablet and run for my life.

The second blast hits as we launch from the stairs and into a study full of leather furniture. Sick realization strikes – we are not alone.

And standing between us and escape, the redhead — holding a gun, its barrel leveled at me.

He says, "Fitting you torched this house, seeing as I torched yours."

Josh pulls the trigger. The gunshot cracks into the roar of the flames rushing up the stairwell behind us. Then hell punches into my arm. Pain radiates into my shoulder and down to my fingertips. Hot blood wells, streaks down my arm as I stagger and slump against Alex.

"Damn. Missed your heart," Josh says, then swings the barrel to point at Alex. "Next bullet's got your name on it."

The next explosion has other ideas. Heaving floorboards send Alex and me tumbling. Alex loosens his hold on me, and directs his roll to crash into Josh. The murderer slams to the floor, and the two fight for the gun. They're a wild tangle of arms and legs, driving fists and knees – this is not a high school scuffle, this is life or death. Alex drives his fist into Josh's jaw, then slams an open-handed chop on the red-head's forearm. The weapon clatters to the floor and skids into my feet.

Crying from pain and fear, I scrabble for the computer I lifted from the basement lab. When I finally get my hand on it, Alex shouts, "Emma, watch out!"

Cradling the little computer to my chest, I fling myself to the floor, narrowly avoiding Josh's kick to my head.

Alex slams into Josh. The two push and shove, mere feet from the staircase. Then Alex uses the same foot sweep he used on his dad on the redhead. Josh makes a mad grab for Alex's arms. Shaking his head, Alex drops him down the staircase, into the fire.

Shrieking bursts from Josh. He flails and rolls, a wild shadow in the flames. Then the blaze takes him and I can't tell the difference between his movements and the fire's advance.

"Come on!" Alex runs barefoot to grab my hand. His grip slides over the blood, then he wraps his fingers around my wrist and jerks me toward the outside wall of the house. Jostling loosens my grip on the computer, only the tips of my fingers keep it from shattering on the floor.

Another blast brings flames into the room, and hurls us out a large window.

Snow rises up in a white rush to cradle me. The cold shoves frigid hurt into my injuries, but I'm beyond caring. The computer clatters to the ground, still intact, and hope-fully with the codes and formulas Alex needs. Our future – because I don't want to live without him – is in this machine. I drag it to me and lay for a second in the snow, drawing huge breaths of fresh air. Tingles spill over my skin when Alex crawls to my side and drapes an arm over me.

"You OK?" he asks, voice unsteady.

"Am I OK?" I look at him, incredulous. "Are *you* OK?"

The image of his body arced from the table is seared into the back of my mind. How can someone go through that and survive?

"I'm fine." His body says otherwise when he works into a sitting position. Gashes and cuts litter his torso in a mad spatter of red. The wound where his father stabbed him leaks blood. But when Alex stands, he's steady and pulls me up with him. "We need to move away, Em. The whole house is gonna come down."

"Your house…" Irrational, maybe, but my mind's had a bit of a scramble.

"It was never mine," he soothes. "That was *his* house."

Maybe it's blood loss. Maybe it's stress. My legs refuse to hold me up. I start to sink toward the snow, gone sloppy and translucent in the heat radiating from the huge blaze.

"I've gotcha," Alex says, and scoops me into his arms.

Exhausted, hurting everywhere, I curl my face into Alex's shoulder and sob.

His father gone. Josh gone. They were monsters at the end, but at one time, Alex's father hadn't been. Josh had at one time been a close friend. Did the crimes they were guilty of warrant their fiery ends?

I let go of the thoughts and cling to Alex. Regardless of what happened, we are together. His love radiates from him, woven into the energy flowing in his body. With my ear pressed to his chest, I hear his heart beating – and know with my entire soul that his heart beats for me.

And mine for him.

Motion jiggles all my hurts as he searches in his pocket. Then he pulls a set of keys from his pocket and presses a code into the fob. In the distance, the gates squeal open.

Sirens bear down on us, colored lights strobe and pulse, dancing on the snowflake-laden air. Heaving a sigh, Alex turns to face the emergency responders flooding the Franks' estate. Face at his shoulder, I catch sight of the old windmill behind the house, its metal blades reflecting the house's flames. Fitting, somehow. The *whump-whump* turns in perfect rhythm with his heartbeat.

A small car appear at the mouth of the estate drive, then turns away, tires squealing its retreat up the hill.

This time, the questions will have to be answered. Policemen pour from their cars carrying notebooks and pens. Ambulances turn the snow to mud as they back around to help us. This time, we won't refuse treatment.

Snow crunches beneath our bare feet, sizzles as it falls on the house. But it can't hide the deer watching from the trees.

Epilogue

Aches still riddle my body days later, making the move to settle Alex into the sunshine house anything but sunny. I dismally regret leaving my pain pills in my bedroom. The gunshot is especially sore, when we move the last of Alex's salvaged things into his room at his grandparents' house. Well, as *he* moves the boxes, and I sit on the bed and pet Renfield. I'm under doctor's orders to do no lifting until my arm heals.

Happy, busy energy radiates through the house; multiple parental-type voices drift up the stairs.

"It's very nice of your grandparents to come back," I say.

Alex says, "It's very nice of your parents to come and meet them."

I work up a smile for him, but it doesn't touch my eyes. We survived his mad father's attempts at killing me, Josh's attempt at killing us both, and still my heart is heavy. My beautiful boyfriend is dying. The shadows are returning under his eyes. Friday looms on the calendar, a black day for me, knowing he doesn't have his formula and no possibility to charge it the way he needs. I glare at the battered remains of the dead tablet computer I dragged from the lab, through the disaster, the hospital, to here – only to find it was fried and useless.

"What's the matter, Emma?"

"It's almost Friday," I say, fighting tears. "The computer, your dad's lab and files are gone."

Sunlight washes his arms where they poke from his short-sleeved shirt, slides down the line of his scars when he comes to the bed. The mattress sinks with his weight when he drops his six-foot-plus frame beside me, then wraps his arms around me. God, I love the feeling of Alex holding me. But there's no electricity. And there won't be anymore.

I bite my lip and snuggle into him.

"If I told you I'll be fine," he asks, "would you believe me?"

"How? How can you be OK?"

Tingles dance over my scalp when he pulls the braid from my hair, then pushes the fall of blond strands over my shoulder. He places a warm, soft kiss on my neck, then gently takes my shoulders and turns me. I slide one leg over his, and straddle his hips. He growls a little and crushes me to him. This kiss is like none of the others. It's intense, urgent, like he knows there are only a few kisses left. Then Alex pulls away suddenly, cheeks flushed, eyes wide.

"Look behind the bed. Under the loose floorboard."

"What?" Why is he playing games? We have days, maybe weeks left together.

"Please just do it, Emergizer."

"Fine." He's learned already, that's the name to use to get his way.

Alex has to help me off his lap, of course, with a cast and a gunshot wound. Then I kneel at the foot of the bed, testing the boards until I find one that wiggles.

"Here," Alex says, "Let me do it."

The boards come up easily, in the dark between the floor

joists sits the leather bag he brought here the first night. I lift it out, the plastic vials clinking like music against each other.

"What about the electrical pulse?" Do I dare to hope?

"My father owned Ascension Labs," he says. "He willed everything to me. They have the same facility that we had at the estate."

"You're going to be OK!"

"I am."

I leave the bag on the floor, launch into his arms, and unsettle Renfield from his spot on Alex's pillows. When we kiss this time, it's a completely different kind of urgency. His hand tangles in my hair, the other slides down my side, and then sneaks up the buttons of my shirt.

I let him undo the first two buttons, because I love the way his lips feel on my skin. As he reaches for the third, an engine rumbles into the driveway.

Alex releases me, a playful pout tugging his full lips down.

"Hey," I say and nip the tip of his nose. "Bree's my best friend. You're going to have to get used to sharing me."

"Every other weekend," he says and winks with his left eye.

"Custody is still up for negotiation."

"Emma!" my mother yells up the stairs. "That door better be open, young lady! Bree and her friend are here."

With all the crazy upheaval, loss and pain in our lives, we know my mother will never change.

"You'll have to get used to that, too," I tell him.

"At least until you go to college." He hooks a finger in my waistband and reels me back into his arms. "Then you're all mine."

"I already am."

Acknowledgments

Massive thanks and mad love go to:

My husband and kids for putting up with my crazy writer behavior. I couldn't do it without them!

My alpha readers and plot buddies: Lexie Hughes, my book writing mental Mini Me with the crazy ideas, fervent love of what I write, and the tears I crave. Judy Spelbring, for getting so lost in reading she forgot to look for those pesky commas, and for suggesting I make Dr Franks even creepier.

My front line readers, Dana and Chris, for the accolades and the "ew gross" comments. Sorry about hurting your soul, Dana!

Amy Plum for the quote that graces the cover.

My agent Gina Panettieri, friend, confidante, tireless champion, typo wrangler and the one who always knew I was a little bit dark.

My editor Amanda Rutter, for loving this story, for taking a chance on me, and for making the process so much fun it doesn't feel like work. And, my publisher for giving me and this story an awesome home and gorgeous cover!

Lastly, you, dear readers. Thank you for picking up this

book. Without readers and books and our community of story fiends this world would be a dreary place indeed!

About the Author

Self-proclaimed nerd, A.E. Rought has spent most of her early life in libraries and bookstores. It's no surprise that she turned to writing shortly after creative arts college. She has novels of varying genres, and different pennames, published since 2006.

aerought.com

"Weird, wise and witty, Blackwood is great fun."
    — *Marcus Sedgwick*

"Unique, heart-wrenching, full of mysteries and twists!"
– *Tamora Pierce, author of* Alanna: The First Adventure

MORE WONDERS IN STORE FOR YOU...